Arthur. C. 3

medicine

STRONG MEDICINE

Novels by Arthur Hailey

STRONG MEDICINE
OVERLOAD
THE MONEYCHANGERS
WHEELS
AIRPORT
HOTEL
IN HIGH PLACES
THE FINAL DIAGNOSIS
RUNWAY ZERO-EIGHT
(with John Castle)

Collected Plays

CLOSE-UP ON WRITING FOR TELEVISION

STRONG MEDICINE

Arthur Hailey

DOUBLEDAY & COMPANY, INC.

GARDEN CITY, NEW YORK

1984

DESIGNED BY LAURENCE ALEXANDER

Library of Congress Cataloging in Publication Data

Hailey, Arthur.
Strong medicine.

I. Title.
PR9199.3.H3S7 1984   813'.54
ISBN 0-385-18014-4
Library of Congress Catalog Card Number 84-8019
Copyright © 1984 by Arthur Hailey

PERSONAL

The Author to His Readers

In 1979, with publication of *Overload*, I announced my retirement. I was tired. My life had been full. I was, and still am, grateful to those millions of readers worldwide who have enriched my life in many ways, including making retirement possible.

In whatever years remained I wanted to spend more time—and travel—with my dear wife Sheila, go fishing, read more books, relax with music, do other things a working writer can't.

What I did not know was that I was near death from six blockages in the coronary arteries—a condition diagnosed soon afterward by my friend and physician, Dr. Edward Robbins of San Francisco, who urged immediate surgery. This was done—a quadruple bypass—by Dr. Denton Cooley and his associates at the Texas Heart Institute, to where my gratitude flows strong.

Sheila was supportive, as she has been through our long and loving marriage. It is more than coincidence in this novel that the names Celia and Sheila come similarly off the tongue.

The aftermath of everything was my revived good health and an abundance of energy—so much of the latter that Sheila said one day, "I think you should write another book."

I took her advice. *Strong Medicine* is the result.

April 5, 1984   A.H.

Diseases, desperate grown,
By desperate appliance are reliev'd,
Or not at all.

SHAKESPEARE, *Hamlet*

We are overwhelmed as it is, with an
infinite abundance of vaunted medicaments,
and here they add a new one.

THOMAS SYDENHAM, M.D. *(1624–89)*

PROLOGUE

1985

In the 747, up forward in first class and half an hour out from London, Dr. Andrew Jordan reached for his wife's hand and held it.

"Stop worrying," he urged her. "Nothing may happen."

"*Something* will happen," she said. "Dennis Donahue will see to that."

Andrew grimaced at the mention of New England's populist U.S. senator. "I was looking forward to lunch," he objected. "Did you need to spoil it by making me nauseous?"

"Be serious, Andrew. Remember there have been deaths. Drug-related."

"You were a long way removed from them."

1

"Just the same, if there are criminal proceedings, I'll be included. I could go to prison."

He tried to buoy their sagging spirits. "It hasn't happened yet, but if you do I promise to visit every day and bring cakes with hacksaw blades inside."

"Oh, Andrew!" She turned toward him, her smile a mixture of love and sadness.

After twenty-eight years of marriage, he thought, how good it was to see your wife, with admiration, as beautiful, intelligent and strong. And, he told himself, he wasn't being sentimental either. He had seen all those qualities, and more, exhibited a thousand times.

"That's nice," a female voice beside them interjected.

Andrew looked up. It was a bright, young, cheerful stewardess, observing them holding hands.

He told her, deadpan, "Love can happen to the elderly, too."

"Really?" The stewardess matched his mocking tone. "That never occurred to me. More champagne?"

"Yes, please."

He caught the girl inspecting him and knew, without being vain, that he still looked good, even to someone young enough to be his daughter. How had that London newspaper columnist described him last week? "The white-haired, handsome and distinguished physician husband of . . . et cetera, et cetera." Though Andrew hadn't said so, at the time he'd rather liked it.

The champagne poured, Andrew sat back. He enjoyed the perquisites which went with first-class travel, even if today they seemed less significant than usual. It was his wife's money which provided those embellishments, of course. While his own income as a busy internist was more than comfortable, he doubted if he would splurge on first-class fare between London and New York, and certainly could never afford the private jet in which his wife, and sometimes Andrew, traveled around North America.

Correction, he reminded himself: *had* traveled until now. What changes lay immediately ahead were far from certain.

Money, though, had never been any kind of issue in their marriage. They had never had the slightest argument about it, and right from the beginning his wife had insisted that what they had, they had together. Their bank accounts were always joint, and though Andrew's contribution nowadays was by far the smaller, neither bothered with comparative arithmetic.

2

His thoughts drifted and they continued to hold hands as the 747 thrummed westward above the Atlantic far below.

"Andrew," his wife said, "you're such a comfort. Always there. And always so strong."

"That's funny," he replied. "Strong is what I was thinking about you."

"There are different kinds of strength. And I need yours."

The usual airline bustle was beginning, preparatory to service of their meal. Stowaway tables were being released, white linen and silverware appearing on them.

After a while his wife said, "Whatever happens, I'm going to fight."

"Haven't you always?"

She was thinking carefully, as usual. "Within the next few days I'll choose a lawyer. It must be someone solid but not flamboyant. Too much showmanship would be a mistake."

He squeezed her hand. "That's my girl."

She smiled back at him. "Will you sit beside me in court?"

"Every day. Patients can fend for themselves until it's done."

"You'd never let that happen, but I would like you with me."

"There are other doctors. Arrangements will be made."

"Maybe," his wife said, "maybe, with the right lawyer, we can pull off a miracle."

Andrew dipped a knife into a helping of caviar that had just been placed before him. However acute their troubles, there was no point in passing up *that*.

"It could happen," he said, spreading the caviar on toast. "We started with a miracle, you and I. And there've been others since, which you've made happen. Why not one more? This time just for you."

"It *would* be a miracle."

"Will be," he corrected gently.

Andrew closed his eyes. The champagne and the altitude had made him sleepy. But in his sleepiness he remembered the first miracle.

Long ago.

ONE

1957–1963

1

Dr. Jordan said quietly, "Your wife is dying, John. She has a few hours more, that's all." He added, conscious of the pale, anguished face of the slight young man before him, still dressed in his factory work clothes, "I wish I could tell you something else. But I thought you'd want the truth."

They were in St. Bede's Hospital in Morristown, New Jersey. Early evening noises from outside—small-town noises—filtered in, barely disturbing the silence between them.

In the dimmed light of the hospital room, Andrew watched the Adam's apple of the patient's husband bob twice convulsively before he managed to get out, "I just *can't* believe it. We're just beginning. Getting started. You know we have a baby."

"Yes, I know."

"It's so . . ."

"Unfair?"

The young man nodded. A good, decent man, hardworking from the look of him. John Rowe. He was twenty-five, only four years younger than Dr. Jordan himself, and he was taking this badly—not surprisingly. Andrew wished he could comfort the other man more. Though Andrew encountered death often enough and was trained to know the signs of death's approach, he still was uncertain about communicating with a dying person's friends or family. Should a doctor be blunt, direct, or was there some subtler way? It was something they didn't teach in medical school, or afterward either.

"Viruses are unfair," he said, "though mostly they don't act the way this has with Mary. Usually they'll respond to treatment."

"Isn't there *anything?* Some drug which could . . . ?"

Andrew shook his head. No point in going into details by answering: *Not yet. So far, no drug for the acute coma of advanced infectious hepatitis.* Nor would anything be gained by saying that, earlier today, he had consulted his senior partner in practice, Dr. Noah Townsend, who also happened to be the hospital's chief of medicine.

7

An hour earlier Townsend had told Andrew, "You've done all you can. There's nothing I'd have done differently." It was then that Andrew sent a message to the factory, in the nearby town of Boonton where John Rowe was working on the swing shift.

Goddam! Andrew's eyes glanced at the elevated metal bed with the still figure. It was the only bed in the room because of the prominent "ISOLATION" notice in the corridor outside. The I.V. bottle on its stand stood behind the bed, dripping its contents—dextrose, normal saline, B-complex vitamins—into Mary Rowe through a needle in a forearm vein. It was already dark outside; occasionally there were rumblings from a storm and it was raining heavily. A lousy night. And the last night of living for this young wife and mother who had been healthy and active only a week ago. Goddam! It *was* unfair.

Today was Friday. Last Monday Mary Rowe, petite and pretty, though clearly unwell, had appeared in Andrew's office. She complained of feeling sick, weak, and she couldn't eat. Her temperature was 100.5.

Four days earlier, Mrs. Rowe told him, she had had the same symptoms plus some vomiting, then the next day felt better and believed the trouble, whatever it was, was going away. But now it had returned. She was feeling terrible, even worse than before.

Andrew checked the whites of Mary Rowe's eyes; they showed a tinge of yellow. Already areas of her skin were showing jaundice too. He palpated the liver, which was tender and enlarged. Questioning elicited that she had been to Mexico with her husband for a brief vacation the previous month. Yes, they had stayed in a small, offbeat hotel because it was cheap. Yes, she had eaten local food and drunk the water.

"I'm admitting you to the hospital immediately," Andrew told her. "We need a blood test to confirm, but I'm as certain as I can be that you have infectious hepatitis."

Then, because Mary Rowe had seemed frightened, he explained that most likely she had consumed contaminated food or water in Mexico, the contamination probably from an infected food handler. It happened frequently in countries where sanitation was poor.

As to treatment, it would be mostly supportive, with adequate fluid intake into the body given intravenously. Complete recovery for ninety-five percent of people, Andrew added, took three to four months, though Mary should be able to go home from the hospital in a matter of days.

With a wan smile, Mary had asked: What about the other five percent?

Andrew laughed and told her, "Forget it! That's a statistic you won't be part of."

Which was where he had been wrong.

Instead of improving, Mary Rowe's condition worsened. The bilirubin in her blood went up and up, indicating increased jaundice, which was obvious from the alarming yellow of her skin. Even more critical, by Wednesday tests revealed a dangerous level of ammonia in the blood. It was ammonia, originating in the intestines, which the deteriorating liver could no longer handle.

Then yesterday her mental state had deteriorated. She was confused, disoriented, didn't know where she was or why, and failed to recognize either Andrew or her husband. That was when Andrew warned John Rowe that his wife was gravely ill.

The frustration at being able to do nothing to help gnawed at Andrew all day Thursday and, in between seeing patients in his office, he kept thinking about the problem, but to no effect. An obstacle to recovery, he realized, was that accumulation of ammonia. How to clear it? He knew that, given the present state of medicine, there was no effective way.

Finally, and unfairly he supposed now, he had taken out his frustration by blowing his stack at the damned drug company saleswoman who had come into his office late in the afternoon. She was a "detail man." Or should it be "detail woman?" Not that he cared. He didn't even remember her name or her appearance, except that she wore glasses and was young, just a kid, and probably inexperienced.

The saleswoman was from Felding-Roth Pharmaceuticals. Afterward Andrew wondered why he had agreed to see her when the receptionist announced that she was waiting, but he had, thinking perhaps he might learn something, though when she started talking about the latest antibiotic her company had just put on the market, his thoughts began wandering until she said, "You're not even listening to me, Doctor," and that had made him mad.

"Maybe it's because I've something better to think about and you're wasting my time."

It was rude, and usually he wouldn't have been that way. But his intense worry about Mary Rowe was coupled with a long dislike of

9

drug companies and their high-pressure selling. Sure, there were some good drugs which the big firms produced, but their huckstering, including sucking up to doctors, was something Andrew found offensive. He had encountered it first in medical school where students—future prescribers, as the drug companies well knew—were sought after, flattered and pandered to by drug firm representatives. Among other things, the drug reps gave away stethoscopes and medical bags which some students accepted gladly. Andrew wasn't one of them. Though he had little money, he preferred to keep his independence and buy his own.

"Maybe you'll tell me, Doctor," the Felding-Roth saleswoman had said yesterday, "what it is that's so all-fired important."

It was then he had let her have it, telling her about Mary Rowe who was critical with ammonia intoxication, and adding caustically that he wished companies like Felding-Roth, instead of coming up with some "me-too" antibiotic which was probably no better or worse than half a dozen others already available, would work on a drug to stop excess ammonia production . . .

He had stopped then, already ashamed of the outburst, and would probably have apologized except that the saleswoman, having gathered up her papers and samples, was on the way out, saying simply as she left, "Good afternoon, Doctor."

So much for yesterday, and Andrew was no closer to being able to help his patient, Mary Rowe.

This morning he had taken a phone call from the head floor nurse, Mrs. Ludlow.

"Dr. Jordan, I'm worried about your patient, Rowe. She's becoming comatose, not responding at all."

Andrew hurried to the hospital. A resident was with Mary Rowe who, by now, was in a deep coma. Although hurrying over was the thing to do, Andrew had known before arriving that no heroic measures were possible. All they could do was keep the intravenous fluids flowing. That, and hope.

Now, near the end of the day, it was clear that hope had been in vain. Mary Rowe's condition seemed irreversible.

Fighting back tears, John Rowe asked, "Will she be conscious again, Doctor? Will Mary know I'm here?"

"I'm sorry," Andrew said. "It isn't likely."

"I'll stay with her, just the same."

10

"Of course. The nurses will be close by, and I'll instruct the resident."

"Thank you, Doctor."

Leaving, Andrew wondered: Thanks for what? He felt the need for coffee and headed for where he knew some would be brewing.

The doctors' lounge was a boxlike place, sparsely furnished with a few chairs, a mail rack, a TV, a small desk, and lockers for attending physicians. But it had the advantages of privacy and constant coffee. No one else was there when Andrew arrived.

He poured himself coffee and slipped into an old, well-worn armchair. No need to stay at the hospital any longer, but he instinctively put off departure for his bachelor apartment—Noah Townsend's wife, Hilda, had found it for him—which was comfortable though sometimes lonely.

The coffee was hot. While letting it cool, Andrew glanced at a *Newark Star-Ledger*. Prominent on the newspaper's front page was a report about something called "Sputnik"—an earth satellite, whatever that might be, which the Russians had recently shot into outer space amid fanfare heralding "the dawn of a new space age." While President Eisenhower, according to the news story, was expected to order speedup of a U.S. space program, American scientists were "shocked and humiliated" by the Russians' technological lead. Andrew hoped some of the shock would spill over into medical science. Though good progress had been made during the twelve years since World War II, there were still so many depressing gaps, unanswered questions.

Discarding the newspaper, he picked up a copy of *Medical Economics*, a magazine that alternately amused and fascinated him. It was said to be the publication read most avidly by doctors, who gave it more attention than even the prestigious *New England Journal of Medicine*.

Medical Economics had a basic function—to instruct doctors in ways to earn the maximum amount of money and, when they had it, how to invest or spend it. Andrew began reading an article: "Eight Ways to Minimize Your Taxes in Private Practice." He supposed he should try to understand such things because handling money, when a doctor finally got to earn some after years of training, was something else they didn't teach in medical school. Since joining Dr.

11

Townsend's practice a year and a half ago, Andrew had been startled at how much cash flowed monthly into his bank account. It was a new and not unpleasant experience. Although he had no intention of letting money dominate him, just the same . . .

"Excuse me, Doctor."

A woman's voice. Andrew turned his head.

"I went to your office, Dr. Jordan. When you weren't there, I decided to try the hospital."

Dammit! It was the same drug company saleswoman who had been in his office yesterday. She was wearing a raincoat, which was soaked. Her brownish hair hung dripping wet, and her glasses were steamed. Of all the gall—to barge in here!

"You seem to be unaware," he said, "that this is a private lounge. Also I don't see salespeople—"

She interrupted. "At the hospital. Yes, I know. But I thought this was important enough." With a series of quick movements she put down an attaché case, removed her glasses to wipe them, and began taking off the raincoat. "It's miserable out. I got soaked crossing the parking lot."

"*What's* important?"

The saleswoman—he observed again that she was young, probably no more than twenty-four—tossed the raincoat onto a chair. She spoke slowly and carefully.

"Ammonia, Doctor. Yesterday you told me you had a hepatitis patient who was dying from ammonia intoxication. You said you wished—"

"I know what I said."

The saleswoman regarded him levelly with clear gray-green eyes. Andrew was aware of a strong personality. She wasn't what you'd call pretty, he thought, though she had a pleasing, high-cheekboned face; with her hair dried and combed she would probably look good. And with the raincoat off, her figure wasn't bad.

"No doubt you do, Doctor, and I'm sure your memory is better than your manners." As he started to say something, she stopped him with an impatient gesture. "What I didn't—couldn't—tell you yesterday is that my company, Felding-Roth, has been working for four years on a drug to reduce ammonia production by intestinal bacteria, a drug that would be useful in a crisis situation like your patient's. I knew about it, but not how far our research people had gone."

12

"I'm glad to hear someone's trying," Andrew said, "but I still don't see—"

"You will if you *listen.*" The saleswoman pushed back several strands of wet hair which had fallen forward on her face. "What they've developed—it's called Lotromycin—has been used successfully on animals. Now it's ready for human testing. I was able to get some Lotromycin. I've brought it with me."

Andrew rose from the armchair. "Do I understand you, Miss . . ." He couldn't remember her name and, for the first time, felt uncomfortable.

"I didn't expect you to remember." Again the impatience. "I'm Celia de Grey."

"Are you suggesting, Miss de Grey, that I give my patient an unknown, experimental drug which has only been tried on animals?"

"With any drug, there has to be one first human being to use it."

"If you don't mind," Andrew said, "I prefer not to be the pioneering doctor."

The saleswoman raised an eyebrow skeptically; her voice sharpened. "Not even if your patient is dying and there isn't anything else? How is your patient, Doctor? The one you told me about."

"Worse than yesterday." He hesitated. "She's gone into a coma."

"Then she *is* dying?"

"Look," Andrew said, "I know you mean well, Miss de Grey, and I'm sorry about the way I spoke when you came in here. But the unfortunate fact is, it's too late. Too late to start experimental drugs and, even if I wanted to, do you have any idea of all the procedures, protocols, all the rest, we would have to go through?"

"Yes," the saleswoman said; now her eyes were blazing, riveting Andrew, and it occurred to him he was beginning to like this forthright, spunky girl-woman. She continued, "Yes, I know exactly what procedures and protocols are needed. In fact, since I left you yesterday I've done little else but find out about them—that, and twist the arm of our director of research to let me have a supply of Lotromycin of which, so far, there's very little. But I got it—three hours ago at our labs downstate, in Camden, and I've driven here without stopping, through this lousy weather."

Andrew began, "I'm grateful," but the saleswoman shook her head impatiently.

"What's more, Dr. Jordan, all the necessary paperwork is taken

13

care of. To use the drug, you would have to get permission from this hospital and the next of kin. But that's all."

He could only stare at her. "I'll be damned!"

"We're wasting time," Celia de Grey said. She had the attaché case open and was pulling out papers. "Please begin by reading this. It's a description of Lotromycin prepared for you by Felding-Roth's research department. And this is a memorandum from our medical director—instructions on how the drug should be administered."

Andrew took the two papers, which seemed to be the first of many. As he began reading, he was immediately absorbed.

Almost two hours had gone by.

"With your patient *in extremis*, Andrew, what have we got to lose?" The voice on the telephone was Noah Townsend's. Andrew had located the chief of medicine at a private dinner party and had described the offer of the experimental drug Lotromycin.

Townsend went on, "You say the husband has already given permission?"

"Yes, in writing. I got the administrator at home. He came to the hospital and had the form typed up. It's signed and witnessed."

Before the signing, Andrew had talked with John Rowe in the corridor outside his wife's room and the young husband reacted eagerly. So eagerly, in fact, that Andrew warned him not to build great hopes or expect too much. The signature on the form was wavery because of John Rowe's shaking hand. But it was there, and legal.

Now Andrew told Noah Townsend, "The administrator is satisfied that the other papers sent by Felding-Roth are in order. Apparently it makes it easier that the drug didn't cross a state line."

"You'll be sure to record all those details on the patient's chart."

"I already have."

"So all you need is my permission?"

"For the hospital. Yes."

"I give it," Dr. Townsend said. "Not that I hold out much hope, Andrew. I think your patient's too far gone, but let's give it the old college try. Now, do you mind if I go back to a delicious roast pheasant?"

As Andrew hung up the phone at the nurses' station from where he had been calling, he asked, "Is everything ready?"

14

The head night nurse, an elderly R.N. who worked part time, had prepared a tray with a hypodermic. She opened a refrigerator and added a clear glass drug container which the Felding-Roth saleswoman had brought. "Yes, it is."

"Then let's go."

The same resident who had been with Mary Rowe this morning, Dr. Overton, was at her bedside when Andrew and the nurse arrived. John Rowe hovered in the background.

Andrew explained Lotromycin to the resident, a burly Texan extrovert, who drawled, "You expectin' a damn miracle?"

"No," Andrew answered curtly. He turned to Mary Rowe's husband. "I want to emphasize again, John, this is a long shot, a *very* long shot. It's simply that in the circumstances . . ."

"I understand." The voice was low, emotion-charged.

The nurse prepared the unconscious Mary Rowe for an injection, which would be intramuscular into the buttocks, as Andrew told the resident, "The drug company says the dose should be repeated every four hours. I've left a written order but I'd like you to . . ."

"I'll be here, chief. And okay, q-4." The resident lowered his voice. "Say, how about a bet? I'll give you even odds against—"

Andrew silenced him with a glare. The Texan had been in the hospital training program for a year, during which time he had proven himself highly competent as a doctor, but his lack of sensitivity was notorious.

The nurse completed the injection and checked the patient's pulse and blood pressure. She reported, "No reaction, Doctor. No change in vital signs."

Andrew nodded, for the moment relieved. He had not expected any positive effect, but an adverse reaction had been a possibility, particularly with an experimental drug. He still doubted, though, that Mary Rowe would survive until morning.

"Phone me at home if she's worse," he ordered. Then, with a quiet, "Good night, John," to the husband, he went out.

It was not until he was in his apartment that Andrew remembered he had failed to report back to the Felding-Roth saleswoman, whom he had left in the doctors' lounge. This time he remembered her name—de Grey. Was it Cindy? No, Celia. He was about to telephone, then supposed that by now she would have found out what had happened. He would talk with her tomorrow.

15

2

Normally on Saturday mornings Andrew saw patients in his office from 10 A.M., then dropped into the hospital around midday. Today he reversed the procedure and was at St. Bede's by 9 A.M.

Last night's storm and rain had been replaced by a fresh, clear morning, cold but sunny.

Andrew was ascending the hospital front steps when, ahead of him, the main door slammed open and Dr. Overton, the resident, appeared to hurl himself out. Overton seemed agitated. His hair was disordered as if he had gotten out of bed in a hurry and forgotten about it. His voice was breathless. He grabbed Andrew's arm.

"Tried to call you. You'd already left. Janitor at your apartment said you were coming. I just had to catch you first."

Andrew pulled his arm away. "What *is* this?"

The resident swallowed hard. "Never mind. Just come on."

Overton, hurrying, preceded Andrew down a corridor and into an elevator. He refused to speak or even look Andrew in the eye as they rode to the fourth floor. The resident hastened from the elevator, Andrew following.

They stopped outside the hospital room where, last night, Andrew had left the unconscious Mary Rowe, her husband, the nurse and the resident.

"In!" Overton motioned impatiently. "Go on in!"

Andrew entered. And stopped. Staring.

From behind him the resident said, "Should've taken my bet, Dr. Jordan." He added, "If I hadn't seen, I wouldn't have believed."

Andrew said softly, "I'm not sure I believe it either."

Mary Rowe, fully conscious, propped up in bed and wearing a blue lacy nightgown, smiled at him. Though the smile was weak, and clearly so was Mary Rowe, her condition was so much in contrast to

16

the deep coma of last night, it seemed a miracle. She had been sipping water; a plastic cup was in her hand. The yellow skin tone, which had deepened yesterday, was noticeably lighter. As Andrew came in her husband stood up, smiling broadly, his hands outstretched.

"Thank you, Doctor! Oh, thank you!" That Adam's apple of John Rowe's bobbed up and down as Andrew took his hand.

From the bed Mary Rowe added a soft but fervent, "Bless you, Doctor!"

It was the resident's turn. Overton pumped Andrew's hand. "Congratulations!" He added, uncharacteristically, "sir." Andrew was surprised to see tears brimming in the burly Texan's eyes.

The head floor nurse, Mrs. Ludlow, bustled in. Normally preoccupied and serious, she was beaming. "It's all around the hospital, Dr. Jordan. Everybody's talking about you."

"Look," Andrew said, "there was an experimental drug, Lotromycin. It was brought to me. I didn't—"

"Around here," the nurse said, "you're a hero. If I were you I wouldn't fight it."

"I ordered a blood test, stat," the resident reported. "It showed ammonia below toxic level. Also, the bilirubin isn't rising, so the rest of the cure will be routine." He added to himself, "Unbelievable!"

Andrew told his patient, "I'm happy for you, Mary." A thought occurred to him. "Has anyone seen that girl from Felding-Roth? Miss de Grey."

"She was around here earlier," Nurse Ludlow said. "She may be at the nursing station."

"Excuse me," Andrew said, and went outside.

Celia de Grey was waiting in the corridor. She had changed her clothes from last night. A soft smile played around her face.

As they regarded each other, Andrew was conscious of a constraint between them.

"You look a lot better with your hair dry," he said.

"And you're not as stern and fierce as yesterday."

There was a pause before he said, "You heard?"

"Yes."

"In there . . ." Andrew motioned toward the hospital room. "In there they've been thanking me. But the one we should all thank is you."

She said, smiling, "You're the doctor."

17

Then suddenly, all barriers down, they were laughing and crying together. A moment later, to his own surprise, he took her in his arms and kissed her.

Over coffee and a shared Danish in the hospital cafeteria Celia de Grey removed her glasses and said, "I telephoned our company medical director and told him what happened. He's talked with some of our research people. They're all happy."

"They have a right to be," Andrew said. "They made a good drug."

"I was also told to ask: Will you write up a case report, including your use of Lotromycin, for publication in a medical journal?"

He answered, "Gladly."

"Naturally, it would be good for Felding-Roth." The saleswoman's tone was businesslike. "That's because we expect Lotromycin to be an important drug and a big seller. But it won't do you any harm either."

Andrew acknowledged with a smile, "Probably not."

He was thoughtful as he sipped his coffee. He knew that through mere chance, a fluke engineered by what he now saw as this remarkable and delightful young woman seated opposite, he had participated in a piece of medical history. Few physicians ever had that opportunity.

"Look," Andrew said, "there's something I want to say. Yesterday, Celia, you told me I had bad manners and you were right. I was rude to you. I apologize."

"Not necessary," she told him briskly. "I liked the way you were. You were worried about your patient and you didn't care about anything else. Your caring showed. But then you're always that way."

The remark surprised him. "How do you know?"

"Because people have told me." Again the swift, warm smile. She had her glasses on again; removing and replacing them seemed a habit. Celia continued, "I know a lot about you, Andrew Jordan. Partly because it's my job to get to know doctors and partly . . . well, I'll get to that later."

This unusual girl, he thought, had many facets. He asked, "What *do* you know?"

"Well, for one thing you were at the top of your medical school class at Johns Hopkins. For another, you did your internship and residency at Massachusetts General—I know only the best get in

18

there. Then Dr. Townsend chose you out of fifty applicants and took you into his practice because he knew you were good. Do you want more?"

He laughed aloud. "*Is* there any?"

"Only that you're a nice man, Andrew. Everybody says so. Of course, there are some negatives about you I've discovered."

"I'm shocked," he told her. "Are you suggesting I'm not perfect after all?"

"You have some blind spots," Celia said. "For instance, about drug companies. You're very prejudiced against us. Oh, I'll agree that some things—"

"Stop right there!" Andrew raised a hand. "I admit the prejudice. But I'll also tell you, this morning I'm in a mood to change my mind."

"That's good, but don't change it altogether." Celia's businesslike tone was back. "There are lots of good things about our industry, and you just saw one of them at work. But there are also things that aren't so good, some that *I* don't like and hope to alter."

"*You* hope to alter." He raised his eyebrows. "Personally?"

"I know what you're thinking—that I'm a woman."

"Since you mention it, yes, I'd noticed."

Celia said seriously, "The time is coming, in fact it's already here, when women will do many things they haven't done before."

"Right now I'm ready to believe that too, especially about you." Andrew added, "You said there was something else to tell me, that you'd get to later."

For the first time Celia de Grey hesitated.

"Yes, there is." Her strong gray-green eyes met Andrew's directly. "I was going to wait until another time we met, but I may as well tell you now. I've decided to marry you."

This extraordinary girl! So full of life and character, to say nothing of surprises. He had never met anyone like her. Andrew started to laugh, then abruptly changed his mind.

One month later, in the presence of a few close friends and relatives, Dr. Andrew Jordan and Celia de Grey were married in a quiet civil ceremony.

3

On the second day of their honeymoon Celia told Andrew, "Ours will be a good marriage. We're going to make it work."

"If you ask me . . ." Andrew rolled over on the beach towel they were sharing, managing to kiss the nape of his wife's neck as he did. "If you ask me, it's working already."

They were on the island of Eleuthera in the Bahamas. Above them was a warm midmorning sun and a few small wispy clouds. A white-sand beach, of which they were the only occupants, appeared to stretch into infinity. An offshore breeze stirred palm fronds and, immediately ahead, cast ripples on a calm, translucent sea.

"If you're talking about sex," Celia said, "we're not bad together, are we?"

Andrew raised himself on an elbow. "Not bad? You're dynamite. Where did you ever learn—?" He stopped. "No, don't tell me."

"I could ask you the same question," she teased. Her hand stroked his thigh as her tongue lightly traced the outline of his mouth.

He reached for her and whispered, "Come on! Let's go back to the bungalow."

"Why not right here? Or in those tall grasses over there?"

"And shock the natives?"

She laughed as he pulled her up and they ran across the beach. "You're a prude! A real prude. Who would have guessed?"

Andrew led her into the picturesque thatched bungalow they had moved into the day before and which was to be theirs for ten days more.

"I don't want to share you with the ants and land crabs, and if that makes me a prude, okay." He slipped off his swim trunks as he spoke.

But Celia was ahead of him. She had shed her bikini and was already lying naked on the bed, still laughing.

An hour later, back on the beach, Celia said, "As I was saying about our marriage . . ."

"It will be a good one," Andrew finished for her. "I agree."

"And to make it work, we must both be fulfilled people."

Andrew was lying back contentedly, hands intertwined behind his head. "Still agree."

"So we must have children."

"If there's any way I can help with that, just let me—"

"Andrew! *Please* be serious."

"Can't. I'm too happy."

"Then I'll be serious for both of us."

"How many children?" he asked. "And when?"

"I've thought about it," Celia said, "and I believe we should have two—the first child as soon as possible, the second two years later. That way, I'll have childbearing done before I'm thirty."

"That's nice," he said. "Tidy, too. As a matter of interest, do you have any plans for your old age—after thirty, I mean?"

"I'm going to have a career. Didn't I ever mention that?"

"Not that I remember. But if you'll recall, my love, the way we leaped into this marriage caper didn't allow much time for discussion or philosophy."

"Well," Celia said, "I did mention my plan about children to Sam Hawthorne. He thought it would work out fine."

"Bully for Sam!—whoever he is." Andrew wrinkled his brow. "Wait. Wasn't he the one at our wedding, from Felding-Roth?"

"That's right. Sam Hawthorne's my boss, the regional sales manager. He was with his wife, Lilian."

"Got it. Everything's coming back."

Andrew remembered Sam Hawthorne now—a tall, friendly fellow, perhaps in his mid-thirties but prematurely balding, and with craggy, strong features that reminded Andrew of the carved faces on Mount Rushmore. Hawthorne's wife, Lilian, was a striking brunette.

Reliving, mentally, the events of three days earlier, Andrew said, "You'll have to make allowance for my having been a little dazed at the time."

One reason, he remembered, was the vision of Celia as she had appeared, in white, with a short veil, in the reception room of a local hotel where they had elected to be married. The ceremony was to be

21

performed by a friendly judge who was also a member of St. Bede's Hospital board. Dr. Townsend had escorted Celia in on his arm.

Noah Townsend was fully up to the occasion, the epitome of a seasoned family physician. Dignified and graying, he looked a lot like the British prime minister, Harold Macmillan, who was so often in the news these days smoothing U.S.–British relations after the preceding year's discords over the Suez Canal.

Celia's mother, a small, self-effacing widow who lived in Philadelphia, was at the wedding. Celia's father had died in World War II; hence Townsend's role.

Under the Bahamas sun, Andrew closed his eyes, partly as relief against the brightness, but mostly to re-create that moment when Townsend brought Celia in . . .

In the month since Celia, on that memorable morning in the hospital cafeteria, had announced her intention to marry him, Andrew had fallen increasingly under what he thought of as no less than her magic spell. He supposed love was the word, yet it seemed more and different—the abandonment of a *singleness* which Andrew had always pursued, and the total intertwining of two lives and personalities in ways that at once bewildered and delighted him. There was no one quite like Celia. No moment with her was ever dull. She remained full of surprises, knowledge, intellect, ideas, plans, all bubbling from that wellspring of her forceful, colorful, independent nature. Almost from the beginning he had a sense of extreme good fortune as if he, through some machinery of chance, had won a jackpot, a prize coveted by others. And he sensed that others coveted Celia as he introduced her to his colleagues.

Andrew had had other women in his life, but none for any length of time, and there had been no one he seriously considered marrying. Which made it all the more remarkable that from the moment when Celia—to put it conventionally—"proposed," he had never had the slightest doubt, hesitation, or inclination to turn back.

And yet . . . it was not until that incredible moment when he saw Celia in her white wedding dress—radiant, lovely, young, desirable, all that any man could ask of a woman and more, far more—it was not until then that, with a flash which seemed an exploding ball of fire within him, Andrew truly fell in love and knew, with the positive certainty that happens few times in any life, that he was incredibly fortunate, that what was happening was for always, and that, despite the cynicism of the times, for himself and Celia there would never be separation or divorce.

It was that word "divorce," Andrew told himself when thinking about it afterward, that had kept him unattached at a time when many of his contemporaries were marrying in their early twenties. Of course, his own parents had provided that rationale, and his mother, who represented (as Andrew saw it) the divorcée *non grata,* was at the wedding. She had flown in from Los Angeles like an aging butterfly, announcing to anyone who would listen that she had interrupted the shedding of her fourth husband to be present at her son's "first marriage." Andrew's father had been her second husband, and when Andrew had inquired about him he was told, "Oh, my dear boy, I hardly remember what he looked like. I haven't seen him in twenty years, and the last I heard, he was an old roué living with a seventeen-year-old whore in Paris."

Over the years Andrew had tried to understand his mother and rationalize her behavior. Sadly, though, he always came to the same conclusion: she was an empty-headed, shallow, selfish beauty who attracted a similar kind of man.

He had invited his mother to the wedding—though he later wished he hadn't—out of a sense of duty and a conviction that everyone should have some feeling for a natural parent. He had also sent a letter about the wedding to the last known address of his father, but there had been no reply, and Andrew doubted if there ever would be. Every three years or so he and his father managed to exchange Christmas cards, and that was all.

Andrew had been the only child of his briefly married parents, and the one other family member he would have liked Celia to meet had died two years earlier. She was a maiden aunt with whom Andrew had lived through most of his boyhood and who, though not well off, had somehow scraped together—without help from either of his parents—the money to sustain Andrew through college and medical school. It was only after her death, when the pathetic remnants of her estate, worth a few hundred dollars, lay exposed in a lawyer's office, that he realized how great the sacrifice had been.

As it was, at the wedding Celia had taken Andrew's mother in stride. Assessing the situation without anything's having to be explained, Celia had been cordial, even warm, though not phonily effusive. Afterward, when Andrew expressed regret about his mother's bizarre behavior, Celia responded, "We married each other, darling, not our families." Then she added, "I'm your family now, and you'll get more love from me than you've ever had in your life before."

Today on the beach Andrew was already realizing this was true.

"What I'd like to do, if you agree," Celia said, continuing their conversation, "is go on working through most of my first pregnancy, then take off a year to be a full-time mother. After that I'll go back to work until the second pregnancy, and so on."

"Sure, I agree," he told her. "And in between being loved and getting you pregnant, I plan to practice a little medicine."

"You'll practice *lots* of medicine, and go on being a fine, caring doctor."

"I hope so." Andrew sighed happily, and a few minutes later fell asleep.

They spent the next few days learning things about each other which they had not had time for previously.

One morning over breakfast, which each day was delivered to their bungalow by a cheerful, motherly black woman named Remona, Celia said, "I love this place. The island, its people, and the quietness. I'm glad you chose it, Andrew, and I'll never forget it."

"I'm glad too," he said.

Andrew's first suggestion for their honeymoon had been Hawaii. But he had sensed a reluctance on Celia's part and switched to what was originally a second choice.

Now Celia said, "I didn't tell you this, but going to Hawaii would have made me sad."

When he asked her why, one more piece of geometry from the past slipped into place.

On December 7, 1941, when Celia was ten years old and with her mother in Philadelphia, her father, a U.S. Navy noncommissioned officer—Chief Petty Officer Willis de Grey—was in Hawaii, aboard the battleship USS *Arizona* at Pearl Harbor. During the Japanese attack that day, the *Arizona* was sunk and 1,102 sailors on the ship were lost. Most died belowdecks; their bodies were never recovered. One was Willis de Grey.

"Oh yes, I remember him," Celia said, answering Andrew's question. "Of course, he was away a lot of the time, at sea. But when he was home on leave the house was always noisy, full of fun. When he

24

was expected it was exciting. Even my little sister Janet felt it, though she doesn't remember him the way I do."

Andrew asked, "What was he like?"

Celia thought before answering. "Big, and with a booming voice, and he made people laugh, and he loved children. Also he was strong—not just physically, though he was that as well, but mentally. My mother isn't; you probably saw that. She relied on my father totally. Even when he wasn't there he'd tell her what to do in letters."

"And now she relies on you?"

"It seemed to work out that way. In fact, almost at once after my father died." Celia smiled. "Of course, I was horribly precocious. I probably still am."

"A little," Andrew said. "But I've decided I can live with it."

Later he said gently, "I can understand about the honeymoon, why you wouldn't choose Hawaii. But have you ever been there—to Pearl Harbor?"

Celia shook her head. "My mother never wanted to go and—though I'm not sure why—I'm not ready yet." She paused before continuing. "I'm told you can get close to where the *Arizona* sank, and look down and see the ship, though they were never able to raise it. You'll think this strange, Andrew, but one day I'd like to go to where my father died, though not alone. I'd like to take my children."

There was a silence, then Andrew said, "No, I don't think it's strange at all. And I'll make you a promise. One day, when we have our children and they can understand, then I'll arrange it."

On another day, in a leaky, weatherbeaten dinghy, while Andrew struggled inexpertly with the oars, they talked about Celia's work.

"I always thought," he commented, "that drug company detail men were always, well, men."

"Don't go too far from shore. I've a feeling this wreck is about to sink," Celia said. "Yes, you're right—mostly men, though there are a few women; some were military nurses. But I'm the first, and still the only, detail woman at Felding-Roth."

"That's an achievement. How did you manage it?"

"Deviously."

In 1952, Celia reminisced, she graduated from Penn State College with a B.S. in chemistry. She had financed her way through college in part with a scholarship and partly from working nights and weekends in a drugstore.

"The drugstore time—passing out prescription drugs with one hand and hair rollers or deodorant with the other—taught me a lot that proved useful later. Oh yes, and sometimes I sold from *under* the counter too."

She explained.

Men, mostly young, would come into the store and loiter uneasily, trying to get the attention of the male druggist. Celia always recognized the signs. She would ask, "Can I help you?" to which the reply was usually, "When will *he* be free?"

"If you want condoms," Celia would say sweetly, "we have a good selection." She would then bring various brands from under the counter, piling the boxes on top. The men, red-faced, would make their purchases and hurriedly leave.

Occasionally someone brash would ask if Celia would help him try the product out. To which she had a stock answer. "All right. Whenever you say. I think I'm over my syphilis by now." While some may have realized it was a joke, clearly no one wanted to take a chance because in each instance she never saw the questioner again.

Andrew laughed, gave up rowing, and let the boat drift.

Armed with her B.S. degree, Celia explained, she applied for a job with Felding-Roth Pharmaceuticals as a junior chemist. She was accepted and worked in the labs for two years.

"I learned some things there—mostly that unless you're a dedicated scientist, lab work is dull and repetitious. Sales and marketing were what interested me. They still do." She added, "It's also where some big decisions are made."

But making a change from lab work to selling proved difficult. Celia tried the conventional route of applying and was turned down. "I was told it was company policy that the only women employed in sales were secretaries."

Refusing to accept the decision, she planned a campaign.

"I found out that the person who would have to recommend a change in policy, if it happened at all, was Sam Hawthorne. You met him at our wedding."

"Your boss, the regional sales maestro," Andrew said. "The one who's stamped approval on our having two kids."

"Yes—so I can keep on working. Anyway, I decided the only way to

26

influence Hawthorne was through his wife. It was risky. It almost didn't work."

Mrs. Lilian Hawthorne, Celia discovered, was active in several women's groups and thus, it seemed, might be sympathetic to another woman's career ambitions. Therefore, in the daytime when Sam Hawthorne was at Felding-Roth, Celia went to see his wife at home.

"I'd never met her," Celia told Andrew. "I had no appointment. I just rang the bell and barged in."

The reception was hostile. Mrs. Hawthorne, in her early thirties and seven years older than Celia, was a strong, no-nonsense person with long, raven-black hair which she pushed back impatiently as Celia explained her objective. At the end Lilian Hawthorne said, "This is ridiculous. I have nothing to do with my husband's work. What's more, he'll be furious when he learns you came here."

"I know," Celia said. "It will probably cost me my job."

"You should have thought of that beforehand."

"Oh, I did, Mrs. Hawthorne. But I took a chance on your being up-to-date in your thinking, and believing in equal treatment for women, also that they shouldn't be penalized unfairly on account of their sex."

For a moment it looked as if Lilian Hawthorne would explode. She snapped at Celia, "You have a nerve!"

"Exactly," Celia said. "It's why I'll make a great saleswoman."

The other woman stared at her, then suddenly burst out laughing. "My God!" she said. "I do believe you deserve it."

And a moment later: "I was about to make coffee, Miss de Grey. Come in the kitchen and we'll talk."

It was the beginning of a friendship which would last across the years.

"Even then," Celia told Andrew, "Sam took some persuading. But he interviewed me, and I guess he liked what he saw, and Lilian kept working on him. Then he had to get the approval of *his* bosses. In the end, though, it all worked out." She looked down at the water in the dinghy; it was now above their ankles. "Andrew, I was right! This thing *is* sinking!"

Laughing, they jumped overboard and swam ashore, pulling the boat behind them.

"When I began work in sales, as a detail woman," Celia told Andrew over dinner that night, "I realized I didn't have to be as good as a man in my job. I had to be better."

"I remember a recent experience," her husband said, "when you were not only better than a man, you were better than this doctor."

She flashed a brilliant smile, removed her glasses, and touched his hand across the table. "I got lucky there, and not just with Lotromycin."

"You take your glasses off a lot," Andrew commented. "Why?"

"I'm shortsighted, so I need them. But I know I look better without glasses. That's why."

"You look good either way," he said. "But if the glasses bother you, you should consider contact lenses. A lot of people are beginning to have them."

"I'll find out about them when we get back," Celia said. "Anything else while I'm at it? Any other changes?"

"I like everything the way it is."

To get where they were, they had walked a mile from their bungalow, hand in hand down a winding, crudely paved road where traffic was a rarity. The night air was warm, the only sounds the chirrup of insects and a cascading of waves on an offshore reef. Now, in a tiny, roughly furnished café called Travellers Rest, they were eating the local standard fare—fried grouper, peas and rice.

While Travellers Rest would not have qualified for the Michelin Guide, it served tasty food for the hungry, the fish freshly caught and prepared in an ancient skillet over a wood fire by their host, a wiry, wizened Bahamian named Cleophas Moss. He had seated Andrew and Celia at a table overlooking the sea. A candle stuck in a beer bottle was between them. Directly ahead were scattered clouds and a near-full moon. "In New Jersey," Celia reminded Andrew, "it's probably cold and rainy."

"We'll be there soon enough. Tell me some more about you and selling drugs."

Her first assignment as a detail woman, Celia related, was to Nebraska where, until then, Felding-Roth had had no sales representation.

"In a way it was good for me. I knew exactly where I stood because I was starting from nothing. There was no organization, few records, no one to tell me whom to call on or where."

"Did your friend Sam do that deliberately—as some kind of test?"

"He may have. I never asked him."

Instead of asking, Celia got down to work. In Omaha she found a small apartment and with that as a base she drove through the state, city by city. In each place she tore out the "Physicians & Surgeons" section from the yellow pages of a phone book, then typed up record sheets and began making calls. There were 1,500 doctors, she discovered, in her territory; later she decided to concentrate on 200 whom she estimated were the biggest prescribers of drugs.

"You were a long way from home," Andrew said. "Were you lonely?"

"Didn't have time. I was too busy."

One early discovery was how difficult it was to get to see doctors. "I'd spend *hours* sitting in waiting rooms. Then, when I'd finally get in, a doctor might give me five minutes, no more. Finally a doctor in North Platte threw me out of his office, but he did me a big favor at the same time."

"How?"

Celia tasted some fried grouper and pronounced, "Loaded with fat! I shouldn't eat it, but it's too good to pass up." She put down her fork and sat back, remembering.

"He was an internist, like you, Andrew. I'd say about forty, and I think he'd had a bad day. Anyway, I'd just started my sales talk and he stopped me. 'Young lady,' he said, 'you're trying to talk professional medicine with me, so let me tell you something. I spent four years in medical school, another five being an intern and resident, I've been in practice ten years, and while I don't know everything, I know so much more than you it isn't funny. What you're trying to tell me, with your inadequate knowledge, I could read in twenty seconds on an advertising page of any medical magazine. So get out!' "

Andrew grimaced. "Cruel."

"But good for me," Celia said, "even though I went out feeling like something scraped off the floor. Because he was right."

"Hadn't the drug company—Felding-Roth—given you any training?"

"Oh, a little. But short and superficial, a series of sales spiels, mostly. My chemistry background helped, though not much. I simply wasn't equipped to talk with busy, highly qualified doctors."

"Since you mention it," Andrew said, "that's a reason why some doctors won't see drug detail men. Apart from having to listen to a canned sales pitch, you can get incorrect information that is dangerous. Some detail men will tell you anything, even mislead you, to get you to prescribe their product."

"Andrew dear, I want you to do something for me about that. I'll tell you later."

"Okay—if I can. So what happened after North Platte?"

"I realized two things. First, I must stop thinking like a salesman and not do any kind of pushy selling. Second, despite doctors knowing more than I did, I needed to find out specific things about drugs that they didn't know, which might be helpful to them. In that way I'd become useful. Incidentally, while attempting all that, I discovered something else. Doctors learn a lot about disease, but they're not well informed about drugs."

"True," Andrew agreed. "What you're taught in medical school about drugs isn't worth a damn, and in practice it's hard enough to keep up with medical developments, never mind drugs. So where prescribing is concerned, it's sometimes trial and error."

"Then there was something else," Celia said. "I realized I must always tell doctors the exact truth, and never exaggerate, never conceal. And if I was asked about a competitor's product and it was better than ours, I'd say so."

"How did you make this big change?"

"For quite a while I had four hours' sleep a night."

Celia described how, after a regular day's work, she would spend evenings and weekends reading every drug manual she could get her hands on. She studied each in detail, making notes and memorizing. If there were unanswered questions, she sought answers in libraries. She made a trip back to Felding-Roth headquarters in New Jersey and badgered former colleagues on the scientific side to tell her more than the manuals did, also what was being developed and would be available soon. Before long her presentations to doctors improved; some doctors asked her to obtain specific information, which she did. After a while she saw that she was getting results. Orders for Felding-Roth drugs from her territory increased.

Andrew said admiringly, "Celia, you're one of a kind. Unique."

She laughed. "And you're prejudiced, though I love it. Anyway, in just over a year the company tripled its business in Nebraska."

"That's when they brought you in from the outfield?"

"They gave someone else who was newer, a man, the Nebraska territory and me a more important one in New Jersey."

"Just think," Andrew said, "if they'd sent you to some other place like Illinois or California we'd never have met."

"No," she said confidently, "we'd have met. One way or another we were destined to. 'Wedding is destiny.'"

He finished the quotation. "'And hanging likewise.'"

They both laughed.

"Fancy that!" Celia said, delighted. "A stuffy head-in-textbook physician who can recite John Heywood."

"The same Heywood, a sixteenth-century writer, who also sang and played music for Henry the Eighth," Andrew boasted, equally pleased.

They got up from the table and their host called over from his woodburning stove, "Dat good fish, you young honeymooners? Erryting okay?"

"Everything's *very* okay," Celia assured him. "With the fish *and* the honeymoon."

Andrew said, amused, "No secrets on a small island." He paid for their meal with a ten-shilling Bahamian note—a modest sum when translated into dollars—and waved away change.

Outside, where it was cooler now, and with the sea breeze freshening, they happily linked arms and walked back up the quiet, winding road.

It was their last day.

As if in keeping with the sadness of departure, the Bahamas weather had turned gloomy. A stratocumulus overcast was accompanied by morning showers while a strong northeast wind whipped whitecaps on the sea and set waves beating heavily onshore.

Andrew and Celia were to leave at midday by Bahamas Airways from Rock Sound, connecting at Nassau with a northbound Pan Am flight which would get them to New York that night. They were due in Morristown the following day where, until they found a suitable house, Andrew's apartment on South Street would be home. Celia, who had been living in furnished rooms in Boonton, had already moved out from there, putting some of her things in storage.

In the honeymoon bungalow which they would leave in less than an hour Celia was packing, her clothes spread out on the double bed. She called to Andrew, who was in the bathroom shaving, "It's been so wonderful here. And this is just the beginning."

Through the open doorway he answered, "A spectacular beginning! Even so, I'm ready to get back to work."

"You know something, Andrew? I think you and I thrive on work.
We have that in common, and we're both ambitious. We'll always be
that way."

"Uh-huh." He emerged from the bathroom naked, wiping his face
with a towel. "No reason not to stop work once in a while, though.
Provided there's a good reason."

Celia started to say, "Do we have time?" but was unable to finish
because Andrew was kissing her.

Moments later he murmured, "Could you please clear that bed?"

Reaching behind, without looking and with one arm around Andrew, Celia began to throw clothes on the floor.

"That's better," he said as they lay down where the clothes had
been. "This is what beds are for."

She giggled. "We could be late for our flight."

"Who cares?"

Soon after, she said contentedly, "You're right. Who cares?" And
later, tenderly and happily, "I care . . ." and then, "Oh, Andrew, I
love you so!"

4

Aboard Pan American Flight 206 to New York were copies of that
day's *New York Times*. Leafing through the newspaper, Celia observed, "Nothing much changed while we were away."

A dispatch from Moscow quoted Nikita Khrushchev as challenging
the United States to a "missile-shooting match." A future world war,
the Soviet leader boasted, would be fought on the American continent, and he predicted "the death of capitalism and the universal
triumph of communism."

President Eisenhower, on the other hand, assured Americans that U.S. defense spending would keep pace with Soviet challenges.

And an investigation into the gangland slaying of Mafia boss Albert Anastasia, gunned down while in a barber's chair at New York's Park-Sheraton Hotel, was continuing, so far without result.

Andrew, too, skimmed the newspaper, then put it away.

It would be a four-hour flight aboard the propeller-driven DC-7B and dinner was served soon after takeoff. After dinner Andrew reminded his wife, "You said there was something you wanted me to do. Something about drug company detail men."

"Yes, there is." Celia Jordan settled back comfortably in her seat, then reached for Andrew's hand and held it. "It goes back to that talk we had the day after you used Lotromycin, and your patient recovered. You told me you were changing your mind about the drug industry, feeling more favorable, and I said don't change it too much because there are things which are wrong and which I hope to alter. Remember?"

"How could I forget?" He laughed. "Every detail of that day is engraved on my soul."

"Good! So let me fill in some background."

Looking sideways at his wife, Andrew marveled again at how much drive and intelligence was contained in such a small, attractive package. In the years ahead, he reflected, he would need to stay alert and informed just to keep up with Celia mentally. Now, he concentrated on listening.

The pharmaceutical industry in 1957, Celia began, was in some ways still too close to its roots, its early origins.

"We started off, not all that long ago, selling snake oil at country fairs, and fertility potions, and a pill to cure everything from headache to cancer. The salesmen who sold those things didn't care what they claimed or promised. All they wanted was sales. They'd guarantee any result to get them."

Often, Celia went on, such nostrums and folk remedies were marketed by families. It was some of the same families who opened early drugstores. Later still, their descendants continued the family tradition and built drug manufacturing firms which, as years went by, became big, scientific and respectable. As it all happened, the crude early selling methods changed and became more respectable too.

"But sometimes not respectable enough. One reason was that fam-

33

ily control persisted, and the old snake-oil, hard-sell tradition was in the blood."

"Surely," Andrew observed, "there can't be many families left that control big drug companies."

"Not many, though some of the original families control large blocks of stock. But what *has* persisted, even with paid executives running the companies, is the out-of-date, less-than-ethical hard sell. Much of it happens when some detail men call on doctors to tell them about new drugs."

Celia continued, "As you know, some detail men—not all, but still too many—will say anything, even lie, to get doctors to prescribe the drugs they're selling. And although drug companies will tell you officially they don't condone it, they know it goes on."

They were interrupted by a stewardess announcing they would land in New York in forty minutes, the bar would be closed soon, and meanwhile would they like drinks? Celia ordered her favorite, a daiquiri, Andrew scotch and soda.

When the drinks were served and they had settled down again Andrew said, "Sure, I've seen examples of what you were talking about. Also I've heard stories from other doctors—about patients being ill or even dying after taking drugs, all because detail men gave false information which the doctors believed." He sipped his scotch, then went on, "Then there's drug company advertising. Doctors are deluged with it, but a lot of the advertising doesn't tell a physician what he ought to know—especially about side effects of drugs, including dangerous ones. The thing is, when you're busy, with patients to see and a lot of other problems on your mind, it's hard to believe that someone from a drug company, or the company itself, is deliberately deceiving you."

"But it happens," Celia said. "And afterward it's swept under the rug and nobody will talk about it. I know, because I've tried to talk about it at Felding-Roth."

"So what's your plan?"

"To build a record. A record no one can argue with. Then, at the proper time, I'll use it."

She went on to explain.

"I won't be calling on you any more, Andrew; that's company policy, so someone else from Felding-Roth will be covering your office and Dr. Townsend's. But whenever you have a detail man—or woman—visit you, from our company or any other, and you discover

34

you're being given wrong information, or not warned about side effects of a drug or anything else you should be told, I want you to write a report and give it to me. I have some other doctors doing the same thing, doctors who trust me, in Nebraska as well as New Jersey, and my file is getting thick."

Andrew whistled softly. "You're taking on something pretty big. Also some risks."

"Someone has to take risks if it's to improve a bad situation. And I'm not afraid."

"No," he said, "I don't believe you ever would be."

"I'll tell you something, Andrew. If the big drug companies don't clean house themselves, and soon, I believe the government will do it for them. There are rumblings in Congress now. If the drug industry waits for congressional hearings, and then new laws with tough restrictions, they'll wish they'd acted first on their own."

Andrew was silent, absorbing what he had just learned and mulling other thoughts. At length he said, "I haven't asked you this before, Celia, but maybe now is a good time for me to understand something about you."

His wife's eyes were fixed on him, her expression serious. Andrew chose his words carefully.

"You've talked about having a career, which is fine by me, and I'm sure you wouldn't be happy without it. But I've had the impression, while we've been together these past weeks, that you want more out of a career than what you're doing now—being a saleswoman."

Celia said quietly. "Yes, I do. I'm going to the top."

"*Right* to the top?" Andrew was startled. "You mean head up a big drug company?"

"If I can. And even if I don't get all the way to the top, I intend to be close enough to have real influence and power."

He said doubtfully, "And that's what you want? Power?"

"I know what you're thinking, Andrew—that power can be obsessive and corrupting. I don't intend to let it be either. I simply want a full life, with marriage and children, but also something more, some solid achievement."

"That day in the cafeteria . . ." Andrew stopped, correcting himself. "That *memorable* day. You said it was time for women to do things they haven't done before. Well, I believe that too; it's already happening in a lot of places, including medicine. But I wonder about

35

your industry—pharmaceuticals. That whole business is conservative and male-oriented—you've said so yourself."

Celia smiled. "Horribly so."

"Then is it ready yet—for someone like you? The reason I'm asking, Celia, is that I don't want to watch, and see you hurt or unhappy, while you throw everything into the effort and then maybe it doesn't work out."

"I won't be unhappy. I'll promise you that." She squeezed Andrew's arm. "It's new for me to have someone care as much as you do, darling, and I like it. And as for your question—no, the industry isn't ready yet, for me or any other women with strong ambition. But I have a plan."

"I should have known you'd have it all figured out."

"First," Celia told him, "I intend to make myself so good at my job that Felding-Roth will discover they can't afford *not* to promote me."

"I'd bet on that. But you said 'first.' Isn't that enough?"

Celia shook her head. "I've studied other companies, their histories, the people who run them, and discovered one thing. Most of those who make it to the top get there on someone else's coattails. Oh, don't misunderstand me—they have to work hard, and be excellent. But early on they select some individual—a little higher up, usually a bit older—who they believe is en route to the top ahead of them. Then they make themselves useful to that person, give him their loyalty, and follow along behind. The point is: when a senior executive gets promoted, he likes someone he's used to, who is capable and whom he can trust, coming up behind."

"At this point," Andrew asked, "have *you* picked someone to follow?"

"I decided some time ago," Celia said. "It's Sam Hawthorne."

"Well, well!" Her husband raised his eyebrows. "One way or another, Sam seems to loom large in our lives."

"In business matters only. So you've no need to be jealous."

"All right. But does Sam know about this decision—that you're hitching to his star?"

"Of course not. Lilian Hawthorne does, though. We've discussed it confidentially and Lilian approves."

"It seems to me," Andrew said, "there's been some womanly plotting going on."

"And why not?" For a moment the inner steel of Celia flashed. "Someday all that may not be needed. But right now the corporate

36

business world is like a private men's club. So a woman must use whatever means she can to become a member and get ahead."

Andrew was silent, considering, then he said, "Until now I hadn't thought about it a lot; I guess most men don't. But what you say makes sense. So okay, Celia, while you're making your way to the top —and I truly believe you just might—I'll be behind you, all the way."

His wife leaned over in her seat and kissed him. "I knew that all along. It's one of the reasons I married you."

They felt the airplane's engines moderate in tempo and the "Fasten Seat Belts" sign came on. Through windows on the port side the lights of Manhattan shimmered in early evening darkness. "In a few minutes," a stewardess announced, "we will be landing at Idlewild International Airport."

Again Celia reached for Andrew's hand.

"And *we'll* be starting our life together," she said. "How can we miss?"

5

On returning to their separate jobs, Andrew and Celia discovered they had each, in differing ways, achieved celebrity status.

Like many important medical developments, the news about Andrew's successful use of Lotromycin took time to circulate but now, some six weeks after Mary Rowe's remarkable recovery, it had been picked up by the national press.

Morristown's tiny *Daily Record* had carried the story first under a heading:

Local Medic Uses Wonder Drug
Patient's "Miracle" Recovery

The *Newark Star-Ledger*, which clearly scanned the local papers in its bailiwick, repeated the item which, in turn, came to the attention of science writers at the *New York Times* and *Time*. When Andrew returned he discovered that urgent phone messages had been left for him to call both publications, which he did. Still more publicity resulted, with *Time*, the more romantically inclined, adding to its report the fact of Andrew and Celia's marriage.

As well as all this, the *New England Journal of Medicine* informed Andrew that, subject to certain revisions, his article on Lotromycin would be published in due course. The suggested revisions were minor and Andrew agreed to them at once.

"I don't mind admitting I'm consumed with envy," Dr. Noah Townsend observed when Andrew told him about the *New England Journal*. Then Andrew's senior partner added, "But I console myself with the luster it's already bringing to our practice."

Later, Townsend's wife Hilda, attractive in her early fifties, confided to Andrew, "Noah won't tell you this, but he's so proud of you that nowadays he's thinking of you like a son—the son we'd both have liked but never had."

Celia, while receiving less personal publicity, found her status at Felding-Roth changed in not-so-subtle ways.

Previously she had been an anachronism, to some a source of curiosity and amusement—the firm's sole saleswoman who, despite an initial and unexpected accomplishment in Nebraska, still had to prove herself over the long term. Not any more. Her handling of Lotromycin, and the continuing publicity which delighted Felding-Roth, had put both the drug and Celia squarely on the road to success.

Within the company her name was now well known to top executives, including Felding-Roth's president, Eli Camperdown, who sent for Celia a day after her return to work.

Mr. Camperdown, a lanky, cadaverous industry veteran in his mid-sixties, who always dressed impeccably and was never seen without a red rose in his buttonhole, received Celia in his ornate office suite on the eleventh floor—executive country—of the Felding-Roth building in Boonton. He attended to the amenities first.

"My congratulations on your marriage, Mrs. Jordan. I hope you'll be happy." He added with a smile, "I also trust that from now on your husband will prescribe nothing but Felding-Roth products."

Celia thanked him and decided the remark about Andrew was merely facetious, so let it go without pointing up her husband's independence where drugs and medicine were concerned.

"You have become something of a legend, young lady," the president continued. "Living proof that an outstanding woman, occasionally, can be every bit as good as a man."

"I hope, sir," Celia said sweetly, "that someday you won't feel the need for that 'occasionally.' I believe you'll see many more women in this business, and some may be even *better* than the men."

For a moment Camperdown seemed taken aback and frowned. Then, recovering his geniality, he said, "I suppose stranger things have happened. We'll see. We'll see."

They continued talking, Camperdown asking questions of Celia about her merchandising experiences. He seemed impressed by her informed, straightforward answers. Then, pulling a watch from a vest pocket, the president glanced at it and announced, "I'm about to hold a meeting here, Mrs. Jordan. It concerns a new drug we intend to market soon after Lotromycin. Perhaps you'd care to stay."

When she agreed that she would, the president called in a half-dozen male staff members who had been waiting outside in a secretary's office. After introductions they all moved to a conference area of the office suite, seating themselves around a table with Camperdown at the head.

The newcomers included the director of research, Dr. Vincent Lord, a recently recruited, youngish scientist; an elderly vice president of sales who was shortly to retire; and four others, including Sam Hawthorne. With the exception of Sam—the only one Celia had met previously—the others regarded her with frank curiosity.

The new drug under consideration, Camperdown explained for Celia's benefit, was not a product developed by Felding-Roth, but had been obtained under license from a West German company, Chemie-Grünenthal.

"It is a sedative, one of the safest ever discovered," the president declared, "and it produces a normal, refreshing sleep without unpleasant morning-after grogginess." The product had no significant side effects, he continued, and was so safe it could be given to small children. The sedative was already on sale, and popular, in almost every major country except the United States. Now, Felding-Roth was fortunate in having the American rights.

The name of the drug, Mr. Camperdown added, was Thalidomide.

Despite Thalidomide's proven safety record, trials of the drug on humans were required in the United States before its sale would be approved by the Food and Drug Administration. "In the circumstances, with all that first-rate foreign data," Camperdown grumbled, "it's a silly, bureaucratic requirement, but we have to live with it."

A discussion followed about where and how the U.S. trials of Thalidomide would be carried out. The director of research, Dr. Lord, favored recruitment of fifty or so physicians in private practice who would give the drug to patients, then report results which Felding-Roth would submit to FDA. "There should be a mix of general practitioners, internists, psychiatrists, and obstetricians," he declared.

The vice president of sales demanded, "How long will all that rigmarole take?"

"Probably three months."

"Could you make it two? We need this product on the market."

"I think so."

Someone else, though, expressed concern about the trials being so widespread. Wouldn't they be simpler and reporting be faster in a concentrated environment such as a hospital?

After several minutes of discussion Camperdown interjected with a smile, "Perhaps our young lady guest has some thoughts on the subject."

"Yes, I have," Celia said.

All heads turned toward her.

She spoke carefully, aware that her presence here was unusual, even privileged; therefore it would be foolish to spoil the opportunity by seeming too assured or brash.

"One thing that could be worrisome," Celia said, "is the suggestion that obstetricians prescribe this drug. This means pregnant women would be taking it, and it's usually advised that pregnancy is not a time for experimenting in any way."

Dr. Lord interrupted testily. "In this case that doesn't apply. Thalidomide has been widely used in Europe and elsewhere, and those taking it have included pregnant women."

"Just the same," Sam Hawthorne put in quietly, "Mrs. Jordan has a point."

Celia continued, "A question which might be asked is this: Who are the people who have the most trouble sleeping, and therefore need a sleeping pill? Well, based on my experience in detailing—visiting hospitals and institutions, as well as doctors—I'd say old people, especially geriatric patients."

She had the group's attention. Several around the table nodded agreement at the last remark. Dr. Lord, his face set stiffly, did not.

"So what I'd recommend," Celia said, "is that our testing of Thalidomide be done in one or two old people's homes. If it's of any use, I know of two of them—one in Lincoln, Nebraska, the other outside Plainfield in this state. Both are well run and efficient, and would keep good records. In both places I've met the doctors in charge and would be glad to contact them."

When Celia had finished there was an uncertain silence. Eli Camperdown broke it. The Felding-Roth president sounded surprised.

"I don't know what the rest of you think, but what Mrs. Jordan has just suggested sounds to me like very good sense."

Having been shown the way, others added their agreement, though Dr. Lord remained silent. Celia immediately sensed an antagonism between herself and the director of research which would persist into the future.

Soon after, a decision was made that Celia would telephone her institutional acquaintances next day and, if they seemed cooperative, the Research Department would take it from there.

As the meeting broke up, Celia left first, amid smiles and friendly handshakes.

A week or so later, having done what was asked, Celia learned through Sam Hawthorne that trials of Thalidomide at both of the old people's homes would soon be under way.

At the time, it seemed the end of a minor incident.

Amid the pressures of their professional lives Andrew and Celia found time to look at houses for sale. One, which Celia found and liked, was at Convent Station, a residential suburb in Morris township, where homes were spaced widely apart and lawns and trees proliferated. As she pointed out when she called Andrew, the house was only two miles from his office and even closer to St. Bede's Hospital. "That's important," Celia declared, "because I don't want you to have to drive a long way, especially when you have night calls and may be tired."

The location would mean a ten-mile commute for Celia on the days she went to Felding-Roth at Boonton, but since most of her sales calls were in other parts of New Jersey, the distance was not important.

But the house, which was a large, unoccupied, neglected, white-

41

frame colonial, shocked Andrew when he saw it. He protested, "Celia, this broken-down old barn isn't for us! Even if we patched it up, which looks impossible, what would we do with five bedrooms?"

"There'd be one for us," his wife explained patiently, "then one each for the children, and after they're born we'll want live-in help, so that's one more." The fifth bedroom, she added, would be for guests. "My mother will be coming to us occasionally, and maybe yours."

Celia also envisaged "a downstairs study-den which the two of us can share, and be together when we bring work home."

Though he had no intention of agreeing to such a wildly impractical idea, Andrew laughed. "You certainly look ahead."

"What neither of us will want," Celia argued, "is the interruption and nuisance of changing homes every few years just because we need more space and didn't plan for it." She looked around her, surveying the cobwebbed, dirt-encrusted lower floor of the house through which they had walked on a Sunday afternoon in January, with pale sunshine glinting through grimy windows. "This place needs scouring, painting, organizing, but it can be beautiful—the kind of home we won't want to leave unless we have to."

"I'm leaving right now," Andrew said, "because what this place needs most is a bulldozer." He added, with rare impatience. "You've been right about a lot of things, but not this time."

Celia seemed undeterred. Putting her arms around Andrew, she stood on tiptoes to kiss him. "I still think I'm right. Let's go home and talk about it."

Later that night, reluctantly, Andrew gave in and next day Celia negotiated the purchase at a bargain price and arranged a mortgage. The down payment created no difficulty. Both she and Andrew had saved money from their earnings over the preceding few years and their combined current incomes were strong.

They moved in near the end of April, and almost at once Andrew conceded he had been wrong about the house. "I already like it," he said on their first day; "I may even get to love it." The renovation had cost less than he expected and results were impressive, even beautiful.

It was a happy time for them both, not least because Celia was, by now, five months pregnant.

6

The birth of Celia and Andrew's first child occurred—as Andrew was apt to tell his hospital colleagues—"precisely according to Celia's schedule."

It happened in August 1958, nine months and one week after their marriage, and the child was a girl, healthy, weighing seven and a half pounds. She was a contented baby who cried hardly at all. They named her Lisa.

During her pregnancy Celia had been firm about birth procedures, which caused an early clash with her obstetrician, Dr. Paul Keating, a fellow staff member of Andrew's at St. Bede's Hospital. Keating, a fussy, middle-aged man who inclined to pomposity, told Andrew at one point, "Your wife is really quite impossible."

"I know what you mean," Andrew sympathized, "but it sure makes life interesting. The funny thing is, what's impossible for some people becomes possible for Celia."

A day or two earlier Celia had informed Dr. Keating, "I've been studying natural childbirth and have begun the exercises which go with it." When the obstetrician smiled indulgently she added, "I'll want to participate actively in labor and be fully aware at the moment of birth. That means no anesthesia. Also, I want no episiotomy."

Keating's smile changed to a frown. "My dear Mrs. Jordan, both those decisions must be taken by your obstetrician during delivery."

"I disagree," Celia said quietly and calmly. "If I concede that, I'm likely to be overruled at a moment when I'm not at my best."

"What if there's an emergency?"

"That's entirely different. If it happened, obviously you'd have to exercise judgment and do what was needed. But afterward you would have to satisfy me, and also Andrew, that an emergency had existed."

43

Dr. Keating grunted noncommittally, then said, "Concerning an episiotomy. You may not realize that cutting the perineum with surgical scissors just before birth prevents a tear when the baby's head emerges—a tear that is painful and heals less easily than a clean surgical cut."

"Oh, I do realize that," Celia said. "And I'm sure you're equally aware of the increasing number of doctors and nurse-midwives who disagree with that view."

Ignoring the obstetrician's growing disapproval, Celia added, "There are plenty of recorded cases where natural tears have healed quickly, whereas episiotomies have not, and have produced infections or months of postpartum pain, or both."

Dr. Keating regarded her dourly. "You seem to know all the answers."

"Not at all," Celia assured him. "It's just that it's my body and my baby."

"Speaking of your body," the obstetrician said, "I'll point out that although it is not the purpose of an episiotomy, the sewing up afterward does maintain vaginal tightness."

"Yes," Celia acknowledged, "I'm aware that vaginal tightness is for the pleasure of my future sex partner. Well, doctor, I don't want any complaints from my husband about a loose vagina, so after my baby is born I'll do exercises to tighten the pelvic muscles."

Soon after, by mutual consent, Celia changed obstetricians and became the patient of Dr. Eunice Nashman, who was older than Dr. Keating but young enough in mind to share many of Celia's ideas.

Subsequent to Lisa's birth Eunice Nashman confided to Andrew, "Your wife is a remarkable woman. There were moments when she was in great pain and I asked if she wanted to change her mind about anesthesia."

Andrew, who had intended to be present at the birth but was called away by a medical emergency involving one of his own patients, asked curiously, "What did she say?"

Dr. Nashman answered, "She just said, 'No, but someone please hold me.' So one of the nurses put her arms around your wife and comforted her, and that was all she needed.

"Then, when your daughter was born, we didn't take the baby away, as usually happens, but just left her lying with Celia, and the two of them together were so at peace it was beautiful to see."

44

As she had said she would, Celia took a year off from work to give her attention and love to Lisa. She also used the time to continue organizing their Convent Station house, which proved to be everything she had foreseen and promised. "I do love it," Andrew observed glowingly one day.

At the same time Celia kept in touch with Felding-Roth. Sam Hawthorne had moved upward to become assistant national sales manager and had promised Celia a job when she was ready to return.

The year was a good one for Felding-Roth Pharmaceuticals, Inc. A few months after the publicity concerning Dr. Andrew Jordan's dramatic use of Lotromycin, the U.S. Food and Drug Administration approved the drug for marketing. Lotromycin went on to become successful and praised worldwide, and one of the more profitable products in Felding-Roth's history. Celia's own contribution to the Lotromycin launch caused executives of the company to endorse Sam Hawthorne's willingness to have her return.

Beyond the company, in terms of history, 1959 was not a spectacular year. Alaska became a state in January, Hawaii in July. To the north, during April, the St. Lawrence Seaway opened. In May, Israel's Premier David Ben-Gurion promised the world that his country would seek peace with its Arab neighbors. Later the same month two monkeys made a 300-mile-high space flight aboard a U.S. army missile, and survived. It was hoped that humans might someday do the same.

One outside event which aroused Celia's attention was a series of hearings, begun during December, by a U.S. Senate subcommittee chaired by Senator Estes Kefauver. During earlier hearings about crime the senator, a Tennessee democrat with presidential ambitions, had gained wide attention and was hungry for more of the same. The target at the new hearings was the pharmaceutical industry.

Most industry officials dismissed Kefauver as a nuisance, but unimportant. The industry's Washington lobby was strong; no long-term effect was expected. Celia, though confiding her opinion only to Andrew, disagreed.

Finally, late in the year, Celia resumed her duties as a detail woman, again with her sales territory in New Jersey. Through contacts at St. Bede's she had found an elderly retired nurse who came to

45

the house daily and took care of Lisa. Typically, Celia tested the arrangement, by going on an out-of-town trip with Andrew and leaving the older woman in charge. It worked well.

Celia's mother, Mildred, occasionally visited from Philadelphia and enjoyed filling in, and getting to know her granddaughter, when the daily nurse was away.

Mildred and Andrew were on excellent terms, and Celia became closer to her mother as time went by, sharing an intimacy they had rarely known in earlier years. One reason, perhaps, was that Celia's younger sister, Janet, was far away—in the Trucial Sheikdoms—having married an oil company geologist, now busy overseas.

Thus, with support from several sources Celia and Andrew were once more able to take pleasure in their separate careers.

In the case of Andrew's career, only one thing marred it slightly, and just how important that worry was, Andrew himself was uncertain. It concerned Noah Townsend.

Andrew's senior partner had, over a handful of widely separated occasions, exhibited what could have been signs of emotional instability. Or perhaps, when Andrew thought about it, bizarre behavior was a more accurate description. What puzzled Andrew was that both characteristics were alien to the nature of the older, dignified physician as Andrew had observed it day by day.

There were three incidents that Andrew knew of.

One was when Noah, during a conversation in his office with Andrew, became impatient because of a telephone call that interrupted him. After a brusque response to the call, he yanked the telephone cord from the wall and hurled the instrument across the office where it hit a file cabinet and broke. Then Noah continued talking as if nothing had happened.

Next day a replacement telephone was on Noah's desk; the fate of the old one was never mentioned.

Some six weeks later Andrew was in Noah's car, with Noah driving. Suddenly, to Andrew's horror, they were hurtling through Morristown with the accelerator floored, skidding around corners, and going through a red light. Andrew shouted a warning, but Noah appeared not to hear. Through extraordinary luck, no accident occurred, and they raced into St. Bede's parking lot, then slid to a halt with a screech of tires. While Andrew was protesting, Noah just shrugged—and the next time Andrew observed Noah driving, it was at a safe speed with normal caution.

A third incident, again widely separated from the others, but the most distressing, involved their office receptionist-secretary, Mrs. Parsons, who had worked for Noah for many years, long before Andrew's arrival. True, Violet Parsons in her mid-sixties was slowing down and was occasionally forgetful. But it was seldom about anything important, and she was good with patients, who liked her. She and Andrew got along well, and her devotion to Noah—close to adoration—was an in-house joke.

Until an incident about a check.

In preparing one for payment of office supplies, Violet made an error. The invoice was for forty-five dollars. She reversed the figures, made out the check for fifty-four dollars, and left it on Noah's desk for him to sign. In practical terms it didn't matter, since the extra amount would have appeared as a credit on the following month's bill.

But Noah stormed into the reception area with the check in his hand and shouted at Violet Parsons, "You stupid bitch! Are you trying to ruin me by giving away my money?"

Andrew, who happened to be entering the office at that moment, could hardly believe what he was hearing. Nor, it seemed, could Violet, who stood up and replied with dignity, "Dr. Townsend, I have never been spoken to in that manner before, and do not intend to have it happen again. I am leaving now and will not be back."

When Andrew tried to intervene, Noah snapped, "Stay out of this!" And Violet said, "Thank you Dr. Jordan, but I no longer work here."

Next day Andrew tried to bring up the subject with Noah, but the older man merely growled, "She wasn't doing her job. I've hired someone else; she starts tomorrow."

If the incidents had been less isolated or more frequent, Andrew might have had greater concern. But, he reasoned, as everyone grew older the pressures of work and daily living could cause tensions to erupt and tempers fray. It was, after all, a human characteristic. Andrew himself felt those pressures at times, with a resultant edginess which he contained. Noah, it seemed, had not contained his.

Still, the incidents troubled Andrew.

Celia's career activities were more upbeat.

In February 1960, on a day when she had left her sales territory to transact some business at Felding-Roth headquarters, Sam Hawthorne summoned her to his office. Sam was in a relaxed mood and greeted Celia cordially. His new responsibilities in national sales did not appear to be wearing him down, she thought—a good sign. Also, in view of her own long-term plans, an optimistic one. Sam's hair, though, was noticeably thinner; by his fortieth birthday, now a year away, he would probably be bald, though the look seemed to suit him.

"I wanted to see you about the national sales meeting," he announced.

Celia already knew that Felding-Roth's biennial sales convention would be held at the Waldorf-Astoria Hotel in New York in April. While private and closed to outsiders, the affair was attended by all company sales people in the United States, plus officers of Felding-Roth subsidiaries abroad. As well, the chairman, president and other senior executives would be present during the three-day proceedings.

"I'm expecting to be there," Celia said. "I hope you're not going to tell me it's for men only."

"Not only is it not men only, but the top brass want you to be one of the speakers."

"I'll do it," Celia said.

Sam observed dryly, "I was sure of *that*. Now, about the subject. I've talked to Eli Camperdown and what he and others would like is for you to describe some of your selling experiences—from a feminine point of view. There's a suggested title: 'A Woman Looks at Pharmaceutical Detailing.'"

"I can't see it on a movie marquee," Celia said, "but it'll do."

"You should keep your talk light, possibly humorous," Sam continued. "Nothing heavy or serious. Nothing controversial. And ten to fifteen minutes should be enough."

Celia said thoughtfully, ". . . I see."

"If you like, you can submit a draft. Then I'll go over it and make suggestions."

"I'll remember that offer," said Celia, who already had ideas about her speech and had no intention of submitting anything.

"Sales in your territory have been excellent," Sam complimented her. "Keep it up!"

"I intend to," she acknowledged, "though some new products would help. By the way, what happened to the one Mr. Camperdown talked about a year ago—Thalidomide?"

"We dropped it. Gave it back to Chemie-Grünenthal. Said thanks but no thanks."

"Why?"

"According to our research people," Sam explained, "it wasn't a good drug. They tried it out in those old people's homes, as you arranged. As a sleep aid it didn't seem to work."

"And that's the end?"

"So far as Felding-Roth is concerned. I just heard, though, that the Merrell Company has taken Thalidomide on. They're calling it Kevadon and they plan a big launching here and in Canada." He added, "With all the success Thalidomide has had in Europe, that's not surprising."

"You sound unhappy," Celia said. "Do you think our company made a mistake?"

Sam shrugged. "Maybe. But we can only sell what our research department approves, and this is one they didn't." He hesitated, then said, "I may as well tell you, Celia, there are a few people around here who are criticizing you because our testing of Thalidomide was limited to old people and wasn't more widespread—as Vincent Lord originally wanted."

"Are you one of the critics?"

"No. At the time, if you remember, I agreed with you."

"I do remember." Celia considered, then she asked, "Is the other criticism important?"

"To you?" Sam shook his head. "I don't think so."

At home, during the evenings and weekends which followed, Celia worked on her sales meeting speech. In the quiet, comfortable study-den she and Andrew enjoyed sharing, she surrounded herself with papers and notes.

Watching her one Sunday, Andrew observed, "You're cooking up something, aren't you?"

"Yes," she admitted, "I am."

"Will you tell me?"

49

"I'll tell you later," Celia said. "If I tell you now, you'll try to talk me out of it."

Andrew smiled and was wise enough to leave it there.

7

"I know that most of you are married," Celia said, looking out over the sea of male faces that confronted her, "so you know how it is with us women. We're often vague, we get mixed up, and sometimes forget things altogether."

"Not you, sharp girl," someone near the front said softly, and Celia smiled swiftly, but continued.

"One of the things *I've* forgotten is how long I'm supposed to speak today. I've a vague notion of someone mentioning ten to fifteen minutes, but that couldn't possibly be right, could it? After all, what woman could make herself intimately known to five hundred men in that short time?"

There was laughter and, from the back of the convention hall, a broad Midwestern voice. "You can have as much of my time as you want, baby!" This was followed by more laughter, wolf whistles, and cries of, "Same here!", "Take all you need, kiddo!"

Leaning closer to the microphone in front of her on the speakers' platform, Celia responded, "Thank you! I was hoping someone would say that." She avoided meeting the eyes of Sam Hawthorne, watching her intently from a few seats away.

It was Sam who, earlier that day, had told Celia, "At the opening of a sales meeting everybody feels their oats. That's why the first day is mostly hype. We try to get all the guys worked up—tell those who are in from the field how great they are, what a topnotch outfit Felding-Roth is, and how happy we are to have them on the team. After that, for the next two days, we get down to more serious business."

"Am I part of the hype?" Celia had asked, having observed from the program that she would be speaking during the afternoon of the first convention day.

"Sure, and why not? You're the only female we have actively selling, a lot of the guys have heard about you, and all of them want to see and hear something different."

Celia said, "I must try not to disappoint them."

At the time, she and Sam had been walking on Park Avenue, shortly after breakfasting at the Waldorf with several others from the company. In an hour the sales convention would begin. Meanwhile they were enjoying the mild and sunny April morning. Clear fresh breezes were sweeping through Manhattan and springtime proclaimed itself in massed tulips and daffodils on Park Avenue's central malls. On either side, as always, were noisy, never ceasing streams of multilane traffic. On sidewalks a tide of hurrying inbound office workers swirled around Sam and Celia as they strolled.

Celia, who had driven in from New Jersey early that morning and would stay for the next two nights at the Waldorf, had dressed carefully for this occasion. She had on a new tailored jacket and skirt of navy blue, with a white ruffled blouse. Celia knew that she looked good and that the combination was a happy blend of business crispness and femininity. She was also glad to have shed the glasses which she had always disliked; contact lenses, suggested by Andrew on their honeymoon, were now a permanent part of her life.

Sam said suddenly, "You decided not to show me a draft of your speech."

"Oh dear!" she acknowledged. "It seems I forgot."

Sam raised his voice to be heard above the traffic. "It might seem that way to others. But not to me, because I know there's almost nothing you forget."

As Celia was about to reply, he silenced her with a gesture. "You don't need to answer that. I know you're different from others who work for me, which means you do things your own way, and so far you've mostly done them right. But I'll offer just a word of warning, Celia—don't overreach. Don't leave caution too far behind. Don't spoil a damn good record by trying to do too much, or move too fast. That's all."

Celia had been silent and thoughtful as they turned, crossed Park Avenue on a green light, and headed back toward the Waldorf. She

51

wondered: would what she had in mind for this afternoon be over-reaching?

Now, with the sales convention under way, and as she faced the entire sales force of Felding-Roth in the Waldorf's Astor Room, she realized she was about to find out.

Her audience was mostly salesmen—detail men—plus supervisors and district managers, all from outposts of the company as far apart as Alaska, Florida, Hawaii, California, the Dakotas, Texas, New Mexico, Maine and places in between. For many it was their only direct contact, every other year, with their superiors at company headquarters. It was a time for camaraderie, the reviving of enthusiasm, the implantation of new ideas and products, and even—for some—a renewal of idealism or dedication. There were also some boisterous high spirits directed toward womanizing and drinking—ingredients found at any sales convention of any industry anywhere.

"When I was invited to speak to you," Celia told her audience, "it was suggested that I describe some of my experiences as a detail woman, and I intend to do that. I was also cautioned not to say anything serious or controversial. Well, I find that impossible. We all know this is a serious business. We are part of a great company marketing important, life-giving products. So we *ought* to be serious, and I intend to be. Something else I believe is that we who are working on the firing line of sales should be able to be frank, honest and, when necessary, critical with each other."

As she spoke, Celia was conscious not only of the large audience of salesmen, but of a smaller one which occupied reserved seats in the front two rows: Felding-Roth's senior executives—the chairman of the board, president, executive vice president, vice president of sales, a dozen others. Sam Hawthorne, his near-bald head standing out like a beacon, was among the others.

Eli Camperdown, as befitted the president and CEO, sat front and center. Beside him was the board chairman, Floyd VanHouten, now elderly and frail, but who had led and shaped the company a decade earlier. Nowadays VanHouten's duties were mainly limited to presiding at directors' meetings, though his influence remained strong.

"I used the word 'critical,'" Celia said into the microphone, "and that—though some of you may not like it—is what I intend to be. The reason is simple. I want to make a positive contribution to this occasion and not be merely ornamental. Also, everything I shall say is within the limits of the title I was handed, which is in the program: 'A Woman Looks at Pharmaceutical Detailing.' "

She had their attention now, and knew it. Everyone was silent, listening.

That had been her worry earlier—whether she could hold this audience. Coming off Park Avenue this morning and entering the crowded, smoky, noisy anteroom where the sales force was assembling, Celia had experienced nervousness for the first time since agreeing to be a convention speaker. Even to herself she admitted the Felding-Roth sales convention was, at least for the time being, essentially a male exercise with its backslapping bonhomie, crude jokes, inane loud laughter, all to a background of unoriginal conversation. Celia lost count of the number of times today she had heard, "Long time, no see!" mouthed as if a novel, just-invented line.

"Just as you do," she went on, "I care very much about this company we work for and the pharmaceutical industry of which we are a part. Both have done fine things in the past and will do more. But there also are things that are wrong, seriously wrong, especially with detailing. I would like to tell you what, in my opinion, these things are and how we could do better."

Glancing down at the two executive rows, Celia detected unease on several faces; one or two people were fidgeting. Quite clearly, what she had said already was not what had been expected. She looked away and gave her attention to other portions of the hall.

"Before we came in here this morning, and again this afternoon, we all saw the banners and the booth which feature Lotromycin. It's a magnificent drug, one of the great breakthroughs in medicine and I, for one, am proud to be selling it."

There was applause and cheers, and Celia paused. Displays in the anteroom outside featured a dozen or so of Felding-Roth's important products, but she had homed in on Lotromycin because of its personal associations.

"If you pick up one of the pamphlets at that booth, as some of you may have already, you'll find it describes the use of Lotromycin by my husband. He's an M.D.—an internist. My husband has had excellent experience with that drug and with some others. He has also had bad experience with drugs, and with detail people who deceived him by describing those drugs falsely. He is not alone. Other doctors—far too many, as I know from reports made to me—have shared the same

53

experience. It is a side to this business which can and should be changed."

Aware that she was reaching rugged ground, Celia faced the audience squarely and chose her words with care.

"As a result of my husband's experiences as a physician, he tells me he has mentally divided the detail men who call on him into three groups—first, those who give him honest information about their companies' drugs, including adverse side effects; second, those who are uninformed and fail to advise him properly about the drugs they are promoting; and third, those who will tell him anything, even lie, to have him prescribe what they are selling.

"I would *like* to say that the first of those three groups—the detail people who are informed and honest—is the largest, and that the other two are small. Unfortunately that isn't true. The second and third groups are far larger than the first. What it adds up to is that the quality of detailing, in terms of full and accurate information, is poor, and that applies to all companies in the pharmaceutical business, including ours."

Celia could now see signs of consternation, not only among executives at the front, but back beyond them. Amid a series of groans someone called out, "Hey, what *is* this?"

She had anticipated the reaction and accepted it as part of a calculated risk. As she continued, her voice was strong and clear.

"I am sure you are asking yourself two questions. One: 'How does she know all that stuff, and can she prove it?' The second: 'Why bring it up now, at a time when we're happy and cozy and don't want to hear unpleasant things?' "

Again a voice from the audience. "You're damn right we're asking!"

"So you should!" Celia shot back. "And you're entitled to an answer, which I'll give."

"Better make it good!"

Something else Celia had gambled on today was that whatever the reaction to her speech, she would be allowed to finish. It seemed to be happening. Despite frowns of displeasure in the executive rows, no one was rising to use authority and cut her off.

"One reason I know what I'm talking about," Celia declared, "is that I used to be a member of that second group—the uninformed. That's because, when I went out selling drugs to doctors, I was inadequately trained. In fact, I was scarcely trained at all. Concerning that, let me tell you a story."

She described the encounter—which she had related to Andrew on their honeymoon—with the North Platte physician who had accused her of having "inadequate knowledge" and ordered her brusquely from his office. Celia told the story well and there was a return to silence as the audience listened. Here and there she saw nods and heard murmurs of agreement. Celia suspected that many in the hall had had similar bruising experiences.

"The doctor was right," she continued. "I didn't have the knowledge to discuss drugs with highly qualified physicians, even though I should have been given it before I went out selling."

She reached behind her to a table and held up a file.

"I mentioned reports from doctors about false information given by detail people. In the nearly four years I have been selling for Felding-Roth I have kept a record of those reports, and it is here. Let me quote examples."

Celia pulled a sheet from the file. "As you know, we have a prescription product called Pernaltone. It is an excellent drug in the treatment of hypertension and one of Felding-Roth's good sellers. *But* it should never be used by patients with rheumatic disease or diabetes. To do so is dangerous; warnings to that effect are in the literature. And yet . . . four doctors in New Jersey, two others in Nebraska, were assured by detail men from this company that Pernaltone was safe for *all* patients, including those with the diseases mentioned. I have the doctors' names if you wish to see them. Of course, those are just the doctors I know about. Obviously there are more, perhaps many more.

"Two of those doctors I spoke of, who were given that misinformation, checked it out and found it to be in error. Two others accepted it in good faith and prescribed Pernaltone for hypertensive patients who were also diabetic. Several of those patients became extremely ill, one of them close to death, though he eventually recovered."

Celia whisked another paper from her file. "A competitor of ours has an antibiotic, Chloromycetin, again a first-rate drug, but for serious infections only, since its possible side effects include damaging, even fatal, blood disorders. Yet—and again I have dates, names, places—the other company's detail men have assured doctors the drug is harmless . . ."

Celia finished with Chloromycetin, then continued, "Now to come back to Felding-Roth . . ."

As she talked, the damning evidence mounted.

"I could go on," Celia said after a while, "but I won't because my file is here for anyone in this company to examine. I *will* answer that second question, though: Why did I bring this up today?

"I brought it up because I could not get attention any other way. I have tried since last year to have someone at headquarters listen to me and go through my file. No one would. I had the strong impression that what I had accumulated was simply bad news that nobody wanted to hear."

Now Celia looked down directly at the two executive rows. "It may be said that what I have done today is headstrong, even foolish. Perhaps it is. But I would like to say that I have done it out of deep conviction and caring—for this company, our industry, and the reputation of both.

"That reputation is being tarnished, yet we are doing little or nothing about it. As most of us know, there are hearings being held at present in the U.S. Congress about the pharmaceutical industry. Those hearings are antagonistic to us, yet few in the industry appear to be taking them seriously. But they *are* serious. Already the press is giving prominence to criticisms; soon there will be a public outcry for reform. I believe that unless we do something ourselves to improve our sales practices and reputation we shall have it done for us by government—in a way that none of us will like and that will be harmful to us all.

"Finally, for all these reasons I urge that our own company take the lead—first in establishing a detailing code of ethics, second in setting up a training and retraining program for us detail people. I have put together my own ideas for such a program." Celia paused and smiled. "If anyone is interested, they too are in my file."

She concluded, "Thank you, and good afternoon."

As Celia gathered up her papers and moved to leave the speakers' platform, there was some feeble handclapping, though it ceased almost at once, with few in the audience seeming inclined to join in. Clearly, most were taking their cue from the executive group at the front, from where there was no applause and facial expressions showed disapproval. The board chairman seemed angry—he was speaking in low tones, heatedly, to Eli Camperdown; the Felding-Roth president nodding as he listened.

The vice president of sales, a New Yorker named Irving Gregson who had been recently promoted, approached her. A forceful man of athletic build, Gregson was normally genial and well liked. But now he was glowering, his face flushed. "Young woman," he declared, "you have been malicious, presumptuous and misguided; also your so-called facts are wrong. You are going to regret it. You will be dealt with later, but for now, I am ordering you to leave this sales convention and not to return."

"Sir," Celia said, "won't you at least look at the material I have—"

"I'll look at nothing!" Gregson's raised voice was audible through the hall. "Get out of here!"

"Good afternoon, Mr. Gregson," Celia said. She turned and walked away, heading for an exit. Her step was firm, head high. She thought, later there would be time for regrets, perhaps deep dejection; for now, she had no intention of leaving this male assemblage defeated, like a weakling. Just the same, she admitted to herself, she *was* defeated, and of course she had known this might happen but hoped that it would not. To Celia, the faults she had described were so obvious and glaring, the reforms so plainly needed, it was hard to see how others could disagree when facts were pointed out.

But they had. And almost certainly her employment by Felding-Roth was ended, or would be shortly. A pity. Sam Hawthorne would probably say she had done what he cautioned her not to do—overreached in trying to achieve too much. Andrew, too, had warned her —on the way back from their honeymoon when she told him about building a file of doctors' reports. She remembered Andrew's words: *"You're taking on something pretty big. Also some risks."* How right he had been! Yet, a principle was involved, and her own integrity, and Celia had decided long ago she would never temporize on that. What was that line from Hamlet she had learned at school? *"This above all: to thine own self be true . . ."* You paid a price for it, though. Sometimes a stiff one.

Moving through the hall, she was aware of sympathetic glances from a few of the men still seated. That was unexpected, after all her criticisms. Not that it made any difference now.

"One moment, please!"

Suddenly, startling her, coming from nowhere, a voice boomed strongly over the p.a. system. "Mrs. Jordan, will you wait?"

Celia hesitated, then stopped as the voice repeated, "Mrs. Jordan, wait!"

57

Turning, she saw with surprise that the voice was Sam Hawthorne's. Sam had left his seat, ascended the speakers' platform, and was leaning over the microphone. Others were startled too. Irving Gregson could be heard exclaiming, "Sam . . . what the hell?"

Sam passed a hand across his head, shiny under the spotlight; it was an unconscious habit when he was thinking a problem through. His craggy face was serious. "If you don't mind, Irving, there's something I'd like to say, and have everyone hear, before Mrs. Jordan goes."

Celia wondered what was coming. Surely Sam wasn't going to endorse her expulsion by telling the world about their conversation of this morning and his warning. It would be out of character. Yet ambition did strange things to people. Was it possible that Sam believed some comment would make him look good in the eyes of the assembled brass?

Looking up at the platform, the vice president of sales asked testily, "What is it?"

"Well," Sam said, close enough to the microphone so his voice could be heard again through the now-silent hall, "I guess you could say, Irving, I'm standing up here to be counted."

"In what way counted?" This time the question was from Eli Camperdown, now also on his feet.

Sam Hawthorne faced the Felding-Roth president, at the same time moving closer to the mike. "Counted with Mrs. Jordan, Eli. And admitting—even though no one else seems willing to—that everything she said is true. As we all damn well know, even while pretending otherwise."

The silence in the hall was awesome. Only minor noises filtered in —the sound of traffic, distantly; a rattle of glassware from a kitchen; muted voices from a corridor outside. It seemed as if everyone was still, rooted, not wanting to move and thereby miss a word. Amid the quiet, Sam continued.

"I'd also like to go on record as wishing I'd had the wit and moral courage to make the speech which Mrs. Jordan did. And there's something else."

Irving Gregson interrupted. "Don't you think you've said enough?"

"Let him finish," Eli Camperdown ordered. "It might as well all hang out."

The sales vice president subsided.

"In particular," Sam Hawthorne went on, "I agree with the opinion that if our industry fails to mend its ways, laws will be passed compelling us to do so. Moreover, those laws will be more restrictive by far than if we accept the good advice we have just heard and clean house ourselves.

"Finally, about Mrs. Jordan. Several times already she has proved her great value to this company. In my opinion she has just done so again, and if we let her leave this room in this way, we're all short-sighted fools."

Celia could scarcely believe what she heard. She had a momentary sense of shame for doubting Sam's motives. What he had just done, she realized, was to put his own job, his ambitions, his promising future at Felding-Roth, all on the line on her behalf.

Still the uncanny silence persisted. There was a shared awareness of a moment of high drama in which no one seemed certain what would happen next.

It was Eli Camperdown who moved first, returning to his seat beside the chairman of the board where the two senior officers began a second urgent, low-voiced conversation. This time Camperdown was doing most of the talking—it seemed, attempting to persuade—while the elderly VanHouten listened. At first the chairman shook his head adamantly, then appeared to relent, and finally shrugged. Camperdown beckoned Irving Gregson to join them.

Since decisions were obviously taking shape at highest level, others waited, though now a buzz of conversation filled the hall.

It diminished as the vice president of sales left the other two and ascended the speakers' platform. He took over the microphone from Sam Hawthorne, who returned to his seat below. Gregson surveyed the sea of curious faces, paused for effect, then permitted himself a broad grin.

"Whatever else you may say about our sales conferences," he declared, "we always promise you they are never dull."

It was the right thing to say and there was a roar of appreciative laughter in which even the dour VanHouten joined.

"I am instructed by our chairman and president," Gregson said, "an instruction in which I personally join, to state that a few moments ago we may all have acted hastily, even unwisely." Again the grin, a pause, and the sales chief continued.

"Many years ago, when I was a small boy and sometimes got into trouble—as all boys do—my mother taught me something. 'Irving,' she said, 'when you've made an ass of yourself and an apology is called for, stand up straight, be a man, and do it handsomely.' My dear mother, rest her soul, is dead; but somehow I can hear her voice saying, 'Irving, my boy, that time is now.'"

Watching and listening, Celia thought: Gregson had style. It was clearly not by accident he had been promoted to the hierarchy of sales.

She realized he was pointing directly at her. "Mrs. Jordan, come this way, please. You too, Sam."

When all three of them were on the platform—Celia dazed, almost unbelieving—Gregson said, "I announced I would apologize, Mrs. Jordan, and I do. We will, after all, consider your suggestions carefully. And now I'll relieve you of that file of yours if you don't mind."

Turning to the audience Gregson said, "I believe you have just witnessed an example of why ours is a great company and will . . ."

The remainder of his remarks were drowned out by applause and cheering and, moments later, executives and others were surrounding Celia, offering congratulations and shaking her hand.

"Why did you risk it?" Sam Hawthorne asked.

"If it comes to that," Celia answered, "why did you?"

It was a week later. Celia and Andrew were spending an evening at the Hawthornes' home and during dinner—a superb meal attesting Lilian Hawthorne's culinary skill—they had avoided the subject of the sales convention and talked of other things. A few days earlier the Russians had announced the shooting down of an American U-2 plane and the capture of its pilot, Gary Powers. Moscow charged that both were spying. The United States at first denied the charge but soon afterward President Eisenhower admitted, red-faced, that it was true. Most Americans, the Hawthornes and Jordans agreed, felt embarrassed too.

In Britain the Queen's sister, Princess Margaret, had set tongues wagging and raised eyebrows by marrying a professional photographer, Antony Armstrong-Jones. The wedding took place in what the press described as a "carnival mood." People were asking: Would the marriage diminish the prestige of the British throne? Andrew emphatically said no.

After dinner they listened to a new recording by Elvis Presley—a pop ballad, "Fame and Fortune." Presley had resumed his career after a year in the U.S. Army, his absence having left his popularity undimmed. The women liked "Fame and Fortune." The men didn't.

Finally, over brandies in the Hawthornes' spacious, artistically decorated living room, it was Sam who introduced the subject, closer to home, that was on all their minds.

Answering Celia's question, he said, "When I followed you onto that platform, maybe I just couldn't resist being part of a dramatic scene."

She objected, "You know it was more than that."

"We all do," Andrew put in. He was leaning back in a comfortable armchair and savoring the brandy; he had had a busy day with patients in a practice that was growing rapidly, and was tired. "You risked everything, Sam—far more than Celia."

"Of course, I'm grateful—" Celia began, but Sam cut her off.

"You don't need to be. If you want the truth, I felt I was being tested." He addressed Andrew. "Your wife had already demonstrated she had more guts, along with greater respect for truth, than anyone else there. I didn't want to fall below her standards." Sam smiled at Celia. "Especially if you're trying to follow me up the ladder at Felding-Roth."

"You *know* about that?"

"I told him," Lilian Hawthorne said. "I'm sorry if I broke your confidence, Celia, but Sam and I don't keep secrets from each other."

"I have a secret," Sam said; "it's about Celia." As the others looked at him curiously, he went on, "She isn't going to be a detail woman anymore."

Andrew chuckled. "You're firing her after all?"

"No. Promoting her. Our company is going to have a Department of Sales Training, just as Celia suggested. She'll help set it up—and will be assistant director."

"Well, hurrah!" Lilian raised her glass. "The men have shown some sense. I'll drink to that."

"If all things were fair," Sam said, "Celia would have been director. But there are some in the company who can't swallow quite that much. Not yet. By the way, it'll be announced tomorrow."

Andrew got up and crossed the room to kiss Celia. "I'm happy for you, darling. You deserve it."

"Well," Celia told them all, "I'm not exactly upset. Thank you, Sam, and I'll settle for 'assistant.' " She added with a smile, "For the time being."

61

They were interrupted by two small, pajama-clad figures who ran, laughing, into the living room. In the lead was Lisa, now twenty months old, lively and inquisitive, whom Andrew and Celia had brought with them and who—so they thought—had been put to bed for the night. Behind her was Juliet, the Hawthornes' four-year-old and only child. Lilian had confided to Celia some time ago that doctors advised her she would never have more children, and she and Sam lavished love on Juliet, who was bright, intelligent and apparently unspoiled. The two little girls had clearly been excited by each other's company.

Lisa hurled herself into her father's arms. She told Andrew, giggling, "Julie chase me."

Lilian got up. "I'll chase you both. Right back to bed." Amid laughter and shrieks the three disappeared in the direction of Juliet's bedroom.

When Lilian returned, Celia said, "All of that reminds me of something. I may need a little time off from that new job after a while, Sam. I seem to be pregnant again."

"This is a night for revelations," Lilian said. "Fortunately there's some booze left, so we can drink to that too." There was, Celia thought, a trace of envy in the other woman's voice.

8

Through the remainder of 1960, and into 1961, Celia immersed herself in teaching the Felding-Roth sales force how to sell.

Her new chief, the director of sales training, was a former division manager from Kansas City named Teddy Upshaw. When introduced, Celia recognized him at once. His had been one of the sympathetic faces when she was about to be ejected from the sales convention at the Waldorf.

Upshaw, a fast-talking, short-statured, dynamic whippet of a man in his late forties, had been selling drugs all his working life. He radiated energy, always hurried from one place to the next, and had a small round head which he nodded frequently during conversations; it gave the impression of a bouncing ball. Before being promoted to management, Upshaw had been the company's top sales producer and confided to Celia that he still missed the life of a traveling salesman, which he described as "like easy breathing," and added, "in this business you don't have to sell dirty to be good because most docs know damned little about drugs, and if you're straight with 'em, and they learn to trust you, you can have all the business you want. Only other thing to remember is to treat the docs like gods. They expect that."

When Celia told Andrew in bed one night about the "gods" remark, he laughed and said, "Smart boss you have. Just remember to treat this doc that way at home." She threw a pillow at him then, after which they wrestled playfully. The wrestling became something more, and they ended up making love. Afterward Andrew rubbed his hands over Celia's belly where her pregnancy was beginning to show and he said, "Take care of this little guy, and remember while he's in there—for you, no drugs of any kind!"

It was a caution he had expressed when she was pregnant with Lisa, and Celia said, "You feel strongly about that."

"Sure do." Andrew yawned. "Now let this god-doc get some sleep."

On another occasion when Teddy Upshaw was talking with Celia he described "dirty selling" as "plain goddam stupid and not needed." Just the same, he admitted, there was plenty of it in the pharmaceutical business. "Don't think you and me are going to stop detail men saying what ain't true, even at Felding-Roth. We won't. What we'll do, though, is show that the other way is smarter."

Upshaw agreed with Celia about the need for sales training. He had been given almost none himself and picked up his scientific knowledge—a surprising amount, as she discovered—by self-education across the years.

The two of them got along well and quickly worked out a division of duties. Celia wrote training programs, a task Upshaw disliked, and he put them into effect, which he enjoyed.

One of Celia's innovations was a staged sales session between a detail man and a doctor, with the former presenting one of Felding-Roth's drugs and the latter asking tough, sometimes aggressive, questions. Usually Teddy, Celia or another staffer played the doctor's role; occasionally, with Andrew's help, a real doctor was persuaded to come in to add reality. The sessions proved immensely popular, both with participants and observers.

All new detail men hired by Felding-Roth were now given five weeks of training, while others already employed were brought to headquarters in small groups for a ten-day refresher. To everyone's surprise, the older hands were not only cooperative but keen to learn. Celia, who also gave regular lectures, was well liked. She discovered that detail men who had been at the Waldorf sales meeting referred to her privately as "Joan of Arc" because, as one explained, "while Jordan wasn't burned for heresy, she came damn close."

When Celia thought about the sales convention she realized, in retrospect, how lucky she had been and how close she had come to wrecking her career. At times she wondered: if Sam Hawthorne had not spoken up, defending her, if she had been expelled from the convention and afterward lost her job, would she have regretted acting as she did? She hoped not. She also hoped she would have the same kind of fortitude in future in whatever other confrontations lay ahead. For the moment, though, she was happy with the outcome.

In her new job Celia saw a fair amount of Sam Hawthorne because, while Teddy Upshaw reported to him officially, Sam took a personal interest in the training program and was aware of Celia's contribution.

Less harmonious was Celia's relationship with the director of research, Dr. Vincent Lord. Because of the need for scientific help with sales training information, the Research Department had to be consulted frequently, something Dr. Lord made clear was an imposition on his time. Yet he refused to delegate responsibility to someone else. During one acerbic session with him Celia was told, "You may have conned Mr. Camperdown and others into letting you build your little empire, but you don't fool me."

Staying calm with an effort, she replied, "It isn't my 'empire,' I'm the assistant, not the director, and would you prefer to have scientific misinformation go out to doctors, the way it used to?"

"Either way," Dr. Lord said, glaring, "I doubt if you would know the difference."

When she reported the conversation to Upshaw, he shrugged and said, "Vince Lord is a first-class prick. But he's a prick who knows his science. Do you want me to talk to Sam and get him kicked in the butt?"

"No," she said grimly. "I'll handle him my own way."

Her way involved collecting more insults, but at the same time learning and, in the end, respecting Vincent Lord's competence. Though only seven years older than Celia—he was thirty-six—his impressive qualifications included a B.S. with honors from the University of Wisconsin, a Ph.D. in chemistry from the University of Illinois, and membership in several scientific honor societies. Vincent Lord had published papers while an assistant professor at U of I, papers describing his own significant discoveries—one concerning oral contraception had led to improvements in the Pill. What everyone expected, Celia learned, was that Dr. Lord eventually would achieve a major breakthrough by developing an important new drug.

But nowhere en route had Vincent Lord learned to be a pleasant human being. Perhaps, Celia thought, it was why he had remained a bachelor, though he was attractive enough physically in an ascetic, austere way.

One day, attempting to improve their relationship, she suggested they use first names, a practice common in the company. He advised her coldly, "It would be better for both of us, Mrs. Jordan, to remember at all times the difference in our status."

Celia continued to sense that the antagonism generated at their first meeting a year and a half earlier would remain a permanent part of their relationship. But despite it, and with Celia's persistence, the contribution of the Research Department to sales training proved substantial.

Not that the plan to raise the standard of detailing was entirely successful or wholly accepted. It wasn't. Celia had wanted to set up a report system, with spot checks of detail men's performance obtained through confidential questionnaires. The questionnaires would be mailed to doctors on whom the detail men called. The suggestion went to the highest level and was vetoed.

Then Celia asked that letters of complaint about detail men sent in by doctors be routed to Sales Training and a record kept. She knew from her own contacts that such letters were mailed in, but no one in the company ever admitted seeing them, and presumably they were buried in some archive, with corrective action, if any, remaining secret. This request, too, was refused.

As Teddy Upshaw patiently explained, "There's certain things the powers-that-be don't want to know. You changed that some because when you stood up at our sales bash and spelled things out, and then Sam rescued you, they just weren't hidden anymore, and the brass had to make the best of what was on their plate. But don't push 'em too far too fast."

It sounded uncannily like the advice Sam Hawthorne had given before her Waldorf speech and Celia retorted, "Someday the government is going to step in and *tell* us what to do."

"You've said that before," Upshaw acknowledged, "and maybe you're right. Also, maybe it's the only way."

They had left it there.

The subject of drugs and the pharmaceutical industry was on other minds elsewhere.

Through much of 1960 the drug business was in the news almost daily—mostly unfavorably. The continuing U.S. Senate hearings, chaired by Senator Kefauver, were proving a gold mine for reporters and unexpected agony for companies like Felding-Roth. Both outcomes were due, in part, to skillful staging by the senator and his staff.

Like all such congressional hearings, much of the emphasis was on politics, with a bias decided in advance. As a Washington reporter, Douglass Cater, wrote, "They . . . move from a preconceived idea to a predetermined conclusion." There was also, on the part of Estes Kefauver and his aides, a constant quest for headlines; thus their presentations were one-sided. The senator proved a maestro at disclosing sensational charges just before reporters had to leave the hearing room to file their stories—11:30 A.M. for afternoon papers, 4:30 P.M. for morning editions. As a result, rebuttals occurred with reporters absent.

Despite the unfairness, certain ugly truths emerged. They revealed excessive pricing of drugs; unlawful collusive price-fixing; illegally rigged bids for government contracts for supplying drugs; misleading advertising to physicians, including minimizing or even ignoring dangerous side effects; infiltration of the Food and Drug Administration by pharmaceutical companies and acceptance by one high-ranking FDA official of "honorariums" totaling $287,000 from a drug firm source.

Newspaper headlines, though sometimes one-sided, zeroed in on some abuses.

SENATORS FIND 1,118% DRUG MARKUP
—Washington Evening Star

SENATE PANEL CITES MARKUP ON DRUGS
Ranging to 7,079%
—New York Times

DRUG PERIL CLAIMED
—Miami Herald

BIG PROFIT FOUND IN TRANQUILIZERS
Chlorpromazine 6 Times Costlier
in U.S. than in Paris
—New York Times

Testimony revealed that drugs which had been discovered and developed in foreign countries were far cheaper in those countries than in the United States. This was absurd, it was pointed out, since the American companies marketing the drugs had incurred no development costs.

In French drugstores, for example, fifty tablets of chlorpromazine cost fifty-one cents compared with three dollars and three cents in the United States. Similarly, the U.S. price of reserpine was three times greater than in Europe where the drug was developed.

Another strange contrast was that American-made penicillin was selling in Mexico for two thirds of its retail price at home. These and other American prices, it was suggested, were high because of unlawful collusion between manufacturers.

PET FOOD SAID BETTER INSPECTED THAN DRUGS
—Los Angeles Times

F.D.A. AIDE'S TALK EDITED BY AD MAN
Drug Firm Slogan Written Into Speech
—New York Times

Testimony disclosed that a speech delivered by an FDA division head at an International Antibiotics Symposium had been sent to a drug company, Pfizer, for prior approval. An advertising copywriter changed the text to include, by inference, a plug for a Pfizer product, Sigmamycin. Later the drug company bought 260,000 reprints of the speech, treating it as an FDA endorsement.

The disagreeable newspaper headlines continued, sometimes on successive days, in big and small cities coast to coast, with TV and radio adding their reports.

All in all, as Celia expressed it to Andrew in December, "It hasn't been a year for boasting about where I work."

At the time, Celia was on leave of absence because their second child had been born in late October, again in accord with Celia's schedule. As Andrew had been confident, it was a boy. They named him Bruce.

Both their lives had been made easier several months before by the advent of a young Englishwoman, Winnie August, who now lived in and took care of the children during their parents' absence. Andrew had found her through an agency that advertised in medical journals. She was nineteen, had previously worked as a shop assistant in London and, as Winnie herself put it, she "wanted to 'ave a workin' 'oliday findin' out what you Yanks are like, then maybe spend a couple o' years down under with the Aussies." She was cheerful, quick and, to Andrew's great joy, whipped up breakfast each morning with lightning speed. "Comes o' practice. Did it for me mum at 'ome," she told him when he complimented her. Winnie also liked children and Lisa adored her. Andrew and Celia hoped that Winnie's departure for Australia would be long delayed.

One other event that came to Celia's attention happened near the end of 1960. The German drug Thalidomide—to be known in the U.S. and Canada as Kevadon—was submitted to the FDA for marketing approval. According to drug industry trade magazines, the Merrell Company, which now had North American rights, had large-scale plans for Thalidomide-Kevadon, believing the drug would be a huge seller, as it was continuing to be in Europe. The company was pressing FDA for swift approval. Meanwhile samples of the drug— officially for "investigative use," though in fact without restriction— were being distributed to over a thousand physicians by enthusiastic Merrell detail men.

The news reminded Celia of her conversation with Sam Hawthorne eight months earlier when he had reported resentment within Felding-Roth because, at Celia's suggestion, Thalidomide had been tested only on old people, then rejected. She wondered briefly if the resentment still remained, then dismissed the subject as unimportant.

She had other business concerns.

Following Bruce's birth Celia returned to work more quickly than she had after Lisa was born and was back at Felding-Roth by mid-December. One reason: it was a busy time in Sales Training. The company was expanding and a hundred more detail men were being taken on—plus, at Celia's urging, some detail women, though only a half dozen. Also contributing to her decision was an infectious sense of national excitement. In November John F. Kennedy had been elected president and it seemed—from the graceful rhetoric at least —as if a new era, stimulating and creative, had begun.

"I want to be part of it all," Celia confided to Andrew. "People are talking about 'a new beginning' and 'history in the making' and saying it's a time to be young and in charge of something. Going back to work means being involved."

"Uh-huh," Andrew had said, almost indifferently, which was un-usual. Then, as if realizing it, he added, "It's okay with me." But Andrew's mind was not really on Celia's endeavors; he was preoccu-pied with a problem of his own.

The problem concerned Dr. Noah Townsend, Andrew's senior partner and the respected chief of medicine at St. Bede's Hospital. Andrew had discovered something about Noah which, ugly and un-pleasant, brought into question the older man's competence to prac-tice medicine.

Dr. Townsend was a drug addict.

9

Noah Townsend, now fifty-eight, had for many years appeared to represent everything a seasoned, experienced physician should be. He was conscientious, treating all who came to him, whether wealthy or poor, with equal concern. His appearance was distinguished; in manner he had always been courtly and dignified. As a result Dr. Townsend had a solid practice with patients who liked him and were

69

loyal—with good reason, since he served them well. His diagnostic skills were regarded as remarkable. Townsend's wife, Hilda, once told Andrew, "I've stood with Noah at a party and he's looked across the room at a complete stranger and told me quietly, 'That man is very ill and doesn't know it,' or another time, 'That woman over there—I don't know her name, but she's going to die in six months.' And he's always been right. Always."

Townsend's patients felt much the same way. Some who exchanged anecdotes about his accurate diagnoses referred to him as "the witch doctor." One even brought back from Africa, as a gift, a witch doctor's mask which Townsend proudly hung on his office wall.

Andrew, too, respected the older doctor's abilities. As well, there had grown up between the two a genuine and warm affection, not least on Andrew's part because Townsend had, in all ways, treated his much younger colleague generously.

Contributing to Andrew's respect was the fact that Noah Townsend stayed up-to-date medically through systematic reading, something many physicians of his age neglected. Yet Andrew had also noticed, over recent months, a certain vagueness at times on Townsend's part, and occasional slurred speech. Then there had been those incidents earlier in the year of Noah's apparently bizarre behavior. The combination of symptoms made Andrew uneasy, though he continued to rationalize that stress and tiredness could be their cause, since both doctors had been working hard, with heavy patient loads.

It was during a November afternoon a month earlier—which Andrew now remembered as beginning for himself a time of agonized soul-searching—that unease and vague suspicion had turned to certainty.

The way it happened was that Andrew wished to discuss their schedule of days off, days when he and Dr. Townsend covered for each other. After checking to be sure no patient was with his colleague, Andrew knocked lightly on Townsend's office door and went in. It was something each of them was used to doing frequently.

Townsend had his back to Andrew and swung around, startled, in his haste failing to conceal what was in the palm of his hand—a sizable pile of tablets and capsules. Even then Andrew might have thought nothing of it, except for the older man's subsequent behavior. Townsend reddened with embarrassment, then with some bra-

70

vado brought his hand to his mouth, shoved the pills inside and with a glass of water flushed them down.

There was no way Townsend could ignore the significance of what Andrew had seen, but he attempted to make light of it. "So you caught me stoking up the furnace! . . . Well, I admit I do it now and then—been under a lot of pressure lately, as you know . . . But never let things get away from me . . . I'm an old-cowhand doctor, m'boy—know too much to ever lose control . . . A damn sight too much." Townsend laughed, a laugh which sounded false. "So don't worry, Andrew—I know where and when to stop."

The explanation did not convince Andrew. Even less convincing was the slurred speech, a slurring which suggested that the pills Noah Townsend had just ingested were not the first he had had that day.

Andrew asked, with a sharpness he immediately regretted, "What were you taking?"

Again the false laugh. "Oh, just a few Dexedrine, some Percodan, a touch of Darvon for added flavor . . . Andrew, what the hell does it matter?" Then, with a touch of belligerence, "Told you I keep it under control. Now, what did you come to see me about?"

With his mind in a turmoil, Andrew mentioned the subject of days off—which now seemed absurdly unimportant—speedily settled what was necessary, and left Noah Townsend's office as quickly as he could. He needed to be alone. To think.

Andrew was horrified at the stew of drugs—there must have been a dozen or fifteen tablets and capsules—which his older colleague had casually downed. According to Noah's own admission, they were stimulants and depressants—drugs which reacted to each other and which no competent doctor would prescribe in combination. While not an expert on addiction, Andrew knew enough to realize the quantity and casualness were hallmarks of someone who was a long way down the addict's road. And prescription drugs taken indiscriminately, as Noah clearly was taking them, could be as dangerous and destroying as any street drug sold illegally.

What to do next? The immediate thing, Andrew decided, was to find out more.

Over the next two weeks he used whatever time he could spare to visit medical reference libraries. St. Bede's had a modest one; Andrew knew of another in Newark. Both had cataloged reports about physicians who became drug addicts and, as he studied the material, the first thing to become evident was the common and widespread nature of the problem. The American Medical Association estimated that some five percent of all physicians were "impaired" because of drug abuse, alcoholism, or related causes. If the AMA admitted to that startling figure, Andrew reasoned, the real one must be higher. Others seemed to agree. Most estimates ranged to ten percent, several to fifteen.

One conclusion reached by all observers was that doctors got into trouble because of overconfidence. They were convinced that their specialized knowledge would let them use drugs without the habit's becoming dangerous, but almost always they were wrong. Noah Townsend's words, ". . . *never let things get away from me . . . know too much to ever lose control . . . I know where and when to stop . . .*" seemed a pathetic echo of what Andrew read.

The point was made that doctors became "successful addicts," undetected for long periods, because of the ease with which they could obtain drugs. How well Andrew knew it! It was something he had discussed with Celia—the fact that physicians could get free supplies of any drug, virtually in unlimited quantity, merely by asking a detail man from the company concerned.

In a way he was ashamed of, yet mentally justified as necessary, Andrew managed to inspect the cupboard in Noah Townsend's office where drug supplies were kept. He did it at a time when Townsend was at the hospital, making grand rounds.

The cupboard should have been locked, but it wasn't. In it, piled high and occupying all available space, was an astounding collection of drugs in manufacturers' containers, including narcotics of which there was a large supply. Andrew recognized some which Townsend had named.

Andrew kept some drugs in his own office, samples of those he prescribed regularly, which he sometimes handed out to patients who he knew were in financial need. But compared with what was here, his own supply was trifling. Nor, for safety reasons, did Andrew ever accumulate narcotics. He whistled softly in amazement. How could Noah be so careless? How had he kept his secret for so long? How did he take the drugs he did and keep control? There seemed no simple answers.

Something else shocked Andrew. He discovered from his researches that no overall program existed either to help doctors in trouble through excessive drug taking, or to protect their patients. The medical profession ignored the problem when it could; when it

72

couldn't, it covered it up by secrecy and closing ranks. No doctor, it seemed, ever reported another doctor for drug addiction. As for a drug-addicted physician losing his license to practice, Andrew couldn't find a record of its happening.

And yet the question haunted him: What about Noah Townsend's patients who, in a way, were also Andrew's because of the shared practice, with each doctor sometimes substituting for the other? Were those patients now at risk? While Townsend seemed normal in his behavior, and while he had made no mistakes medically so far as Andrew knew, would that condition continue? Could it be relied on? Would Noah someday, because of drugs, misdiagnose or fail to see an important symptom he should have caught? And what of his even larger responsibility as chief of medicine at St. Bede's?

The more Andrew thought, the more the questions multiplied, the more elusive were any answers.

In the end he confided in Celia.

It was early evening, a few days before Christmas. Celia and Andrew were at home and, with Lisa's excited help, had been decorating their tree. It was Lisa's first awareness of "Kissmus," as she called it; all three were loving the experience. Eventually, with his daughter almost asleep from excitement and fatigue, Andrew gently carried her to bed. Afterward he stopped briefly in the adjoining bedroom where Bruce, the baby, was sleeping soundly in his crib.

When Andrew returned to the living room, Celia had mixed a scotch and soda. "I made it a stiff one," she said as she handed him the glass. "I think you need it."

As he looked at her inquiringly, she added, "Lisa was good for you tonight; you were more relaxed than I've seen you in weeks. But you're still troubled. Aren't you?"

Surprised, he asked, "It shows that much?"

"Darling, we've been married four years."

He said feelingly, "They've been the best four years of my life." While he drank his scotch Andrew studied the Christmas tree and there was a silence while Celia waited. Then he said, "If it was that obvious, why didn't you ask me what was wrong?"

"I knew you'd tell me when you were ready." Celia sipped a daiquiri she had made for herself. "Do you want to tell me? Now?"

"Yes," he said slowly. "Yes, I think I do."

"My God!" Celia said in a whisper when Andrew had finished. "Oh, my God!"

"So you see," he told her, "if I've been less than a barrel of laughs, there's been good reason."

She came to him, putting her arms around him, her face against his, holding him close. "You poor, poor darling. What a burden you've been carrying. I had no idea. I'm so sorry for you."

"More to the point—be sorry for Noah."

"Oh, I am. I really am. But I'm a woman, Andrew, and you're the one who means most to me. I can't, I *won't*, see you go on this way."

He said sharply, "Then tell me what to do."

"I *know* what to do." Celia released herself and turned to face him. "Andrew, you have to share this. You *have* to tell someone, and not just me."

"For instance—who?"

"Isn't it obvious? Someone at the hospital—someone with authority who can take some action, and help Noah too."

"Celia, I *can't*. If I did, it would be talked about, brought out in the open . . . Noah would be disgraced. He'd be removed as chief of medicine, God knows what would happen about his license, and either way it would *break* him. I cannot, simply *cannot*, do that."

"Then what's the alternative?"

He said glumly, "I wish I knew."

"I want to help you," Celia said. "I really do, and I have an idea."

"I hope it's better than the last one."

"I'm not sure the last was wrong. But if you won't talk about Noah Townsend specifically, why not talk to someone in the *abstract*. Sound them out. Discuss the subject generally. Find out how other people at the hospital feel."

"Do you have anyone in mind?"

"Why not the administrator?"

"Len Sweeting? I'm not sure." Andrew took a turn around the room, considering, then stopped beside the Christmas tree. "Well, at least it's an idea. Thanks. Let me think about it."

"I trust that you and Celia had a good Christmas," Leonard Sweeting said.

"Yes," Andrew assured him, "we did."

74

They were in the hospital administrator's office with the door closed. Sweeting was behind his desk, Andrew in a chair facing it.

The administrator was a tall, lanky ex-lawyer who might have been a basketball player but instead had the unlikely hobby of pitching horseshoes, at which he had won several championships. He sometimes said the championships had been easier than getting doctors to agree about anything. He had switched from law to hospital work in his twenties and now, in his late forties, seemed to know as much about medicine as many physicians. Andrew had come to know Len Sweeting well since their joint involvement in the Lotromycin incident four years earlier, and on the whole respected him.

The administrator had thick, bushy eyebrows which moved up and down like vibrating brushes every time he spoke. They moved now as Sweeting said briskly, "You said you had a problem, Andrew. Something you need advice about."

"Actually it's a physician friend of mine in Florida who has the problem," Andrew lied. "He's on staff at a hospital down there and has uncovered something he doesn't know how to deal with. My friend asked me to find out how we might handle the same situation here."

"What kind of situation?"

"It has to do with drugs." Briefly Andrew sketched out a mythical situation paralleling his own real one, though being careful not to make the comparison too close.

As he spoke he was aware of a wariness in Sweeting's eyes, the earlier friendliness evaporating. The administrator's heavy eyebrows merged into a frown. At the end he pointedly stood up.

"Andrew, I have enough problems here without taking on one from another hospital. But my advice is to tell your friend to be very, *very* cautious. That's dangerous ground he's treading on, especially in making an accusation against another doctor. Now, if you'll excuse me . . ."

He knew. With a flash of intuition Andrew realized that Len Sweeting knew precisely what he had been talking about, and whom. The Florida-friend gambit had not fooled Sweeting for an instant. *God knows how,* Andrew thought, *but he's known for longer than I have.* And the administrator wanted no part of it. All he wanted, quite clearly at this moment, was to get Andrew out of his office.

Something else. If Sweeting knew, then others in the hospital must know too. Almost certainly that meant fellow physicians, some of them a great deal senior to Andrew. And *they* were doing nothing either.

Andrew stood up to go, feeling naïve and foolish. Len Sweeting came with him to the door, his friendliness returned, his arm around the younger man's shoulders.

"Sorry to have to hurry you away like this, but I have important visitors due—big donors to hospitals who we hope will give us several million dollars. As you're aware, we really need that kind of money. By the way, your boss will be joining us. Noah is a tremendous help with fund-raising. Seems to know everybody, and everybody likes him. There are times I wonder how this hospital could continue functioning without our Dr. Townsend."

So there it was. The message, plain and unequivocal: *Lay off Noah Townsend.* Because of Noah's connections and moneyed friends, he was too valuable to St. Bede's for any scandal to intrude. *Let's cover it up, fellas; maybe if we pretend the problem isn't there, it will go away.*

And of course, if Andrew attempted to repeat what Sweeting had just conveyed to him, the administrator would either deny the conversation had taken place or claim his remarks were misinterpreted.

In the end, which was later the same day, Andrew decided he could only do what everyone else was doing—nothing. He resolved, though, that from now on and as best he could, he would watch his senior colleague closely and try to ensure that Noah's medical practice or his patients did not suffer.

When Andrew told Celia about the chain of events and what he had decided she looked at him strangely. "It's your decision and I can understand why you made it. All the same, it may be something you'll regret."

10

Dr. Vincent Lord, director of research for Felding-Roth Pharmaceuticals, Inc., was a mixed-up—an unkind person might say "messed-up"—personality. A scientific colleague had observed wryly, "Vince behaves as if his psyche is whirling in a centrifuge, and he's not sure how it will come out—or how he wants it to."

That such an assessment should be made at all was in itself paradoxical. At the relatively young age of thirty-six, Dr. Lord had reached a plateau of success which many dream of but few attain. But the fact that it *was* a plateau, or seemed to be, kept him worrying and wondering about how he got there and whether anything significant lay beyond it.

What might also be said of Dr. Lord was that if there had not been disappointments in his life, he would have invented them. Expressed another way: Some of his disappointments were more illusory than real.

One of them was that he had not received the respect he believed he deserved from the academic-scientific community, which was snobby about drug company scientists—regarding them generally, though often erroneously, as second-raters.

Yet it had been Vincent Lord's own personal, free choice, three years earlier, to move from an assistant professorship at the University of Illinois over to industry and Felding-Roth. However, strongly influencing that choice were Lord's frustration and anger at the time —both directed at the university—the anger persisting even now to the point where it had become a permanent corroding bitterness.

Along with the bitterness he sometimes asked himself: Had he been hasty and unwise in leaving academia? Would he have become a more respected international scientist had he stayed where he was, or at least moved to another university somewhere else?

The story behind it all went back six years, to 1954.

That was when Vincent Lord, a graduate student at U of I, became "Dr. Lord," with a Ph.D. in organic chemistry. The doctorate was a good one. The university's chemistry school at Champaign-Urbana was acknowledged as among the finest in the world, and Lord had proved himself a brilliant student.

His appearance fitted the concept of a scholar. His face was thin, sensitive, delicately boned and, in a way, agreeable. Less agreeable was that he rarely smiled and often wore a worried frown. His vision was poor, perhaps from years of intense studying, and he wore rimless glasses through which dark green eyes—Lord's strongest feature—looked out with alertness mingled with suspicion. He was tall and lean, the last because food held no interest for him. He regarded meals as a waste of time and ate because his body required it; that was all. Women attuned to sensitive men found Vincent Lord attractive. Men seemed divided, either liking or detesting him.

His field of expertise was steroids. This included male and female hormones—testosterone, estrogen, progesterone—which affect fertility, sexual aggressiveness and birth control, and during that period of the fifties when the Pill was just beginning to be used, the subject of steroids commanded wide scientific and commercial interest.

After earning his Ph.D., and since his work on steroid synthesis was going well, it seemed logical for Dr. Lord to take a two-year postdoctoral fellowship, also at U of I.

The university was cooperative, financing for a "postdoc" was obtained readily from a government agency, and the two years passed amid continued scientific success and only minor personal problems. The problems arose from Lord's habit, close to an obsession, of looking over his shoulder mentally and asking himself: *Did I do the right thing?*

He brooded: Had he made a mistake by remaining "in-house" at U of I? Should he have cut loose and gone to Europe? Would Europe have supplied a more rounded education? The questions—most of them unnecessary—multiplied persistently. They also made him moody and bad-tempered, a trait that would persist and lose him friends.

And yet—another facet of the paradoxical prism which was Vincent Lord—he had a high opinion of his worth and work, an opinion that was wholly justified. Therefore it did not surprise him when, at the end of his two-year "postdoc," the University of Illinois offered

78

him a post as assistant professor. He accepted. Again he remained "in-house." Again, as time went by, he brooded over that latest decision, repeating the torture of his earlier questions.

An angel looking into Vincent Lord's soul might well have wondered—*Why?*

During Lord's time as an assistant professor his reputation as a steroid expert burgeoned, not only at U of I but far beyond. In slightly more than four years he published fifteen scientific papers, some in prestigious publications including the *Journal of the American Chemical Society* and *Journal of Biological Chemistry*. It was an excellent record, considering his low-totem-pole status at the university.

And *that* was something which infuriated Dr. Lord, increasingly as time went on.

In the arcane world of scholarship and science, promotions are seldom speedy and almost always painfully slow. The next upward step for Vincent Lord would be to associate professor—a tenured appointment, tenure itself equating a laurel wreath or lifetime financial security, whichever way you looked at it. Associate professorship was also a signal saying, *You have made it. You are one of the elite of academia. You have something which cannot be taken away, and are free to work as you choose, with only limited interference from above. You have arrived.*

Vincent Lord wanted that promotion badly. And he wanted it *now*. Not in another two years, the remaining period which, as the mills of academia ground, he would normally have to wait.

Thus, wondering why the idea hadn't occurred to him sooner, he decided to seek accelerated promotion. With his record, he reasoned, it should be a snap, a mere formality. Full of confidence, he prepared a bibliography, telephoned for an appointment with the dean the following week, and when the appointment was arranged, dispatched the bibliography to precede him.

Dean Robert Harris was a small man, wizened and wise, though his wisdom included doubts of his own ability to make the Socratic decisions frequently required of him. Basically a scientist, he still kept his hand in with a small laboratory, and attended scientific meetings several times each year. Most of his working hours though, were taken up with chemistry school administration.

On a morning in March 1957 Dean Harris was in his office, turning pages of Dr. Vincent Lord's bibliography and wondering why it had been sent. With someone as temperamental and unpredictable as Lord there could be a dozen reasons. Well, he would find out soon. The subject of the bibliography was due to arrive in fifteen minutes.

Closing the bulky folder which he had read fully and carefully— the dean was by nature conscientious—he leaned back in the armchair behind his desk, musing on facts and his private, personal instincts about Vincent Lord.

The man had genius potential. No doubt of it. If the dean had not known that already, he would have learned it from his recent reading of Lord's published work and reviews and accolades concerning it. In his chosen field Vince Lord could, and probably would, scale the Parnassus heights. With reasonable luck, which scientists like other mortals needed, some splendid discovery might well be in his future, bringing renown to himself and U of I. Everything seemed positive, all signals set at green. And yet . . .

Dr. Vincent Lord at times made Dean Harris feel uneasy.

The reason was not the high-strung temperament exhibited by Lord; that and brilliance quite often went together and in tandem were acceptable. Any university—the dean sighed as he thought about it—was a cauldron of animus and jealousies, often over unimportant issues argued with surprising pettiness.

No, it was something else, something more—a question raised once before and recently raised again. It was: Did the seeds of intellectual dishonesty, and therefore scientific fraud, lie somewhere deep in Vincent Lord?

Nearly four years earlier, in the first year of Dr. Lord's assistant professorship, he had prepared a scientific paper on a series of experiments which, as Lord described them, produced exceptional results. The paper was close to being published when a colleague at U of I, a more senior organic chemist, let it be known that while attempting to repeat the experiments and results described by Dr. Lord, he could not do so; his results were different.

An investigation followed. It showed that Vincent Lord had made mistakes. They appeared to be honest mistakes of misinterpretation, and Lord's paper was rewritten and later published. It did not, however, create the stir scientifically which the originally stated results— had they been correct—would have caused.

In itself the incident had no significance. What had happened to

Dr. Lord occasionally happened to the best of scientists. All made mistakes. But if a scientist later discovered an error of his own, it was considered normal and ethical to announce the error and correct any published work.

What was different in Lord's case was an intuition, a suspicion among his peers based on Lord's reaction when confronted, that he had known about the errors, probably discovered after his paper was prepared, but had kept quiet, hoping no one else would notice.

For a while there were rumblings on campus about moral sense and ethics. Then, following a series of unchallenged and praised discoveries by Vincent Lord, the rumblings died down, the incident apparently forgotten.

Dean Harris had almost forgotten too. Until a conversation two weeks earlier at a scientific conference in San Francisco.

"Listen, Bobby," a professor from Stanford University and long-time crony had told Harris over drinks one evening, "if I were you I'd keep an eye on your guy Lord. Some of us have found his two latest papers nonrepeatable. His syntheses are okay, but we don't get those spectacular yields he claims."

When pressed for more details, the informant added, "I'm not saying Lord isn't honest, and we all know he's good. But there's an impression around that he's a young man in a hurry, maybe too much of a hurry. You and I both know what that can mean, Bobby—once in a while cutting corners, interpreting data the way you *wish* it to come out. It adds up to scientific arrogance and danger. So what I'm saying is: For the good of U of I, and your own good, watch out!"

A worried, thoughtful Dean Harris nodded his thanks for the advice.

Back at Champaign-Urbana he had summoned the chairman of Dr. Lord's department and repeated the San Francisco conversation. The dean then asked: What about those two last published papers of Vince Lord's?

Next day the department chairman was back in the dean's office with an answer. Yes, Dr. Lord acknowledged there was some dispute about his latest published results; he intended to run the experiments again and, if appropriate, would publish a correction.

On the face of it—fair enough. Yet, overhanging the conversation was the unspoken question: *Would Lord have acted if someone else had not brought attention to the subject?*

Now, two weeks later, Dean Harris was again pondering that question when his secretary announced, "Dr. Lord is here for his appointment."

"So that's it," Vincent Lord concluded ten minutes later. He was seated, facing the dean across his desk. "You've seen my record in the bibliography, Dean Harris. I believe it's more active and impressive than that of any other assistant professor in this school. In fact, no one else comes close. I've also told you what I'm planning for the future. Putting all of it together, I believe accelerated promotion is justified and I should have it now."

The dean placed his hands together, surveyed Dr. Lord across his fingertips and said with some amusement, "You do not appear to suffer from an underestimation of your own worth."

"Why should I?" The answer was quick and sharp, devoid of humor. Lord's dark green eyes were fixed intensely on the dean. "I know my record as well as anyone. I also know other people around here who are doing a damn sight less than I am."

"If you don't mind," Dean Harris said with a touch of sharpness himself, "we will leave other people out of it. Others are not the issue. The issue is you."

Lord's thin face flushed. "I don't see why there's an issue at all. The whole thing seems perfectly clear. I thought I had just explained it."

"Yes, you did explain. Quite eloquently." Dean Harris decided he would not be provoked into being less than patient. After all, Lord was right about his record. Why *should* he be falsely modest and pretend? Even the aggressiveness could be excused. Many scientists —as one himself, the dean understood—simply did not have time to school themselves in diplomatic niceties.

So should he agree to Lord's request for fast promotion? No. Dean Harris knew already that he wouldn't.

"You must realize, Dr. Lord," he pointed out, "that I alone do not make decisions about promotions. As dean I must depend heavily on advice from a faculty committee."

"That's a—" Lord blurted out the words and stopped.

A pity, the dean thought. *If he'd said "a load of crap" or something similar I'd have had an excuse for ordering him from my office. But this is a formal occasion, as he remembered just in time, and we will keep it that way.*

"A promotion supported by you is always accepted." Vincent Lord scowled as he corrected himself. He hated being subservient to this dean whom he considered an inferior has-been scientist, now a pathetic paper pusher. Unfortunately he was a paper pusher with the authority of the university behind him.

Dean Harris did not reply. What Lord had said about his support of any promotion was true, but that was because he never took a position on one until he was sure it would be acceptable to the faculty. Though a dean was the senior member of a faculty, the faculty as a whole had more power than a dean. Which was why he knew he would never get Lord's promotion agreed to at this point, even if he pushed it.

By now, gossip about those two most recent published papers of Vincent Lord's was undoubtedly circulating through the campus. Gossip, plus questions about ethics, plus the earlier, four-year-old incident which had been almost forgotten but now would be revived.

There was no point, the dean reasoned, in delaying announcement of a decision already taken.

"Dr. Lord," he stated quietly, "I will not recommend you for accelerated promotion at this point."

"Why not?"

"I do not believe the reasons you have given are sufficiently compelling."

"Explain 'compelling'!"

The words had been snapped out like a command and there were limits to patience, the dean decided. He replied coldly, "I believe it would be better for both of us if this interview were ended. Good day!"

But Lord made no attempt to move. He remained seated in front of the dean's desk, glaring. "I'm asking you to reconsider. If you don't, you may regret it."

"In what way might I regret it?"

"I could decide to leave."

Dean Harris said, and meant it, "I would be sorry to see that happen, Dr. Lord, and your departure would be a loss. You have brought credit to the university and will, I believe, continue to. On the other hand"—the dean permitted himself a thin smile—"I believe that even after your departure this institution would survive."

Lord rose from the chair, his face flushed with anger. Without a word he stalked from the office and slammed the door behind him.

Reminding himself, as he had so many times before, that part of his

83

job was to deal calmly and fairly with un-calm, talented people who often behaved unreasonably, the dean returned to other work.

Unlike the dean, Dr. Lord did not put the matter from his mind. As if a recording were implanted in his brain, he replayed the interview over and over, growing increasingly bitter and angry until he came to hate not only Harris, but the entire university.

Vincent Lord suspected—even though the subject had not been mentioned at the interview—that those minor changes he was having to make in his two most recently published papers had something to do with his rejection. The suspicion increased his anger because, as he saw it, the matter was trivial compared with his overall scientific record. Oh yes, he conceded even to himself, he knew how those errors had occurred. He *had* been impatient, overenthusiastic, in a hurry. He had, *for the absolute briefest time,* let wishful thinking about results overrule his scientific caution. But he had since vowed never to let anything similar happen again. Also, the incident was past, he would shortly publish corrections, so why *should* it be considered? Petty! Trivial!

At no point did it occur to Vincent Lord that it was not the incidents themselves, including the one four years ago, that his critics were concerned with, but certain symptoms and signals about his character. In the absence of such reasoning and understanding by Dr. Lord, his bitterness continued festering.

Consequently when, three months later during a scientific meeting in San Antonio, he was approached by a representative of Felding-Roth Pharmaceuticals with an invitation to "come aboard"—a euphemism for an offer of employment—his reaction, while not immediately positive, was at least, "Well, maybe."

The approach itself was not unusual. The big drug firms were constantly on the lookout for new scientific talent and monitored carefully all published papers originating in universities. In the case of something interesting, a congratulatory letter might be written. Then, following through, scholarly gatherings where drug company people met academic scientists on neutral ground were useful points of contact. In all these ways, and well before the San Antonio meeting, Vincent Lord's name had been considered and selected as a "target."

More specific talks followed. What Felding-Roth wanted was a scientist of highest caliber in his field to head a new division to develop steroids. From the beginning, the company representatives treated Dr. Lord with deference and respect, an attitude which pleased him and which he saw as a pleasant contrast to what he considered his shabby treatment by the university.

The opportunity, from a scientific point of view, was interesting. So was the salary offered—fourteen thousand dollars a year, almost twice as much as he was earning at U of I.

To be fair to Vincent Lord, it could have been said that money itself held almost as little interest for him as did food. His personal needs were simple; he never had difficulty living on his university pay. But the drug firm's money was one more compliment—a recognition of his worth.

After thinking about it for two weeks, Dr. Lord accepted. He left the university abruptly, with minimal goodbyes. He began work at Felding-Roth in September 1957.

Almost at once an extraordinary thing occurred. In early November the drug firm's director of research collapsed over a microscope and died of a massive cerebral hemorrhage. Vincent Lord was in place and available. He had the needed qualifications. He was appointed to the vacant post.

Now, three years later, Dr. Lord was solidly entrenched at Felding-Roth. He continued to be respected. His competence was never questioned. He ran his department efficiently, with minimal outside interference, and despite Lord's private personality problems, relations with his staff were good. Equally important, his personal scientific work was going well.

Most others, in the circumstances, would have been happy. Yet for Vincent Lord there was that perpetual looking-backward syndrome, the doubts and soul-searching about long-ago decisions, the anger and bitterness—as impassioned as ever—about his refused promotion at U of I. The present held problems too, or so he thought. Outside his department, he was suspicious of others in the company. Were they undermining him? There were several people whom he disliked and distrusted—one of them that pushy woman. Celia Jordan received altogether too much attention. Her promotion had been unwelcome to him. He saw her as a competitor for prestige and power.

There was always the possibility, which he hoped for, that the Jordan bitch would overreach, be toppled, and disappear. As far as Dr. Lord was concerned, it could not happen too soon.

Of course, none of this would matter, not even the insult in the past at U of I, and no one would come close to Vincent Lord in power and respect if a certain event occurred which now seemed likely.

Like most scientists, Vince Lord was inspired by the challenge of the unknown. Also like others, he had long dreamed of achieving, personally, a major breakthrough, a discovery which would push back dramatically the frontiers of knowledge and place his name in the honor roll of history.

Such a dream now seemed attainable.

After three years of persistent, painstaking work at Felding-Roth, work which he knew to be brilliantly conceived, a chemical compound was at last in sight which could become a revolutionary new drug. There was still a great deal to be done. Research and animal experiments were needed over two more years at least, but preliminaries had been successful, the signposts were in place. With his knowledge, experience and scientific intuition, Vincent Lord could see them clearly.

Of course, the new drug when marketed would make an undreamed-of fortune for Felding-Roth. But that was unimportant. What *was* important was what it would do to the worldwide reputation of Dr. Vincent Lord.

A little more time was all he needed.

Then he would show them. *By God, he would show them all!*

11

Thalidomide exploded!

As Celia said much later, "Though none of us knew it then, nothing in the drug industry would ever be quite the same again after the facts about Thalidomide became well known."

Developments started slowly, unnoticed except locally, and—in the minds of anyone involved at the beginning—unconnected with a drug.

In West Germany, in April 1961, physicians were startled by an outbreak of phocomelia—a rare phenomenon in which babies are born tragically deformed, without arms or legs, instead having tiny, useless, seal-like flippers. The previous year two cases had been reported—even that an unprecedented number since, as one researcher put it, "two-headed children have been more common." Now, suddenly, there were dozens of phocomelic babies.

Some mothers, when shown the children to whom they had given birth, screamed in revulsion and despair. Others wept, knowing that, as one put it, "my son could never feed himself unaided, bathe himself, attend to basic sanitary requirements, open a door, hold a woman in his arms, or even write his name."

Among the mothers, several committed suicide; far more required psychiatric help. A formerly devout father cursed God. "I spit and shit upon him!" Then he corrected himself. "There *is* no God. How could there be?"

And still the cause of the phocomelia outbreak remained unknown. (The word, it was explained, is from the Greek—*phoke* meaning "seal"; *melos* is "limb.") One study suggested the cause might be radioactive fallout from atom bombs. Another, that a virus was at work.

Many of the babies had other defects as well as missing limbs. Ears were absent or deformed; hearts, bowels and other organs were incomplete or didn't function as they should. Some babies died—"the lucky ones," as one observer wrote.

Then, in November 1961, two doctors working independently and unknown to each other—a pediatrician in Germany and an obstetrician in Australia—linked phocomelia to the drug Thalidomide. Soon afterward, it was established that the drug was indeed the cause of the defective births.

Australian authorities, acting swiftly, ordered Thalidomide off the market during the same month the connection became known. West Germany and Britain withdrew the drug a month later, in December. But in the United States it was two months more until, in February 1962, the Thalidomide-Kevadon application was withdrawn from the FDA. Canada, inexplicably, left the drug on sale until March —four months later than the Australian withdrawal and time for many more individuals, including pregnant women, to take it.

Celia and Andrew, who followed the grim story by reading scientific publications as well as the regular press, discussed it frequently.

One night at dinner Celia said, "Oh, Andrew, how glad I am you wouldn't let me take *any* drugs during pregnancy!" A few minutes earlier she had looked with love and gratitude at their own two healthy, normal children. "I could have taken Thalidomide. I hear there are doctors' wives who did."

Andrew said quietly, "I had some Kevadon myself."

"*You* did?"

"I was given samples by a detail man."

Jolted, Celia said, "But you didn't use them?"

Andrew shook his head. "I'd like to say I had a suspicion about the drug, but it wouldn't be true. I simply forgot they were there."

"Where are the samples now?"

"Today I remembered them. I pulled them out. There were several hundred tablets. I read somewhere that more than two and a half million were distributed to American doctors. I've flushed mine down the toilet."

"Thank God."

"I'll second that."

In the months that followed, more news about Thalidomide continued to flow in. It was estimated that twenty thousand deformed babies were born in twenty countries, though the exact number would never be known.

In the United States the number of phocomelia births was low—an estimated eighteen or nineteen—because the drug had never been approved for general use. Had it been approved, the number of armless and legless American babies would probably have reached ten thousand.

"I guess we all owe a debt to that woman Kelsey," Andrew commented to Celia on a Sunday in July 1962. He was at home, relaxing, a newspaper spread out before him in the den they shared.

"Kelsey" was Dr. Frances Kelsey, an FDA medical officer who, despite intense pressure from the drug firm which planned to market Thalidomide-Kevadon, used bureaucratic tactics to delay it. Now, declaring she'd had scientific reasons for doubting the drug's safety all along, Dr. Kelsey was a national heroine. President Kennedy had awarded her the President's Gold Medal for Distinguished Service, the country's highest civilian decoration.

"As it turned out," Celia said, "what she did was right, and I agree about being grateful. But there are some who say she got the medal for doing nothing, just putting off making a decision, which is always the safe thing for a bureaucrat to do, and now she's claiming to have had more foresight than she really did. Also, it's feared that what Kennedy has done will mean that in the future, *good* drugs that are truly needed will be delayed by others at FDA who'd like a medal too."

"What you have to understand," Andrew said, "is that all politicians are opportunists and Kennedy's no exception, nor is Kefauver. Both of them are using the publicity about Thalidomide for their own advantage. Just the same, we need *some* kind of new law because whatever else Thalidomide did, it sure as hell showed that your industry, Celia, can't regulate itself and that parts of it are rotten."

The remark was prompted by revelations, following investigations into the drug firms responsible for Thalidomide, of duplicity, callousness, greed, cover-up and incompetence, revelations that seemed to surface almost daily.

Celia acknowledged sadly, "I wish I could argue with you. But no one in their right mind could."

Surprisingly, and despite the political maneuvering that preceded it, some good legislation did emerge and was signed into law by President Kennedy in October 1962. While far from perfect, and with provisions which later would deny valuable new drugs to those in desperate need of them, the new law provided consumer safe-

89

guards that had not existed "B.T."—which was how many in the drug
industry would in future identify the era of "before Thalidomide."

Also in October the news reached Celia that Eli Camperdown,
president and CEO of Felding-Roth, who had been ill for several
months, was dying. The cause was cancer.

A few days after she heard, Sam Hawthorne summoned Celia to his
office. "Eli has sent a message. He would like to see you. He's been
taken home from the hospital and I've arranged for you to be driven
there tomorrow."

The house was five miles southwest of Morristown at Mount Kemble Lake. Located at the end of a long driveway and shielded from
outside view by trees and heavy shrubbery, it was large and old, with
a frontage of fieldstone which had weathered and taken on a green
patina. From the outside the interior looked dark. Inside, it was.

A stooped, elderly butler let Celia in. He led her to an ornate
drawing room furnished with heavy period pieces and asked her to
wait. The house was quiet, with no sounds of activity. Perhaps, Celia
thought, it was because Eli Camperdown lived alone; she knew he
had been a widower for many years.

In a few minutes a uniformed nurse appeared. In contrast to the
surroundings, she was young, pretty and brisk. "Will you please come
with me, Mrs. Jordan. Mr. Camperdown is expecting you."

As they climbed a wide, curving staircase with deep carpeting
Celia asked, "How is he?"

The nurse said matter-of-factly, "Very weak and in a good deal of
pain, though we use sedation to help him with that. Not today,
though. He said he wished to be alert." She looked at Celia curiously.
"He's been looking forward to your coming." Near the head of the
staircase the nurse opened a door and motioned Celia in.

At first Celia had difficulty in recognizing the gaunt figure propped
up by pillows in the large four-poster bed. Eli Camperdown, who not
long since had seemed the embodiment of strength and power, was
now emaciated, wan and fragile—a caricature of his former self. His
eyes, sunk in their sockets, regarded Celia as his face twisted in an
attempt to smile. When he spoke his voice was low and reedy. "I'm
afraid advanced cancer isn't pretty, Mrs. Jordan. I hesitated about

90

letting you see me like this, but there are things I wanted to say to you directly. I thank you for coming."

The nurse had brought a chair before leaving them alone and Celia sat in it beside the bed. "I was glad to come, Mr. Camperdown. I'm just sorry you are ill."

"Most of my senior people call me Eli. I'd be glad if you would do that."

She smiled. "And I'm Celia."

"Oh yes, I know. I also know you've been important to me, Celia." He raised a frail hand and motioned to a table across the room. "There's a *Life* magazine over there, some papers with it. Would you pass them to me?"

She found the magazine and papers and brought them. With effort, Eli Camperdown began leafing through the issue of *Life* until he found what he was seeking.

"Perhaps you've seen this."

"The article about Thalidomide, with the photos of deformed babies? Yes, I have."

He touched the other papers. "These are more reports and photographs; some haven't reached the public yet. I've been following the case closely. It's awful, isn't it?"

"Yes, it is."

They were silent, then he said, "Celia, you know I'm dying?"

She answered gently, "Yes, I know."

"I made the damn doctors tell me. I've a week or two, at best; perhaps only days. It's why I had them bring me home. To finish here." As she started to speak, he stopped her with a gesture. "No, hear me out."

He paused, resting. Clearly the effort made so far had tired him. Then he went on.

"This is selfish, Celia. None of it will do those poor, innocent children any good." His fingers touched the photos in the magazine. "But I'm glad I'm dying without that on my conscience, and the reason I don't have it there is you."

She protested, "Eli, I believe I know what you're thinking, but when I suggested . . ."

He continued as if not hearing her. "When we at Felding-Roth had that drug, we planned to push it hard. We believed it would be big. We were going to test it widely, then pressure the FDA to pass it. Maybe it *would* have passed. Our timing would have been different;

91

there could have been another examiner. There's not always logic to these things."

He paused again, mustering his strength and thoughts. "You persuaded us to do the tests on old people; because of that, no one under sixty took it. It didn't work. We dropped it. Afterward I know there was criticism of you . . . But if it had happened . . . the way we intended in the beginning . . . then I'd have been responsible . . ." Again his fingers found the photos in the magazine. "I'd have died with that terrible thing upon me. As it is . . ."

Celia's eyes were misty. She took his hand and told him, "Eli, be at peace."

He nodded and his lips moved. She leaned closer to hear what he was saying. "Celia, I believe there is something you have: a gift, an instinct, for judging what is right . . . Big changes are coming in our business, changes I won't see . . . Some in our company believe you are going far. That's good . . . So I'll give you some advice, my last advice . . . Use your gift, Celia. Trust your good instincts. When you have power, be strong to do what you believe . . . Don't let lesser people dissuade you . . ."

His voice drifted off. A spasm of pain contorted his face.

Celia turned, aware of movement behind her. The young nurse had come into the room quietly. She had a syringe on a tray which she put down beside the bed. Her movements were efficient and quick. Leaning over her patient she asked, "Is it pain again, Mr. Camperdown?" As he nodded feebly, she rolled back the sleeve of his pajamas and injected the syringe's contents into his arm. Almost at once his facial tension eased, his eyes closed.

"He'll drift now, Mrs. Jordan," the nurse said. "I'm afraid there isn't much point in your staying." Again she regarded Celia curiously. "Did you finish your talk? It seemed important to him."

Celia closed the *Life* magazine and put it, with the papers, back where she had found it.

"Yes," she said. "Yes, I think so."

Somehow—though not from Celia, who kept her own counsel—a report of her encounter with Eli Camperdown filtered through the company. As a result she found herself regarded with a mixture of curiosity, respect, and occasionally awe. No one, including Celia, had any illusion that some exceptional insight had prompted her suggestion five years earlier about Felding-Roth's testing of Thalidomide, testing that turned out to be unsuccessful. But the fact was, the route the company took had saved it from what could have been disaster, and Celia's contribution to that route was cause enough for gratitude.

Only one person in the company's top echelon failed to acknowledge Celia's role. The director of research, although he was one of those who had originally urged wide testing of Thalidomide—including giving it to obstetricians, which Celia specifically opposed—chose to keep quiet about that portion of his involvement with the drug. Instead he reminded others that his had been the decision to turn it down when it failed during testing on old people. His statement was true, though incomplete.

There was, however, little time for prolonged discussion. The death of Eli Camperdown occurred two weeks after Celia visited him. In newspapers the following day, November 8, 1962, the Camperdown obituaries were respectfully long, though even longer were those for Mrs. Eleanor Roosevelt, who also had died the day before. As Celia said to Andrew, "It seems as if two pieces of history ended together—one that was big history, the other smaller, but which I was part of."

The death of the Felding-Roth president resulted in changes within the company, as a new president was named by the board of directors, and others moved up the promotion ladder. Among those affected were Sam Hawthorne, who became a vice president and national sales manager, while Teddy Upshaw, to his great joy, was appointed sales manager of over-the-counter products, marketed by the company's Bray & Commonwealth division. "A smashing chance with O-T-C to do some really drag-'em-in, knock-'em-down selling" was how Teddy described his impending move excitedly to Celia and told her, "I've recommended that you get my job, though I have to tell you there are still some around here who don't like the idea of a woman being director of anything." He added, "To be honest, I used to feel that way myself, but you changed my mind."

Another eight weeks passed during which Celia functioned as head of sales training in everything except title. Day by day her frustration at the unfairness increased. Then, on a morning in early January, Sam Hawthorne walked into her office unannounced and beaming. "By

93

God, we did it!" he declared. "I had to plunge my sword into the entrails of a few male diehards, and blood has flowed, but word has now come down. You are director of this bailiwick and, what is more important, Celia, you are officially on the company's fast track."

TWO

1963–1975

TWO

1965-196

1

Being on the fast track at Felding-Roth meant much the same as it did at other companies. You had been selected as a candidate for senior management and would be given better than normal opportunities to learn the business and to prove yourself. Of course, not everyone on the fast track made it to the finish line. There were others on the track. Competition was keen. Also, a name could be removed at any time.

Celia realized all this. She also knew that, as a woman, she had overcome an extra hurdle of prejudice which men didn't have to. The need for double achievement made her keener still.

Which is why it seemed unfortunate that the 1960s were already proving a dry, non-innovative period for the prescription drug business.

"It's happened before," Sam Hawthorne said when Celia raised the subject. "Look, we've just gone through twenty years of miracle drugs—antibiotics, new heart medicines, the Pill, tranquilizers, all the rest. Now we're in a flat spell before the next big scientific breakthrough."

"How long a flat spell?"

Sam rubbed his bald head thoughtfully. "Who knows? Could be two years, could be ten. Meanwhile, our Lotromycin is selling well and we're developing improved versions of existing drugs."

Celia said pointedly, "Don't you mean developing 'me-toos'? Copying the successful drugs of our competitors? Playing molecular roulette by changing them just enough so we can't be sued for infringing someone's patent?"

Sam shrugged. "If you choose to use our critics' language, maybe so."

"Speaking of critics, isn't it true they accuse us of wasting research effort on 'me-too' drugs, effort we ought to use in more productive, beneficial ways?"

"And isn't it time you realized this industry is criticized for every-

97

thing?" An edge of sharpness crept into Sam's voice. "Especially by people who don't know or care that 'me-too' drugs keep companies like ours afloat when nothing much is happening in science. There have always been gaps. Do you know that after vaccination for small-pox began to be used successfully, scientists took another hundred years to find out why it worked?"

Though the conversation depressed Celia, she discovered after-ward that other pharmaceutical companies were experiencing the same dry period, with little that was new or exciting being devel-oped. It was an industry-wide phenomenon which—though no one knew it then—would last until the 1970s, eventually proving Sam an accurate prophet.

Meanwhile, through most of 1962, Celia continued to work suc-cessfully as director of sales training. Until November.

"I sent for you," Sam told Celia on an afternoon in late November, with the two of them seated in his oak-paneled office, "to tell you you're getting a new assignment. And, oh yes, it's also a promotion."

Celia waited. When Sam said nothing more, she sighed and smiled. "You know perfectly well I'm dying of curiosity, but you're going to make me ask the question, so I will. Okay, Sam: what's my new job?"

"General manager of over-the-counter products. You're to be in overall charge of Bray & Commonwealth. Teddy Upshaw, who used to be your boss, will now report to you." Sam smiled. "Celia, I hope you're suitably happy and impressed."

"Oh, I am! I really am, Sam. Thank you!"

He looked at her shrewdly. "Amid that enthusiasm, do I detect a reservation?"

"No reservation." Celia shook her head decisively. "It's just that . . . Well, the fact is, I know nothing about our over-the-counter business."

"You're not unique," Sam said. "I used to have the same gap in knowledge until I served a couple of years in O-T-C territory. In some ways it's like going to a foreign country." He hesitated. "Or crossing the tracks to another side of town."

"The less reputable side?"

"Could be."

What they both knew was that Felding-Roth, like other big phar-maceutical firms, erected a wall between the prescription drug portion of its business, which was considered prestigious, and its O-T-C activities which frequently were not. On each side of the wall all activities were separate. Each side had its own administration, research staff, and sales force; there was no liaison between the two.

This policy of separation was why Felding-Roth kept alive the name Bray & Commonwealth—originally a small, independent drug house. It had been acquired by Felding-Roth many years earlier and was now concerned solely with non-prescription products. In the public mind Bray & Commonwealth had no connection with Felding-Roth, and the parent company preferred it that way.

"Bray & Commonwealth will be an educational experience," Sam told Celia. "You'll learn to care about cough remedies, hemorrhoid ointments and shampoos. Also, O-T-C is part of the whole drug scene —a big part, and it makes a bundle of money. So you have to know about it, how it works, and why."

He continued, "Something else is that you may have to suspend your critical judgments for a while."

She said curiously, "Would you explain that?"

"You'll find out."

Celia decided not to press the point.

"There's one more thing I should tell you," Sam said. "The Bray & Commonwealth division has been stagnating and our O-T-C line needs new initiative, new ideas." He smiled. "Maybe the ideas of a strong, imaginative, occasionally abrasive woman—Yes, what is it?"

The last remark was to his secretary, an attractive young black woman who had come in and was standing at the open doorway.

When she failed to answer immediately Sam said, "Maggie, I told you I didn't want to be—"

"Wait!" Celia said. She had seen what Sam did not—that tears were streaming down the secretary's face. "Maggie, what's wrong?"

The girl spoke with an effort, words emerging between sobs. "It's the President . . . President Kennedy has been shot . . . in Dallas . . . It's all over . . . on the radio."

Hurriedly, with a look combining horror and unbelief, Sam Hawthorne snapped on a radio beside his desk.

Forever after, like most others of her generation, Celia would remember precisely where she was and what she was doing at that terrible moment. It was a shattering, numbing introduction to the

99

apocalyptic days which followed, a time of ended hopes and deep dejection. Whether Camelot had been real or illusory, there was a sense of something lost for always; of a new beginning which suddenly went nowhere; of the impermanence of everything; of the unimportance of lesser concerns including—for Celia—her own ambitions, and talk and thought of her new job. The hiatus ended, of course, and life moved on. It moved on, for Celia, to the head offices of Bray & Commonwealth Inc., wholly owned subsidiary of Felding-Roth Pharmaceuticals, located in a four-story plain brick building a mile and a half from the parent company headquarters. There, some two weeks later, in her new modest but comfortable office, she met with Teddy Upshaw, the division sales manager, to review over-the-counter products.

Through the preceding week Celia had immersed herself in papers—financial statements, sales data, research reports, personnel files—all relating to her new appointment. As she read on, she realized what Sam Hawthorne had told her was true. The division had been stagnating under uninspired leadership. It *did* need new initiative and ideas.

At the beginning of her talk with Upshaw, Celia said, "Teddy, a plain, blunt question. Do you resent my sitting here and your having to report to me? Does it matter that our roles have been reversed?"

The whippetlike sales chief appeared surprised. "Matter? My God, Celia, I couldn't be happier! You're what this division needed. When I heard you were moving over, I felt like cheering. Ask my wife! The night after I got the news, we drank your health." Teddy's energetic, bouncing head punctuated his remarks. "As to resenting you, no my dear, I'm just a salesman—a damn good one, but that's all I'll ever be. But you've the brains to give me something good, a whole lot better than what we have, to sell."

Celia was moved by the reaction. "Thank you, Teddy," she said. "I like you too. We can be good for each other."

"Damn right!"

"You've been on both sides of this business," she pointed out. "Prescription drugs and O-T-C. Tell me what you see as differences between them."

"It's pretty basic. O-T-C is mostly hype." Teddy glanced at papers spread around the office. "I guess you've discovered that from studying costs."

"Just the same, I'd like to hear your version."

He looked at her inquiringly. "Confidentially? No holds barred?"

She nodded. "That's the way I want it."

"All right then, look at it this way. As we both know, a prescription drug costs millions to research and takes five, six years before it's ready for selling. With an O-T-C item, you need six months or less to formulate the stuff, and the cost is peanuts. After that the big money goes for packaging, advertising, sales."

"Teddy," Celia said, "you have a knack of getting to the core of things."

He shrugged. "I never kid myself. What we're selling around here ain't from Louis Pasteur."

"Yet overall, the industry's O-T-C drug sales are shooting up and up."

"Like a goddam rocket! Because it's what the great American public wants, Celia. People who've got something wrong with 'em— mostly something minor which time would take care of if they had the sense to leave it alone—those people want to treat themselves. They like playing doctor, and that's where we come in. So if that rocket is going up anyway, why shouldn't all of us—Felding-Roth, you, me—go up there with it, hitching to the tail?" He paused, considering, then went on. "Only trouble right now is, we ain't got firm hold of that tail—we're not getting the share we could have of the market."

"I agree about market share," Celia said, "and I believe we can change that. As to O-T-C drugs themselves, surely they have a *little* more value than you say."

Teddy raised his hands as if the answer didn't matter. "A little maybe, but not much. There are a few good things—like aspirin. As to others, the main thing is they make people *feel* good, even if it's only in their minds."

She persisted, "Don't some of the common cold remedies, for instance, do more than ease the mind?"

"Nah!" Teddy shook his head emphatically. "Ask any good doctor. Ask Andrew. If you or I get a cold, being on the inside track so to speak, what's the best thing we should do? I'll tell you! Go home, put our feet up and rest, drink lots of liquids, take some aspirin. That's *all* there is to do—until science finds a cure for the common cold, which is still a long hard march from here, the way I hear it."

Despite the seriousness, Celia laughed. "You never take *any* cold medicine?"

"Never. Luckily, though, there's lots who do. Armies of hopefuls who pay out half a billion dollars every year trying to cure their uncurable colds. And you and me, Celia—we'll be out there selling 'em what they want, and the nice thing is, none of it'll do 'em harm." A note of caution crept into Teddy's voice. "Of course, you understand I wouldn't talk like this to anyone outside. I'm doing it now because you asked me, we're private, and we trust each other."

"I appreciate the frankness, Teddy," Celia said. "But feeling the way you do, doesn't it sometimes bother you, doing this kind of work?"

"The answer's no for two reasons." He ticked them off on fingers. "Number one, I'm not in the judgment business. I take the world the way it is, not the way some dreamers think it ought to be. Number two, somebody's gonna sell the stuff, so it might as well be Teddy Upshaw." He regarded Celia searchingly. "It bothers you, though, doesn't it?"

"Yes," she acknowledged. "Occasionally, it does."

"Did the brass tell you how long you'd stay in Bray & Commonwealth?"

"Nothing was said. I suppose it could be indefinitely."

"No," Teddy assured her. "They won't leave you here. You'll have this job for a year, probably, then move on. So stick it out, baby! In the end it's worth it."

"Thank you, Teddy," Celia said. "I'll take your advice, though I hope to do a great deal more than stick it out."

Despite being a working wife and mother, Celia was determined never to neglect her family, and especially to remain close to Lisa, now five, and Bruce who was three. Each weeknight, on her return home and before dinner, she spent two hours with the children—a schedule Celia adhered to no matter how important were the office papers she brought home in a briefcase for later study.

During the evening of the day on which she had her talk with Teddy Upshaw, Celia continued what she had begun a few days earlier—reading to Lisa, and to Bruce when he would sit still long enough to listen, from *Alice's Adventures in Wonderland*.

Bruce was quieter than usual tonight—he was tired and had the beginnings of a head cold with a runny nose—and Lisa, as always, was listening raptly as the story described Alice waiting by a tiny door to a

102

beautiful garden, a door which Alice was too large to enter, and hoping she would find . . .

> . . . a book of rules for shutting people up like telescopes: this time she found a little bottle . . . ("which certainly was not here before," said Alice), and tied round the neck of the bottle was a paper label, with the words "DRINK ME" beautifully printed on it in large letters.

Celia put the book down while she wiped Bruce's nose with a tissue, then read on.

> It was all very well to say "Drink me," but the wise little Alice was not going to do *that* in a hurry. "No, I'll look first," she said, "and see whether it's marked '*poison*' or not." . . . She had never forgotten that, if you drink much from a bottle marked "poison," it is almost certain to disagree with you, sooner or later.
>
> However, this bottle was *not* marked "poison," so Alice ventured to taste it, and finding it very nice (it had, in fact, a sort of mixed flavor of cherry-tart, custard, pineapple, roast turkey, toffee, and hot buttered toast), she very soon finished it off.
>
> "What a curious feeling!" said Alice. "I must be shutting up like a telescope."
>
> And so it was indeed: she was now only ten inches high . . .

Lisa interjected, "She shouldn't have drunk it, Mommy, should she?"

"Not in real life," Celia said, "but this is a story."

Lisa insisted firmly, "I still don't think she should have drunk it." Her daughter, Celia had observed before, was already a person of strong opinions.

"You're dead right, honey," Andrew's voice behind them said cheerfully; he had come in quietly and unnoticed. "Never drink anything you're not sure about unless your doctor prescribes it."

They all laughed, the children embraced Andrew enthusiastically, and he kissed Celia.

"Right now," Andrew said, "I prescribe an end-of-day martini." He asked Celia, "Join me?"

"Sure will."

"Daddy," Lisa said, "Brucie has a cold. Can you make it go away?"

"No."

"Why not?"

"Because I'm not a cold doctor." He picked her up and hugged her. "Feel me! I'm a warm doctor."

Lisa giggled. "Oh, Daddy!"

"It's uncanny," Celia said. "This is almost a replay of a conversation I had today."

Andrew put Lisa down and began to mix martinis. "What conversation?"

"I'll tell you over dinner."

Celia put *Alice* on a shelf until the next evening and prepared to take the children to bed. An aroma of curried lamb floated in from the kitchen while, in the adjoining dining room, Winnie August was setting Andrew and Celia's places for dinner. *What did I ever do,* Celia thought, *to have such a wonderful, satisfying, happy life?*

"Teddy's absolutely right about its being useless to treat colds with anything except liquids, rest and aspirin," Andrew said after Celia told him of the discussion in her office that morning.

The two of them had finished dinner and taken their coffee to the living room. He went on, "I tell my patients, if they have a cold and treat it properly it will last seven days. If they don't, it will last a week."

Celia laughed and Andrew poked at a log fire he had lighted earlier, restoring it to flame.

"But Teddy's in error," Andrew said, "about so-called cold remedies not doing any harm. A lot of them *are* harmful, some dangerous."

"Oh, really!" she objected. "Surely 'dangerous' is exaggerating."

He said emphatically, "It isn't. In trying to cure a cold you may make other, more serious things that are wrong with you a whole lot worse." Andrew crossed to a bookshelf and pulled down several volumes, their pages flagged with slips of paper. "I've been doing some reading about this lately." He turned pages of the books.

"In most cold remedies," Andrew said, "there's a mishmash of ingredients. One's a chemical called phenylephrine; it's in what are advertised as decongestants to relieve a stuffy nose. Mostly, phenylephrine doesn't work—there isn't enough used to be effective

104

—but it *does* raise blood pressure, which is harmful for anyone, and dangerous for those who have high blood pressure already."

He referred to a page of notes. "Plain, simple aspirin, just about all medical researchers agree, is the best thing for a cold. But there are aspirin substitutes, heavily advertised and bought, which contain a chemical, phenacetin. It can cause kidney damage, maybe irreversible damage, if taken too often and too long. Then there are antihistamines in cold tablets—there shouldn't be; they increase mucus in the lungs. There are nose drops and nasal sprays more harmful than good —" Andrew stopped. "Do you want me to go on?"

"No," Celia said, and sighed. "I get the picture."

"What it comes down to," Andrew said, "is that if you have saturation advertising you can make people believe anything and buy anything."

"But cold aids do help a cold," she protested. "You hear people say so."

"They only *think* they help. It's all a delusion. Maybe the cold was getting better. Maybe it was psychological."

As Andrew put the books away, Celia remembered something another doctor, a veteran general practitioner, had told her when she was a detail woman. *"When patients come to me complaining of a cold, I give 'em placebos—harmless little sugar pills. A few days later they'll come back and say, 'Those pills worked wonders; the cold has gone.' "* The old G.P. had looked at Celia and chuckled. *"It would have gone anyway."*

The memory, and Andrew's comments, had the flavor of truth and now, in contrast to her earlier mood, Celia was depressed. Her new responsibilities were opening her eyes to things she wished she didn't have to know. What was happening, she wondered, to her sense of values? She realized what Sam had meant when telling her, *"You may have to suspend your critical judgments for a while."* Would it really be necessary? And could she? Should she? Still pondering the questions, she opened the briefcase she had brought home and spread papers around her.

Also in the briefcase was something Celia had forgotten until then —a sample package of Bray & Commonwealth's "Healthotherm," an O-T-C product introduced some twenty years earlier and still sold widely as a chest rub for children with colds; it had a strong, spicy smell described in advertising as "comforting." Celia had brought it

105

home, knowing Bruce had a cold, and intending to use it. Now she asked Andrew, "Should I?"

He took the package from her, read the table of ingredients, and laughed. "Darling, why not? If you want to use that ancient greasy goo, it won't do Brucie the slightest harm. Won't do him any good, either, but it'll make *you* feel better. You'll be a mother *doing something.*"

Andrew opened the package and inspected the tube inside. Still amused, he said, "Maybe that's what Healthotherm is all about. It isn't for the kids at all; it's for their mothers."

Celia was about to laugh herself, then stopped and looked at Andrew strangely. Two thoughts had jumped into her mind. The first: yes, she *would* have to suspend critical judgments for a while; no doubt about it. As to the second thought, Andrew had just tossed out a good—*No, much better than that!*—a splendid, excellent idea.

2

"No," Celia told the advertising agency executives across the table. "No, I don't like any of it."

The effect was instant, like the sudden dousing of a fire. If there had been a temperature indicator in the agency conference room, Celia thought, it would have swung from "warm" to "frigid." She sensed the quartet of advertising men making a hasty, improvised assessment of how they should react.

It was a Tuesday in mid-January. Celia and four others from Bray & Commonwealth were in New York, having driven in from New Jersey that morning for this meeting at Quadrille-Brown Advertising. Sam Hawthorne, who had been in New York the night before, had joined them.

Outside, it was a mean, blustery day. The Quadrille-Brown agency was located in Burlington House on Avenue of the Americas where snarled traffic and scurrying pedestrians were combating a treacherous mixture of snow and freezing rain.

The reason for this meeting, in a forty-fourth-floor conference room, was to review the Bray & Commonwealth advertising program—a normal happening after a major change in management. For the past hour the program had been presented with showmanship and ceremony—so much of both that Celia felt as if she were on a reviewing stand while a regiment paraded by.

Not an impressive regiment, though, she had decided. Which prompted her comment, just received with shock.

At the long mahogany table at which they were seated, the agency's middle-aged creative man, Al Fiocca, appeared pained; he stroked his Vandyke beard and shifted his feet, perhaps as a substitute for speech, leaving the next move to the youngish account supervisor, Kenneth Orr. It was Orr, smooth of speech and natty in a blue pinstripe suit, who had been the agency group's leader. The third agency man, Dexter Wilson, was the account executive and had handled most of the detailed presentation. Wilson, a few years older than Orr and prematurely gray, had the earnestness of a Baptist preacher and now looked worried, probably because a client's displeasure could cost him his job. Advertising executives, Celia knew, earned large rewards but lived precarious lives.

The fourth member of the agency quartet, Bladen—Celia hadn't caught his first name—was an assistant account executive. (Was there anyone in the business, she wondered, who didn't have an important-sounding title?) Bladen, who seemed little more than a youth, had been busy helping move storyboards and artwork around for viewing by the company representatives headed by Celia.

Additional agency people—probably another dozen—had come and gone as segments of the presentation succeeded one another. The most recent segment had been for Healthotherm—a new advertising proposal begun before Celia's arrival on the O-T-C scene.

The others with Celia from Bray & Commonwealth were Grant Carvill, who headed marketing; Teddy Upshaw, representing sales; and Bill Ingram, a young product manager. Carvill, a stolid longtime company man in his fifties, was competent but unimaginative; Celia had decided that sometime soon she would move him sideways to another job. Ingram, boyish, with unruly red hair and only a year out of Harvard Business School, was apparently keen and energetic, but otherwise an unknown quantity.

107

Sam Hawthorne, as an officer of Felding-Roth, was senior to them all. The ad agency president, in acknowledgment of Sam's presence, had looked in briefly to say hello.

But Sam, in announcing during a telephone call to Celia the day before that he would attend the advertising review, had made his own role clear. "I'll just be sitting in, observing. Because you've a big responsibility to which you're new, and a lot of dollars are involved, the brass over here will feel more comfortable if someone from the parent company keeps an eye on what's happening and reports back. But I won't intervene and it's your show."

Now Celia glanced at Sam, wondering if he agreed or not with her comment of a moment earlier. But Sam's face was impassive, revealing nothing, as had been the case all morning.

"All right, Mr. Orr," Celia said briskly, addressing the account supervisor, "you can stop wondering about how to react, and how to handle me. Let's have plain talk about the advertising, why I don't like it, and why I think this agency, whose work I'm familiar with, can do a whole lot better."

She sensed a stirring of interest among the advertising group and even, perhaps, relief. All eyes, including those of her own people, were focused on her.

Kenneth Orr said smoothly, "We're all delighted to listen, Mrs. Jordan. There is nothing among what you've seen which anyone in the agency is cemented to. As to new ideas, we'll be happy to produce them, or develop yours."

"I'm glad about the cement," Celia said with a smile, "because my feeling about what we've seen is that everything would have been good ten years ago but is out of tune with here and now. I'm also wondering—to be fair—if some of that is because of instructions and restrictions from our company."

She was aware of Orr and Dexter Wilson looking at her sharply, with respect. But it was Bladen, the young dogsbody, who blurted out, "Gosh, that's just the way it was! Whenever anybody around here came up with a 'with it' idea, or wanted to jazz up your old products—"

The account supervisor cut in sharply, "That will do!" He glared at his subordinate. "We do not blame a client for shortcomings in our advertising. We are professionals who accept responsibility for what goes out from here. Furthermore, you will never refer to 'old products' in that tone. Mrs. Jordan, I apologize."

"That's a load of horseshit!" The remark shot out from Celia's side of the table before she had time to answer Orr. It came from young Bill Ingram, whose face had flushed red in sudden anger, matching his hair. He went on, "They *are* old products and we all know it, so what's wrong with saying so? No one's suggested discarding them, but they sure can stand jazzing up. So if we're going to have plain talk, the way Mrs. Jordan said, let's have it."

There was an awkward silence which Kenneth Orr broke. "Well, well!" With an eyebrow raised, he seemed divided between surprise and amusement. "It seems that youth has spoken up for youth." He turned to Celia. "Do you mind?"

"No. It may even help us progress."

Behind Celia's attitude today was her opinion, gained from a study of Bray & Commonwealth files, that past advertising *had* been inhibited by overly cautious, status-quo policies, an inhibition she intended to shed.

"To begin, I'd like to discuss Healthotherm," she told the others. "I believe the new advertising that's proposed, as well as our old advertising, takes the wrong approach."

With a mental salute to Andrew, Celia went on, "All our advertising, going back years because I've checked, shows children smiling, feeling better, happier, after Healthotherm has been applied to them, rubbed on their chests."

The account executive, Dexter Wilson, asked mildly, "Isn't that what's supposed to happen?" But Kenneth Orr, watching Celia's face intently, waved his colleague to silence.

"Yes, it happens," Celia answered. "But it isn't the children, happy or otherwise, who go into stores and *buy* Healthotherm. It's their mothers. Mothers who want to be *good mothers*, who want to *do something* to make their sick children feel better. Yet, in our advertising a mother is either not in view or is merely in the background. What I would like to see, right up front, is a *happy mother*, a relieved mother, a mother who, when her child was ill, did something to help and now feels good about it. We should use the same approach for the print media and television."

Suddenly there were approving nods around the table. Celia wondered: Should she add Andrew's comment, *"Maybe that's what Healthotherm is all about. It isn't for the kids at all; it's for their mothers."* She decided not. She also put resolutely from her mind

Andrew's description, "that ancient greasy goo" which, he claimed, would do neither harm nor good.

Kenneth Orr said slowly, "That's interesting. Very interesting."

"It's more than interesting," Bill Ingram injected. "It's damn good. Do you think so, Howard?" The question was to Bladen, so now Celia had the missing first name.

The young agency man nodded eagerly. "Sure do. What we'd have is a kid in the background—I guess you'd have to show one somewhere. But momma right up front, and not too smoothy a momma. Her hair a bit ruffled, maybe her dress a touch untidy. As if she'd been working, sweating, worrying, in the kid's sickroom."

Ingram picked it up. "Yes, make her *real.*"

"But happy," Bladen said. "She's relieved, not worrying any more because she knows her kid's okay, thanks to Healthotherm. That's a must. Mrs. Jordan put her pinkie on it there."

"We can work out the details," Orr observed. He smiled at Celia. "Mrs. Jordan, there seems a consensus that you have something promising."

"And something else, Mrs. Jordan," Bill Ingram said. "At our end we ought to change the product a bit. Then we could call it 'New Healthotherm.'"

The account executive, Dexter Wilson, nodded. "That always helps."

"New Healthotherm." Teddy Upshaw mouthed the words as if trying them on, then affirmed, "Yep! Be good for our sales guys out front. Give 'em a new angle, something fresh to talk about."

Grant Carvill, the Bray & Commonwealth marketing man, leaned forward. Celia had the impression he felt the decision process was passing him by, therefore he should say something.

"Changing the product won't be difficult," Carvill volunteered. "The chemists do it by revising an ingredient. Just something minor, not critical, maybe a difference in the perfume."

"Great!" Bladen said. "Now we're cooking."

In a separate compartment of her mind, Celia wondered if all this was really taking place, and how she would have felt about it only a short time ago. Well, she reasoned, for better or worse she had accepted Sam Hawthorne's advice and suspended critical judgments. How long would she have to go on doing it? If Teddy Upshaw was right in his prediction about her moving on from O-T-C, it would be merely for a year. Celia observed that Sam was smiling and wondered at what.

Her thoughts returned to her responsibilities. Observing the two young men, Howard Bladen and Bill Ingram, Celia had an instinct about whom she would be working with closely in the future, both at Bray & Commonwealth and Quadrille-Brown Advertising.

Even in her most sanguine moments Celia had not expected her merchandising program for New Healthotherm—the "happy-momma" plan, as it became known to company insiders—to produce the astounding results it did. As Teddy Upshaw declared cheerfully during a private session in her office, "Celia, baby, it's dynamite!" He added, "I knew all along you were good, but you turned out to be a friggin' genius."

Within a month of launching a TV, radio and print campaign orchestrated by Quadrille-Brown Advertising, sales of Healthotherm had multiplied by six. Moreover, in the fourth week a fresh flood of wholesale orders made clear this was merely a beginning. Sure enough, within another month the previous high had doubled, with still further gains predicted.

The success of Celia and New Healthotherm were duly noted at Felding-Roth corporate headquarters. Consequently, through the remainder of 1964 when plans were developed to revitalize other Bray & Commonwealth products, approval of the expense was automatic. As Sam Hawthorne explained, "We still want to know what's going on, Celia—after all, we might learn something over here—but while you continue producing, you'll be given freedom to operate your way."

Celia's way consisted of creating new images for elderly, existing products.

One of them had been known simply as B&C Shampoo. At Celia's suggestion the old name was retained, but in minuscule type with a large new added name—EMBRACE. Immediately below and almost as prominent was the slogan: *As Gentle As Your Dream Lover.*

Not only was the slogan remembered by those who saw EMBRACE advertised, and those who bought it, but—to the delight of all concerned with sales—it was bandied around to become a national catchphrase. TV comics milked the line for laughs. Parodies appeared in newspapers—among them an editorial page feature in

The Wall Street Journal, criticizing a White House tax plan and headed:

No Gentle Embrace From Your Dream President

This, and more, brought EMBRACE shampoo unprecedented attention and sales exploded.

Again, the Quadrille-Brown agency developed the advertising program for EMBRACE, but this time under the direction of Howard Bladen, promoted from assistant to full account executive. Young Bladen had also played a role in New Healthotherm, eventually eclipsing the earnest, worried Dexter Wilson who simply disappeared from view, so Celia never did learn whether he had left the agency or was pastured to a lesser account.

Similarly, at the Bray & Commonwealth end of the equation, the youthful Bill Ingram had been moved up by Celia to become marketing director, replacing the veteran Grant Carvill. For Carvill another slot was found where he was now—as someone said unkindly—"counting paper clips until early retirement."

Ingram, taking his cue from Celia, came up with innovative marketing ideas. It was Ingram, also, who brought to her the news that a small pharmaceutical firm in Michigan was available for purchase. "They have several products, Mrs. Jordan, but the only interesting one is System 5, a liquid cold medicine, a decongestant. As you know, that's a gap in our own line, something we don't have. If we could buy the Michigan company, dump their other products and take over System 5, we could build it into something big."

Remembering Andrew's views about all cold medicines, she asked, "Is System 5 any good?"

"I had our chemists check it out. They say it's okay. Nothing world-shaking, and no better than we could produce ourselves, starting from scratch if we needed to." Ingram ran a hand through his perpetually untidy red hair. "But System 5 does what it's supposed to and it's already on the market with a reasonable sales base, so we wouldn't start from zero."

"Yes, that's important."

Celia was aware that economics were on the side of adapting an O-T-C product which had some acceptance already, rather than introducing something entirely new. Not only was any new item incredibly costly to launch, but most new products failed, often taking their supporters down to obscurity with them.

"Give me a written report with all the details, Bill," she instructed. "I'll look them over. If I think it's a good idea, I'll talk to Sam."

A few days later Celia did think it a good idea and made a recommendation to buy the Michigan company—and thereby the cold medication System 5. As a result the small company was quietly acquired through an intermediary law firm, the vendors unaware of whom the lawyers represented. Such methods were standard, since announcing that a major drug house was interested would have pushed the purchase price sky high.

Soon after, the other products of the acquired company were sold off and the Michigan plant closed. Manufacture of System 5, and a few of the people working with it, were transferred to Bray & Commonwealth's New Jersey plant.

Bill Ingram was charged with improving and expanding sales of System 5.

He began by ordering a striking, modern package design in orange and gold, an attractive matching plastic container to replace the green glass bottle in which the medicine had been sold previously, and renaming it System 500.

"Those extra numbers," he argued, when reporting to Celia, "will imply we've strengthened the product at the same time we redesigned it. Matter of fact, our chemists are making a change or two in formulation so manufacturing will be more efficient."

Celia studied the material presented, then said, "I suggest an extra line of copy immediately beneath the name." She scribbled on a sheet of paper:

System 500
The SYSTEMATIC Cold Fighter

and passed it to Ingram.

He regarded her admiringly. "Brilliant! It'll make people feel they can be *organized* in getting rid of their colds. They'll love it!"

Celia thought, *Forgive me, Andrew!* She reminded herself once more, *All this is only for a year*—then remembered how quickly time had gone by and that it was already a year and a half since her transfer to Bray & Commonwealth. *I've become so engrossed,* she reflected, *sometimes I forget about moving back to the prescription drug side. Besides, what's happening here is fun.*

Bill Ingram was continuing, enthusiastically as usual. "In another

113

six months, when the new packaging has taken hold, we can launch the tablets."

"What tablets?"

He looked pained. "You haven't read my memo?"

Celia pointed to a stack of papers on her desk. "It's probably in there. So tell me."

"Okay. Tablets are just another way of selling System 500. Ingredients will be the same, the effect the same. But we'd advertise separately and get double exposure. Of course, we *will* dilute the ingredients for the children's version. That one will be called System 50, the smaller figure showing . . ."

"Yes," Celia said. "Yes, I get the idea—smaller figure, smaller people." She laughed.

"Next winter," Ingram went on, undeterred, "when whole families are down with colds, my memo suggests we introduce a large, family-size System 500 bottle. If that catches on, we'd follow with an even larger one—in the trade they call it an 'Oh-my-God!' size."

"Bill," Celia said, still laughing. "You're getting to be too much! But I like it. How about System 500 in aspic?"

"For the carriage trade?" Now he was laughing with her. "I'll work on it."

And while Celia and O-T-C were meshed fructiferously, events elsewhere moved on as always—with tragedy, comedy, conflict, nobility, sadness, laughter and human folly—bounding or shuffling onstage, sometimes as entities, occasionally all together.

The British and French announced confidently, as they had on and off for a hundred and fifty years, that work would shortly begin on a Channel tunnel. Jack Ruby, killer of President Kennedy's assassin, Oswald, was found guilty and sentenced to death. President Johnson succeeded, where Kennedy had failed, in having a strong civil rights bill passed by Congress. Four saucy, charming Liverpudlians with the unlikely title of the Beatles were causing their music and a cult dubbed "Beatlemania" to sweep the world.

In Canada, during a nationwide wrangle combining anger and silliness, the country adopted a new national flag. Winston Churchill, who had appeared likely to survive forever, died at ninety. And in the United States something called the Gulf of Tonkin resolution, relating to a faraway country, Vietnam, was eased through Congress

114

with little attention paid, and less awareness that its consequences would alienate a generation and tear America asunder.

"I want to watch the TV news tonight," Andrew told Celia on an evening in August 1965. "There's been rioting and burning in a place called Watts. It's part of Los Angeles."

They were at home for a family evening, which both of them cherished, though recently such occasions were fewer since Celia's work now required her to travel, and sometimes she was away for days at a time. Because of this, and to compensate, the children joined their parents for the evening meal whenever possible.

Celia liked the children, also, to see their grandmother, though—to general regret—the visits from Mildred were less frequent nowadays, due to her failing health. Asthma had long been a problem for Celia's mother, and lately it had worsened. Andrew suggested that Mildred come to live with them, where he could take care of her, but she declined, preferring her independence and the modest Philadelphia home where she had lived since Celia was small.

Andrew's mother, who had moved to Europe, was seldom heard from and, despite invitations, had never been to visit. She had not seen her grandchildren and apparently had no wish to. "When she hears from us, we remind her that she's old," Andrew observed. "She'd prefer not to have that happen, so I think we'll leave her alone."

Celia sensed the sadness behind Andrew's remark.

Andrew's long-estranged father had died; the news reached them, by merest chance, several months after it happened.

As to younger family members, Lisa was now seven and in second grade at school. She continued to exhibit a strong personality, took her schoolwork seriously, and had a special pride in her growing vocabulary, though sometimes straining it. Referring to an American history lesson, she told Celia, "We learned about the American Constipation, Mommy," and on another occasion when explaining a circle, "The outside is the encumbrance."

Bruce—now almost five—showed, in contrast, a gentleness and sensitivity, partly offset by a droll sense of humor. Celia was prompted to observe once to Andrew, "Brucie can be hurt easily. He'll need more protecting than Lisa."

"Then he must do what I did," Andrew responded, "and marry a strong, good woman." He said it tenderly and Celia went to him and hugged him.

115

Afterward she said, "I see a lot of *you* in Brucie."

Of course, the two of them bickered occasionally, and there had been a serious quarrel or two during eight years of marriage, but no more than was normal between husbands and wives, nor did the minor wounds they inflicted fail to heal quickly. Both knew they had a good marriage and did all they could to protect and preserve it.

The children were with them when they watched, on TV, the rioting in Watts.

"My God!" Andrew breathed, as scene followed awful scene—of burning, looting, destruction, brutality, injury and death, savage fighting between embittered blacks and beleaguered police in the wretched, degrading, segregated ghetto slum of Charcoal Alley. It was a living nightmare of poverty and misery the world ignored, except at moments like this when Watts obligingly provided drama for the TV networks, which it would continue to do for five more dreadful days and nights. "My God!" Andrew repeated. "Can you believe this is happening in our own country?"

All of them were so riveted to the TV screen that not until near the end did Celia observe Bruce who was shaking, quivering, sobbing silently, with tears streaming down his face. She went to him at once and held him, urging Andrew, "Switch it off!"

But Bruce called out, "No, Daddy! No!" and they continued watching until the terrible scenes were done.

"They were hurting people, Mommy!" Bruce protested afterward.

Still comforting him, Celia answered, "Yes, Brucie, they were. It's sad and it's wrong, but it sometimes happens." She hesitated, then added, "What you're going to find out is that things like what you saw *often* happen."

Later, when the children were abed, Andrew said, "It was all depressing, but you gave Brucie the right answer. Too many of us live in cocoons. Sooner or later he has to learn there's another world outside."

"Yes," Celia said. She went on thoughtfully, "I've been wanting to talk to you about cocoons. I think I've been in one myself."

A swift smile crossed her husband's face, then disappeared. He asked, "Could it be an O-T-C cocoon?"

"Something like that. I know that some of what I've been doing involves things you don't approve of, Andrew—like Healthotherm and System 500. You haven't said a lot. Have you minded very much?"

"Maybe a little." He hesitated, then went on. "I'm proud of you, Celia, and what you do, and it's the reason I'll be glad when someday you go back to the prescription medicines side of Felding-Roth, which we both know is a whole lot more important. Meanwhile, though, there are things I've come to terms with. One is, people will go on buying snake oil whether you or others produce it, so it doesn't make a helluva difference who does. And something else: If people didn't buy O-T-C potions and went to doctors instead, we'd all be swamped—we couldn't cope."

"Aren't you rationalizing?" Celia asked doubtfully. "Just because it's me?"

"If I am, why not? You're my wife, and I love you."

"That goes both ways." She leaned over to kiss him. "Well, you can stop rationalizing, darling, because I've decided that O-T-C and I have been together long enough. Tomorrow I intend to ask for a change."

"If it's what you really want, I hope you get it."

But Andrew's response was reflexive, automatic. The mental depression produced by the televised scenes from Watts had stayed with him. So had a crucial personal problem, not related to Celia or his family—a problem that had already caused him anguish and would not, could not go away.

"The dilemma is," Sam Hawthorne told Celia next day, "you've been too successful—or, rather, far more successful than anyone expected. You are a goose producing golden eggs, which is why you've been left alone at Bray & Commonwealth."

They were in Sam's office at Felding-Roth headquarters—a meeting arranged at Celia's request and at which she had just asked for a transfer from her O-T-C duties.

"I have something here which may interest you," Sam said. Reaching across his desk, he shuffled several file folders, pulled one free from the others and opened it. From the other side of the desk Celia could see that it contained financial statements.

"This hasn't been circulated yet, but the board of directors will see it soon." Sam put his finger on a figure. "When you went over to Bray & Commonwealth, revenues from that division were ten percent of all Felding-Roth sales. This year the figure will be fifteen percent, with profit up proportionately." Sam closed the folder and smiled.

117

"Of course, you were helped a little by a falloff in prescription drugs sales. Just the same, it's a tremendous achievement, Celia. Congratulations!"

"Thank you." Celia was pleased. She had expected the figures to be favorable, though not as outstanding as those Sam had just reported. She considered briefly, then told him, "I think O-T-C will keep its momentum, and Bill Ingram has become very good. Since, as you just said, prescription sales are down, maybe I could help out there."

"You will," Sam said. "I promise it. Also, we may have something special and interesting for you. But be patient for a few months more."

3

Andrew faced the hospital administrator grimly. They were in Leonard Sweeting's office and both were standing. Tension hung in the air between them.

It was a Friday, close to noon.

"Dr. Jordan," the St. Bede's administrator said formally—his voice taut, his expression serious—"before you go any further, let me caution you to be absolutely certain of what you are saying and to consider the consequences which may follow."

"Goddammit!" Andrew, who was short-tempered from a sleepless night, was ready to explode. "Do you think I haven't done that?"

"I imagined you had. I wanted to be sure." As usual, Sweeting's thick, bushy eyebrows moved up and down rapidly as he spoke.

"All right—here it is again, Leonard, and this time I'm making it official." Continuing, Andrew chose his words carefully, the sentences wrenched reluctantly from his heart.

"My partner, Dr. Noah Townsend," Andrew said, "is up on the medical floor at this moment where he is seeing patients. To my personal knowledge, Dr. Townsend is under the influence of drugs, to which he is addicted. In my opinion he is incompetent to practice medicine and may be endangering patients' lives. Further, also to my personal knowledge, a patient died needlessly in this hospital this week because of an error by Noah Townsend when he was impaired by drugs."

"Jesus!" At the final sentence the administrator had paled. Now he pleaded, "Andrew, can you at least leave that last bit out?"

"I can't and I won't! I also demand that you do something immediately." Andrew added savagely, "Something you should have done four years ago when we both knew what was happening, but you and others chose to keep your mouths closed and your eyes averted."

Leonard Sweeting growled, "I *have* to do something. Legally, after what you've told me, I have no choice. But as to what's past, I know nothing about it."

"You're lying," Andrew said, "and both of us know it. But I'll let that go because at the time I was as bad, and as gutless as you. What I'm concerned about is now."

The administrator sighed. He said, half to himself, "I guess this had to break open sometime." Then, moving to his desk, he picked up a telephone.

A secretary's voice rattled in the instrument and Sweeting instructed, "Get me the chairman of the board downtown. Whatever he's doing, tell his people to break into it. This is urgent. When you've done that, you and anyone else out there get on phones and summon a meeting of the medical executive committee. The meeting will be held immediately in the boardroom." Sweeting glanced at a clock. "Most heads of services should be in the hospital now."

As the administrator put down the phone he grimaced wearily, then his manner softened. "This is a bad day, Andrew. For all of us, and for the hospital. But I know you've done what you felt you had to."

Andrew nodded dully. "What happens next?"

"The executive committee will meet in a few minutes. You'll be called in. Meanwhile wait here."

Somewhere outside a noontime whistle sounded.

Time. Wait. Waiting.

Andrew mused dejectedly: Waiting was what he had done too much of. He had waited too long. Waited until a patient—a young patient, who should have lived for many more years—had died.

119

After his discovery, four years and eight months earlier, that Noah Townsend was a drug addict, Andrew had kept watch as best he could on the older physician—the objective being to ensure that no medical mishap or crucial misjudgment occurred. And while there were limits, obviously, to the closeness of Andrew's scrutiny, he was satisfied that no serious malpractice problem had existed.

As if recognizing and accepting his colleague's concern, Noah would often discuss his difficult cases, and it was evident that, drugs or not, the elderly doctor's diagnostic skills were continuing to function.

On the other hand, Dr. Townsend became noticeably more careless about taking drugs, not bothering with the concealment from Andrew he had practiced earlier, and showing increasing signs of the drugs' effects—glazed eyes, slurred speech and shaky hands—both at the office and St. Bede's. He left dozens of sample bottles of prescription drugs lying around in his office, not even taking the trouble to put them out of sight, and he would dip into them—occasionally when Andrew was with him—as if they contained candy.

Sometimes Andrew wondered how Townsend could continue to be a drug addict, yet function as well as he appeared to. Then Andrew reasoned: habit died hard, and so did instincts. Noah had been practicing medicine for so many years that much of what he did— including diagnoses which could be difficult for others—came easily to him. In a way, Andrew thought, Noah was like a flawed machine which goes on running of its own momentum. But a question was: How long would the momentum last?

Still, at St. Bede's, no one else appeared to share Andrew's concern. However, in 1961—a year after Andrew's discovery about Noah and the first, abortive session with Leonard Sweeting—Noah Townsend did step down as chief of medicine, also quitting the hospital's medical board. Whether the changes were Townsend's own idea or the result of a quiet suggestion, Andrew never found out. Also, from then on, Townsend led a less active social life, staying at home more than in the past. And at the office he eased up on his patient load, mostly referring new patients to Andrew and a new young doctor, Oscar Aarons, who had joined their practice.

From time to time Andrew still worried about Noah and patients, but because there seemed no major problem, Andrew had—as he saw it now—simply drifted along, doing nothing, waiting for something to happen, yet nurturing a wishful belief it never would.

Until this week.

The climax, when it came, arrived with shattering suddenness.

At first Andrew had only partial, disconnected information. But soon afterward, because of his suspicions and inquiries, he was able to piece events together in their proper sequence.

They began on Tuesday afternoon.

A twenty-nine-year-old man, Kurt Wyrazik, appeared in Dr. Townsend's office complaining of a sore throat, nausea, persistent coughing and feeling feverish. An examination showed his throat to be inflamed; temperature was 102 and respiration rapid. Through his stethoscope, Noah Townsend's clinical notes revealed, he heard suppressed breath sounds, lung rales, and a pleural friction rub. He diagnosed pneumonia and instructed Wyrazik to go to St. Bede's Hospital where he would be admitted immediately and where Townsend would see him again, later in the day.

Wyrazik was not a new patient. He had been in the office several times before, beginning three years earlier. On that first occasion he had also had an inflamed throat and Townsend had given him, there and then, a shot of penicillin.

In the days that followed the injection, Wyrazik's throat returned to normal but he developed an itchy body rash. The rash indicated that he was hypersensitive to penicillin; therefore that particular drug should not be given him again because future side effects might be severe or even catastrophic. Dr. Townsend made a prominent, red-starred note of this in the patient's medical record.

Wyrazik had not, until that time, known about his allergy to penicillin.

On a second occasion, when Wyrazik arrived with a minor ailment, Noah Townsend was away and Andrew saw him. Reading the patient's file, Andrew observed the warning about penicillin. At that point it did not apply, since Andrew prescribed no medication.

That—about a year and a half earlier—was the last time Andrew saw Wyrazik alive.

After Noah Townsend sent Wyrazik to St. Bede's, Wyrazik was installed in a hospital room where there were three other patients. Soon afterward he was given a normal workup by an intern who took

121

a medical history. This was routine. One of the questions the intern asked was, "Are you allergic to anything?" Wyrazik replied, "Yes—to penicillin." The question and answer were recorded on the patient's hospital chart.

Dr. Townsend kept his promise to see Wyrazik later at the hospital, but before that he telephoned St. Bede's, instructing that the patient be given the drug erythromycin. The intern complied with the order. Since, with most patients, it was normal to use penicillin to treat pneumonia, it appeared that Townsend had either read the allergy warning in his file, or had remembered it—perhaps both.

That same day, when he visited Wyrazik in the hospital, Townsend would have—or should have—read the intern's notes, thus receiving a further reminder about the penicillin allergy.

The patient's own background had some relevance to what happened, or failed to happen, later.

Kurt Wyrazik was a mild, unobtrusive person, unmarried and without close friends. Employed as a shipping clerk, he lived alone and was in every sense a "loner." No one visited him while he was in the hospital. Wyrazik was American-born; his parents had been Polish immigrants. His mother was dead. His father lived in a small town in Kansas with Kurt's older sister, also unmarried. The two were the only people in the world with whom Kurt Wyrazik had close ties. However, he did not inform them that he was ill and in St. Bede's.

Thus the situation remained until the second day of Wyrazik's stay in the hospital.

On the evening of that second day, around 8 P.M., he was seen again by Dr. Townsend. At this point also, Andrew had some indirect connection with the case.

Noah Townsend, of late, had taken to visiting his hospital patients at unorthodox hours. As Andrew and others reasoned afterward, he may have done so to avoid meeting medical colleagues in the daytime, or it may have been his general disorientation due to drugs. It so happened that Andrew was also at St. Bede's that evening, dealing with an emergency for which he had been called from home. Andrew was about to leave the hospital as Townsend arrived, and they spoke briefly.

Andrew knew at once from Noah Townsend's demeanor and speech that the older physician was under the influence of drugs and had probably taken some quite recently. Andrew hesitated but, since he had been living with the situation for so long, reasoned that nothing harmful would happen; therefore he did nothing. Later Andrew would blame himself bitterly for that omission.

As Andrew drove away, Townsend took an elevator to the medical floor where he saw several patients. The young man, Wyrazik, was the last.

What went on in Townsend's mind at that point could only be guessed at. What *was* known was that Wyrazik's condition, while not critical, had worsened slightly, with his temperature higher and breathing difficult. It seemed likely that Townsend, in his befuddled state, decided the earlier medication he had prescribed was not working and should be changed. He wrote out new orders and, leaving Wyrazik, delivered them personally to the nursing station.

The new orders were for six hundred thousand units of penicillin every six hours, injected intramuscularly, with the first injection to be given at once.

Because of the absence, through illness, of a senior nurse, the night nurse on duty was junior and new. She was also busy. Seeing nothing unusual in Dr. Townsend's order, she carried it out promptly. She had not seen, nor did she read then, the earlier notes in the patient's chart; hence she was unaware of the warning about penicillin allergy.

Wyrazik himself, when the nurse reached him, was both feverish and sleepy. He did not ask what was being injected into him, nor did the nurse volunteer the information. Immediately after giving the injection the nurse left Wyrazik's room.

What happened next had to be partly conjecture; the other part was based on a report from another patient in the room.

Given the known effects of penicillin in the circumstances, Wyrazik would, within moments, have experienced severe apprehension accompanied by sudden itching all over his body, and his skin would have turned fiery red. In a continuing swift process he would have gone into anaphylactic shock with rapid swelling and distortion of his face, eyes, mouth, tongue and larynx, all accompanied by sounds of choking, wheezing and other desperate noises from the chest. The swelling of the larynx, most critical of all, would have blocked the airway to the lungs, preventing breathing, followed —mercifully, after pain and terror—by unconsciousness, then death. The entire process would occupy five minutes or perhaps a little more.

If emergency treatment had been used, it would have consisted of a massive injection of adrenaline and an urgent tracheotomy—a surgical cut through the neck into the windpipe—to get air into the lungs. But it was never called for, and when help arrived it was too late.

Another patient in the room, observing thrashing and hearing choking noises from the adjoining bed, pressed a bell push urgently to call back the nurse. But when she came Kurt Wyrazik had already died—unaided and alone.

The nurse immediately paged a resident. She also paged Dr. Townsend in the hope that he was still in the hospital. He was, and arrived first.

Townsend took charge, and again the reasoning behind his actions had to be conjectured.

What seemed most likely was that a realization of what had happened penetrated his befuddled state and, with an effort of will, he cleared his head and began what—except for Andrew's intervention later—would have been a successful cover-up. It must have been clear to him that the nurse did not know about the penicillin allergy. It was also possible that, with some extraordinary luck, the two incriminating items—the earlier entry on the patient's chart concerning the allergy, and the penicillin injection—might not be connected. So if he could pass off the death as occurring from natural causes, the true cause might not attract attention. It also could not have escaped Townsend's notice that Kurt Wyrazik was without close friends, the kind likely to ask prying questions.

"Poor fellow!" Townsend told the nurse. "His heart gave out. I was afraid it might happen. He had a weak heart, you know."

"Yes, Doctor." The young nurse was immediately relieved that she was not being blamed for anything. Also, even now, Noah Townsend was an impressive, seasoned figure of authority whose pronouncement she did not question. Nor was it questioned by the resident who had been called, and who returned to other duties after finding there was an "attending" on the scene; therefore he was not needed.

Townsend sighed and addressed the nurse. "There are things we have to do after a death, young lady. Let's you and me get on with them."

One of the things was to complete a death certificate in which Noah Townsend recorded the death as due to "acute heart failure secondary to pneumonia."

124

Andrew learned about Kurt Wyrazik's death by chance on Thursday morning.

Passing through the office reception area which he, Townsend, and Dr. Aarons shared, Andrew heard Peggy, the receptionist who had replaced the departed Violet Parsons, refer on the telephone to "Dr. Townsend's patient who died last night." Soon after, Andrew encountered Townsend and said sympathetically, "I hear you lost a patient."

The older man nodded. "Very sad. It was a young fellow; you saw him once for me. Wyrazik. He had a bad case of pneumonia, also a weak heart. His heart gave out. I was afraid it might."

Andrew might have thought no more about the matter; the death of a patient, while regrettable, was not unusual. But there was something awkward in Townsend's manner which aroused a sense of vague disquiet. The feeling prompted Andrew, an hour or so later when Townsend had left the office, to pull out Wyrazik's medical file and read it. Yes, now he remembered the patient and, going through the file, Andrew noticed two things. One was a notation about a penicillin allergy, which did not seem significant. The other was the absence of any reference to heart disease, which did.

Still not overly concerned, but curious, Andrew decided to make discreet inquiries about Wyrazik's death at the hospital later in the day.

That afternoon he went to the records office at St. Bede's. Wyrazik's chart and other documents had been sent there from the medical floor after the patient's death.

Andrew read the last entry on the medical chart first—the cause of death, as recorded by Dr. Townsend—then worked backward through the file. Almost at once the order, in Townsend's handwriting, for six hundred thousand units of penicillin leaped out at him, striking Andrew like a thunderbolt. Equally shattering was the nurse's notation that the penicillin had been administered and, as time sequences showed, it was shortly before Wyrazik died.

Andrew read the rest of the file—including the intern's note about penicillin allergy and the earlier order for erythromycin—in a daze. When he returned the file to a records clerk his hand was shaking, his heart pounding.

Questions hurled themselves. *What to do? Where to go next?*

Andrew went to the morgue to view Wyrazik's body.

In death the eyes were closed, the dead man's features composed.

Except for a slight bluish, cyanotic tinge to the skin which could have been from other causes, there were no telltale signs of the anaphylactic shock which, Andrew now believed, had killed this young man needlessly.

He asked the morgue attendant who accompanied him, "Has an autopsy been ordered?"

"No, sir." Then the man added, "There's a sister who's supposed to be coming from Kansas. There's to be cremation after she gets here."

Andrew's thoughts were in turmoil. Remembering his earlier experience with the hospital administrator, he was still uncertain about what to do next. Clearly, something must be done, but what? Should he sound a warning about the need for an autopsy? One thing Andrew was sure of: an autopsy would show there had been no heart failure. But even without an autopsy the entries on the patient's chart were damning evidence.

By now it was early evening, most senior people in the hospital had gone home, and there was little choice but to wait until next day.

Throughout that night, while Celia slept beside him, unaware of her husband's problem, he lay awake as courses of action chased themselves around his mind. Ought he to go before colleagues in the hospital with what he knew, or would impartial proceedings be more assured if he went to authorities outside? Should he confront Noah Townsend first and hear Noah's explanation? But then Andrew realized the futility of this, as Noah's personality had clearly changed, even more than appeared on the surface—the result of his drug addiction over years.

The Noah Andrew had once known and respected, and at moments loved, was upright and honorable, holding the strongest views about ethics and medicine, so that he would never have condoned in himself or others the awful professional negligence, followed by subterfuge, which he had just practiced. The old Noah Townsend would have stood up, confessed and taken the consequences, no matter how harsh. No, a personal confrontation would accomplish nothing.

Over it all, Andrew had a sense of great sadness and of loss.

In the end he decided wearily that he would keep what he knew within the family of the hospital. If other, outside action needed to be taken, then others in the hospital must decide. Next morning in his office he took time to write a detailed summation of what he knew. Then, shortly before noon, he went to St. Bede's and confronted the administrator.

126

4

If he closed his eyes, Andrew thought, he might well imagine he was at a PTA meeting at the children's school, or perhaps in the boardroom of a nuts-and-bolts industrial company making everyday, routine decisions.

The words flowed past him.

"May I have a resolution on that?"

"Mr. Chairman, I propose . . ."

"Is there a seconder?"

". . . second that."

". . . been proposed and seconded . . . Those in favor of the resolution . . ."

A chorus of *"aye."*

"Against?"

Silence.

". . . declare the resolution carried. By unanimous decision the hospital privileges of Dr. Noah Townsend are suspended . . ."

Could this truly be the way it happened? This prosaic, formal, minor-key accompaniment to deepest tragedy. Were these petty, pecksniffian phrases the best that could be found to signal the sudden, grievous ending of a lifetime's work, a once dedicated man's career?

Andrew was not ashamed to find that tears were coursing down his face. Aware that others seated around the hospital boardroom table were watching, he made no attempt to hide them.

"Dr. Jordan," the chairman of the medical board executive committee said considerately, "please believe me that the rest of us share your great sadness. Noah was, and is, our friend and colleague too. We respect you for doing what you have, which we are well aware was difficult. What we have done was equally difficult, but equally necessary."

Andrew nodded, unable to speak.

The chairman was Dr. Ezra Gould. He was a neurologist and the chief of medicine, having succeeded Noah Townsend in that office three years earlier. Gould was small and soft-spoken, but quietly strong and greatly respected at St. Bede's. The others on the committee were heads of services—surgery, obstetrics and gynecology, pathology, pediatrics, radiology, several more. Andrew knew most of them fairly well. They were decent, sensitive, caring people, but doing what they had to, even though, in Andrew's view, their action had been delayed too long.

"Mr. Chairman," Leonard Sweeting said, "I should inform the committee that in anticipation of its decision I prepared a notice which will go immediately to the entire hospital—nursing stations, admitting office, pharmacy, and so on. In it I took the liberty of describing Dr. Townsend's suspension as being 'because of health reasons.' I believe that's more discreet than anything specific. Is that agreeable?"

Gould glanced inquiringly at the others. There were murmurs of assent.

"It's agreeable," Gould said.

"I would also urge," the administrator continued, "that the details of what has passed here be discussed outside this room as little as possible."

Leonard Sweeting had guided the committee on procedure from the moment the meeting's purpose had been made known—to the shock and consternation of the senior doctors summoned here so hurriedly. Sweeting had also, before the meeting began, had a hurried telephone consultation with the hospital chairman, a veteran local lawyer, Fergus McNair, whose practice was in Morristown. The conversation had been in Andrew's presence and, while hearing only one side of it, Andrew did catch the chairman's emphatic final words which rattled in the phone receiver, "Protect the hospital."

"I'll do my best," the administrator had said.

After that Sweeting had gone into the boardroom, which adjoined his office, closing the door behind him and leaving Andrew alone. In a few minutes the door reopened and Andrew was summoned in.

All faces around the boardroom table were deadly serious.

"Dr. Jordan," the chairman, Dr. Gould, had said, "we have been informed of the nature of your charges. Please tell us what you know."

Andrew had repeated what he had told the administrator earlier, at times referring to his notes. Following his statement there were a few questions and some discussion, but not much. Leonard Sweeting then produced the hospital's file on the deceased Kurt Wyrazik, which was passed around and the patient's chart, with its damning entries, examined amid doleful head shaking.

Andrew had the clear impression that although members of the committee had not expected today's disclosures to unfold as they had, the subject itself was no surprise to them.

The formal resolution had come next, stripping Noah Townsend of his long-held status at St. Bede's.

Now the chief of pediatrics, a gaunt, slow-speaking New Englander, said, "Something we haven't discussed is what's to happen concerning the young man who died."

"Knowing what we do," the administrator answered, "it's essential that an autopsy be performed. Just before this meeting I spoke by telephone with the deceased's father in Kansas—a sister is on the way here—and the father has given the necessary permission. So the autopsy will be done today." Sweeting glanced at the head of pathology, who signified assent.

"All right," the pediatrics chief persisted, "but what do we tell his family?"

"Quite frankly," Sweeting said, "because of the legal issues involved, that is a delicate, potentially volatile subject. I suggest you leave a decision on it to Dr. Gould, to me, and to Mr. McNair who will be here shortly and who will also advise us legally." He added, "Perhaps, later on, we will report back to this committee."

Dr. Gould asked the others, "Is that all right?" There were nods of agreement and also, it seemed, a sense of relief.

Perhaps. Andrew thought: it was the operative word. *Perhaps . . . we will report back to this committee. And perhaps we won't.*

What the hospital, in the persons of Leonard Sweeting and his boss Fergus McNair, would undoubtedly like was for everything to be hushed up, and for young Kurt Wyrazik, the innocent victim, to be cremated and forgotten. In a way, Andrew supposed, you couldn't blame Sweeting or McNair. They had their responsibilities. And if all this came to a malpractice case in court, a jury award or financial settlement could be horrendous. Whether insurance would cover it,

Andrew had no idea and didn't care. The only thing he was sure of was that he would not be part of a cover-up himself.

There had been a buzz of conversation and the chairman rapped a gavel for attention.

"Now," Dr. Gould said, "we come to the hardest part." He glanced around the room. "I will have to go to Noah Townsend and tell him what has been decided here. I understand he is still in the hospital. Is there anyone who chooses to come with me?"

Andrew said, "I'll come with you." It was, he thought, the very least that he could do. He owed that much to Noah.

"Thank you, Andrew." Gould nodded his appreciation.

In the calm of later, quiet reflection, and despite the pathetic, strident scene that followed, Andrew had an instinct that Noah Townsend had been waiting for them and was relieved to see them come.

As Dr. Ezra Gould and Andrew stepped out of an elevator on the medical floor, to their right were a busy corridor, patients' rooms and a nursing station. At the end of the corridor Townsend was standing, doing nothing, appearing to be looking into space.

As the two of them approached, he moved his head and then, observing them, seemed to shrink into himself. He turned away, but a moment later abruptly changed his mind. Swinging back, his features twisted in the parody of a smile, he held out his wrists, both close together.

"Did you bring handcuffs?" Townsend asked.

Gould seemed nonplused, then said, "Noah, I have to talk to you. Let's go somewhere private."

"Why bother with privacy?" The response was close to a shout and it appeared as if Townsend had raised his voice deliberately; a nurse and several patients turned their heads in curiosity. "Isn't the whole hospital going to know before the day is out?"

"Very well," Gould said quietly. "If you insist, we'll do it here. It is my duty to tell you, Noah, that the medical board executive committee has held a meeting. With the greatest regret it was decided to suspend your hospital privileges."

"Do you have any idea"—Townsend's voice was still raised—"how long I've been part of this hospital and how much I've done for it?"

"I'm aware that it's been many years and we all know you've done

130

a great deal." Gould was uncomfortably conscious of still more people listening. "Please, Noah, can't we . . ."

"Doesn't all of that count for something?"

"In this case, unfortunately no."

"Ask Andrew here how much I've done! Go on, ask him!"

"Noah," Andrew said. "I told them about Wyrazik. I'm sorry, but I had to."

"Ah, yes! Wyrazik." Townsend nodded several times with jerky movements of his head; he spoke more softly. "That poor young fellow. He deserved better. I'm sorry about Wyrazik too. I truly am."

Then suddenly, embarrassingly, the elderly physician broke down and began to blubber. Violent sobs shook his body. They were punctuated by incoherent phrases. ". . . first time . . . ever made mistake . . . surely overlooked . . . won't happen . . . promise you . . ."

Andrew reached for Townsend's arm but Ezra Gould was ahead of him. Grasping it, Gould said firmly, "Noah, let's get out of here. You're not well. I'm going to take you home."

Still shaken by sobs, Townsend allowed himself to be eased toward the elevators. Curious glances followed them.

Gould turned to Andrew. Pushing Townsend slightly ahead, the chief of medicine said quietly, "Andrew, stay here. Find out which patients Noah saw today and check any orders he may have written. Do it quickly. There must be no repetition of . . . You understand?"

Andrew nodded. "Yes."

Reluctantly he watched the other two go.

When they reached the elevators Townsend began screaming and shouting hysterically, trying to resist. Suddenly, incredibly, something within him seemed to have collapsed, reducing him to a shard of his former self, a broken figure, stripped of all dignity and stature. As an elevator door opened Gould shoved Townsend roughly, hurriedly inside. Even when the door closed the screaming could be heard. Then it faded as the elevator descended, leaving Andrew standing alone amid the silence.

That evening, after dinner, Andrew received a telephone call at home from Ezra Gould.

"I want to see you," the chief of medicine said. "Tonight. Where would be most convenient? I'll come to your house if you wish."

131

"No," Andrew said. "Let's make it at the hospital." He had not felt equal yet to telling Celia about Noah and though, as she always did, Celia sensed something wrong, she had not pressed him for the reason.

When Andrew arrived at St. Bede's, Dr. Gould was in the tiny office which the hospital set aside for his use. "Come in," he said. "And close the door."

Opening a desk drawer, Gould produced a bottle of scotch and two glasses. "It's against the rules and I do this rarely. But I feel a need tonight. Will you join me?"

Andrew said gratefully, "Yes, please."

Gould poured the drinks, added ice and water, and they drank in silence.

Then Gould said, "I've been with Noah almost since I left you. There are several things you should know. The first is—since it will affect your practice and Noah's patients—Noah Townsend will never practice medicine again."

"How is he?" Andrew asked.

"Make that 'where is he?' and I'll answer." Gould swirled the remaining liquid in his glass. "He's been committed to a private psychiatric hospital in Newark. In the opinion of those competent to know, he's unlikely ever to leave."

As Gould described the events of the afternoon and early evening his voice was strained. At one point he commented grimly, "I hope I never go through anything like this again."

After leaving Andrew, when Gould and Townsend reached the main floor of St. Bede's the chief of medicine managed to hustle Townsend, still screaming, into an unoccupied treatment room where Gould locked the door and telephoned urgently for a staff psychiatrist. When the psychiatrist arrived, between them they subdued Townsend and sedated him. Obviously, in his condition Townsend could not be taken home so the psychiatrist had done some hasty telephoning, after which Townsend was removed by ambulance to the institute in Newark. Gould and the psychiatrist accompanied him.

By the time they arrived at the psychiatric hospital, the sedation had worn off and Townsend became violent, necessitating his being restrained in a straitjacket. "Oh, Christ, it was awful!" Gould took out a handkerchief and wiped his face.

At that point, more or less, it became evident that Noah Townsend had become insane.

As Ezra Gould described it, "It was as if somehow Noah had been living—for a long time and because of his drug addiction, of course— as an empty shell. God knows how he managed to keep going, but he did. Then, suddenly, what happened today caused the shell to crumple . . . and there was nothing functioning inside and, the way it looks now, nothing salvageable either."

An hour ago, Gould continued, he had been to see Noah Townsend's wife.

Andrew was startled. Amid all that had occurred in the past few days, he had given no thought to Hilda. He asked, "How has she taken it?"

Gould considered before answering. "It's hard to say. She didn't talk a lot and she didn't break down. I got the impression she's been expecting something to happen, though never knowing what. I think you'd better see her yourself tomorrow."

"Yes," Andrew said. "I will."

Gould hesitated. Then, looking at Andrew directly, he said, "There's one more thing you and I have to discuss, and that's the dead man, Wyrazik."

"I may as well tell you now," Andrew said firmly, "I have no intention of being part of any cover-up."

"All right," Gould acknowledged; his voice sharpened. "Then let me ask you this: What do you propose doing? Are you going to make a public statement, maybe to the press? After that will you volunteer as a prosecution witness in a malpractice suit? Will you help some ambulance-chasing lawyer on a fat contingency fee take away from Townsend's wife whatever money Noah had accumulated for their old age? Will you load this hospital with damages far in excess of any insurance we carry, and which could break us financially, so we might have to reduce our services or close?"

Andrew protested, "None of that may happen."

"But it *could*. You've read enough about sharp lawyers to know what they can do in court."

"That isn't my problem," Andrew insisted. "What's important is the truth."

"The truth is important to us all," Gould answered. "You don't have a monopoly on that. But sometimes the truth can be shaded for

133

decent reasons and in special circumstances." His voice became persuasive. "Now listen carefully, Andrew. Hear me out."

The chief of medicine paused, gathering his thoughts, then said, "The dead man's sister, Miss Wyrazik, arrived this afternoon from Kansas. Len Sweeting saw her. She's a nice ordinary woman, he says, quite a bit older than her brother was, and of course she's sorry about his death. But the two of them weren't close, haven't been for many years, so for her it's not a shattering bereavement. There's a father back in Kansas, but he has Parkinson's. It's advanced; he hasn't long to live."

Andrew said, "I don't see what all this—"

"You will. Just listen!"

Again Gould paused before continuing. "Wyrazik's sister is not here to make trouble. She hasn't asked a lot of questions. She even volunteered the statement that her brother's health was never good. She wants his remains cremated, and afterward she'll take the ashes back to Kansas. But she does have problems about money. When Len talked to her he discovered that."

"Then she's entitled to be helped. Surely that's the least—"

"Exactly! We're all agreed on that, Andrew. What's more, financial help can be arranged."

"How?"

"Len and Fergus McNair have worked it out. They've been busy this afternoon. Never mind all details; you and I don't need to know them. But the fact is, our insurers—who've been talked to confidentially—have an interest in seeing this thing ended quietly. Wyrazik, it appears, was sending money to Kansas to help pay medical expenses for his father. Those amounts can be continued, maybe augmented. Wyrazik's funeral expenses will be paid. And there can be a pension, not enormous but sufficient, for the sister for the remainder of her life."

"How will you explain that to her without admitting liability? Supposing she becomes suspicious?"

"I imagine it's a risk," Gould said, "though Len and McNair don't seem to think so, and they're lawyers after all. They believe they can handle it discreetly. Also, I suppose, it has to do with the kind of woman Miss Wyrazik is. The most important thing: this way there won't be any ridiculous multimillion dollar settlements."

"I suppose," Andrew said, "what's ridiculous or isn't depends on your point of view."

The chief of medicine gestured impatiently. "Try to remember this: There's no wife involved, no children with future education to be considered—just a dying old man and one middle-aged woman who's going to be taken care of reasonably." Gould stopped, then asked abruptly, "What were you thinking?" At the last remark Andrew had smiled.

"A cynical thought. If Noah *had* to kill a patient, he couldn't have picked one who'd be more accommodating."

Gould shrugged. "Life's full of chances. This happens to be one that broke our way. Well?"

"Well what?"

"Well, are you going to make a public statement? Will you call the press?"

Andrew said irritably, "Of course not. I never intended to. You knew that perfectly well."

"Then what else is there? You've already behaved correctly in bringing what you knew to the hospital's attention. Further than that you're not involved. You will not be a party to any settlement. You are not being asked to lie and if, for any reason, all this blew open and you were questioned officially, naturally you'd tell the truth."

"If that's my position," Andrew queried, "what about yours? Will you tell Miss Wyrazik the real cause of her brother's death?"

"No," Gould answered curtly. Then he added, "That's why some of us are in this deeper than you. And maybe why we deserve to be."

In the ensuing silence Andrew thought: What Ezra Gould had just said was an admission, subtle but clear, that Andrew had been right, and others wrong, four years ago when Andrew tried to bring Noah Townsend's drug addiction out in the open but was rebuffed. Andrew was certain now that Leonard Sweeting had told others of their conversation at that time.

Undoubtedly the admission was the only one that ever would be made; such things were never inserted in a written record. But at least, Andrew reasoned, something had been learned—by himself, Sweeting, Gould and others. Unfortunately their learning came too late to help either Townsend or Wyrazik.

So where, Andrew asked himself, did he go from here? The answer seemed to be: Nowhere.

What Gould had been saying did, on the whole, make sense. It was also true that Andrew was not being asked to lie, though he was being asked to keep quiet so, in that sense, he *was* sharing in a cover-up. On

135

the other hand, who else was there to tell, and what would be gained from doing so? No matter what happened, Kurt Wyrazik could not be brought back to life, and Noah Townsend—tragically but necessarily —had been removed from the scene and would menace no one else.

"All right," Andrew told the chief of medicine, "I'll do nothing more."

"Thank you," Gould acknowledged. He looked at his watch. "It's been a long day. I'm going home."

Andrew went to see Hilda Townsend the following afternoon.

Townsend was age sixty-three, Hilda four years younger. For a woman of her age, she was attractive. She had kept her figure in good shape. Her face was firm. Her hair, while entirely gray, was cut stylishly short. Today she was dressed smartly in white linen slacks and a blue silk blouse. Around her neck she wore a thin gold chain.

Andrew had expected her to show signs of strain, perhaps of weeping. There were none.

The Townsends lived in a small but pleasant two-storied house on Hill Street, Morristown, not far from the medical office at Elm and Franklin to which, on fine-weather days, Noah Townsend had often walked. There were no servants in the house and Hilda let Andrew in herself, preceding him to a sitting room. It was a room, furnished in soft browns and beiges, which overlooked a garden.

When they were seated, Hilda said matter-of-factly, "Would you like something, Andrew? A drink? Tea, perhaps?"

He shook his head. "No, thanks." Then he said, "Hilda, I don't know what else to say except—I'm terribly sorry."

She nodded, as if the words were expected, then asked, "Were you dreading this? Coming here to see me?"

"A little," he admitted.

"I thought so. But there's no need. And don't be surprised or shocked because I'm not weeping, or wringing my hands, or doing any of those other emotional, womanly things."

Uncertain how to respond, he simply said, "All right."

As if she had not heard, Hilda Townsend went on, "The fact is, I've done them all, done them so often, and for so long, that now they're far behind me. For years I shed so many tears that my supply ran dry. I used to think that little pieces of my heart were breaking off while I watched Noah destroy himself. And when I couldn't make him un-

136

derstand or even listen, I came to think that all of my heart was gone and only an inner piece of stone was left. Does any of that make sense?"

"I think so," Andrew said, and thought: How little each of us knows of the sufferings of other people! For years Hilda Townsend must have lived behind a wall of loyal concealment, a wall which Andrew had neither known of nor suspected. He remembered, too, Ezra Gould's words of the night before. *"She didn't talk a lot . . . I got the impression she's been expecting something to happen, though never knowing what."*

"You knew about Noah and the drugs," Hilda said. "Didn't you?"

"Yes."

Her voice became accusing. "You're a doctor. Why did you do nothing?"

"I tried. At the hospital. Four years ago."

"And no one there would listen?"

"Something like that."

"Could you have tried harder?"

"Yes," he said. "Looking back now, I think I could have."

She sighed. "You probably wouldn't have succeeded." Abruptly she switched subjects. "I went to see Noah this morning, or rather *tried* to see him. He was raving. He didn't know me. He doesn't know anyone."

"Hilda," Andrew said gently, "is there anything I can do, *anything*, to help you?"

She ignored the question. "Does Celia feel any guilt about what's happened?"

The question startled him. "I haven't told her yet. I will this evening. But as to guilt—"

"She should!" The words were spoken savagely. In the same tone, Hilda went on, "Celia is a part of that greedy, ruthless, money-coining, high-pressure drug business. They do anything to sell their drugs, to get doctors to prescribe them and people to use them, even if the drugs aren't needed. *Anything!"*

Andrew said quietly, "No pharmaceutical company forced Noah to take the drugs he did."

"Maybe not directly." Hilda's voice rose. "But Noah took drugs, and so do others, because the companies *surround* doctors with them! They deluge them! With sleazy, oh-so-clever, limitless advertising, page after page in medical magazines which doctors have to

137

read, and with an avalanche of mail, and with free trips and hospitality and booze—all of it designed to make doctors *think* drugs, *always* drugs, still *more* drugs! The companies, every one of them, swamp doctors with free samples, telling them they can have any drug they want, in whatever quantity, and just by asking! No restrictions, never any questions! *You* know it, Andrew." She stopped. "I want to ask you something."

He told her, "If I can answer, I will."

"Lots of salesmen—detail men—came into the office. Noah saw them all the time. Don't you think that *some* of them, maybe *all* of them, knew how much he was taking drugs, were aware he was an addict?"

Andrew considered. He thought of the untidy profusion of drugs, all in manufacturers' containers and packages, in Noah's office. "Yes," he answered. "Yes, I think it's likely that they knew."

"Yet it didn't stop them, did it? *Bastards!* They just went on delivering. Giving Noah anything he wanted. Helping him destroy himself. That's the rotten, filthy business your wife is in, Andrew, and I *loathe* it!"

"There's something in what you've said, Hilda," he acknowledged. "Maybe a lot. And while it isn't the whole picture, I'd like you to know I understand your feelings."

"Do you?" Hilda Townsend's voice mixed contempt and bitterness. "Then explain them to Celia sometime. Maybe she'll consider changing to another line of work."

Then, as if a pent-up force had at last broken free, she put her head in her hands and began to cry.

5

The mid-to-late-1960s was a time when women's lib became a phrase on many lips and a fixture in the news. In 1963 Betty Friedan had published *The Feminine Mystique,* a declaration of war on "the second-class citizenship of women." Her book became the *vade mecum* of the women's movement and the Friedan voice was now heard frequently. Germaine Greer and Kate Millett joined the movement, adding literary and artistic style. Gloria Steinem effectively combined women's advocacy with journalism and feminist politics.

Women's lib had its mockers. Abbie Hoffman, a counterculture celebrity of the period, declared, "The only alliance I would make with the women's lib movement is in bed." And historians, reminding the world that few things are ever new, pointed out that in 1792 in England, one Mary Wollstonecraft courageously published *A Vindication of the Rights of Woman,* arguing, "Tyrants and sensualists . . . endeavor to keep women in the dark, because the former only want slaves, and the latter a plaything."

But many in the 1960s took the movement seriously, and thoughtful men explored their consciences.

Celia's attitude to women's lib was approving and sympathetic. She bought copies of *The Feminine Mystique* and gave them to several male executives at Felding-Roth. One was Vincent Lord, who returned the book with a scribbled note, "I have no use for this rubbish." Sam Hawthorne, influenced by his wife Lilian, an ardent libber herself, was more sympathetic. He told Celia, *"You're* proof that this company has no sex discrimination."

She shook her head in disagreement. "I had to claw my way to where I am, Sam—with your help, but also fighting male prejudice, and you know it."

"But you don't have to do that anymore."

"That's because I've proved myself as a producer, and I'm useful. Which makes me a freak, an exception. Also, you know how little support there is whenever I argue for more women on the detail force."

He laughed. "Okay, I concede, but attitudes are changing. Apart from that, you're still the best example a man could have for treating women as equals."

Despite her private advocacy, Celia took no active part in women's lib. She decided—selfishly, as she admitted to herself—that, first, she didn't need it personally; second, she didn't have the time.

Celia's working time continued to be occupied with O-T-C products at Bray & Commonwealth. Despite Sam's promise of a change to other duties, no new assignment seemed in sight for Celia, and his urging to "be patient for a few months" proved an underestimate.

Meanwhile, at home, Celia shared with Andrew the anguish following Noah Townsend's breakdown and committal to a mental institution. As time went on, the prediction of Dr. Gould that Noah would never be discharged seemed increasingly and sadly to be true.

Andrew had told Celia of Hilda Townsend's tirade about drug companies and excessive free samples, and was surprised to find her sympathetic. "Hilda's right," Celia said. "The amount of free drugs handed out *is* crazy and I guess we all know it. But competition made the scene the way it is. Now, no one company could cut back without being at a disadvantage."

"Surely," Andrew remonstrated, "drug companies could get together and make some agreement to cut back."

"No," Celia said. "Even if they wanted to, that would be collusion and against the law."

"Then how about a case like Noah's? Where drug company detail people must have known, or at least had a good idea, that Noah was heavily on drugs. Should they have kept feeding his habit the way they did?"

"Noah was an addict, but he was still a doctor," Celia pointed out. "And you know perfectly well, Andrew, doctors can get all the drugs they want, one way or another. If Noah hadn't got his from detail people he'd simply have written prescriptions, which maybe he did as well as getting samples." She added with some heat, "Besides, when the medical profession does nothing about doctors who become addicts, why should pharmaceutical companies be expected to be different?"

"A fair question," Andrew conceded, "for which I don't have an answer."

Then, in August of 1967, Celia's reassignment happened.

Preceding it, one significant event occurred near the end of 1966. Sam Hawthorne was promoted to executive vice president, making it clear that unless something accidental intervened, Sam would some-day soon be at the head of Felding-Roth. Thus, Celia's judgment ten years earlier when choosing a mentor in the company seemed close to being proved correct.

It was Sam who eventually sent for her and told her with a smile, "Okay, your O-T-C servitude is over."

Sam was now in a palatial office with a comfortable conference area, and instead of one secretary outside his door, his new job rated two. At a previous meeting he confided to Celia, "Damned if I know how I keep them busy. I think they dictate letters to each other."

Now Sam announced, "I'm offering you the post of Latin-American Director for Pharmaceutical Products. If you accept you'll operate from here, though you'll be away a bit, with quite a lot of travel." He regarded her interrogatively. "How would Andrew feel about that? And you about the children?"

Without hesitation Celia answered, "We'll work it out."

Sam nodded approvingly. "I expected that was what you'd say."

The news delighted and excited her. Celia was well aware that international business in pharmaceuticals was becoming increasingly important. The opportunity was excellent, even better than she had hoped for.

As if reading her mind, Sam said, "International is where the fu-ture is for sales. So far we've barely probed beneath the surface, in Latin America especially." He waved a hand in dismissal. "Go home now. Share the news with Andrew. Tomorrow we'll get down to details."

Thus began five years which proved a Rubicon in Celia's career. It also, far from making the Jordans' family life more difficult, immea-surably enriched it. As Celia was to write later in a letter to her sister Janet, "All of us benefited in ways we never expected. Andrew and I because we had more real togetherness when Andrew traveled with me than we ever did at home, where both of us were busy with our separate working lives. And the children gained because when they

141

traveled too, it enlarged their education and made their thinking international."

From the beginning, when Celia brought home the news about her new appointment, Andrew was happy for her and supportive. He was relieved that her time with O-T-C was over, and if he had doubts about family separations which her new work would entail, he kept them to himself. His attitude, like Celia's, was: *We'll make it work.*

Then, thinking about it more, Andrew decided he would use the opportunity to take some time away from the pressures of medicine and travel with Celia when he could. Andrew, now just a year away from being forty, was determined to profit from the lesson of Noah Townsend whose breakdown, he believed, began with overwork and too much stress. Andrew had watched other doctors, too, become obsessed with their profession to the exclusion of all else, to the detriment of themselves and their families.

In the medical practice he had joined as a newly qualified internist eleven years earlier—the year before he and Celia met and were married—Andrew was now senior partner. The second doctor, Oscar Aarons, a stocky, brisk and bustling Canadian with a lively sense of humor, had proved to be an asset in whom Andrew had great confidence, and he enjoyed their burgeoning friendship. A third internist, Benton Fox, a twenty-eight-year-old with excellent credentials, had been with them for just a month and was already working well.

When Andrew told Celia of his intention to travel with her sometimes she was overjoyed; as it worked out, he went along on South American journeyings several times a year. Occasionally, depending on school arrangements, one or both of the children traveled too.

All of it was made easier by some fortunate arrangements at home. Winnie August, their young English housekeeper-cum-cook, having long ago abandoned her plan to move on to Australia, and being virtually a member of the Jordan family after seven years, was married in the spring of '67. Incredibly, her husband's last name was March. As Winnie put it, "If it 'ad to be another month, I should be glad it ain't December."

When Andrew learned that Hank March, a likable, energetic man who worked at various outdoor jobs, was looking for steady employment, he offered him a post as chauffeur-gardener and general handyman. Since live-in accommodation would be included, the offer was accepted with appreciation from both Winnie and Hank. For his part, Andrew continued to be grateful for Celia's foresight in insisting, shortly after their marriage, that they buy a large house.

Within a short time Hank seemed as indispensable as his wife, now Winnie March.

Thus Andrew and Celia could leave home, with or without the children, confident their interests would be taken care of in their absence.

One note of family sadness intruded at this time. Celia's mother, Mildred, died of respiratory failure after a severe asthma attack. She was sixty-one.

Her mother's death affected Celia greatly. Despite the strength and support of Andrew and the children, she experienced a sense of "aloneness" which persisted long afterward, though the feeling, Andrew assured her, was entirely normal.

"I've seen it happen in patients," he said. "The death of a second parent is like severing an umbilical cord to our past. No matter how much we grow up, while at least one parent is alive there's always a sense of having someone to fall back on. When both are gone, we know we are truly on our own."

Celia's younger sister, Janet, flew to Philadelphia for the funeral, though leaving her busy oilman husband and their two small children in the Middle East. Afterward, Janet and Celia had a few days together in Morristown, each promising they would try to make mutual visits more frequently in future.

6

The sights and sounds of faraway places fascinated Andrew. While Celia transacted her Latin-American business with regional functionaries at outposts of Felding-Roth, he explored the offbeat intrica-

143

cies of foreign cities or savored scenes of rural life outside. The Parque Colón of Buenos Aires became familiar, as did great herds of grazing cattle on the Argentine pampas. So did Colombia's Bogotá, surrounded by mountain grandeur, where downward-sloping streets, the *calles*, carried streams of icy water from the Andes, and ancient mule carts jousted with modern autos for a share of space. In Costa Rica, Andrew came to know the Meseta Central, the country's heartland and, beyond it, dense broadleaf forests where mahogany and cedar grew. From Montevideo's narrow, congested Old City streets there were journeys into Uruguay's valleys, the air fragrant with the scent of verbena and aromatic shrubs. There was Brazil's dynamic São Paulo city, on the edge of the Great Escarpment and, behind it, wide grassy plains with rich red-purple earth, the *terra roxa*.

When the children were traveling, Andrew took them along on his explorations. At other times he reconnoitered, then Celia joined him when her work permitted.

One of Andrew's pleasures was bargaining in native shops and making purchases. The drugstores—*droguerias*—often with their wares crowded into tiny spaces, fascinated him. He talked with pharmacists and occasionally managed to hold conversations with local doctors. He already had a smattering of Spanish and Portuguese and his use of both languages improved with practice. Celia was learning the languages too; at times they helped each other.

Despite it all, not every trip was a success. Celia worked hard. Sometimes, trying to solve local problems against an unfamiliar background was a strain. The result was tiredness and normal human frictions which led, on one occasion, to the fiercest, most bitter fight of Andrew and Celia's marriage, a collision of wills and viewpoints they were unlikely to forget.

It happened in Ecuador and, like most husband-and-wife quarrels, this one started off low-key.

They were staying, with Lisa and Bruce, in the capital, Quito, a high mountain city in a cupped palm of the Andes, and a place of vicious contrasts—mostly between religion and reality. On the one hand was a profusion of ornate churches and monasteries with golden altars, carved choir stalls, crucifixes of silver and ivory, and monstrances vulgar with encrusted jewels. On the other was dirty, barefoot poverty and a peasantry undoubtedly the poorest on the

144

continent with wages—for those lucky enough to find work—of some ten cents a day.

Also in contrast to the poverty was the Hotel Quito, an excellent hostelry in which the Jordan family had a suite. It was to the suite that Celia returned in the early evening, after a generally frustrating day spent with the Felding-Roth *gerente local,* Señor Antonio José Moreno.

Moreno, fat and complacent, had made clear that any visit by a head office functionary was not only an unwelcome intrusion on his territory, but an affront to his personal competence. Moreover, whenever Celia suggested changes in procedures, he had given her what she now knew to be a standard Latin-American response, *"En este país, así se hace, Señora."* When Celia suggested that an attitude of "In this country that is how it is done" could sanctify inefficiency and sometimes be unethical, she was met by the same bland rejoinder and a shrug.

One of Celia's concerns was the inadequate information being given to Ecuadorian physicians about Felding-Roth drugs, in particular their possible side effects. When she pointed this out, Moreno argued, "The other companies do it like this. So do we. To say too much about things which perhaps are not going to happen would be *perjudicial* to us."

While Celia had authority to issue orders, she knew that Moreno, as the man on the spot and a successful sales entrepreneur, would interpret them later—aided by differences of language—as he chose.

Now, in the hotel suite living room, her frustrations still seething, she asked Andrew, "Where are the children?"

"In bed and asleep," he answered. "They decided to go early. We had a grueling day."

The fact of not seeing Lisa and Bruce, to which she had been looking forward, as well as what seemed a coolness in Andrew's tone, irritated Celia and she snapped, "You're not the only one who had a lousy day."

"I didn't say it was lousy, just grueling," he observed. "Though for me there *were* unpleasant portions."

Though neither realized it, the high altitude of Quito—more than nine thousand feet above sea level—was having an effect on them both. In Celia it produced a physical weariness, worsening her already downbeat mood. And Andrew had a sharpened acuity, an

145

aggressive edginess, in contrast to his normal easygoing ways at home.

Celia said, " 'Unpleasant portions!' I don't know what you're talking about."

"I'm talking about that!" Andrew jabbed a finger, pointing to a collection of pharmaceutical bottles and packages on a side table.

With an expression of distaste, she told him, "I've had enough of that stuff for one day, so I suggest you get those out of here."

"You mean you're not interested?" His tone was sarcastic.

"Dammit! No!"

"Frankly, I didn't expect you to be. Because what I have here is about drug companies and it's unpleasant." Andrew picked up a small plastic container. "Today, as well as taking the children out, I did some shopping and asked questions."

Flipping open the container top, he poured tablets into his hand and held them out. "Do you know what these are?"

"Of course I don't!" Dropping into a chair, Celia peeled off her shoes and left them where they fell. "What's more, I don't care."

"You should care! Those are Thalidomide and I bought them today in a local *drogueria*—without a prescription."

The reply jolted Celia and the sharp exchange might have ended there, except that Andrew went on, "The fact that I could buy them, *five years after they should have been withdrawn,* and buy other dangerous drugs marketed here without proper warnings because there are no government agencies to insist on adequate labeling, is typical of the don't-give-a-damn attitude of American drug firms, including your own precious Felding-Roth!"

The injustice, as Celia saw it, when she had spent a large part of her day attempting to change what Andrew had just criticized, inflamed her to hot anger. It also robbed her of all reason. Instead of telling Andrew, as she had intended to do later that evening, of her frustration with Antonio José Moreno, she threw back at him her version of Moreno's answer. "What the hell do *you* know about local problems and regulations? What right have *you* to come here and tell Ecuador how to run this country?"

Andrew's face went white. "The right I have is that I'm a *doctor!* And I know that pregnant women who take these tablets will have babies with flippers instead of arms. Do you know what the pharmacist told me today? He said, yes he *had* heard about Thalidomide, but he didn't know these tablets were the same thing because they're

146

called *Ondasil*. And in case *you* don't know, Celia, or don't *want* to know, Thalidomide has been sold by drug companies under *fifty-three different names.*"

Without waiting for a response, he stormed on, "Why always so many different names for drugs? Certainly not to help patients or their doctors. The only reason anyone can think of is to sow confusion and aid the drug firms when there's trouble. Speaking of trouble, look at this!"

Selecting another bottle, Andrew held it out. Celia could read the label: Chloromycetin.

"If you bought this in the U.S.," he declared, "there'd be a published warning about possible side effects, especially fatal blood dyscrasias. Not here, though! Not a word!"

From the collection on the table he chose one more. "I got this today, too. Take a look at Felding-Roth's Lotromycin, which you and I both know about. We also know it shouldn't be used by anyone with impaired kidney function, or by pregnant women, or women breast-feeding infants. But is there a printed warning saying so? Not on your life! Who cares if a few people suffer or die here because they haven't been cautioned? After all, it's only Ecuador, a long way from New Jersey. Why should Felding-Roth care? Or Celia Jordan?"

She screamed back at him, *"How dare you say that to me!"*

Now Andrew lost control.

"I dare," he answered fiercely, "because I've seen you change. Change little by little over eleven years. From having decent feelings and ideals and caring, to not caring quite so much, then relaxing while you helped push useless over-the-counter junk, and now moving on to this—using phony head-in-the-sand excuses to justify something which you *know* is evil, but won't concede, even to yourself." His voice rose. "What happened to that idealistic girl who first brought me Lotromycin and wanted to raise the ethics of the drug business, the same one who stood up, straight and strong, at a New York sales meeting and criticized dishonest detailing? You want to know what happened to her? I think she sold out."

Andrew stopped, then inquired scathingly, "Were ambition and promotion worth it?"

"You *bastard!*" Acting instinctively, without rational thought, Celia reached down and, seizing one of the shoes she had dropped moments earlier, threw it hard at Andrew. Her aim was unerring. The shoe's stiletto heel struck him on the left side of his face, opening a

147

gash from which blood spurted. But Celia failed to see. Blind to all else, she hurled venomous words.

"What gives *you* the right to be so goddam holy about morals and ideals? What happened to *yours?* Where were your precious ideals when you did nothing about Noah Townsend, *and let him go on practicing medicine for nearly five years, when all that time he was high on drugs, and a danger to himself and others?* And don't blame the hospital! *Their* inaction doesn't excuse you! You know it!

"And what about that patient," Celia stormed on, "the young one, Wyrazik? Was it really Noah who killed him, or was it *you?* You, because when you could have done *something* about Noah, you did *nothing,* and left doing *anything* until too late. Do you ever lie awake nights wondering about that, and feeling guilty? Because you *should!* And do you ever wonder if there weren't some other patients Noah killed during those five years, others you don't know about, *and who died because of your neglect?* Do you hear me, *you self-righteous hypocrite? Answer!"*

Abruptly Celia stopped. Stopped, not only because she had run out of words, but because she had never seen such anguish as on Andrew's face. Her hand went to her mouth.

She said softly, to herself, in horror, "Oh, my God! What have I done!"

Then it was not just anguish in Andrew's expression which she saw, but sudden shock at something happening behind her. Following his gaze, Celia wheeled. Two small pajama-clad figures had come into the room. In their uncontrolled fury, both parents had forgotten Lisa and Bruce in the bedroom next door.

"Mommy! Daddy!" It was Lisa's voice, choked with tears.

Bruce was sobbing uncontrollably.

Celia rushed toward both, arms outstretched, in tears herself. But Lisa was faster. Dodging her mother, she went to Andrew.

"Daddy, you're hurt!" She saw the shoe, which had blood on the heel, and cried out, "Mommy, how *could* you!"

Andrew touched his face, which was still bleeding. Blood seemed everywhere—on his hands, his shirt, the floor.

Now Bruce joined Lisa, clinging to his father while Celia watched helplessly, guiltily, standing back.

It was Andrew who resolutely broke the impasse.

"No!" he told the children. "Don't do this! You must not take sides! Your mother and I have been foolish. Both of us were wrong, and

148

we're ashamed, and all of us will talk about it later. But this is still one family. We belong together."

Then, suddenly, all four of them were holding each other, emotionally, as if they never wanted to be separate again.

Soon after it was Lisa, aged ten, who broke away and, going to a bathroom, brought back wet towels with which, competently, she wiped her father's face and washed away the blood.

Much later, when the children were again in bed and sleeping, Andrew and Celia came together, making love with a passionate, wild abandon, greater by far than they had experienced for a long time. Near the peak of their frantic coupling, Celia cried out, "Deeper! Deeper! Hurt me!" And Andrew, relinquishing all gentleness, seized her, crushed her, and thrust himself into her, roughly, crudely, deeply, again and again.

It was as if their earlier fierceness had released passions other than anger, passions which suddenly coalesced.

Afterward, though exhausted, they talked far into the night and again next day. "It was the kind of talk," Andrew said later, "which we've needed to have, yet both of us put off."

What each conceded was that, for the most part, there had been unpleasant truths in the other's accusations.

"Yes," Celia admitted, "I *have* relaxed some standards I once had. Not all, or even most, but some. And there *have* been times I've put my conscience in my pocket. I'm not proud of it, and I'd like to say I'll go back to the way things were before, but I have to be honest—at least in this—and say I'm not certain if I can."

"I guess," Andrew said, "all of it goes with growing older. You think you're wiser, more seasoned, and you are. But you've also learned along the way that there are obstacles and practicalities which idealism won't ever conquer, so you ease up on ideals."

"I intend to try to do better," Celia said. "I really do. To make sure that what happened to us here will not be wasted."

"I guess that goes for us both," Andrew said.

Earlier he had told Celia, "You touched a nerve when you asked if I lie awake sometimes, wondering about Wyrazik's death and perhaps some others. Could I have saved Wyrazik by acting sooner about Noah? Yes, I could, and it's no good saying otherwise and living with delusions. The only thing I *can* say is that there isn't anyone who's been years in medicine who doesn't have something in the past to look back on and know he could have done better, and perhaps saved somebody who died. Of course, it shouldn't happen often, but if it does, the best you can do is hope that what you learned you'll use later on for the benefit of someone else."

A postscript to what happened was that next day Andrew had three stitches in his face, put there by a local *médico* who observed with a smile as his patient left, "Probably a scar stays, Doctor. It will serve as a reminder to your wife." Since Andrew had earlier described the cut as the result of a fall while climbing, it merely showed that Quito was a small place where gossip traveled fast.

"I feel terrible about that," Celia said. It was a few hours later and they were having lunch with the children.

"No need to," Andrew reassured her. "There was a moment when I felt like doing the same thing. But you were the one who happened to have a shoe handy. Besides, my aim isn't nearly as good as yours."

Celia shook her head. "Don't joke about it."

It was then that Bruce, who had been silent through the meal, spoke up and asked, "Will you get a divorce now?" His small, serious face was tightly set, reflecting worry, making it clear the question had been weighing on him for some time.

Andrew was about to answer flippantly when Celia stopped him with a gesture. "Brucie," she said gently, "I promise and swear to you that as long as your father and I live, that will never happen."

"That goes for me too," Andrew added, and their son's face lighted up in a radiant smile, as did Lisa's beside him.

"I'm glad," Bruce said simply, and it seemed a fitting end to a nightmare which was past.

There were other, happier journeys the family shared during the lustrum spent by Celia with International Sales. As to Celia's career, the period proved overall successful, enhancing her reputation at Felding-Roth headquarters. She even, despite opposition within the company, managed to achieve some headway in having the labeling of Felding-Roth drugs sold in Latin America come closer to the precise standards required by law in the United States. However, as she admitted frankly to Andrew, the progress was "not much."

"The day will come," Celia predicted, "when someone will bring this whole subject out into the open. Then, either new laws or public

150

opinion will compel us to do what we should have been doing all along. But that time isn't yet."

An idea whose time *had* come was encountered by Celia in Peru. There, a large part of the Felding-Roth sales force was composed of women. The reason, Celia learned, was not liberation; it was sales. In Peru it is considered rude to keep a woman waiting; therefore in doctors' offices detail women were ushered into a doctor's presence quickly, ahead of male competitors who might have to wait for hours.

The discovery prompted a long memorandum from Celia to Sam Hawthorne urging recruitment of more detail women on Felding-Roth's U.S. sales force for the same reason. "I remember from my own time as a detail woman," Celia wrote, "that while sometimes I had to wait to see doctors, at other times they saw me quickly, and I think it was because I was a woman, so why not use that to our advantage?"

In a subsequent discussion Sam put the question: "Isn't what you're suggesting a way of advancing women for the wrong reason? That's not women's lib. That's just using women's femininity."

"And why not?" Celia shot back. "Men have used their masculinity for centuries, often to women's disadvantage, so it's our turn now. Anyway, man or woman, we're all entitled to make the most of what we have."

In the end, Celia's memo was taken seriously and began a process in Felding-Roth which, during the years that followed, was copied enthusiastically by other drug houses.

And during all this time, beyond the pharmaceutical business, outside events marched on. The tragedy of Vietnam was taking shape and worsening, with young Americans—the cream of a generation—being slain by tiny people in black pajamas, and no one really knowing why. A rock-music cult called "Woodstock Nation" flared briefly, then burned out. In Czechoslovakia the Soviet Union brutally extinguished freedom. Dr. Martin Luther King, Jr., and Robert Kennedy were savagely assassinated. Nixon became President, Golda Meir prime minister of Israel. Jackie Kennedy married Aristotle Onassis. Eisenhower died. Kissinger went to China, Armstrong to the moon, Edward Kennedy to Chappaquiddick.

Then, in February 1972, Sam Hawthorne, at age fifty-one, became president and chief executive officer of Felding-Roth. His accession to power was sudden, and occurred at a difficult, critical period in the company's history.

151

7

Sam Hawthorne, in the jargon of the times, was a Renaissance man. He had a multiplicity of interests, indoors and out, intellectual and athletic.

He was at heart a scholar who, despite heavy involvement in business, managed to keep alive a lifelong, well-informed love of literature, art and music. In foreign cities, no matter how great the pressures of work Sam would somehow find time to visit bookstores, galleries and concerts. In painting he favored the Impressionists, inclining to Monet and Pissarro. In sculpture his great love was Rodin. Lilian Hawthorne once told a friend that in Paris, in the garden of the Rodin Museum, she had seen her husband stand silent for fifteen minutes contemplating "The Burghers of Calais," much of the time with tears in his eyes.

In music, Sam's passion was Mozart. A proficient pianist himself, though not a brilliant one, he liked to have a piano in his hotel suite while on trips and play something from Mozart, perhaps the Sonata No. 11 in A—the grave and clear Andante, the quickening Menuetto, and finally the joyous Turkish Rondo, sending his spirits soaring after a tiring day.

The fact that he had a piano in what was usually a luxury suite was because he paid for such things himself. He could afford to. Sam was independently wealthy and owned a substantial amount of Felding-Roth stock, having inherited it from his mother who died when he was young.

His mother had been a Roth, and Sam was the last member of either the Felding or Roth clan to be involved in company management. Not that his family connections had made much, if any, difference to his career; they hadn't, particularly as he neared the top.

What Sam had achieved was through ability and integrity, and the fact was widely recognized.

At home, Sam and Lilian Hawthorne's marriage was solid and both adored Juliet, now fifteen and apparently unspoiled despite the adoration.

In athletics Sam had been a long-distance runner in college and still enjoyed an early morning run several times a week. He was an enthusiastic and fairly successful tennis player, though the enthusiasm was stronger than his style. Sam's greatest asset on the court was a vicious volley at the net, making him a popular doubles partner.

But dominating all outside interests, sporting or cerebral, was the fact that Sam Hawthorne was an Anglophile.

For as long as he could remember he had loved visiting England, and felt an admiration and affinity for most things English—traditions, language, education, humor, style, the monarchy, London, the countryside, classic cars. In line with the last preference, he owned and drove to work each day a superb silver-gray Rolls-Bentley.

Something else that held Sam's high opinion was British—not just English—science, and it was this conviction that prompted an original, daring proposal during the opening months of his Felding-Roth presidency.

In a confidential, written submission to the board of directors he set out some stark, unpleasant facts.

"In drug research and production—our *raison d'être*—our company is in a barren, dispiriting period which has extended far beyond the 'flat spell' experienced by this industry generally. Our last major breakthrough was with Lotromycin, nearly fifteen years ago. Since then, while competitors have introduced major, successful new drugs, we have had only minor ones. Nor do we have anything startling in sight.

"All this has had a depressing effect on our company's reputation and morale. Equally depressing has been the effect on finances. It is the reason we reduced our dividend last year, an action which caused the value of our stock to plummet, and it is still out of favor with investors.

"We have begun internal belt tightening, but this is not enough. In two to three years, if we fail to produce a strong, positive program for the future we will face a financial crisis of the gravest kind."

What Sam did *not* say was that his predecessor as president and CEO, who had been dismissed after a confrontation with the board,

153

had followed a top-level policy of "drift" which, in large part, had reduced Felding-Roth Pharmaceuticals to its present sorry state.

Instead, and having set the stage, Sam moved on to his proposal.

"I strongly and urgently recommend," he wrote, "that we create a Felding-Roth Research Institute in Britain. The institute would be headed by a topflight British scientist. It would be independent of our research activities in the United States."

After more details he added, "I profoundly believe the new suggested research arm would strengthen our most critical resource area and hasten discovery of the important new drugs our company so desperately needs."

Why Britain?

Anticipating the question, Sam proceeded to answer it.

"Traditionally, through centuries, Britain has been a world leader in basic scientific research. Within this century alone, consider some of the great discoveries which were British in origin and which changed our way of life dramatically—penicillin, television, modern radar, the airplane jet engine, to name just four.

"Of course," Sam pointed out, "it was American companies which developed those inventions and reaped commercial benefits—this because of the unique ability of Americans to *develop and market,* an ability the British so often lack. But the original discoveries, in those and other instances, were British.

"If you asked me for a reason," he continued, "I would say there are fundamental, inherent differences between British and American higher education. Each system has its strengths. But in Britain the differences produce an academic and scientific curiosity unmatched elsewhere. It is that same curiosity we can, and should, harness to our advantage."

Sam dealt at length with costs, then concluded, "It can be argued that embarking on a major costly project at this critical time in our company's existence is reckless and ill-advised. And, yes, a new research institute will be a heavy financial burden. But I believe it would be even more reckless, even more ill-advised, to continue to drift and *not* take strong, positive, daring action for the future—action which is needed *now!*"

Opposition to Sam Hawthorne's plan surfaced with astounding speed and strength.

The proposal was, as someone put it, "scarcely out of the Xerox machine" and beginning to circulate among company directors and a few senior officers when Sam's telephone began ringing, the callers forceful with objections. "Sure the Brits have had their scientific glories," one director argued, "but nowadays American achievements far exceed them, so your whole contention, Sam, is laughable." Others focused on—as one board member expressed it heatedly— "the absurd and backward-looking notion of locating a research center in an effete, run-down, has-been country."

"You'd have thought," Sam confided to Lilian a few evenings later over dinner, "that I'd suggested canceling the Declaration of Independence and taking us back to colonial status."

Something Sam was learning quickly was that holding the company's top job neither gave him carte blanche to do as he wished nor freed him from the shifting sands of corporate politics.

A practicing expert in company politics was the director of research, Vincent Lord, also an immediate objector to Sam's proposal. While agreeing that more money should be spent on research, Dr. Lord described the idea of doing so in Britain as "naïve" and Sam Hawthorne's view of British science as "kindergarten thinking, founded on a propaganda myth."

The unusually strong, even insulting words were in a memo addressed to Sam, with a copy to a friend and ally of Vince Lord's on the board of directors. On first reading the memo, Sam burned with anger and, leaving his office, sought out Vincent Lord on the research director's own ground.

Walking on impeccable polished floors through the research division's glass-lined, air-filtered corridors, Sam was reminded of the many millions of dollars, virtually limitless sums, expended by Felding-Roth on research equipment—modern, computerized, gleaming, occasionally mysterious—housed in pleasant, spacious laboratories and served by an army of white-coated scientists and technicians. What was here represented an academic scientist's dream, but was a norm for any major pharmaceutical company. The money poured into drug research was seldom, if ever, stinted. It was only the specifics of expenditure which occasionally, as now, became a subject for argument.

Vincent Lord was in his paneled, book-lined, brightly lighted office. The door was open and Sam Hawthorne walked in, nodding casually to a secretary outside who had been about to stop him—

155

then, seeing who it was, changed her mind. Dr. Lord, in a white coat over shirtsleeves, was at his desk, frowning as he so often did, at this moment over a paper he was reading. He looked up in surprise, his dark eyes peering through rimless glasses, his ascetic face showing annoyance at the unannounced intrusion.

Sam had been carrying Lord's memo. Putting it on the desk, he announced, "I came to talk about this."

The research director made a halfhearted gesture of rising, but Sam waved him down. "Informal, Vince," Sam said. "Informal, and some face-to-face, blunt talking."

Lord glanced at the memo on his desk, leaning forward short-sightedly to confirm its subject matter. "What don't you like about it?"

"The content and the tone."

"What else *is* there?"

Sam reached for the paper and turned it around. "It's quite well typed."

"I suppose," Lord said with a sardonic smile, "now that you're head honcho, Sam, you'd like to be surrounded by 'yes men.'"

Sam Hawthorne sighed. He had known Vince Lord for fifteen years, had grown accustomed to the research director's difficult ways, and was prepared to make allowances for them. He answered mildly, "You know that isn't true. What I want is a reasoned discussion and better causes for disagreeing with me than you've given already."

"Speaking of reasoning," Lord said, opening a drawer of his desk and removing a file, "I strongly object to a statement of yours."

"Which one?"

"About our own research." Consulting the file, Lord quoted from Sam's proposal about the British institute. "'While our competitors have introduced major, successful new drugs, we have had only minor ones. Nor do we have anything startling in sight.'"

"So prove me wrong."

"We have a number of *promising* developments in sight," Lord insisted. "Several of the new, young scientists I've brought in are working—"

"Vince," Sam said, "I know about those things. I read your reports, remember? Also, I applaud the talent you've recruited."

It was true, Sam thought. One of Vincent Lord's strengths across the years had been his ability to attract some of the cream of scientific newcomers. A reason was that Lord's own reputation was still high, despite his failure to achieve the major discovery that had been expected of him for so long. Nor was there any real dissatisfaction with Lord's role as research director; the dry spell was one of those misfortunes that happened to drug companies, even with the best people heading their scientific sides.

"The progress reports I send to you," Lord said, "are always weighted with caution. That's because I have to be wary about letting you and the merchandising gang become excited about something which is still experimental."

"I know that," Sam said, "and I accept it." He was aware that in any drug company a perpetual tug-of-war existed between sales and manufacturing on the one hand and research on the other. As the sales people expressed it, "Research always wants to be a hundred and ten percent sure of every goddam detail before they'll say, 'Okay, let's go!' " Manufacturing, similarly, was eager to gear up for production and not be caught out by sudden demands when a new drug was required in quantity. But, on the other side of the equation, researchers accused the merchandising arm of "wanting to rush madly onto the market with a product that's only twenty percent proven, just to beat competitors and have an early lead in sales."

"What I'll tell you now, and what isn't in my reports," Vincent Lord informed Sam, "is that we're getting excitingly good results with two compounds—one, a diuretic, the other an anti-inflammatory for rheumatoid arthritis."

"That's excellent news."

"There's also our application for Derogil pending before the FDA."

"The new anti-hypertensive." Sam knew that Derogil, to control high blood pressure, was not a revolutionary drug but might become a good profit maker. He asked, "Is our application getting anywhere?"

Lord said sourly, "Not so you'd notice. Those puffed-up nincompoops in Washington . . ." He paused. "I'm going there again next week."

"I still don't think my statement was wrong," Sam said. "But since you feel strongly, I'll modify it when the board meets."

Vincent Lord nodded as if the concession were no more than his due, then went on, "There's also my own research on the quenching of free radicals. I know, after all this time, you believe nothing will come of it—"

157

"I've never said that," Sam protested. "Never once! At times you choose to disbelieve it, Vince, but there are some of us here who have faith in you. We also know that important discoveries don't come easily or quickly."

Sam had only a sketchy idea of what the quenching of free radicals involved. He knew the objective was to eliminate toxic effects of drugs generally, and was something Vincent Lord had persevered with for a decade. If successful, there would be strong commercial possibilities. But that was all.

"Nothing you've told me," Sam said, getting up, "changes my opinion that creating a British research center is a good idea."

"And I'm still opposed because it's unnecessary." The research director's reply was adamant, though as an afterthought he added, "Even if your plan should go ahead, we must have control from here."

Sam Hawthorne smiled. "We'll discuss that later, if and when." But in his mind, Sam knew that letting Vincent Lord have control of the new British research institute was the last thing he would permit to happen.

When Lord was alone, he crossed to the outer door and closed it. Then, returning, he slumped in his chair disconsolately. He sensed that the proposal for a Felding-Roth research institute in Britain would go ahead despite his opposition, and he saw the new development as a threat to himself, a sign that his scientific dominance in the company was slipping. How much farther would it slip, he wondered, before he was eclipsed entirely?

So much would have been different, he reflected gloomily, if his own personal research had progressed better and faster than it had. As it was, he wondered, what did he have to show for his life in science?

He was now forty-eight, no longer the young and brilliant wizard with a newly minted Ph.D. Even some of his own techniques and knowledge, he was aware, were out of date. Oh, yes, he still read extensively and kept himself informed. Yet that kind of knowledge was never quite the same as *original involvement* in the scientific field in which your expertise developed—organic chemistry in his own case; developed to become an art, so that always and forever after you had instinct and experience to guide you. In the new field of

158

genetic engineering, for example, he was not truly comfortable, not as at home in it as were the new young scientists now pouring from the universities, some of whom he had recruited for Felding-Roth.

And yet, he reasoned—reassured himself—despite the changes and fresh knowledge, the possibility of a titanic breakthrough with the work he had been doing still was possible, still could come at any time. Within the parameters of organic chemistry an answer existed —an answer to his questions posed through countless experiments over ten long years of grinding research.

The quenching of free radicals.

Along with the answer Vincent Lord sought would come enormous therapeutic benefits, plus unlimited commercial possibilities which Sam Hawthorne and others in the company, in their scientific ignorance, had so far failed to grasp.

What would the quenching of free radicals achieve?

The answer: something essentially simple but magnificent.

Like all scientists in his field, Vincent Lord knew that many drugs, when in action in the human body and as part of their metabolism, generated "free radicals." These were elements harmful to healthy tissue, and the cause of adverse side effects and sometimes death.

Elimination, or "quenching," of free radicals would mean that beneficial drugs, *other drugs,* which previously could not be used on humans because of dangerous side effects, could be taken by anyone with impunity. And restricted drugs, hitherto used only at great risk, could be absorbed as casually as aspirin.

No longer need physicians, when prescribing for their patients, worry about toxicity of drugs. No longer need cancer patients suffer agonies from the near-deadly drugs which sometimes kept them alive, but equally often tortured, then killed them from some other cause than cancer. The beneficial effects of those and all other drugs would remain, but the killing effects would be nullified by the quenching of free radicals.

What Vincent Lord hoped to produce was *a drug to add to other drugs,* to make them totally safe.

And it was all possible. The answer existed. It was there. Hidden, elusive, but waiting to be found.

And Vincent Lord, after ten years' searching, believed he was close to that elusive answer. He could smell it, sense it, almost taste the nectar of success.

But how much longer? *Oh, how much longer* would he have to wait?

Abruptly he sat upright in his chair and, with an effort of will, expunged his downcast mood. Opening a drawer of his desk, he selected a key. He would go now—once more—he decided, to the private laboratory, a few steps down the hall, where his research work was done.

8

Vincent Lord's friend and ally on the Felding-Roth board of directors was Clinton Etheridge, a successful and prominent New York lawyer who had pretensions to scientific knowledge. The pretensions were based on the fact that, for two years as a young man, Etheridge had been a medical student before deciding to switch to law. As an acquaintance cynically described the changeover, "Clint diagnosed where the big money was and prescribed a route to it directly."

Etheridge was now fifty-three. The fact that his brief, incomplete medical studies had taken place more than a quarter century earlier never deterred him from making confident pronouncements on scientific matters, delivered in his best courtroom manner with an implication that they should be preserved on stone.

It suited Vincent Lord's purposes to flatter Etheridge by appearing to treat him as a scientific equal. In this way the research director's own views were often placed before the Felding-Roth board of directors with the bonus, for Vince Lord, of a lawyer's skilled persuasiveness.

Not surprisingly, at a board meeting called to consider Sam Hawthorne's proposal for a British research institute, Clinton Etheridge led off for the opposition.

The meeting was at Felding-Roth's Boonton headquarters. Fourteen of the total complement of sixteen directors—all men—were assembled around the boardroom's traditional walnut table.

Etheridge, who was tall, slightly stooped and cultivated a Lincolnesque image, began genially. "Were you hoping, Sam, that if this pro-British thing goes through, they'll be so pleased with you over there, you'll be invited to tea at Buckingham Palace?"

Sam joined in the general laughter, then shot back, "What I'm really after, Clint, is a long weekend at Windsor Castle."

"Well," the lawyer said, "I suppose it's an attainable objective, but in my opinion the *only* one." He became serious. "What you've proposed seems to me to overlook the tremendous scientific capability and achievements of our own country—your country too."

Sam had thought about this meeting in advance and had no intention of letting the argument get away from him. "I haven't overlooked American achievements in science," he objected. "How could I? They're all around us. I simply want to supplement them."

Someone else injected, "Then let's use our money to supplement them here."

"The British themselves," Etheridge persisted, "have fostered a myth about science on their little island somehow being superior. But if that's true, why does Britain have its so-called 'brain drain'—with so many of their best people hotfooting it over *here*, to join in U.S. research?"

"They mostly do it," Sam answered, "because our facilities are better, and more money is available for staff and equipment. But your question, Clint, supports my argument. This country welcomes British scientists *because* of their high quality."

"In your opinion, Sam," Etheridge asked, "what area of scientific research, relating to this industry, is at present most important?"

"Without question, genetic engineering."

"Exactly." The lawyer nodded, satisfied with the answer. "And isn't it true—and I speak with some scientific knowledge, as you know—that the United States has led the world, and continues to, in this genetic field?"

Sam was tempted to smile, but didn't. For once, the pseudoscientist had allowed himself to be mis-briefed.

"Actually, Clint," Sam said, "it isn't true. As long ago as 1651, in Britain, William Harvey studied the development of the chick in the egg, and so laid the foundations of genetic studies. Also in England, the study of biochemical genetics was begun in 1908. In between

161

there were other discoveries, with a good deal of work by an American geneticist, Dr. Hermann Muller, in the 1920s and onward. But a crowning achievement, sometimes referred to as 'an explosion in genetic science,' was also in England—at Cambridge in 1953, when Doctors Watson and Crick discovered the structure of the DNA molecule for which they won a Nobel Prize." Now Sam smiled. "Dr. Watson, incidentally, was American-born, which shows that basic science is international."

Several of the directors chuckled and Etheridge had the grace to look rueful. He acknowledged, "As we lawyers say, there are questions you wish you hadn't asked." Then, undeterred, he added, "Nothing that's been said changes my view that American science is second to none; further, that our own research quality will suffer if we spread ourselves too thin by setting up shop in another country."

There were murmurs of agreement until another director, Owen Norton, rapped his knuckles sharply on the table to command attention. He received it at once.

Norton, a prestigious, authoritarian figure in his mid-seventies, was chairman and major stockholder of a communications empire that included a TV network. It was generally agreed that Felding-Roth was fortunate to have him on its board. Now, having gained attention, he spoke forcefully in a loud, rasping voice.

"May I remind all of you that we are discussing—or should be—the serious and important problems which beset this company. We chose Sam Hawthorne as president, believing he would give leadership, ideas and guidance. So he has come up with a proposal embodying all three, and what is happening here? We are being urged by Clint and others to dismiss it out of hand. Well, I for one, will not."

Owen Norton glanced at Etheridge, with whom he had clashed at board meetings before, and his voice became sarcastic. "I also believe, Clint, you should save your juvenile, flag-waving polemics for a jury which is less well informed than the members of this board."

There was a momentary silence during which Sam Hawthorne reflected on how much it might surprise outsiders to discover that corporate board meetings were seldom conducted on the high intellectual level which many might expect. While weighty and sometimes wise decisions could be arrived at, there was often a surprising amount of low-level argument and petty bickering.

"What the hell does it matter, anyway," Norton continued, "whose science is superior—Britain's or ours? That isn't the point."

162

A director asked, "Then what is?"

Norton pounded the table with a fist. "Diversification! In any business, including mine, it's sometimes an advantage to have a second 'think tank,' completely separate from and independent of any existing one. And maybe the best way to get that separation is to put an ocean between the two."

"It's also a way," someone else said, "of letting costs get out of hand."

For nearly an hour the debate continued, with more opposition surfacing and alternative ideas being put forward. But there was support for Sam's proposal from several directors, support which Owen Norton's stand had strengthened, and in the end the opposition dissipated. Finally the original proposal was approved by a vote of thirteen to one, Clinton Etheridge the sole dissenter.

"Thank you, gentlemen," Sam acknowledged. "I truly believe that something productive will come from this decision."

Later the same day he sent for Celia.

"You're moving on," he told her without time-wasting preliminaries. "The International Division is now behind you. Your new job is special assistant to the president and you'll be my right hand in setting up a British research institute."

"All right," Celia acknowledged; the news delighted her, but she kept her tone as brisk as Sam's. He was showing signs, she thought, of some of the pressures which inevitably were crowding him. He was now almost totally bald, only a thin fringe of hair remaining. From her own point of view, Celia reasoned, there would be time for celebration tonight when she shared her news with Andrew.

She asked, "When do I start?" Mentally she was calculating how long it would take to hand over her Latin-American responsibilities. A month should be enough.

"I'd prefer to make it this afternoon," Sam answered. "But we'll have to arrange an office for you, so let's say 9 A.M. tomorrow."

"This new assignment you have," Sam explained to Celia next day, "won't last long. Your main job will be to help get our British research institute established, staffed and operating. I'd like to have that done in a year, though sooner would be better. As soon as possible after that, we'll find you something else."

The priorities, Sam continued, were to find and appoint a British

163

scientist who would head the institute, to decide where in Britain it should be located, then to buy or lease a building—preferably an existing one capable of being adapted quickly to its new purpose.

Everything was to be on an urgent basis—which was the reason for pulling Celia so suddenly from International. Sam personally would spearhead the search for a prestigious, capable scientific director, though Celia would help as needed. As to the other matters, Celia would handle those, coming up with recommendations for Sam and others to consider.

Both Sam and Celia would leave for Britain the following week. Before then, however, they would consult with Vincent Lord who, despite his opposition to the project, was well informed about British science and scientists and might have names of candidates to suggest.

The consultation with Dr. Lord took place a few days later in Sam's office, with Celia present.

To Celia's surprise, Vince Lord was cooperative, even friendly as far as that capability lay within him. Sam, who understood more of the background than Celia, realized why. With Felding-Roth now committed to research in Britain, Lord wanted to control it. But Sam still was determined not to have that happen.

"I've prepared a list," Lord informed them, "of people who could be potential candidates. You'll have to approach them discreetly because they are either professors at universities or are employed by our competitors."

Sam and Celia examined the list, which contained eight names. "We'll be discreet," Sam promised, "but we'll also move quickly."

"While you're over there," Lord said, "here's something else you might look into." From a file he extracted a batch of papers and letters clipped together. "I've been corresponding with a young scientist at Cambridge University. He's been doing some interesting work on mental aging and Alzheimer's disease, but he's run out of money and wants a grant."

"Alzheimer's," Celia said. "That's when the brain stops functioning, isn't it?"

Lord nodded. "Part of the brain. Memory disappears. The condition starts slowly and gets worse."

Despite the research director's earlier aversion to Celia, he had come to accept her as a fixture in the company, and influential; therefore continued antagonism would be pointless. The two had

164

even progressed to using first names—at first a touch awkwardly, but by now with ease.

Sam took the letters from Lord, glanced through them and read aloud, "Dr. Martin Peat-Smith." Passing them to Celia, he asked Lord, "Do you recommend a grant?"

The research director shrugged. "It's a long shot. Alzheimer's has baffled scientists since 1906 when it was first diagnosed. What Peat-Smith is doing is studying the aging process of the brain, hoping to find a cause of Alzheimer's while he does."

"What are his chances?"

"Slim."

"We might put up some money," Sam said. "If we have time, I'll talk with him. But other things come first."

Celia, who had been studying the letters, asked, "Is Dr. Peat-Smith a possible candidate for institute director?"

Lord looked surprised, then answered, "No."

"Why not?"

"For one thing, he's too young."

Celia looked down at what she had been reading. "He's thirty-two." She smiled. "Weren't you about that age, Vince, when you came here?"

He replied tautly, some of his normal irritation surfacing. "The circumstances were different."

"Let's talk about these other people," Sam said. He had gone back to the original list. "Vince, brief me on them."

9

June 1972. London was a blaze of pageantry and color. Celia reveled in it.

In public parks and gardens a multitude of flowers—roses, lilacs, azaleas, irises—filled the air with fragrance. Tourists and Londoners basked in warm sunshine. Trooping the Color—the military celebration of the Queen's birthday—was a vivid, dazzling performance to the music of massed bands. In Hyde Park, elegantly attired riders cantered on Rotten Row. Nearby, along the Serpentine, children happily fed ducks which competed for water space with splashing bathers. At Epsom the Derby had been run against a background of tradition, style and hoopla, victory going to the colt Roberto and jockey Lester Piggott, riding to his sixth Derby win.

"Being here at this time doesn't feel like work," Celia told Sam one day. "I feel as if I should pay the company for the privilege."

She was staying at the Berkeley in Knightsbridge from where, for the past several weeks, she had traveled to more than a dozen possible locations for the Felding-Roth research institute. Celia was alone, since Andrew had not been able to leave his practice to come with her. Sam and Lilian Hawthorne were at Claridge's.

It was to Claridge's, the Hawthornes' suite, that Celia brought her news and an opinion during June's third week.

"I've traveled all over the country, as you know," she told Sam, "and I believe the best place for us to set up shop is at Harlow, Essex."

Lilian said, "I've never heard of it."

"That's because Harlow was a little village," Celia explained. "Now it's something called a 'new town,' one of thirty-odd established by the British Government, which is trying to get people and industry out of big cities."

She went on, "The location fits all our requirements. It's near London, has fast rail service, good roads, and an airport close by. There's housing and schools, with open countryside around—a wonderful place for staff to live."

Sam asked, "How about a building?"

"I've some news about that too." Celia consulted notes. "A company called Comthrust, which makes small communications equipment—intercom systems, burglar alarms, that kind of thing—built a plant at Harlow but ran into money problems. So now they can't afford the plant, which has roughly the square footage we want. It's never been occupied, and Comthrust is looking for a quick cash sale."

"Could the building be converted to labs?"

"Easily." Celia unfolded several blueprints. "I've brought the plans. I've also talked with a contractor."

"While you co-workers are poring over that dull stuff," Lilian announced, "I'm going shopping at Harrods."

166

Two days later Sam and Celia drove together to Harlow. As Sam threaded a rented Jaguar through early morning traffic out of London, heading north, Celia read that day's *International Herald Tribune.*

Vietnam peace talks, which had been stalled, would soon resume in Paris, a front-page report predicted. In a Maryland hospital, a bullet had been removed successfully from the spine of Governor George Wallace of Alabama, shot a month before by a would-be assassin. President Nixon, offering his own assessment of the Vietnam war, assured Americans, "Hanoi is losing its desperate gamble."

One item, from Washington, D.C., which appeared to receive unusual attention, described a burglary—a break-in at Democratic Party national headquarters at a place called Watergate. It seemed a minor matter. Celia, uninterested, put the newspaper away.

She asked Sam, "How have your latest interviews been going?"

He grimaced. "Not well. You've made better progress than I."

"Places and buildings are easier than people," she reminded him.

Sam had been working his way through Vincent Lord's list of potential candidates to head the research institute. "Most of them I've seen so far," he confided to Celia, "are a little too much like Vince—set in their ways, status-conscious, with their best research years probably behind them. What I'm looking for is someone with exciting ideas, highly qualified of course, and possibly young."

"How will you know when you've found someone like that?"

"I'll know," Sam said. He smiled. "Maybe it's like falling in love. You're not sure why. When it happens, you just know."

The twenty-three miles between London and Harlow were amid increasing traffic. Then, leaving the A414 main road, they entered an area of wide grass boulevards with pleasant homes, separated in many cases by open fields. The industrial areas were discreetly apart, concealed from residential and recreational portions of the town. Some old structures had been preserved. As they passed an eleventh-century church, Sam stopped the car and said, "Let's get out and walk around."

"This is ancient ground," Celia told him as they strolled, surveying the combined rural-modern scene. "Old Stone Age relics have been found from two hundred thousand years ago. The Saxons were here; the name Harlow is from Saxon words meaning 'the hill of the army.'

And in the first century A.D., the Romans had a settlement and built a temple."

"We'll try to add some history ourselves," Sam said. "Now, where's that plant we've come to see?"

Celia pointed to the west. "Over there, behind those trees. It's in an industrial park called Pinnacles."

"Okay, let's go."

By now it was midmorning.

Sam surveyed the silent, unoccupied building as he halted the Jaguar outside. A portion of it, intended as showroom and offices, was of concrete and glass, divided into two floors. The remainder, a metal-clad steel frame, was on one level and designed as a spacious workshop. Even from the outside, Sam could see that what Celia had reported was true—the whole could be readily converted to research laboratories.

A short distance ahead of them another car was parked. Now a door opened and a pudgy middle-aged man got out and approached the Jaguar. Celia introduced him as Mr. LaMarre, a real estate company representative she had arranged to have meet them.

After shaking hands, LaMarre produced a bunch of keys and jangled them. "No sense in buying the barn without looking at the hay," he said amiably. They moved to the main doorway and went in.

A half hour later Sam took Celia aside and told her quietly, "It'll do very well. You can let this man know we're interested, then instruct our lawyers to get started with negotiations. Tell them to wind up everything as quickly as possible."

While Celia went back to talk with LaMarre, Sam returned to the Jaguar. A few minutes later, when she rejoined him, he said, "I forgot to tell you that we're going on to Cambridge. Because Harlow is halfway there, I arranged to meet Dr. Peat-Smith—he's the one doing research on brain aging and Alzheimer's disease, who has asked for a grant."

"I'm glad you found time for him," Celia said. "You thought you might not."

After an hour's drive through more countryside, in bright sunshine, they entered Trumpington Street, Cambridge, soon after midday. "This is a lovely, venerable town," Sam said. "That's Peterhouse on your left—the oldest college. Have you been here before?"

168

Celia, fascinated by a succession of ancient, historic buildings cheek by jowl, answered, "Never."

Sam had stopped en route to telephone and arrange luncheon at the Garden House Hotel. Martin Peat-Smith would join them there.

The picturesque hotel was in an idyllic location, close to the "Backs"—the landscaped gardens that provide a superb rear view of many colleges—and alongside the River Cam on which boaters in punts poled their leisurely, sometimes uncertain way.

In the hotel lobby Peat-Smith spotted them first and came forward. Celia had a swift impression of a stocky, solidly built young man with a shock of untidy blond hair that needed trimming, and a sudden, boyish smile that creased a rugged, square-jawed face. Whatever else Peat-Smith might be, she thought, he wasn't handsome. But she had a sense of facing a strong, purposeful personality.

"Mrs. Jordan and Mr. Hawthorne, I presume?" The incisive, cultured but unaffected voice matched Peat-Smith's ingenuous appearance.

"That's right," Celia responded. "Except, in terms of importance, it's the other way around."

The quick smile once more. "I'll try to remember that."

As they all shook hands, Celia noticed Peat-Smith was wearing an old Harris Tweed jacket with patched elbows and frayed cuffs, and unpressed, stained gray slacks. Instantly reading her mind, he said without embarrassment, "I came directly from the lab, Mrs. Jordan. I do own a suit. If we meet out of working hours, I'll wear it."

Celia flushed. "I'm embarrassed. I apologize for my rudeness."

"No need." He smiled disarmingly. "I just like to clear things up."

"A good habit," Sam pronounced. "Shall we go in to lunch?"

At their table, which provided a view of a rose garden and the river beyond, they ordered drinks. Celia, as usual, had a daiquiri, Sam a martini, Peat-Smith a glass of white wine.

"I have a report from Dr. Lord about your current research," Sam said. "I understand you've asked for a grant from Felding-Roth which would let you continue it."

"That's right," Peat-Smith acknowledged. "My project—the study of mental aging and Alzheimer's disease—is out of money. The university doesn't have any, at least not for allocation to me, so I've had to look elsewhere."

Sam assured him, "That's not unusual. Our company does give

grants for academic research if we think it's worthwhile, so let's talk about it."

"All right." For the first time Dr. Peat-Smith showed a trace of nervousness, probably, Celia thought, because a grant was important to him. He asked, "To start with Alzheimer's—how much do you know about it?"

"Very little," Sam said. "So assume we know nothing."

The young scientist nodded. "It isn't one of the fashionable diseases—at least, not yet. Also there's no knowledge, only theories, about what causes it."

"Doesn't it affect old people mostly?" Celia asked.

"Those over fifty—yes; more particularly the age group over sixty-five. But Alzheimer's *can* affect someone younger. There have been cases in people aged twenty-seven."

Peat-Smith sipped his wine, then continued. "The disease begins gradually, with lapses of memory. People forget simple things, like how to tie their shoelaces, or what a light switch is for, or where they usually sit at mealtime. Then, as it gets worse, more and more memory goes. Often the person can't identify anyone, even their husband or wife. They may forget how to eat and have to be fed; when thirsty, they may not know enough to ask for water. They're often incontinent, in bad cases violent and destructive. Eventually they die of the disease, but that takes ten to fifteen years—years which are hardest on anyone living with an Alzheimer's victim."

Peat-Smith paused, then told them, "What goes on in the brain can be seen after autopsy. Alzheimer's hits nerve cells in the cortex—where senses and memory are housed. It twists and severs nerve fibers and filaments. It litters the brain with tiny bits of a substance called plaque."

"I've read something about your research," Sam said, "but I'd like you to tell us yourself what direction you're taking."

"A genetic direction. And because there are no animal models for Alzheimer's—so far as we know, no animal gets the disease—my studies with animals are on the chemistry of the mental aging process. As you're aware, I'm a nucleic acid chemist."

"My chemistry is a little rusty," Celia said, "but as I understand nucleic acids, they're the 'building blocks' of DNA which make up our genes."

"Correct, and not so rusty." Peat-Smith smiled. "And it's likely that big future medical advances will come when we understand the

170

chemistry of DNA better, showing us how genes work and why they sometimes go wrong. That's what I'm researching now, using young and old rats, trying to find differences, varying with age, between the animals' mRNA—messenger ribonucleic acid—which is a template made from their DNA."

Sam interjected, "But Alzheimer's disease and the normal aging process are two separate things, right?"

"It appears so, but there may be overlapping areas." As Peat-Smith paused, Celia could sense him organizing his thoughts, as a teacher would, into simpler, less scientific words than he was accustomed to using.

"An Alzheimer's victim may have had, at birth, an aberration in his DNA, which contains his coded genetic information. However, someone else, born with more normal DNA, can change that DNA by damaging its environment, the human body. Through smoking, for example, or a harmful diet. For a while, our built-in DNA repair mechanism will take care of that, but as we get older the genetic repair system may slow down or fail entirely. Part of what I'm searching for is a reason for that slowing . . ."

At the end of the explanation, Celia said, "You're a natural teacher. You enjoy teaching, don't you?"

Peat-Smith appeared surprised. "Doing some teaching is expected at a university. But, yes, I enjoy it."

Another facet of this man's interesting personality, Celia thought. She said, "I'm beginning to understand the questions. How far are you from answers?"

"Perhaps light-years away. On the other hand we might be close." Peat-Smith flashed his genuine smile. "That's a risk that grant givers take."

A maître d' brought menus and they paused to decide about lunch. When they had chosen, Peat-Smith said, "I hope you'll visit my laboratory. I can explain better there what I'm trying to do."

"We were counting on that," Sam said. "Right after lunch."

While they were eating, Celia asked, "What is your status at Cambridge, Dr. Peat-Smith?"

"I have an appointment as a lecturer; that's more or less equivalent to assistant professor in America. What it means is that I get lab space in the Biochemistry Building, a technician to help me, and freedom to do research of my choice." He stopped, then added, "Freedom, that is, if I can get financial backing."

"About the grant we're speaking of," Sam said. "I believe the amount suggested was sixty thousand dollars."

"Yes. It would be over three years, and is the least I can get by on—to buy equipment and animals, employ three full-time technicians, and conduct experiments. There's nothing in there for me personally." Peat-Smith grimaced. "All the same, it's a lot of money, isn't it?"

Sam nodded gravely. "Yes, it is."

But it wasn't. As both Sam and Celia knew, sixty thousand dollars was a trifling sum compared with the annual expenditures on research by Felding-Roth Pharmaceuticals or any major drug firm. The question, as always, was: Did Dr. Peat-Smith's project have sufficient commercial promise to make an investment worthwhile?

"I get the impression," Celia told Peat-Smith, "that you're quite dedicated on the subject of Alzheimer's. Was there some special reason that got you started?"

The young scientist hesitated. Then, meeting Celia's eyes directly, he said, "My mother is sixty-one, Mrs. Jordan. I'm her only child; not surprisingly, we've always been close. She's had Alzheimer's disease for four years and become progressively worse. My father, as best he can, takes care of her, and I go to see her almost every day. Unfortunately, she has no idea who I am."

Cambridge University's Biochemistry Building was a three-storied red-brick neo-Renaissance structure, plain and unimpressive. It was on Tennis Court Road, a modest lane where no tennis court existed. Martin Peat-Smith, who had come to lunch on a bicycle—a standard form of transportation in Cambridge, it appeared—pedaled energetically ahead while Sam and Celia followed in the Jaguar.

At the building's front door, where they rejoined him, Peat-Smith cautioned, "I think I should warn you, so you're not surprised, that our facilities here are not the best. We're always crowded, short of space"—again the swift smile—"and usually short of money. Sometimes it shocks people from outside to see where and how we work."

Despite the warning, a few minutes later Celia was shocked.

When Peat-Smith left them alone briefly, she whispered to Sam, "This place is *awful*—like a dungeon! How can anyone do good work here?"

On entering, they had descended a stairway to a basement. The

172

hallways were gloomy. A series of small rooms leading off them appeared messy, disordered, and cluttered with old equipment. Now they were in a laboratory, not much bigger than the kitchen of a small house, which Peat-Smith had announced was one of two that he worked in, though he shared both with another lecturer who was pursuing a separate project.

While they were talking, the other man and his assistant had come and gone several times, making a private conversation difficult.

The lab was furnished with worn wooden benches, set close together to make the most of available space. Above the benches were old-fashioned gas and electrical outlets, the latter festooned untidily, and probably unsafely, with adapters and many plugs. On the walls were roughly made shelves, all filled to capacity with books, papers and apparently discarded equipment, amid it, Celia noticed, some outmoded retorts of a type she remembered from her own chemistry work nineteen years earlier. A portion of bench was a makeshift desk. In front was a hard Windsor chair. Several dirty drinking mugs could be seen.

On one bench were several wire cages, inside them, twenty or so rats—two to a cage, and in varying states of activity.

The floor of the laboratory had not been cleaned in some time. Nor had the windows, which were narrow, high up on a wall, and providing a view of the wheels and undersides of cars parked outside. The effect was depressing.

"No matter how it all looks," Sam told Celia, "never forget that a lot of scientific history has been made here. Nobel Prize winners have worked in these rooms and walked these halls."

"That's right," Martin Peat-Smith said cheerfully; he had returned in time to hear the last remark. "Fred Sanger was one of them; he discovered the amino acid structure of the insulin molecule in a lab right above us." He saw Celia looking at the old equipment. "In academic labs we never throw anything away, Mrs. Jordan, because we never know when we'll need it again. Out of necessity, we improvise and build much of our own equipment."

"That's true of American academia too," Sam said.

"Just the same," Peat-Smith acknowledged, "all this must be quite a contrast to the kind of labs you're both used to."

Remembering the spacious, immaculate, and richly equipped laboratories at Felding-Roth in New Jersey, Celia answered, "Frankly, yes."

173

Peat-Smith had brought back two stools. He offered the Windsor chair to Celia, one of the stools to Sam, and perched on the second himself.

"It's only fair to tell you," he said, "that what I'm attempting here involves not just problems of science, but enormously difficult techniques. What has to be found is a means of transferring information from a brain cell nucleus to the machinery of the cell that makes proteins and peptides . . ."

Warming to his exposition, he drifted into scientific jargon. ". . . take a gross mixture of mRNA from young and old rats and put it into a cell-free system . . . RNA templates are allowed to produce proteins . . . a long strand of mRNA may code for many proteins . . . afterwards, proteins are separated by electrophoresis . . . a possible technique could use a reverse transcriptase enzyme . . . then if the RNA and DNA's don't combine, it will mean the old rat has lost that genetic capability, so we'll begin learning which peptides are changing . . . eventually, I'll be seeking a single peptide . . ."

The talk continued for more than an hour, interspersed by shrewd, detailed questioning from Sam that impressed Celia. Although Sam had no scientific training, during his years with Felding-Roth he had absorbed much on-the-scene science and the effect of it showed.

Throughout, Peat-Smith's enthusiasm transmitted itself to them both. And while he spoke—clearly, concisely, and from what was plainly a disciplined, orderly mind—their respect grew.

Near the end of the discussion the scientist pointed to the rats in cages. "These are only a few. We have several hundred others in our animal room." He touched a cage and a large rat, which had been sleeping, stirred. "This old man is two and a half years old; that's equivalent to seventy in a human. This is his last day. Tomorrow we'll sacrifice him, then compare his brain chemistry with that of a rat born a few days ago. But to find answers we need it will take a lot of rats, a lot of chemical analysis, and a lot more time."

Sam nodded his understanding. "We're aware of the time factor from our own experience. Now to summarize, Doctor—how would you express your long-term goal?"

Peat-Smith considered before answering. Then he said carefully, "To discover, through continuing genetic research, a brain peptide which enhances memory in younger people but, as those same people grow older, is not produced in the human body anymore. Then, having found and isolated such a peptide, we'll learn to produce it by

174

genetic techniques. After that, people of all ages can be given it to minimize memory loss, forgetfulness—and perhaps eliminate mental aging altogether."

The quiet summation was so impressive, so profoundly confident, yet in no way boastful, that neither visitor seemed inclined to break the silence that followed. Celia, despite the dismal surroundings, had a sense of sharing in a moment to be remembered, and of history being made.

It was Sam who spoke first. "Dr. Peat-Smith, you now have your grant. It is approved, as of this moment, in the amount you asked."

Peat-Smith appeared puzzled. "You mean . . . it's that simple . . . just like that?"

It was Sam's turn to smile. "As president of Felding-Roth Pharmaceuticals I have a certain authority. Once in a while it gives me pleasure to exercise it." He added, "The only condition is the usual one, implicit in these arrangements. We'd like to keep in touch with your progress and have first crack at any drug you may produce."

Peat-Smith nodded. "Of course. That's understood." He still seemed dazed.

Sam extended his hand, which the young scientist took. "Congratulations and good luck!"

It was a half hour later and teatime in the Biochemistry Building. At Martin's invitation—the three of them had, by now, progressed to first names—they had gone upstairs to where tea and biscuits were being served from tea trolleys in the foyer. Balancing their cups and saucers, the trio moved on to a faculty "tearoom" which, as Martin explained, was a social focal point for scientists who worked there and their guests.

The tearoom, as austere and inelegant as the remainder of the building, had long tables with wooden chairs and was crowded and noisy. The scientists were of all shapes, sexes, sizes and ages, but fragments of conversation that could be overheard were decidedly *un*scientific. One discussion was about official parking places, an elderly faculty member arguing heatedly that favoritism to someone junior was depriving him of his tenurial rights. Alongside, a bearded, white-coated enthusiast reported a "sensational" sale by a Cambridge wine merchant; an available Meursault was recommended.

Another group was dissecting a new movie playing in town—*The Godfather,* starring Marlon Brando and Al Pacino.

After some maneuvering and exchanging places with others, Martin Peat-Smith managed to find a corner for his group.

"Is it always like this?" Celia asked.

Martin seemed amused. "Usually. And almost everyone comes here. It's the only time some of us get to see each other."

"It does appear to me," Sam said, "that your setup in this building doesn't allow much privacy."

Martin shrugged. "That can be a nuisance at times. But you get used to it."

"But *should* you have to get used to it?" When there was no answer, Sam went on, lowering his voice to avoid being heard by others nearby, "I was wondering, Martin, if you'd be interested in pursuing the same work you're doing now, but under superior conditions, and with more facilities and help."

A half smile played over the scientist's face as he asked, "Superior conditions where?"

"What I'm suggesting," Sam said, "as no doubt you've guessed, is that you leave Cambridge University and come to work with us at Felding-Roth. There would be many advantages for you, and it would be in Britain where we're planning—"

"Excuse me!" As Martin cut in, he appeared concerned. "May I ask you something?"

"Of course."

"Is the offer of a grant from your company conditional on this?"

Sam answered, "Absolutely not. You already have the grant, to which there are no strings attached, other than the one we agreed. On that I give you my word."

"Thank you. For a moment I was worried." The full and boyish smile returned. "I don't wish to be rude, but I think it will save us both time if I tell you something."

It was Celia who said, "Go ahead."

"I'm an academic scientist and I intend to remain one," Martin declared. "I won't go into all the reasons, but one is freedom. By that, I mean freedom to do the kind of research I want, without commercial pressures."

"You'd have freedom with us . . ." Sam began. But he stopped as Martin shook his head.

176

"There'd be commercial factors to consider. Tell me honestly—wouldn't there?"

Sam admitted, "Well, from time to time, some. We're in business, after all."

"Exactly. But here there *are* no commercial considerations. Just pure science, a search for knowledge. For myself, I want to keep it that way. Will you have more tea?"

"Thank you, no," Celia said. Sam shook his head. They rose to go.

Outside, on Tennis Court Road and standing by the rented Jaguar, Martin told Sam, "Thank you for everything, including the job offer. And you too, Celia. But I'll stay at Cambridge which, apart from this building"—he glanced behind him and grimaced—"is a beautiful place."

"It's been a pleasure," Sam said. "And about working for us, though I regret your decision, I understand it."

He got into the car.

From the seat beside him, with the window down, Celia told Martin, "Cambridge *is* a beautiful place. I've never been here until today. I wish I had time to see more."

"Hey, hold it!" Martin said. "How long are you staying in Britain?" She considered. "Oh, probably another two weeks."

"Then why not come back for a day? It's easy to get here. I'd be happy to show you around."

"I'd like that very much," Celia said.

While Sam started the car, they arranged the visit for ten days later —the Sunday after next.

In the Jaguar, driving back to London, Celia and Sam were silent, busy with their own thoughts, until they were clear of Cambridge and on the A10, headed south.

Then Celia said quietly, "You want him, don't you? You want him to head our research institute."

"Of course." Sam answered tersely, frustration in his voice. "He's outstanding, my guess is a genius, and he's the best I've seen since coming here. But dammit, Celia, we won't get him! He's an academic, and he'll stay one. You heard what he said, and it's obvious nothing will change his mind."

"I wonder," Celia said thoughtfully. "I just wonder about that."

10

The days that followed were filled, for Sam and Celia, with more arrangements for the physical aspects of the Felding-Roth research institute at Harlow. But the activity, while necessary, was unsatisfying. The frustration they shared—a conviction that Dr. Martin Peat-Smith would be the best possible choice as the institute's director, but Sam's equal certainty that Martin would never agree to move from the academic world to industry—hung over them as a pervasive disappointment.

During the week after their journey to Cambridge, Sam declared, "I've seen several other candidates, but none are of the caliber of Peat-Smith. Unfortunately, he's spoiled me for everyone else."

When Celia reminded Sam that she would be seeing Martin for a second time the following Sunday, for her conducted tour of Cambridge, Sam nodded gloomily. "Of course, do what you can, but I'm not optimistic. He's a dedicated, determined young man who knows his own mind."

Then Sam cautioned Celia, "Whatever you do when you talk to Martin, don't bring up the subject of money—I mean the kind of salary we'd pay if he came to work for us. He knows, without our saying so, that it would be big, compared with what he's getting now. But if you talk about it, and make it sound as if we believe he can be bought, he'll think we're just two more brash Americans, convinced that everything in this world can be had with dollars."

"But Sam," Celia objected, "if Martin came to work for Felding-Roth, you'd have to discuss salary at some point."

"At some point, yes. But not initially, because money would never be the key issue. Believe me, Celia, I know how sensitive these academic types can be, and if—as you believe—there's a chance Martin might change his mind, let's not blow it by being crass!"

"As a matter of interest," Celia queried, "what *are* the figures?"

Sam considered. "According to information I have, Martin is earning about two thousand four hundred pounds a year; that's six thousand dollars, more or less. To begin, we'd pay him four or five times that amount—say, twenty-five to thirty thousand dollars, plus bonuses."

Celia whistled softly. "I didn't know the gap was so wide."

"But academic people know. And, knowing it, they still choose academia, believing there's more intellectual freedom, and for scientific people more 'purity of research' in a college environment. You heard Martin when he talked about 'commercial pressures,' and how he would resent them."

"Yes, I did," Celia said. "But you argued with him, and said the pressures weren't great."

"That's because I'm on the industry side of the fence and it's my job to think that way. But in private, between you and me, I'll admit that maybe Martin's right."

Celia said doubtfully, "I agree with you about most things. But I'm less sure about all that."

It was an unsatisfactory conversation, she felt, and brooded about it afterward. She also resolved, as she put it to herself, to get a "second opinion."

On Saturday, the day before she was due to go to Cambridge, Celia talked by telephone with Andrew and the children, as she had done at least twice weekly during her month-long stay in Britain. Both they and she were excited by her impending homecoming, now less than a week away. After the usual family talk, Celia told Andrew about Dr. Peat-Smith, the disappointment concerning him, and her exchanges on the subject with Sam.

She also informed Andrew that she was meeting Martin the following day.

"Do *you* think he might change his mind?" Andrew inquired.

"I've an instinct it could happen," Celia answered. "Perhaps under certain circumstances, though I've no idea what they might be. What I *don't* want to do, when we talk tomorrow, is handle things badly."

There was a silence on the telephone and she could sense her husband ruminating, turning things over in his mind. Then he said, "Sam's partly right in what he's said, but maybe not altogether. In my experience you'll never insult anyone by letting them know they

179

have a high monetary value. In fact, most of us rather like it, even if we have no intention of accepting the money offered."

"Keep talking," Celia said. She respected Andrew's wisdom, his knack of going directly to the nub of any situation.

He continued, "From what you tell me, Peat-Smith is a straightforward person."

"Very much so."

"In that case, I suggest you deal with him the same way. By being complicated, trying to outguess him, you could defeat your own purpose. Besides, deviousness isn't your style, Celia. Be yourself. That way, if it seems natural to talk money—or anything else—just do it."

"Andrew darling," she responded, "what would I do without you?"

"Nothing important, I hope." Then he added, "Now that you've told me about tomorrow, I'll admit to feeling a mite jealous about you and Peat-Smith."

Celia laughed. "It's strictly business. It will stay that way."

Now it was Sunday.

Alone, in a first class no-smoking compartment aboard an early morning London-to-Cambridge train, Celia allowed her head to fall back against the cushion behind her. Relaxing, she began using the hour-and-a-quarter journey to order her thoughts.

Earlier, she had taken a taxi from her hotel to Liverpool Street Station—a grim, cast-iron-and-brick Victorian legacy, frenetically busy from Mondays through Fridays but quieter at weekends. The quietness meant that few people were aboard the diesel-electric train as it rumbled from the station, and Celia was glad of her solitude.

Mentally she reconstructed the past two weeks' events and conversations, wondering once more whose advice she should take today—Andrew's or Sam's. The meeting with Martin, while outwardly social, could be important for Felding-Roth as well as for herself. Sam's warning came back to her: *"Let's not blow it by being crass!"*

The rhythmic sound of wheels over rails lulled her, and the journey passed swiftly. As the train slowed and pulled into Cambridge, Martin Peat-Smith—his welcome expressed in that broad, cheerful smile —was waiting on the station platform.

At age forty-one, Celia knew she looked good. She also felt it. Her soft brown hair was trimmed short, her figure slim and firm, her high-cheekboned face tanned and healthy from recent weeks out of doors and the unusually benevolent British summer, which was continuing today.

Nowadays her hair held beginning strands of gray. This reminder of time passing rarely bothered her, though occasionally she camouflaged the gray with a color rinse. She had used the rinse the night before.

She was dressed for a summer's day in a cotton voile dress of green and white, with a lacy petticoat beneath. She had on white, high-heeled sandals and a broad-brimmed white straw hat. The entire outfit had been bought in London's West End the preceding week because, when packing in New Jersey, it had not occurred to her she would need such warm-weather clothes in Britain.

As she stepped down from the train she was aware of Martin's admiring gaze. For a moment he seemed lost for words, then, taking her extended hand, he said, "Hello! You look wonderful, and I'm glad you came."

"You look pretty good yourself."

Martin laughed and flashed a boyish smile. He was wearing a navy-blue blazer, white flannels and an open-necked shirt. "I promised you I'd wear my suit," he said. "But I found this old outfit which I haven't had on for years. It seemed less formal."

As they walked from the station, Celia linked her arm in his. "Where are we going?"

"My car's outside. I thought we'd drive around a bit, then walk through some colleges, and later we'll have a picnic."

"It all sounds great."

"While you're here, is there anything else you'd like to do or see?"

She hesitated, then said, "Yes, there is one other thing."

"What's that?"

"I'd like to meet your mother."

Martin, surprised, turned his head to look at her. "I can take you to my parents' home right after we've done our tour. If you're sure that's what you want."

"Yes," she said, "it's what I want."

Martin's car was a Morris Mini Minor of indeterminate age. After they squeezed themselves in, he drove circuitously through old Cambridge streets and parked on Queen's Road by the "Backs." He told Celia, "We walk from here." Leaving the car, they followed a footpath to King's Bridge over the River Cam.

At the bridge, Celia stopped. Shading her eyes from the bright morning sun, she said with awe, "I've seldom seen anything more lovely."

Beside her, Martin announced quietly, "King's College Chapel—the noblest view of all."

Immediately ahead were serene lawns and shady trees. Beyond was the great chapel—a vision of turrets, sturdy buttresses and lofty spires rising over a glorious vaulted roof and stained-glass windows. The pale stone buildings of colleges on either side conveyed a complementary sense of history and nobility.

"Let me do my tour guide act," Martin said. "It goes like this: We're an old foundation. In 1441, King Henry VI began what you see here, and Peterhouse, over to the south, is even older. It started 'the Cambridge quest for knowledge' in 1284."

Without thinking, Celia said impulsively, "How could anyone who truly belongs here ever leave this place?"

Martin answered, "Many never have. There were great scholars who lived and worked at Cambridge until they died. And some of us —younger and living—have a similar idea."

For two more hours they alternately walked and rode, and in the process Celia imbibed the lore and love of Cambridge. Place names stayed with her: Jesus Green, Midsummer Common, Parker's Piece, Coe Fen, Lammas Land, Trinity, Queens', Newnham. The list seemed endless, as did Martin's knowledge. "As well as scholars who stayed, others have taken this place elsewhere," he told her. "One was an M.A. from Emmanuel College, John Harvard. There's another place of learning named after him." He gave his familiar, twisted grin. "I forget just where."

At length, as they eased back into the Mini, Martin asserted, "I think that will do. We'll save anything else for another time." Abruptly, his face became serious. "Do you still want to see my parents? I have to warn you—my mother won't know either of us, or why we're there. The effect can be depressing."

"Yes," Celia said, "I still want to."

The terraced house, small and undistinguished, was in a district called the Kite. Martin parked on the street outside and used a key to go in. From a small, dimly lighted hallway he called out, "Dad! It's me, and I have a guest."

There was a sound of shuffling footsteps, a door opened, and an elderly man, wearing a faded sweater and baggy corduroy trousers, appeared. As he came closer, Celia was startled by the physical resemblance between father and son. The older Peat-Smith had the same stocky solidity as Martin, a similar rugged, square-jawed face—though more seamed with age—and even a quick, shy smile as they were introduced seemed a duplicate of Martin's.

When the older man spoke, the similarity ceased. His voice revealed a discordant, coarse, provincial twang; his sentences, roughly framed, suggested little education.

"Pleased to meet yer," he told Celia. And to Martin—"Din't know as you was comin', son. Only just got yer ma dressed. She ain't bin none too good today."

"We won't stay long, Dad," Martin said, and told Celia, "The Alzheimer's has been a big strain on my father. That's often the way it is—it's harder on the families than the patient."

As they moved into a modest, nondescript living room, Peat-Smith, Senior, asked Celia, "Yer wan' a cuppa?"

"That's tea," Martin translated.

"Thank you, I'd love some tea," Celia said. "I'm thirsty after our tour."

While Martin's father walked into a tiny kitchen, Martin went to kneel beside a gray-haired woman who was seated in a baggy armchair with a flowered cover. She had not moved since they came in. Putting his arms around her, he kissed her tenderly.

Once, Celia thought, the older woman had been beautiful and even now was handsome in a faded way. Her hair was neatly combed. She was wearing a simple beige dress with a row of beads. At her son's kiss she appeared to respond a little, and gave the slightest smile, but not, it seemed, of recognition.

"Mother, I'm your son, Martin," Martin said; his voice was gentle. "And this lady is Celia Jordan. She's from America. I've been showing her around Cambridge. She likes our little town."

"Hello, Mrs. Peat-Smith," Celia said. "Thank you for letting me visit your home."

The gray-haired woman's eyes moved, again with that tantalizing hint of understanding. But Martin told Celia, "There's nothing there, I'm afraid. No memory left at all. But where my mother's concerned I allow myself to be non-scientific and keep trying to get through."

"I understand." Celia hesitated, then asked, "Do you think that if

183

your research progresses, if you discover something important soon, there might be a chance . . ."

"Of helping her?" Martin answered decisively, "Absolutely none. No matter what's discovered, nothing will revive a dead brain cell. I've no illusions about that." Standing, he looked down at his mother sadly. "No, it's others who'll be helped someday soon. Others who haven't advanced this far."

"You're sure of that, aren't you?"

"I'm sure some answers will be found—by me or someone else."

"But you'd like to be the one who finds them."

Martin shrugged. "Every scientist would like to be first in making a discovery. That's human. But,"—he glanced toward his mother— "it's more important that *someone* discover the cause of Alzheimer's."

"So it's possible," Celia persisted, "that someone other than you could get there first."

"Yes," Martin said. "In science that can always happen."

Peat-Smith, Senior, came in from the kitchen with a tray containing a teapot, cups and saucers, and a milk jug.

When the tray was set down, Martin put his arm around his father. "Dad does everything for mother—dresses her, combs her hair, feeds her, and some other things less pleasant. There was a time, Celia, when my father and I weren't the closest of friends. But we are now."

"Tha's right. Used ter have a lot of hot arguments," Martin's father said. He addressed Celia. "You want milk in the tea?"

"Yes, please."

"Was a time," the older man said, "when I din't think much of all them scholarships Martin an' his ma was set on. I wanted 'im to go to work wi' me. But 'is ma got the best of it an', the way it worked out, 'e's been a good lad to us. Pays for this place, an' most else we need." He glanced at Martin, then added, "An' over at that college, I hear he ain't done bad."

"No," Celia said, "he hasn't done badly at all."

It was almost two hours later.

"Is it okay to talk while you're doing that?" Celia inquired from the comfortably cushioned seat where she was reclining.

"Sure. Why not?" As he spoke, Martin, who was standing, thrust a long punt pole away from him; it found purchase on the river's

184

shallow bottom, and the awkward flat-bottomed craft they were sharing glided easily upstream. Martin seemed to do everything well, Celia thought, including handling a punt—something at which few people were skilled, judging by others they had passed on the river and who, by comparison, were bumbling their way along.

Martin had rented the punt at a Cambridge boatyard and they were now on their way to Grantchester, three miles southward, for what would be a late picnic lunch.

"This is personal," Celia said, "and maybe I shouldn't ask. But I was wondering about the difference between you and your father. For example, the way you each speak—and I don't just mean being grammatical . . ."

"I know what you mean," Martin said. "When my mother was talking, before she forgot how to, she spoke much the same way. In *Pygmalion,* Bernard Shaw called it an 'incarnate insult to the English language.' "

"I remember that from *My Fair Lady,* " Celia reminisced. "But you managed to avoid it. How?"

"It's one more thing I owe my mother. Before I explain, though, there's something you have to understand about this country. In Britain, the way people speak has always been a class barrier, a social distinction. And despite some who'll tell you otherwise, it still is."

"In the academic world too? Among scientists."

"Even there. Perhaps especially there."

Martin busied himself with the punt pole while considering his next words.

"My mother understood that barrier. Which was why, when I was very small, she bought a radio and made me sit for hours in front of it, listening to the BBC announcers. She told me, 'That's the way you'll speak, so start copying those people. It's too late for your Dad and me, but not for you.' "

Listening to Martin's pleasant and cultured, though unaffected, voice, Celia said, "It worked."

"I suppose so. But it was one of many other things she did, including finding out what interested me at school, then discovering what scholarships there were, and making sure I went after them. That was when we had those fights at home my father talked about."

"He believed your mother was overreaching?"

"He thought I should be a stonemason, like him. My father be-

185

lieved in that English rhyme that Dickens wrote." Martin smiled as he quoted:

> *"O let us love our occupations,*
> *Bless the squire and his relations,*
> *Live upon our daily rations,*
> *And always know our proper stations."*

"But you don't hold a grudge against your father for that?"

Martin shook his head. "He simply didn't understand. For that matter, nor did I. Only my mother understood what could be accomplished through ambition—and through me. Perhaps you realize now why I care so much about her."

"Of course," Celia said. "And now that I know, I feel the same way."

They lapsed into a contented silence as the punt progressed upriver between green banks and leafy trees on either side.

After a while, Celia said, "Your father said you pay for most of what both your parents need."

"I do what I can," Martin acknowledged. "One thing I do is send in an agency nurse two mornings a week. It gives my father a break. I'd like to use the nurse more often, but . . ." He shrugged, left the sentence unfinished, and expertly brought the punt alongside a grassy bank under the shade of a willow tree. "How's this for a picnic site?"

"Idyllic," Celia said. "Straight from Camelot."

Martin had packed a hamper with some prawns, a Melton Mowbray pork pie, a fresh green salad, strawberries and thick, yellow Devonshire cream. There was wine—a respectable Chablis—and a thermos of coffee.

They ate and drank with gusto.

At the end of the meal, over coffee, Celia said, "This is my last weekend before going home. It couldn't have been nicer."

"Was your trip here a success?"

About to reply with a platitude, she remembered Andrew's advice on the telephone and answered, "No."

"Why not?" Martin sounded surprised.

"Sam Hawthorne and I found the ideal director for the Felding-Roth research institute, but he didn't want the job. Now, everyone else seems second-rate."

After a silence, Martin said, "I presume you're talking about me."

186

"You know I am."

He sighed. "I hope you're going to forgive me for that delinquency, Celia."

"There's nothing to forgive. It's your life, your decision," she assured him. "It's simply that, thinking about it just now, there were two things . . ." She stopped.

"Go on. What two things?"

"Well, a little while ago you admitted you'd like to be first in finding answers about Alzheimer's and mental aging, but others might get there ahead of you."

Martin leaned back in the punt, facing Celia; he had folded his blazer behind him and was using it as a pillow. "Others are doing similar research to mine. I know of someone in Germany, another in France, a third in New Zealand. They're all good people and we're pursuing the same objectives, exploring the same trail. It's impossible to know who, if anyone, is ahead."

"So it's a race that you're in," Celia said. "A race against time." Unconsciously, her voice had sharpened.

"Yes. But that's the way science is."

"Do any of those others you mentioned have better facilities or more staff than you?"

He considered. "Probably 'yes' to both in Germany. I don't know about the other two."

"How much laboratory space do *you* have now?"

"Altogether"—Martin calculated mentally—"about a thousand square feet."

"Then wouldn't it help you get closer, faster, to what you're searching for if you had *five times that space*, plus equipment to go into it— everything you needed, and all for your project—plus a staff of maybe twenty people working for you, instead of two or three? Wouldn't *that* move things along, and not only find the answers, but get you to them first?"

Suddenly Celia was aware that the mood between them had changed. This was no longer a social occasion; whatever innocence there had been had fled. Subtly, it was now a challenge of intellect and wills. Well, she thought, this was why she had come to Britain, and to Cambridge today.

Martin was staring at her in amazement. "Are you serious about all that? Five thousand square feet and *twenty* people!"

"Dammit! Of course I'm serious." She added impatiently, "Do you think, in the pharmaceutical business, we play games?"

"No," he said, still staring, "I didn't think that. You said there were two things. What's the other?"

Celia hesitated. Should she go on? She sensed that what she had just said had made a deep impression on Martin. Would she now destroy that, wiping out any advantage gained? Then, once more, she remembered Andrew.

"I'll put this crudely and bluntly, in the usual crass American way," Celia said, "and I'm saying that because I know dedicated researchers like you aren't motivated by money and can't be bought. But if you worked for Felding-Roth, became director of our institute and brought your project with you, you'd most likely be paid twelve thousand pounds a year, plus bonuses, which can be substantial. I've reason to believe that's about five times what you're earning now. Furthermore, having met your parents and knowing what you do for them, and having an idea that there's more you'd like to do, I think you could use that extra cash. You could certainly send a nurse in more than twice a week, move your mother to better surroundings . . ."

"That's enough!" Martin had sat up and was glaring at her; he had become intensely emotional. "Damn you, Celia! I know what money can do. What's more, don't hand me that bilge about people like me not caring for it. I care like hell, and what you've just told me is mind-boggling. You're trying to undermine me, tempt me, take advantage . . ."

She snapped, "That's ridiculous! Take what advantage?"

"Of meeting my parents, for one thing. Seeing how they live and how much I care. So, using that, you're offering me a golden apple, playing Eve to my Adam." He glanced around them. "In Paradise, too."

"It isn't a poisoned apple," Celia said quietly, "and there's no serpent in this boat. Look, I'm sorry if—"

Martin cut her off savagely. "You're not sorry at all! You're a businesswoman who's good at her job—bloody good; I can testify to that! But a businesswoman going all out, no holds barred, to get what she wants. You're quite ruthless, aren't you?"

Now Celia was surprised. "Am I?"

He answered emphatically, "Yes."

"All right," Celia said; she would give back as good as she got, she decided. "Supposing I am. And supposing all of what you said is true. Isn't it what *you* want too? The answers to Alzheimer's! That brain peptide you're searching for! Scientific glory! Is any of that *cheating* you?"

"No," Martin said, "whatever else it is, it isn't cheating." He gave his twisted smile, though this time with a touch of sourness. "I hope they pay *you* well, Celia. As a crass American, which is what you called yourself, you do one helluva job." He stood up and reached for the punt pole. "It's time to go."

They returned downstream in silence, Martin thrusting the punt forward with a fierceness he had not shown on the outward journey. Celia, busy with her thoughts, wondered if she had gone too far. Near the town and the boatyard, Martin stopped his poling and let the craft drift. From his perch on the stern above her, he regarded Celia solemnly.

"I don't know the answer. I only know you've unsettled me," he told her. "But I still don't know."

It was early evening when Martin dropped Celia at the Cambridge railway station and they said a formal, somewhat strained, goodbye. Celia's return train was a painfully slow local which stopped at almost every station, and it was past 11:30 P.M. by the time she arrived at the London terminus, this time King's Cross. She took a taxi to the Berkeley, reaching the hotel shortly before midnight.

During most of the journey Celia reconstructed the day's events, especially her own part in them. What had jolted her, as much as anything, was Martin's cutting accusation: *You're quite ruthless, aren't you?* Was she ruthless? Looking in a mental mirror, Celia admitted that perhaps she was. Then she corrected herself: *Not "perhaps." Make that "certainly."*

But, she reasoned, wasn't *some* ruthlessness necessary? Necessary —especially for a woman—to have carved a career, as Celia had, and to have made it to where she was? *Yes. Of course!*

Furthermore, she reminded herself, ruthlessness was not—or, rather, need not be—equated with dishonesty. In essence it was a commitment to be tough in business, to make unpleasant hard decisions, fight through to the essentials, and dispense with an excess of worry concerning other individuals. Equally to the point: If her own

189

responsibilities increased in future, she would need to be even tougher, even more ruthless, than before.

Why, then, if being ruthless was a fact of business life, had Martin's remark so bothered her? Probably because she liked and respected him, and therefore wished him to feel the same way about her. Well, did he? Celia wondered about that briefly, then decided obviously not, after their showdown of this afternoon.

However, did Martin's opinion of her really matter? The answer: *no!* One reason: there was still something of the child in Martin, even at thirty-two. Celia had once heard someone say of research scientists, "They spend so much of their lives becoming more and more educated that they have time for little else and, in some ways, stay children forever." For sure, some of that seemed true of Martin. Celia knew that she was much more a person of the world than he.

What *was* important, then? Not Martin's personal feelings, nor Celia's either, but the *outcome* of today.

True? *Yes*, again.

As to that outcome—Celia sighed within her—she wasn't optimistic. In fact, she almost certainly did, to use Sam's phrase, "blow it by being crass." The more she thought about that, the less she liked what she had done, the more the memories of the day depressed her. The downbeat mood persisted as far as the hotel.

In the lobby of the Berkeley she was greeted by a uniformed concierge. "Good evening, Mrs. Jordan. Did you have a pleasant day?"

"Yes, thank you." In her mind she added: *Just some parts of it.*

In turning to reach for her key, the concierge gathered up several message forms which Celia accepted. She would read them later in her room.

Then, about to turn away, she heard, "And, oh yes, Mrs. Jordan. This one came in a few minutes ago. A gentleman phoned. I took it down myself. It doesn't seem to make much sense, but he said you'd understand."

Tired, and without interest, Celia glanced at the slip of paper. Then her eyes were riveted.

The message read:

TO EVERY THING THERE IS A SEASON INCLUDING CRASS AMERICANS BEARING GIFTS. THANK YOU.
I ACCEPT.   —MARTIN.

190

Unusually, and to the frowning disapproval of the concierge, the staid lobby of the Berkeley echoed to a loud and piercing cry from Celia.

"Yippee!"

11

A few days before Celia's Sunday tour of Cambridge, Sam and Lilian Hawthorne had left Britain for a brief visit to Paris and from there had flown directly to New York on Saturday. Therefore it was not until Monday, at 3:30 P.M. London time, that Celia reached Sam by telephone in his office at Felding-Roth, New Jersey.

When she informed him of the news about Martin Peat-Smith, he reacted enthusiastically, telling her, "I'm delighted, though astounded. Celia, you're incredible! How the devil did you do it?"

She had been expecting the question and said cautiously, "I'm not sure you'll like this." Then she reported her conversation with Martin about money, and how that, as much as anything else, had influenced his change of mind.

At the other end of the line, Sam moaned audibly. "Oh, shit!—if you'll pardon me." Then he said, "I was the one who warned you not to mention money, and how could I have been so wrong?"

"You couldn't have known," she assured him. "I just probed, and uncovered some of Martin's problems. By the way, he called me ruthless for doing that."

"Never mind! What you did produced the result we wanted. I should have done the same, but didn't have your insight and persistence."

Celia thought, *You also didn't have Andrew to advise you.* Aloud, she said, "Sam, for goodness' sake stop blaming yourself! It isn't necessary."

"All right, I will. But I'll make you a little pledge."

She asked, "What's that?"

"If ever, someplace down the road, you and I differ on a matter of judgment that's important, you have my permission to remind me of this incident, and that your judgment was right and mine wrong."

"I hope it never happens," Celia said.

Sam changed the subject. "You're coming home this week, aren't you?"

"The day after tomorrow. I love London, but I love Andrew and the children more."

"Good! As soon as you're home, you'd better take some days off to be with them. But then, in a few weeks, I'll want you back in Britain again. There'll be more things to do in setting up the institute; also we'll need to hire an administrator. Martin's research skills are too important to waste on organization and office work."

"I agree," Celia said, "and all of that sounds fine."

"Something else that's fine," Sam said, "is that during the few days I had in Paris last week I acquired the American rights to a new French drug for Felding-Roth. It's still experimental and won't be ready for at least two years. But it looks extremely promising."

"Congratulations! Does it have a name?"

"Yes," Sam said. "It's called Montayne. You'll hear much more about it later."

The remainder of 1972 and into '73 was, for Celia, an exciting, stimulating time. She made five more trips to Britain, each of several weeks' duration. On two of them, Andrew joined her for part of the time; on another, Lisa and Bruce flew over. While Andrew was in Britain he and Martin met; the two men liked each other and later Andrew told Celia, "The only thing Martin needs is a woman like you to share his life. I hope he finds one."

While the children were visiting her, and during times when she was not working, Celia, Lisa and Bruce inspected the sights of London to—in Celia's words—"exhaustion point."

Bruce, now twelve, revealed himself as a history addict. As he explained it one Sunday morning while the three of them walked around the Tower of London, "It's all *there*, Mom, for anybody to find out—what went right, and all the mistakes. You can *learn* so much from what's already happened."

"Yes, you can," Celia said. "Unfortunately, most of us don't."

192

Bruce's fascination with history continued during a second tour of Cambridge, conducted, this time for the children, by Martin Peat-Smith. Celia met regularly with Martin during her working trips to Britain, though their total time together was not great because each was busy in differing ways.

Martin, now that his decision to join Felding-Roth was made, showed himself very much in charge, and aware of his requirements of equipment and staff. He recruited another nucleic acid chemist, a young Pakistani, Dr. Rao Sastri, who would be second-in-command on the scientific side. There were specialist technicians, including a cell culture expert and another skilled in electrophoretic separation of proteins and nucleic acids. A woman animal care supervisor would safeguard the hundreds of rats and rabbits to be used in experiments.

During visits to Harlow, Martin discussed the location of laboratories, staff, and equipment in the building where conversion work was already under way. However, such visits were brief, and until the institute was ready Martin would continue research in his Cambridge lab. Apart from the necessary excursions to Harlow, Martin insisted that his time not be taken up by administrative matters which others could handle—a strategy already endorsed by Sam Hawthorne and implemented by Celia.

Celia hired an administrator whose name was Nigel Bentley. A smallish, confident, sparrowlike man in his mid-fifties, Bentley had recently retired from the Royal Air Force where, with the rank of squadron leader, he was in charge of the administrative side of a large RAF hospital. The ex-officer's qualifications for the new post were excellent; he also understood what was expected of him.

In Celia's presence, Bentley told Martin, "The less I bother you, sir —in fact, the less you see of me—the better I'll be doing my job." Celia liked the statement, also the "sir," which was a gracious way of making clear that Bentley understood what the relationship between himself and the much younger scientist was expected to be.

In between trips to Britain, and while Celia was back in the United States, a personal milestone—at least, as she saw it—occurred in her life. That was in September 1972 when Lisa, at age fourteen, excitedly left home to enter boarding school. The school was Emma Willard in upstate New York, and the whole family accompanied Lisa on her odyssey. At home during dinner the night before, Celia asked Andrew nostalgically, "Where did all those years go?"

But it was Lisa—ever practical—who answered. "They happened

while you were getting all those promotions at work, Mommy. And I've figured out that I'll just be graduating from college when you get to sit in Mr. Hawthorne's chair."

They all laughed at that, and the good time extended through the next day when they, with other parents, families and new girls, were initiated into the beauty, enlivening spirit, and traditions of Emma Willard School.

Two weeks later Celia returned once more to Britain. Sam Hawthorne, deeply involved with other requirements of the company presidency, was now leaving almost all details of the British scene to her.

Eventually, in February 1973, the Felding-Roth Research Institute (U.K.) Limited was officially opened. At the same time, Dr. Martin Peat-Smith's research project into Alzheimer's disease and the mental aging process was transferred from Cambridge to Harlow.

It had been decided, as a matter of company policy, that no other research would be embarked on in Britain for the time being. The reasoning, as Sam confided it to the board of directors at a meeting in New Jersey, was that "the project we now have is timely, damned exciting, and with big commercial possibilities; therefore we should concentrate on it."

No public fanfare was made about the Harlow opening. "The time for fanfare," declared Sam, who had flown over for the occasion, "is when we have something positive to show, and that isn't yet."

When *would* there be something positive?

"Allow me two years," Martin told Sam and Celia during a relaxed private moment. "There ought to be some progress to report by then."

After the institute's opening, Celia's visits to Britain became fewer and shorter. For a while she went, as Sam's representative, to help smooth out initial working problems. But, mostly, Nigel Bentley seemed to be justifying the confidence placed in him by his appointment as administrator. From Martin, as months went by, there was no specific news except, via Bentley, that research was continuing.

At Felding-Roth's New Jersey headquarters, Celia continued as special assistant to the president, working on other projects Sam gave her.

It was during this period that, on the national scene, the putrescent boil of Watergate burst. Celia and Andrew, like millions of others worldwide, watched the parade of events nightly on television and were caught up in the unfolding drama's fascination. Celia reminisced about how, a year earlier when driving to Harlow with Sam, she had dismissed the first published report of a Watergate burglary as insignificant.

Near the end of April, while tension mounted, two haughty presidential aides—Haldeman and Ehrlichman—were thrown to the wolves by President Nixon in an attempt to save himself. Then, in October, adding to Nixon's and the nation's misery, Vice President Agnew was ejected from office for other corruption, unconnected with Watergate. Finally, ten months later, Nixon himself reluctantly became the first American President to resign. As Andrew remarked, "Whatever else history may say, at least he'll be in *The Guinness Book of Records.*"

Nixon's successor promptly granted his predecessor a pardon-in-advance against criminal prosecution and, when asked if it was all tit-for-tat politics, proclaimed, "There was no deal."

Watching and hearing the statement on TV, Celia asked Andrew, "Do you believe that?"

"No."

She said emphatically, "Nor do I."

Around the same time—less significant on the larger scene, but important to the Jordan family—Bruce, too, left home to enter prep school—the Hill School, at Pottstown, Pennsylvania.

Through the entire period and into 1975 the fortunes of Felding-Roth, while not spectacular, maintained an even keel. They were helped by two products developed in the company's own laboratories—an anti-inflammatory for rheumatoid arthritis and a beta-blocker called Staidpace, a medicine to slow heartbeat and reduce blood pressure. The arthritis drug was only moderately successful but Staidpace proved an excellent, lifesaving product which became widely used.

Staidpace would have contributed even more to Felding-Roth revenues had its United States approval not been delayed by the Food and Drug Administration for what seemed an unconscionable time—in the company's view, two years longer than necessary.

At FDA's Washington headquarters there seemed, in the frustrated words of Felding-Roth's research director, Vincent Lord, "an infectious unwillingness to make a decision about anything." The opinion was echoed by other drug firms. Reportedly, one senior FDA official exhibited proudly on his desk a plaque with the famed promise of

France's Marshal Pétain in World War I, *"They shall not pass."* It appeared to sum up neatly the attitude of FDA's staff to any new drug application.

It was about this time that the phrase "drug lag"—describing the non-availability in the United States of beneficial drugs in use elsewhere—began to be used and gain attention.

Yet, always, a routine reply to any plea for faster action on new drug approvals was: "Remember Thalidomide!"

Sam Hawthorne tackled this attitude head-on in a speech to an industry convention. "Strong safety standards," he declared, "are necessary in the public interest, and not long ago, too few of them existed. But pendulums swing too far, and bureaucratic indecision has now become a national disservice. As to critics of our industry who point back to Thalidomide, I point forward to this: The number of Thalidomide-deformed babies is now exceeded by the number of those who have suffered or died because effective drugs, held back by American regulatory delays, are failing to reach them in their time of need."

It was tough talk and the beginning of what would be a fiercely argued, pro-and-con debate extending over many years.

At Felding-Roth, one keenly anticipated project was now on "hold."

The deal made by Sam for the American rights to a new French drug, Montayne, still had not reached a point where tests for safety and efficacy, as required by law, could begin in the United States. Thus there was a long way to go even before a new drug application could be made to FDA.

Montayne was a drug to combat morning sickness in pregnant women; it held great promise, especially for working women whom it would free from a burden that made life difficult and sometimes threatened their employment. The drug's discoverers—Laboratoires Gironde-Chimie, a reputable house—were convinced they had something of highest quality and safety, as shown by unusually extensive tests on animals and volunteer humans. The tests, the Paris-based firm informed Felding-Roth, had so far produced excellent results and no adverse side effects. Still, as the head of Gironde-Chimie explained in a personal letter to Sam:

196

Because of past occurrences, and the nature fragile of this drug, we have need of being extremely prudent. Therefore we have decided to make a few more series of tests on different types of animals, and also more humans. This will take a little more of time.

In the climate of the times, Sam agreed, the additional precautions seemed wise. Meanwhile, Felding-Roth continued to wait for a green light from the French before beginning their own work on Montayne.

THREE

1975–1977

1

While Dr. Vincent Lord had some problems which were imaginary, he also had others that were real.

One was the FDA.

The Food and Drug Administration, with headquarters just outside Washington, D.C., represented a labyrinthine obstacle course which any new pharmaceutical drug and its sponsors had to run before the drug was approved for general use. Some drugs were never approved; they failed to complete the course. And since sponsors of drugs were almost always the companies which discovered, manufactured, and eventually sold them to the public, the big drug firms and FDA were, more often than not, locked in a combative state. That state ranged, according to the issue of the moment, from intellectual-scientific skirmishing to all-out war.

As far as Vince Lord was concerned, it was war.

Part of his job at Felding-Roth was to deal, or supervise dealings, with the FDA. He loathed it. He also disliked, and in some cases despised, the people who worked there. Adding to his problem was that, to achieve anything at all at FDA, he had either to subdue those feelings or keep them to himself. He found both things difficult, at times impossible.

Of course, Dr. Lord was prejudiced. So were others, from other drug firms, who dealt with FDA.

Sometimes that prejudice was justified. Sometimes not.

This was because laws and custom required the FDA to be several things at once.

It was a guardian of the public's health, its duty to protect the innocent from excessive avarice, incompetence, indifference, or carelessness, all of which sins were at times committed by pharmaceutical companies whose bottom line was profit. The reverse of that was FDA's function as a ministering angel: the covenant to make available, with utmost speed, those new and splendid drugs—from

201

the same pharmaceutical companies—which lengthened life or shortened pain.

Another agency role was to be a whipping boy for critics—drug firms, consumer groups, journalists, authors, lawyers, lobbyists, other special interests—who accused FDA of being either too rigid or too lenient, depending on what camp the critics lived in. As well, the FDA was used regularly as a political platform by self-serving and self-righteous congressmen and senators who sought an easy way to get their names in print and on TV.

Coupled with all this, the FDA was a bureaucratic mess—overcrowded, in critical areas understaffed, its medical and scientific experts overworked and underpaid.

Yet the amazing thing was, amid all these roles, hindrances, and critics, the FDA did its job—on the whole—remarkably well.

But without question there were glitches, and the so-called drug lag was one of them.

Just how bad the drug lag was depended, like so much else surrounding the FDA, on your point of view. But that it existed, even the FDA itself conceded.

Vincent Lord suffered through an example of the drug lag during the attempt by Felding-Roth to gain approval for United States marketing of Staidpace, a heart and blood-pressure medicine already in use in Britain, France, West Germany and several other countries.

The FDA required that before Staidpace could go on American drugstore shelves and be prescribed by doctors, there must be additional, thorough, American testing of the product's safety and efficacy. And it was a good requirement. Nobody argued against it, including Vincent Lord and others at Felding-Roth.

What they did protest—after all the required testing had been done successfully, and results submitted to the FDA—was two extra years of petty, indecisive quibbling by the government agency.

In 1972 Felding-Roth delivered its Staidpace NDA—new drug application—to FDA headquarters in a truck. The NDA consisted of 125,000 printed pages, contained in 307 volumes, enough to fill a small room. All this material was required by law and included information covering two years of U.S. testing on animals and humans.

Although the information supplied was as complete as anyone could make it, there was an unspoken awareness on both sides that no one at FDA could possibly read it all. Similar amounts of material were received, with great frequency, from other manufacturers seeking approval of other drugs.

From the FDA's medical-scientific staff, a reviewer was selected to oversee and adjudicate the Staidpace submission. He was Gideon R. Mace, M.D., who had been with FDA a year.

Dr. Mace would be assisted by scientific specialists in the agency— that is, whenever they could spare time from work on other drugs.

Another part of the procedure was that, as FDA's examination proceeded, scientists from Felding-Roth would be called in, perhaps to explain some of the submitted material or to add even more. This was normal.

What proved to be less normal were the work habits and attitude of Dr. Mace. His pace was snail-like—slow even for the FDA. He was also petty, unreasonably querulous, and mean.

This was how the name of Gideon Mace came to be added to the list of people at FDA whom Vincent Lord despised.

Lord had personally overseen the Staidpace application and believed it to be as complete and thorough as any ever submitted by the company. Therefore, as months went by with no decision made, Lord's frustration grew. Then when Mace was finally heard from it was about trifling points, and later—as one of Lord's assistants put it —"he seemed to query every damn comma, sometimes having nothing to do with science." Equally maddening was that several times when Mace imperiously demanded extra data, it developed that what was being sought was already in the original submission. Mace simply hadn't looked for it or even asked whether it was there. When the facts were pointed out, he took still more weeks to acknowledge them—and then did so ungraciously.

After a good deal of this, Vincent Lord took over from his staff and began doing what he disliked most—going to the FDA himself.

The agency headquarters was in an inconvenient location—on Fishers Lane in Maryland, some fifteen miles north of Washington, an hour's tedious drive from the White House or Capitol Hill. It was housed in a plain brick building, shaped like an "E" and built cheaply in the 1960s without benefit of architectural imagination.

The offices, where seven thousand people worked, were mostly tiny and crowded. Many were windowless. Others had so many occupants and were filled with so much furniture, it was hard to move around. What little space remained was filled with paper. Paper was everywhere. Piles of it, reams of it, stacks of it, tons of it. Paper beyond imagination. The mailroom was a paper nightmare, each day subjected to an avalanche of more, moving two ways, though outgoing paper seldom equaled the inward flow. In corridors, messengers pushed delivery trolleys loaded down with still more paper.

Dr. Gideon Mace worked in a room, not much better than a cupboard, on the tenth floor. In his late fifties, Mace was lanky and long-necked; people made unkind remarks about giraffes. He was red-faced, with a heavily veined nose. He wore rimless glasses and squinted through them, suggesting that his prescription needed changing. His manner was brusque. In conversation he could be sarcastic, and acidity came to him easily. Dr. Mace usually wore an ancient gray suit which needed pressing, and a faded tie.

When Vincent Lord went to see him, Mace had to clear papers from a chair before the Felding-Roth research director could sit down.

"We seem to be having trouble over Staidpace," Lord said, making an effort to be friendly. "I've come to find out why."

"Your NDA is sloppy and disorganized," Mace said. "Also, it doesn't tell me nearly enough that I need to know."

"In what way is it disorganized?" Lord asked. "And what more do you need to know?"

Mace ignored the first question and answered the second. "I haven't decided yet. But your people will hear."

"When will we hear?"

"When I'm ready to tell you."

"It would be helpful and perhaps save time," Lord said, managing to subdue his anger, but only just, "if you could give me some idea of where we both have problems."

"I don't have problems," Gideon Mace said. "You do. I'm doubtful about the safety of your drug; it could be carcinogenic. As to saving time, I'm unconcerned about that. There's no hurry. We have lots of time."

"You may have," Lord retorted. "But how about people with heart disease who'll be using Staidpace? Many heart patients need that drug now. It's already saving lives in Europe where we gained approval for it long ago. We'd like to have it do the same thing here."

Mace smiled thinly. "And just by coincidence, make Felding-Roth a potful of money."

Lord bridled. "That part never concerns me."

204

"If you say so," Mace said skeptically. "But from where I'm sitting, you sound more like a salesman than a scientist."

Still Vincent Lord contained himself. "You mentioned safety a moment ago. As you must know from our NDA, side effects have been minimal, none dangerous, and there has been no trace of carcinogens. So will you tell me the basis of your doubts?"

"Not now," Mace said. "I'm still thinking about them."

"And meanwhile making no decision."

"That's right."

"Under law," Lord reminded the FDA official, "you have a time limit of six months . . ."

"Don't lecture me on regulations," Mace said testily. "I know them. But if I turn down your NDA temporarily, and insist on more data, the calendar goes back to zero."

And it was true. Such procedural delaying tactics were used at FDA—sometimes with good reason, Vincent Lord conceded mentally, but at other times on an official's whim or merely to postpone decisions.

Having reached the outer limit, Lord said, "Not making decisions is always the *safe* route for a bureaucrat, isn't it?"

Mace smiled but didn't answer.

In the end, the meeting produced nothing but an increase of frustration for Vincent Lord. It did, however, cause him to make a decision: he would find out more—as much as he could—about Dr. Gideon R. Mace. Sometimes that kind of information could be useful.

Over the next few months, Lord had reason to make several other visits to Washington and FDA headquarters. Each time, through casual questions put to Mace's colleagues in the agency and discreet research outside, he managed to learn a surprising amount.

In the meantime, Mace had faulted one of Felding-Roth's studies concerning Staidpace—a series of field tests on patients with heart problems. Plainly relishing his power, Mace ruled that the entire test sequence should be done again. Lord could see no valid reason for repeating the work; it would take a year and be costly, and he could have objected. But he also realized that any such objection might be self-defeating, resulting either in the Staidpace NDA's being stalled indefinitely or in the drug's rejection. Therefore, reluctantly, Vincent Lord gave orders for the testing program to be done again.

Soon afterward he informed Sam Hawthorne of the decision, and reported what he had found out about Gideon Mace. The two were in Sam's office.

"Mace is a failed doctor," the research director said. "He's also an alcoholic, he's in money trouble, partly because he's paying alimony to two wives, and he moonlights by working evenings and weekends, helping in a private medical practice."

Sam weighed what had been said. "What do you mean by 'a failed doctor'?"

The research director consulted notes. "Since getting his medical degree, Mace has worked in five different cities where he was employed by other physicians. After that, he was in practice on his own. As far as I can learn from those who know him, all those arrangements broke down because Mace doesn't get along with people. He didn't like the other doctors and, about quitting private practice, he says frankly he didn't like his patients."

"From the sound of it," Sam said, "they probably didn't love him. Why was he hired at FDA?"

"You know the FDA situation. They have trouble getting *anybody.*"

Sam said, "Yes, I do." Medical-scientific recruiting at FDA was a problem of long standing. Government salaries were notoriously low, and an M.D. employed by FDA received less than half of what he or she could earn in private practice. In the case of scientists, the gap between those employed at FDA and drug company scientists with similar qualifications was even wider.

There were other factors. One was professional prestige.

In medical-scientific circles, working for FDA was not regarded as impressive. An appointment to the government's National Institutes of Health, for example, was much more sought after.

Something else affecting M.D.'s at FDA was the absence of what most working doctors enjoyed—direct, "hands on" contacts with patients. There was only—as Sam once heard it described—"the vicarious practice of medicine through reading other people's case reports."

Again remarkably, and despite those limitations, the agency's ranks contained many highly qualified, dedicated professionals. But inevitably there were others. The unsuccessful. The soured and alienated who preferred comparative solitude to meeting many people. The dedicated self-protectors, avoiding difficult decisions. Alcoholics. The unbalanced.

206

Clearly, as both Sam and Vince Lord saw it, Dr. Gideon Mace was one of these.

Sam asked, "Is there anything I can do? Like going to the commissioner?"

Lord answered, "I don't advise it. FDA commissioners are political; they come and go. But bureaucrats stay, and have long memories."

"What you're saying," Sam said, "is that we might win with Staidpace but lose out badly later on."

"Exactly."

"What about Mace's alcoholism?"

Lord shrugged. "Heavy drinking broke up his marriages, I hear. But he copes. He comes to work. He functions. He may keep a bottle in his desk, but if he does, no one I've talked to has seen him dipping into it."

"Is the moonlighting, working in a private practice, against regulations?"

"Apparently not, if Mace confines it to his free time, even though he may be tired next day when he comes to work. Other doctors at FDA do the same thing."

"Then there's no way we can touch Mace?"

"Not now," Lord said. "But he still has all that alimony to pay, and money troubles make people do strange things. So I'm going to keep watching. Who knows, something may turn up."

Sam regarded the research director thoughtfully. "You've become a good company man, Vince. Handling this, which isn't pleasant. Looking out for all our interests. I'd like you to know that I appreciate it."

"Well . . ." Lord looked surprised, though not displeased. "I hadn't thought of it that way. All I've wanted is to nail that bastard, and have Staidpace approved. But maybe you're right."

Vincent Lord, reflecting later, supposed that what Sam had said about his being a company man was true. Lord was now in his eighteenth year at Felding-Roth and, even if you didn't expect it to happen, in that length of time certain loyalties built up. Also, nowadays, introspective thoughts about whether he had been right or wrong in leaving academia for industry occupied him less than they once had. Much more of his thinking was directed toward his continuing research on the quenching of free radicals—whenever he could

207

free himself from other responsibilities in the department. The answers Lord sought were still elusive. But he knew they were there. He would never, *never* give up.

And there was a new incentive to his research. That was the company's institute in Britain where Peat-Smith, whom Vincent Lord had not yet met, was concentrating on the mental aging process. It was a competition. Who—Lord or Peat-Smith—would achieve a breakthrough first?

It had been a disappointment to Lord when he had not been given authority over Felding-Roth research in Britain as well as in the United States. But Sam Hawthorne had been adamant about that, insisting that "over there" be independent and operate on its own. Well, Lord reasoned, as things had turned out, perhaps that was best after all. From rumors seeping back from Britain, it seemed that Peat-Smith was getting nowhere, had come up against a scientific brick wall. If true, Lord was divorced from any responsibility.

Meanwhile, on the American pharmaceutical scene there was much to do.

As to Dr. Gideon Mace, the opportunity Vincent Lord had hoped for—to "get" Mace—did arrive eventually, though not soon enough to help Staidpace which, after more delays and quibbling, was at last approved and went on sale in 1974.

It was in January 1975, a day after he had returned from Washington, having been there to visit FDA about another matter, that Lord received an unusual telephone call. "There's a man on the phone," his secretary announced, "who won't give his name. But he's persistent and says you'll be glad if you speak to him."

"Tell him to go to—no, wait!" Curiosity was inbred in Lord. "Put him on."

Into the phone he said curtly, "Whoever you are, say what you want quickly, or I'll hang up."

"You've been collecting information about Dr. Mace. I have some." The male voice sounded young, also educated.

Lord was instantly curious. "What kind of information?"

"Mace has broken the law. With what I have, you could send him to jail."

"What makes you think I'd want to?"

"Look," the voice said; "you wanted me to be quick, but you're the one who's futzing around. Are you interested or not?"

Lord was cautious, remembering that telephone conversations could be taped. "How has Dr. Mace broken the law?"

"He used confidential FDA information to make a profit for himself on the stock market. Twice."

"How can you prove that?"

"I have papers. But if you want them, Dr. Lord, I'll expect to be paid. Two thousand dollars."

"Doesn't peddling that kind of information make you as bad as Mace?"

The voice said calmly, "Perhaps. But that isn't the issue."

Lord asked, "What's your name?"

"I'll tell you when we meet in Washington."

2

The bar was in Georgetown. It was elegantly decorated in subtle shades of red, beige and brown, with handsome bronze accoutrements. It was also, plainly, a rendezvous for homosexuals. Several faces looked up interestedly as Vincent Lord came in; he sensed himself being appraised and it made him uncomfortable. But before the feeling could persist, a young man who had been seated alone in a booth got up and came toward him.

"Good evening, Dr. Lord. I'm Tony Redmond." He smiled knowingly. "The voice on the telephone."

Lord muttered an acknowledgment and allowed his hand to be shaken. He had instantly recognized Redmond as an FDA employee; Lord recalled having seen him several times during other trips to Washington, though could not remember precisely where. Redmond, in his mid-twenties, had short, curly brown hair, baby-blue eyes with prominent lashes, and was in other ways good-looking.

He led the way back to the booth where they sat down, facing each

209

other. Redmond already had a drink. Motioning, he asked, "Will you join me, Doctor?"

Lord said, "I'll order myself." He had no intention of making this a friendly occasion. The sooner he finished what he had come here to do, the better he would like it.

"I'm an FDA medical technician," Redmond volunteered. "I've seen you come in and out of our department several times."

Now Lord had the younger man pinpointed. He worked in the same general area as Gideon Mace. It would explain, in part, how he had come by the information he had been touting.

Since the original call from the person now revealed as Redmond, there had been two further phone conversations. In one they discussed money. Redmond had been firm in repeating his original demand for two thousand dollars in exchange for documents he claimed to have. During the last call they had arranged this meeting, Redmond choosing the place.

A few days before, at Felding-Roth headquarters, Lord had gone to see Sam Hawthorne in the president's office. "I need two thousand dollars," the research director had said, "and I don't want to have to account for it."

When Sam raised his eyebrows, Lord continued, "It's for some information I believe the company should have. If you insist, I'll give you details, but in my opinion you're better off not knowing."

"I don't like this kind of thing," Sam objected, then asked, "Is anything dishonest involved?"

Lord considered. "I suppose it's unethical—a lawyer might say borderline-illegal. But I assure you we're not stealing anything—like another company's secrets."

Sam still hesitated, and Lord reminded him, "I said I'd tell you if you wish."

Sam shook his head. "Okay, you'll have the money. I'll authorize it."

"When you do," Lord said carefully, "it would be best if as few people as possible were involved. I was thinking that Mrs. Jordan doesn't need to know."

Sam said irritably, "I'll decide that." Then he conceded, "All right, she won't know."

Lord was relieved. Celia Jordan had a way of asking penetrating questions. Also, she might disagree with what he proposed to do.

Later the same day Vincent Lord received a company check. A

voucher showed the amount to be reimbursement for "special travel expenses."

Lord converted the check to cash before leaving Morristown for Washington, and had brought the cash with him to this bar. It was in a pocket of his jacket, in an envelope.

A waiter came to the booth. His manner matched that of Redmond, whom he addressed as "Tony." Lord ordered himself a gin and tonic.

"A nice place, don't you think?" Redmond observed when the waiter had gone. "It's considered chic. People who come here are mostly from government and the university."

"I don't give a damn who comes here," Lord said. "Let me see those papers."

Redmond countered with, "Did you bring the money?"

Lord nodded curtly and waited.

"I suppose I can trust you," Redmond said. There was a briefcase on the seat beside him which he opened; from it he removed a large manila envelope. He passed the envelope to Lord. "It's all in there."

Lord's drink arrived as he began to study the envelope's contents. He sipped twice while reading.

Ten minutes later he looked across the table and said grudgingly, "You've been thorough."

"Well," Redmond acknowledged, "that's the first nice thing you've said to me." His face creased in a knowing smile.

Lord sat silently, weighing possibilities.

The scenario concerning Dr. Gideon Mace was clear. Redmond had sketched in some of it during the phone talks. The papers Lord was reading explained the rest.

It hinged on United States patent laws, generic drugs, and FDA procedures. Vincent Lord was familiar with all three.

When the patent on any major pharmaceutical drug expired—normally seventeen years after patent registration—a number of small manufacturers sought to produce that drug in generic form, afterward selling it at a cheaper price than the originating company. When that happened, the cash rewards to a generic company could be counted in the millions.

However, before *any* generic drug could be manufactured, application had to be made to the FDA, and approval given. This held true even if the same type of drug was already on the market, with FDA approval long since given to its original developer.

211

The procedure by which a generic company was authorized to manufacture and sell a previously patented drug was known as an abbreviated new drug application—ANDA for short.

For any important drug whose patent was about to run out, a dozen or more ANDA's, from different generic manufacturers, might be filed with FDA. And, as with regular NDA's, such as Felding-Roth's for Staidpace, ANDA processing took time.

Exactly how FDA dealt with all of these ANDA's internally was never entirely clear. What *was* clear was that one approval was usually announced first. The others followed later, usually singly, sometimes at widely spaced intervals.

Thus, the manufacturing company that was first to receive approval of an important ANDA had an enormous advantage over competitors, with the probability of matching rewards. Also if that company's stock happened to be traded, it could jump in value, sometimes doubling overnight.

However, because small generic companies were not listed on major exchanges, such as the New York Stock Exchange, their shares were traded on the Over-the-Counter market. Thus while professional traders might notice a sudden price surge in an O-T-C stock, the public mostly didn't, and individual O-T-C stocks rarely garnered headlines in daily newspapers or *The Wall Street Journal*.

For all these reasons it was a situation made to order for someone dishonest and "in the know." That same someone, aware of which generic company was about to receive approval of an ANDA, could make a lot of money quickly by buying the company's shares low before FDA made the ANDA announcement and selling them high immediately after.

Dr. Gideon Mace, inside FDA and privy to confidential information, had done just that. Twice. The proof was in photocopies which Vincent Lord held in his hand. It was all there:

—broker's "buy" and "sell" transaction slips on which the customer's name appeared as Marietta Mace. Lord had already learned from Redmond that this was Mace's spinster sister, obviously a stand-in for Mace as a precaution, but one which hadn't worked;

—two dated FDA announcements of ANDA approvals affecting generic companies called Binvus Products and Minto Labs. Both names corresponded to shares described on the brokerage slips;

—two canceled checks of Gideon Mace's, payable to his sister and *for the exact bottom-line amounts on the two brokerage "buy" orders;*

—two bank statements belonging to Gideon R. Mace, showing large deposits shortly after the dates of the "sell" orders.

Lord had done a quick penciled calculation on the envelope in front of him. Mace, after his sister had deducted what appeared to be a ten percent commission, had reaped a total net profit of some sixteen thousand dollars.

Perhaps more. It was possible that Mace had done something similar, more often—this being something a criminal investigation would reveal.

"Criminal" was the operative word. Precisely as Redmond had promised in his original phone call, if Dr. Mace were exposed, he would almost certainly go to jail.

Lord had been about to ask Redmond how all the material was obtained, then changed his mind. The answer was not hard to guess. Most likely, Mace had kept everything in his desk at FDA, perhaps believing it to be a safer place than at home. But Redmond, who was clearly resourceful, could have found a way of getting into the desk in Mace's absence. Of course, Redmond must have had suspicions to begin with, but an overheard phone call would have been sufficient to set them off.

How could Gideon Mace, Lord wondered, have been so incredibly stupid? Stupid in believing he could do what he had and not be caught. Stupid in trading shares in a name identical with his own, then keeping incriminating papers in a place where someone like Redmond could reach and copy them. But then, clever people often did foolish things.

Lord's thoughts were interrupted by Redmond's voice, petulant. "Well, do you want all that stuff? Do we do business, or don't we?"

Without speaking, Lord reached into his jacket for the envelope containing the money and handed it to Redmond. The younger man lifted the envelope flap, which was unsealed. As he withdrew the cash and handled it, his eyes and face lighted with pleasure.

"You'd better count it," Lord said.

"I don't need to. You wouldn't cheat me. This is too important."

For some time Lord had been conscious of another young man, seated on a bar stool a few yards distant, who had occasionally glanced their way. Now he looked at them again, and this time Redmond returned the look and smiled, holding up the money before putting it away. The other smiled back. Lord felt a sense of distaste.

Redmond said cheerfully, "I guess that's it, then."

"I just have one question," Vincent Lord told him. "It's something I'm curious about."

"Ask away."

Lord touched the manila envelope whose contents he had bought. "Why did you do this to Dr. Mace?"

Redmond hesitated. "Something he said to me."

"Like what?"

"If you must know," Redmond said, his voice shrill and spiteful, "he called me a lousy fag."

"What's wrong with that?" Lord said as he rose to go. "You *are* one, aren't you?"

Before leaving the bar, he glanced back. Tony Redmond was glaring after him, his face contorted, white with rage.

For a week Vincent Lord debated within himself what to do, or not to do. He had still not decided when he encountered Sam Hawthorne.

"I hear you were in Washington," Sam said. "I presume it had something to do with that money I authorized."

Lord nodded. "Presumption right."

"I'm not one for playing games," Sam said. "And if you think you're protecting me, forget it! I've a natural curiosity. I want to know."

"In that case I need to get some papers from my office safe," Lord told him. "I'll bring them to you."

A half hour later, when he had finished reading, Sam whistled softly. His face was troubled. "You realize," he told the research director, "that if we don't do something about this immediately, we're accessories to a crime."

"I suppose so," Lord said. "But whatever we do, if it comes out in the open it will be messy. We'd have to explain how we got those papers. Also, at FDA, no matter who was right or wrong, they'd hate us and never forget."

"Then why in hell did you get us into this?"

Lord answered confidently, "Because what we have here will be useful, and there are ways of handling it."

Lord was unperturbed; for reasons he was unclear about, he felt at ease in this situation, and in control. He had decided now, within the past few minutes, what was the best course to pursue.

He told Sam, "Look, there was a time when I thought something like this would help move Staidpace along, but that problem is behind us. There *will* be other problems, though, and other drugs, and other NDA's we'll want approved without the unreasonable delay we had with Staidpace."

Sam said, shocked, "Surely you're not suggesting . . ."

"I'm not suggesting anything. Except that sooner or later we're certain to come up against Mace again and, if he gives us trouble, we've ammunition we can use. So let's do nothing now, and save it until then."

Sam was already standing. While considering what had just been said, he moved restlessly around the room. At length he growled, "You may be right. But I don't like it."

"Neither will Mace," Lord said. "And permit me to remind you that he is the criminal, not us."

Sam seemed about to say something more, but Lord spoke first. "When the time comes, let *me* do the dirty work."

As Sam nodded reluctantly, Lord added silently to himself, *I might even enjoy it.*

3

Early in 1975, Celia was again promoted.

Her new job was as director of pharmaceutical sales, a post that made her a divisional vice president and positioned her one notch below the vice president for sales and marketing. For anyone who had begun working in sales as a detail person, it was an excellent achievement. For a woman it was extraordinary.

But there was one thing Celia noticed nowadays. Within Felding-Roth, the fact that she was a woman no longer seemed to matter. Her sex was taken for granted. She was judged—as she had always wanted to be—on how well she performed.

Celia had no illusions that this acceptance held true in a majority of business firms, or for women generally. But it showed, she believed, that a woman's chances of reaching the top echelons of business were growing and would improve still more. As with all social changes, there had to be pioneers, and Celia realized that she was one.

However, she still took no part in activist movements, and some of the newcomers to women's rights groups embarrassed her with their stridency and clumsy political pressures. They appeared to view any questioning of their rhetoric—even an honest difference of opinion by a man—as chauvinist. Also apparent was that many such women, without achievements of their own, were using women's activism as substitute careers.

Although, in her new job, Celia would have less direct contact with Sam Hawthorne than she'd had for the preceding three years, Sam made it clear that she still had access to him at any time. "If you see something in the company that's important and wrong, or think of something we ought to be doing and aren't, I want to hear about it, Celia," Sam told her during her last day as special assistant to the president. And Lilian Hawthorne, during a pleasant dinner for Celia and Andrew at the Hawthornes' home, had raised a glass and said, "To you, Celia—though selfishly I wish you weren't moving on because you made life easier for Sam, and now I'll worry about him more."

Also at dinner that night was Juliet Hawthorne, now nineteen and home briefly from college. She had become a beautiful, poised young woman who seemed to have suffered not at all from the attention lavished on an only child. Escorting her was a pleasant, interesting young man whom Juliet introduced as "Dwight Goodsmith, my boyfriend. He's studying to be a lawyer."

Celia and Andrew were impressed with both young people, Celia reflecting how short a time ago it seemed that Juliet and Lisa, as small children in pajamas, had chased each other through this same room where they were dining.

After Lilian's toast to Celia, Sam said with a smile, "What Celia doesn't know yet, because I only approved a memo about it late today, is the real promotion. She now has her own parking slot on the catwalk level."

"My God, Daddy!" Juliet said, and to her friend: "That's like being selected for the Hall of Fame."

The so-called catwalk level was the top floor of a garage and parking structure alongside the Felding-Roth headquarters building. The level was reserved for the company's most senior officers who could park their cars, then use a convenient glassed-in ramp to reach the opposite story of the main building where a private elevator whisked them to the eleventh floor and "executive country."

Sam was one of those who used the catwalk level and parked his silver-gray Rolls-Bentley there each day, preferring it to a chauffeured limousine to which, as president, he was entitled.

Others in the company with lesser status used lower parking levels, then had to take an elevator downward, cross to the other building in the open, and go up again.

There was more good-natured banter about Celia's "double elevation" before the evening ended.

In their car going home, Andrew, who was driving, said, "It turned out to be a wise decision you made, years ago, to hitch your career to Sam's."

"Yes," Celia said, then added, "lately I've been concerned about him."

"Why?"

"He's more driven than he used to be, and he agonizes when something doesn't go right, though I suppose both things go with big responsibility. But there are also times when he's secretive, as if there are things he's worrying about but doesn't want to share."

"You've enough responsibility of your own," Andrew reminded her, "without taking on Sam's psyche too."

"I suppose so. You get wiser every day, Dr. Jordan." Celia squeezed her husband's arm gratefully.

"Quit making sexual advances to the driver," Andrew told her. "You're distracting him."

A few minutes later, he asked, "Speaking of hitching careers to stars, what's happened to that young man who hitched his to yours?"

"Bill Ingram?" Celia laughed; she always remembered the first time Ingram had come to her favorable attention—at the Quadrille-Brown advertising meeting in New York. "Bill has been working in International as Latin-American Director—the job I had. Now we're thinking of bringing him to pharmaceutical sales with a promotion."

"Nice," Andrew said. "Looks as if he made a good star-choice too."

Amid Celia's happiness about her promotion, a note of grief intruded. Teddy Upshaw died, while working at his desk, from a heart attack.

Teddy had remained as O-T-C sales manager, having found his niche, which he filled successfully and happily. At his death he was less than a year from retirement. It grieved Celia that she would never again hear Teddy's lively voice, watch his energetic stride, or see his bouncing-ball head while he talked enthusiastically.

Celia, with Andrew, and others from the company, attended Teddy's funeral and accompanied the cortege to the graveside. It was a miserable, blustery March day, with showers of freezing rain, and the mourners huddled in their coats while sheltering under wind-besieged umbrellas.

Some, including Celia and Andrew, went to the Upshaws' home afterward, and it was there that Teddy's widow, Zoe, took Celia aside.

"Teddy admired you so much, Mrs. Jordan," Zoe said. "He was proud to work for you, and he used to say that as long as you were at Felding-Roth, the company would always have a conscience."

Celia, moved by the words, remembered the first day she had become aware of Teddy—fifteen years earlier, immediately after her speech to the Waldorf sales convention, when she had been ordered from the meeting hall in apparent disgrace. His was one of the few sympathetic faces she had seen on the way out.

"I loved Teddy, too," she told the other woman.

Afterward Andrew asked, "What was it Mrs. Upshaw said to you?"

Celia told him, adding "I haven't always lived up to Teddy's ideal. I remember that fight, the argument, you and I had in Ecuador when you pointed out some places where I'd ignored my conscience, and you were right."

"We were both right," Andrew corrected her, "because you brought up some things that I'd done, or hadn't done, too. But none of us is perfect, and I agree with Teddy. You *are* Felding-Roth's conscience, I'm proud of you for it, and I hope you'll stay that way."

The following month brought better news, for the world at large and, in a narrower sense, for Felding-Roth.

The war in Vietnam was over. It was a crushing defeat for America, a nation not accustomed to defeats. Yet, the tragic slaughter had ceased and the task ahead—formidable but less bloody—was the healing of national wounds, more divisive and bitter than any since the Civil War.

"In our lifetimes the bitterness won't end," Andrew predicted one evening, after he and Celia had watched on television the final, humiliating exodus of Americans from Saigon. "And historians, two centuries from now, will still be arguing the rights and wrongs about our being in Vietnam."

"I know it's selfish," Celia said, "but all I can think of is, thank heaven it finished before Brucie was old enough to go!"

A week or two later, the hierarchy of Felding-Roth was cheered by news from France that the drug Montayne had been approved for manufacture and sale in that country. It meant that under the licensing agreement between Felding-Roth Pharmaceuticals and Laboratoires Gironde-Chimie, American testing of Montayne would now begin.

As to the drug's purpose, Celia had suffered some unease on first learning that it was intended for pregnant women, to be taken early in their pregnancy when nausea and morning sickness were most prevalent—conditions which Montayne would banish. Celia, like others, had strong memories of Thalidomide and its awful aftermath. She also remembered how glad in retrospect she had been that during both of her own pregnancies Andrew had insisted she take no drugs at all.

She had confided her concern to Sam, who was understanding and sympathetic. "When I first heard about Montayne," he admitted, "my reaction was the same as yours. But since then I've learned more about it, convincing me it's a splendidly effective, yet totally safe drug." Since Thalidomide, Sam pointed out, fifteen years had passed during which time there had been enormous progress in pharmaceutical research, including scientific testing of new drugs. As well, government regulations in 1975 were stricter by far than in the 1950s.

"Many things change," Sam insisted. "For example, there was a time when the idea of using anesthetics during childbirth was fiercely opposed by some who believed it would be dangerous and destructive. In the same way there can, and must, be safe drugs for use during pregnancy. Montayne is simply one whose time has come."

219

He urged Celia to keep an open mind until she had examined all the data. She promised that she would.

The importance of Montayne to Felding-Roth was underlined soon afterward when the vice president and comptroller, Seth Feingold, confided to Celia, "Sam has promised the board that Montayne will give us a big boost moneywise, which we sure as hell need. This year our balance sheet looks like we're candidates for a welfare handout."

Feingold, a sprightly, white-haired company veteran, was past retirement age, but was retained because of his encyclopedic knowledge of Felding-Roth finances and an ability to juggle money in tight situations. Over the past two years he and Celia had become friends, their closeness aided by the fact that Andrew had successfully treated Feingold's wife for arthritis. The treatment freed Mrs. Feingold from pain she had suffered over several years.

"My wife thinks your husband could change water into wine," the comptroller had informed Celia one day. "Now that I know you better, I've a similar feeling about his wife."

Continuing to discuss Montayne, he said, "I've talked with Gironde-Chimie's financial people, and the Frenchies believe their drug will be an enormous profit builder for them."

"Even though it's early, all of us in sales are gearing up for the same thing here," Celia assured him. "But especially for you, Seth, we'll try a little harder."

"Attagirl! Speaking of trying harder, some of us are wondering how hard those Brits are working in our research center over there. Or are they loafing, spending most of their time having tea breaks?"

"I haven't heard much lately . . ." Celia began.

"I haven't heard *anything,*" Feingold said. "Except it's costing us millions, like the money's going in a bathtub with the plug out. That's one reason why our balance sheet is a disaster area. I'm telling you, Celia, a lot of people around here, including some members of the board, are worried about that British caper. Ask Sam."

As it turned out, Celia did not need to ask Sam because he sent for her a few days later. "You may have heard," he said, "that I'm taking a lot of flak about Harlow and Martin Peat-Smith."

"Yes," she answered. "Seth Feingold told me."

Sam nodded. "Seth is one of the doubters. For financial reasons he'd like to see Harlow shut down. So would a growing number on the board, and I'm expecting tough questions from shareholders at the annual meeting." He added moodily, "Some days I feel like letting it happen."

Celia reminded him, "It's not much more than two years since the Harlow research started. You had faith in Martin."

"Martin predicted at least *some* positive result within two years," Sam answered. "Also there are limits to faith when we're hemorrhaging dollars and I have the board and shareholders on my back. Another thing—Martin's been obstinate about progress reports. He just won't make any. So I need some assurance there really *is* progress and that it's worthwhile going on."

"Why not go to see for yourself?"

"I would, except that right now I can't take the time. So I want you to go, Celia. As soon as you can, and then report back to me."

She said doubtfully, "Don't you think Vince Lord is better qualified?"

"Scientifically, yes. But Vince is too prejudiced. He opposed doing research in Britain, so if Harlow closed it would prove him right, and he couldn't resist recommending it."

Celia laughed. "How well you know us all!"

Sam said seriously, "I know you, Celia, and I've learned to trust your judgment and your instincts. Just the same, I urge you—no matter how much you like Martin Peat-Smith—if you need to be tough and ruthless in your recommendation, do it! How soon can you go?"

"I'll try for tomorrow," Celia said.

4

When Celia arrived at London's Heathrow Airport in the early morning for a two-day visit, no time was wasted. A waiting limousine transported her directly to the Felding-Roth Research Institute

221

where she would review with Martin Peat-Smith and others what she now thought of mentally as "the Harlow equation."

After that, having reached a decision about what to recommend to Sam, she would fly home.

During her first day at Harlow she was made pointedly aware that the mood, with almost everyone she met, was upbeat. From Martin downward, Celia was assured how well the research on mental aging was progressing, how much had been learned already, and how hard —and as a coordinated team—all concerned were working. Only occasionally were there flashes—like fleeting, accidental glimpses through the doorway of a private donjon—of what seemed to her like doubt or hesitancy. Then they were gone, or instantly denied, leaving her to wonder if she had imagined them after all.

To begin, on that first day Martin walked with her through the labs, explaining work in progress. Since their last meeting, he explained, he and others working with him had fulfilled their initial objective of "discovering and isolating an mRNA which is different in the brains of young animals compared with old ones." He added, "This will probably, in time, be found equally true of human beings."

The scientific jargon flowed.

". . . extracted mRNA from the brains of rats of varying ages . . . afterward the extraction incubated with 'broken cell' preparations of yeast with radioactive amino acids added . . . the yeast system manufactures the animal brain peptides which become mildly radioactive also . . . next, separate them by means of their electric charge, on special gels . . . following that, use an X-ray film and, where bands appear, we have a peptide . . ."

Like a conjurer producing a rabbit from a hat—*voilà!*—Martin slid several eight-by-ten negatives across a lab bench where he and Celia had paused. "These are films of the chromatograms."

As Celia picked them up, they seemed to be almost clear, transparent films, but Martin commanded, "Look closely and you'll see two columns of dark lines. One is from the young rat, the other from the old. Notice . . ." He pointed with a finger. "Here and here on the young rat column are at least nine peptides no longer being produced in the older animal's brain." His voice rose with excitement as he declared, "Now we have positive evidence that the brain RNA, and probably the DNA, change during the aging process. This is *terribly important.*"

"Yes," Celia said, but wondered silently: was it really a triumph

222

justifying more than two years of combined effort here at enormous expense?

A reminder of the expense was all around—the spacious labs and modern offices, all with modular dividers permitting rearrangement when desired; the unobstructed corridors; a cozy conference room; and, in the elaborately equipped labs, a wealth of stainless steel and modern benches, the latter manufactured from synthetics—no wood allowed because, in scientific terms, wood was dirty. Air conditioning removed airborne impurities. Lighting was bright without glare. A pair of incubation rooms housed massive glass-faced incubators, specially designed to hold racks of petri dishes containing bacteria and yeast. Still other rooms had double-entry doors with "Danger: Radiation Hazard" signs outside.

The contrast to the Cambridge laboratories that Celia had visited with Martin was startling, though a few familiar things remained. One was paper—a prodigious quantity piled high and untidily on desks, Martin's in particular. You could change a scientist's background, she thought, but not his work habits.

As they moved away from the bench and the chromatograms, Martin continued explanations.

"Now that we have the RNA, we can make the corresponding DNA . . . then we must insert it into the DNA of living bacteria . . . try to 'fool' the bacteria into making the required brain peptide . . ."

Celia attempted to absorb as much as she could at high speed.

Near the end of their inspection, Martin opened a door to a small laboratory where a white-coated, elderly male technician was confronting a half-dozen rats in cages. The technician was wizened and slightly stooped, with only a fringe of hair surrounding his head, and wore old-fashioned pince-nez secured by a black cord worn around the neck. Martin announced, "This is Mr. Yates, who is about to do some animal dissections."

"Mickey Yates." He extended his hand. "I know who you are. Everybody does."

Martin laughed. "That's right, they do." He asked Celia, "May I leave you here for a few minutes? I have to make a phone call."

"Of course." When Martin had gone, closing the door behind him, she told Yates, "If it won't bother you, I'd like to watch."

"Won't bother me at all. First, though, I have to kill one of these little buggers." He motioned to the rats.

With quick, deft movements, the technician opened a refrigerator and, from the freezing compartment, took out a smallish, clear plastic box with a hinged lid. Inside was a slightly raised platform with a tray beneath containing crystalline material from which wisps of evaporation rose. "Dry ice," Yates said. "Put it in there just before you came."

Opening one of the cages, he reached in and expertly grasped a large, squirming white-gray rat which he transferred to the plastic box, then closed the lid. Celia could now see the rat, on the small platform inside.

"Because of the dry ice, in there it's a CO_2 environment," Yates said. "You know what that means?"

Celia smiled at the elementary question. "Yes. Carbon dioxide is what we all breathe out after we've used the air's oxygen. We couldn't live on it."

"Nor can chummy there. He's just about a goner."

While they watched, the rat jerked twice, then was still. A minute passed. "He's stopped breathing," Yates said cheerfully. After another thirty seconds he opened the plastic box, removed the unmoving creature and pronounced, "Dead as a doornail. But it's a slow way to do it."

"Slow? It seemed quick to me." Celia was trying to remember how rats were killed during her own laboratory days, but couldn't.

"It's slow when you've got a lot to do. Dr. Peat-Smith likes us to use the CO_2 box, but there's another way that's faster. This one." Yates reached down. Opening a cupboard beneath the lab bench, he produced a second box, this time metal. The design differed from the first in that one end of the box had a small round aperture cut into it while immediately above was a hinged, sharp knife. "This here's a guillotine," Yates said, still cheerfully. "The French know how to do things."

"But messily," Celia responded. Now she remembered; she had seen rats killed in a similar kind of device.

"Oh, it ain't that bad. And it's fast." Yates glanced over his shoulder at the closed door, then, before Celia could object, he took a fresh rat from a cage and swiftly thrust it in the second box, its head protruding through the round hole. As if slicing bread, he pushed the hinged knife down.

There was a soft crunching sound, another which might have been a cry, then the rat's head fell forward as blood spurted from arteries

224

in the severed neck. Celia, despite her familiarity with laboratories and research, felt sick.

Yates casually tossed the rat's body, still bleeding and twitching, into a trash receptacle and picked up the head. "All I have to do now is remove the brain. Fast and painless!" The technician laughed. "I didn't feel a thing."

Angry and disgusted at once, Celia said, "You did *not* have to do that for me!"

"Do what?" It was Martin's voice behind her. He had come in quietly, and now took in the scene. After a moment, and with equal quietness, he instructed, "Celia, please wait outside."

As Celia left, Martin was glaring at Yates and breathing heavily.

While she waited, through the intervening door she heard Martin's angrily raised voice. "Don't *ever again!* . . . not if you want to go on working here . . . my orders, always to use the CO_2 box which is painless, *no other way!* . . . get that other monstrosity out of here or break it up . . . I will not have cruelty, do you understand?"

She heard the voice of Yates saying weakly, "Yessir."

When Martin emerged, he took Celia's arm and escorted her to the conference room where they were alone, a thermos jug of coffee between them, from which Martin poured.

"I'm sorry that happened; it shouldn't have," he told her. "Yates got carried away, probably because he isn't used to having an attractive woman watch him at work—at which he's very good, incidentally, and it's the reason I brought him here from Cambridge. He can dissect a rat's brain the way a surgeon would."

Celia said, her mild annoyance past, "It was a small thing. It doesn't matter."

"It matters to me."

She said curiously, "You care about animals, don't you?"

"Yes, I do." Martin sipped coffee, then said, "It's impossible to do research without inflicting some pain on animals. Human needs come first, and even animal lovers have to accept that. But the pain should be kept to a minimum, which you ensure by an attitude of caring; otherwise it's all too easy to become callous. I've reminded Yates of that. I don't think he'll forget."

The incident made Celia like and respect Martin even more than before. But, she reminded herself, likes or dislikes must not affect her purpose here.

"Let's get back to your progress," she said briskly. "You've talked

225

about differences in the brains of young and old animals, also your plans to synthesize a DNA. But you haven't yet isolated a protein—the peptide you're looking for, the one that counts. Correct?"

"Correct." Martin gave his swift, warm smile, then continued confidently. "What you just described is the next step, also the toughest. We're working on it, and it will happen, though of course it all takes time."

She reminded him, "When the institute opened, you said, 'Allow me two years.' You expected to have something positive by then. That was two years and four months ago."

He seemed surprised. "Did I really say that?"

"You certainly did. Sam remembers. So do I."

"Then it was reckless of me. Working, as we are here, at the frontier of science, timetables can't apply." Again Martin seemed untroubled, yet Celia detected strain beneath the surface. Physically, too, Martin seemed out of condition. His face was pale; his eyes suggested fatigue, probably from long hours of work; and there were lines on his face which had not been there two years ago.

"Martin," Celia said, "why won't you send progress reports? Sam has a board of directors he must satisfy, and shareholders . . ."

The scientist shook his head, for the first time impatiently. "It's more important that I concentrate on research. Reports, so much writing and paperwork, take up valuable time." He asked abruptly, "Have you read John Locke?"

"At college, a little."

"He wrote that man makes discoveries by 'steadily intending his mind in a given direction.' A scientific researcher must remember that."

Celia abandoned the subject for the time being, but raised it later that day with the administrator, ex-Squadron Leader Bentley, who suggested a different reason for the absence of reports.

"You should understand, Mrs. Jordan," Nigel Bentley said, "that Dr. Peat-Smith finds it excruciatingly difficult to put *anything* in writing. A reason is that his mind moves forward so quickly that what was important to him yesterday may be out of date today, and even more so tomorrow. He is actually embarrassed by things that he wrote earlier—two years ago, for example. He sees them as naïve even though, at the time, they may have been incredibly perceptive. If he could have his way, he'd wipe out everything he's written in the

226

past. It's a trait not uncommon in scientists. I've encountered it before."

Celia said, "Tell me some more things I should know about the scientific mind." They were sharing the privacy of Bentley's modest but neatly organized office where Celia was having increasing respect for this competent, sparrowlike man she had chosen to run the research institute's business side.

Nigel Bentley considered, then began, "Perhaps the most important thing is that scientists stay so long in the educational process, become so involved in their chosen, sometimes narrow, specialties, that they come to the realities of everyday life much later than the rest of us. Indeed, some great scholars never come to grips with those realities at all."

"I've heard it said that they stay, in some ways, childlike."

"Precisely, Mrs. Jordan, and in certain areas very much that way. It's why one sees, so often, childish behavior in academic circles—petty squabbles and the like, over trivial issues."

Celia said thoughtfully, "I would not have thought any of that was true of Martin Peat-Smith."

"Possibly not, within those specific limits," Bentley acknowledged. "But in other ways."

"Tell me."

"Well, something Dr. Peat-Smith has great trouble with is small decisions. Some days, as one might put it, he can't decide which side of the street to walk on. As an example, he agonized for weeks over which one of two technicians we employ should have preference in going on a three-day course in London. It was a minor matter, something you or I would have decided in a few minutes and, in the end, because my superior couldn't reach a decision, I made it for him. All this, of course, is in total contrast to Dr. Peat-Smith's mainstream purpose—his scientific clarity and dedication."

"You're making several things much clearer," Celia said. "Including why Martin hasn't sent reports."

"There's something else I believe I should point out," Bentley volunteered. "It may even have a bearing on your visit."

"Go ahead."

"Dr. Peat-Smith is a leader and, as with any leader, it would be a mistake for him to show weakness or exhibit doubts about the progress being made here. If he did, the morale of those working with him would collapse. And something else: Dr. Peat-Smith has been used to working alone, at his own pace. Now, suddenly, he has huge responsibilities, with many people depending on him, as well as other pressures—subtle and not so subtle—including your own presence, Mrs. Jordan, here and now. All those things are an enormous strain on any individual."

"Then there *are* doubts about the work being done," Celia said. "Serious doubts? I've been wondering."

Bentley, who was facing Celia across his desk, put the tips of his fingers together and regarded her across them. "In working here I have an obligation to Dr. Peat-Smith, but an even larger responsibility to you and Mr. Hawthorne. Therefore I must answer your question—yes."

"I want to know about those doubts," Celia said. "In detail."

Bentley answered, "I lack the scientific qualifications." He hesitated, then went on, "It would be irregular, perhaps, but I believe you should speak privately with Dr. Sastri and instruct him, as you have authority to do, to open up totally and frankly."

Dr. Rao Sastri, as Celia knew, was the nucleic acid chemist—a Pakistani, formerly a Cambridge colleague—whom Martin had recruited as his scientific second-in-command.

"This is too important to worry about what's regular or isn't, Mr. Bentley," she said. "Thank you. I'll do as you suggest."

"Is there any other way in which I can help?"

Celia considered. "Martin quoted John Locke at me today. Is he a Locke disciple?"

"Yes, and so am I." Bentley gave a small, tight smile. "The two of us share a conviction that Locke was one of the finer philosophers and guides this world has ever known."

"I'd like something of Locke's to read tonight," Celia said. "Can you get it for me?"

Bentley made a note. "It will be waiting for you at your hotel."

It was not until late afternoon, during her second day at Harlow, that Celia was able to have her talk with Dr. Sastri. In between that and her session the previous day with Nigel Bentley, she talked with others at the institute who were consistently cheerful and optimistic in their views about the Harlow research scene. Yet still Celia had a sense of something being held back, an instinct that those she had met were being less than forthright with her.

Rao Sastri proved to be a handsome, dark-skinned, articulate and fast-speaking young man, still in his twenties. Celia knew he had a Ph.D. and a brilliant scholastic record, and both Martin and Bentley had assured her the institute was fortunate in having him. Sastri and Celia met in an annex to the plant cafeteria, a small room normally used by senior staff for working lunches. After shaking hands with Sastri, and before they sat down, Celia closed the door for privacy.

She said, "I believe you know who I am."

"Indeed, Mrs. Jordan. My colleague Peat-Smith has spoken of you frequently, and kindly. At this time I am honored to meet you." Sastri's speech was cultured and precise, with a Pakistani lilt. He also smiled frequently, though at times switching off the smile with a trace of nervousness.

"I am happy to meet you also," Celia said, "and wish to discuss with you the progress of research here."

"It is wonderful! Truly marvelous! A jolly good show all around."

"Yes," Celia acknowledged, "others have told me the same. But before we go on I would like to make clear that I am here on behalf of Mr. Hawthorne, the president of Felding-Roth, and exercising his authority."

"Oh, dear! My goodness! I wonder what is coming now."

"What is coming, Dr. Sastri, is that I am asking you—ordering you, in fact—to be totally frank with me, holding back nothing, including any doubts you have, and which so far you may have kept entirely to yourself."

"All this is damned awkward," Sastri said. "Also not entirely fair, as I pointed out to Bentley when he informed me of this line you would be taking. I do, after all, have an obligation to Peat-Smith, who is a decent chap."

"You have an even bigger obligation to Felding-Roth," Celia told him sharply, "because the company pays your salary—a good one—and is entitled to your honest professional opinions in return."

"I say, Mrs. Jordan! You don't mess about, do you?" The young Pakistani's tone mixed shock and awe.

"Messing about—as you eloquently put it, Dr. Sastri—takes time, which I don't have a lot of, since I'm returning to America tomorrow. So please tell me exactly where, in your opinion, our institute research is, and where it's going."

Sastri raised both hands in a submissive gesture, and sighed. "Very well. The research is *not* very far along. And, in my humble opinion and that of others in this project, it is going nowhere."

"Explain those opinions."

"In more than two years, all that has been achieved is to confirm a theory that there are brain DNA changes during aging. Oh yes, it is an interesting accomplishment, but beyond it we are facing a damned blank wall which we do not have techniques to penetrate, may not have for many years, and *even then* the peptide Peat-Smith has postulated may not be behind the wall."

Celia queried, "You do not accept that postulation?"

"It is my colleague's *theory*, Mrs. Jordan. I admit I shared it." Sastri shook his head regretfully. "But, in my inmost heart, no longer."

"Martin informed me," Celia said, "that you have proved the existence of a unique RNA and should be able to make the corresponding DNA."

"Which is, by golly, true! But perhaps what you were *not* told is that the isolated material may be *too large*. The mRNA strand is long, and codes for many proteins, possibly forty altogether. It is therefore unusable—just 'nonsense' peptides."

Celia reached into her scientific memory. "Can the material be cleaved? Each peptide isolated?"

Sastri smiled; his voice assumed a superior edge. "*There* is the blank wall. There are no techniques to take us further. Possibly in ten years from now . . ." He shrugged.

For another twenty minutes they talked science, Celia learning that, of the group of scientists now working at Harlow on the mental aging project, only Martin remained a true believer that it would produce worthwhile results.

At the end she said, "Thank you, Dr. Sastri. You've told me what I crossed the Atlantic to find out."

The young man nodded sadly. "I have done my duty as you insisted. But I will not sleep well tonight."

"I don't expect to either," Celia said. "But that's a price which people like you and me pay sometimes—for being where we are."

5

At Martin's invitation, Celia went to his home for drinks during her second and last evening at Harlow. Afterward they would go on to dinner which she had arranged at the Churchgate Hotel where she was staying.

Martin lived in a small semidetached house about two miles from the Felding-Roth Institute. The house, while modern and functional, was similar to dozens of others nearby which appeared to Celia to have been assembled on a mass-production line.

When she arrived, by taxi, Martin escorted her to a tiny living room and, as on other occasions, she was aware of his admiring inspection. For the brief trip to Britain she had traveled lightly, wearing a tailored suit during daytimes, but tonight had on a Diane von Furstenberg wraparound dress in an attractive brown and white print, with a single strand of pearls. Her soft brown hair was stylish in the short, blunt cut of the day.

On the way in from the front hall Celia stepped over or around five animals—a friendly Irish setter, a growling English bulldog, and three cats. Within the living room was a parrot on an open perch.

She laughed. "You really *are* an animal lover."

"I suppose I am," Martin smilingly agreed. "I enjoy having animals around and I'm a sucker for homeless cats." The cats seemed to know this and followed him slavishly.

Celia knew that Martin lived alone, with a "daily" woman coming to clean. The living-room furniture was minimal, consisting mainly of a leather armchair with a reading light beside it, and three bookcases, crammed with scientific volumes. Some bottles, mixes and ice were set out on a small table. Martin waved her to the armchair and began mixing drinks.

"I've the makings of a daiquiri, if that's what you'd like."

"I'd like it," Celia said, "and I'm touched you should remember."
She wondered if they would be as relaxed and friendly at the evening's end. As on earlier occasions, she was aware of Martin's physical attractiveness as a man, yet before coming here she had reminded herself of Sam Hawthorne's parting words: *"No matter how much you like Martin . . . if you need to be tough and ruthless . . . do it!"*

"I'll be seeing Sam the day after tomorrow," Celia said. "I have to make a recommendation about the future of the Harlow institute, and I'd like to know what you think it should be."

"That's easy." He handed her a daiquiri. "You should urge a continuance of our present research for another year, longer if necessary."

"There *is* opposition to continuing. You know that."

"Yes." The confidence which Martin had shown ever since Celia's arrival was still in evidence. "But then, there are always shortsighted people, unable to see the big picture."

"Is Dr. Sastri shortsighted?"

"I'm sorry to say it—yes. How's the drink?"

"Fine."

"Rao came here an hour ago," Martin said. "He wanted to see me because he felt I should know everything he told you this afternoon. Rao has a strong sense of honor."

"And?"

"He's wrong. Totally wrong. So are the others who have doubts."

Celia asked, "Can you refute *factually* what Sastri says?"

"Of course not!" Martin's impatience flashed, as it had yesterday. "All scientific research is based on theory. If we had facts instead, we wouldn't need to research. What *is* involved is informed, professional judgment and some instinct; some call the combination scientific arrogance. Either way, it's a conviction of being on the right track, knowing that only time—in this case a *short time*—is standing between you and what you're searching for."

"Time and a great deal of money," Celia reminded him. "Also the question of whether yours, or Sastri's and some others, is the right judgment."

Martin sipped a scotch and water he had poured himself and paused, considering. Then he said, "Money is something I don't like to think about more than I have to, especially money made from selling drugs. But you mentioned it first, so I'll tell you this now

232

because maybe it's the only way I can get through to you, to Sam, and others like you."

Celia watched Martin intently, listening carefully, wondering what was coming.

"Even in what you think of as my scientific remoteness," he said, "I know that Felding-Roth is in deep trouble. If things don't improve within the next few years, the company could go under." He asked sharply, "Right or wrong?"

Celia hesitated, then nodded. "Right."

"What *I* can do, *given a little more time,* is save your company. Not only save it, but make it productive, acclaimed and enormously rich. That's because, at the end of my research, there will be important medication—a drug." Martin grimaced before going on. "Not that I care about any commercial outcome. I don't. I'm also embarrassed to be talking about it now. But when it happens, what *I* want accomplished will happen too."

The statement, Celia thought, had the same impressive effect as another made by Martin in his Cambridge lab the day of their first meeting. At that time, Sam had felt that effect too. But the earlier statement, made more than two years ago, had not been fulfilled. Why, she asked herself, should today's be different?

Celia shook her head. "I don't know. I just don't know."

"Dammit, I *know* mine is the right judgment!" Martin's voice rose. "We're close—*so close!*—to finding a means to improve the quality of aging and retard brain deterioration, and maybe prevent Alzheimer's disease as well." He gulped what remained of the drink in his hand and slammed down the glass. *"How in hell can I convince you?"*

"You can try again over dinner." Celia glanced at her watch. "I believe we should go now."

The food at the Churchgate Hotel, while good, ran to large portions—too large for Celia. After a while she toyed with what remained on her plate, moving it around without eating, while she considered what to say next. Whatever it was would be important. Knowing it, she held back, hesitating, preparing her words carefully.

Meanwhile the ambience was pleasant.

More than six centuries before the Churchgate existed as a hotel, its site had been occupied by a chantry house—a priest's dwelling—

233

which, in Jacobean times, became a private home. Some portions of the Jacobean structure still remained in the charming hotel building, enlarged and refurbished when Harlow changed from a village to a town after World War II. The dining room was one of the historic holdovers.

Celia liked the room's atmosphere—its low ceiling, upholstered window benches, white and red napery and pleasant service, including the placement of food at each table before diners were called in from an adjoining lounge-bar where earlier they had received menus and placed their orders.

Tonight, Celia had one of the window benches. Martin sat facing her.

Through the meal they continued the conversation begun at Martin's house, Celia listening, interjecting an occasional question, as Martin talked science confidently. But fresh in her memory were the words of Nigel Bentley, spoken yesterday. *"Dr. Peat-Smith is a leader and, as with any leader, it would be a mistake for him to show weakness or exhibit doubts . . ."*

Did Martin, despite that persistent outward confidence, have an inward, private uncertainty? Celia considered a tactic to help her find out. It was an idea developed from the book she had read last night, after its delivery to the hotel—a promise fulfilled by Nigel Bentley.

Having calculated and weighed her words, she looked at him directly and said, "An hour ago, when we were talking at the house, you said you had scientific arrogance."

He riposted, "Don't misunderstand that. It's positive, not negative —a combination of knowledge, willingness to criticize one's own work, yet conviction also—something a successful scientist must have to survive."

As he said it, Celia wondered if for the first time there was the slightest crack, a hint of weakness, in the confident façade. She wasn't sure, but pressed on.

"Is it possible," she insisted, "that scientific arrogance, or whatever else you call it, can go too far; that someone can become so convinced of what they *want* to believe that they indulge in wishful thinking which becomes unshakable?"

"Everything's possible," Martin answered. "Though not in this case."

But his voice was flat, with less conviction than previously. Now she

234

was sure. She had probed his weakness, and he was close to concession, perhaps to breaking point.

"I read something last night," Celia said. "I wrote it down, even though I think you may know of it." Her purse was beside her. From it she extracted a sheet of hotel stationery and read aloud:

> "Error is not a fault of our knowledge, but a mistake of our judgment . . . Those who cannot carry a train of consequences in their heads; nor weigh exactly the preponderancy of contrary proofs and testimonies . . . may be easily misled to assent to positions that are not probable."

There was a silence which, after a moment, Celia filled, aware she was being relentless, even cruel. "It's from *An Essay Concerning Human Understanding* by John Locke. The man you believe in and revere."

"Yes," he said, "I know."

"So isn't it likely," she persisted, "that *you* are not weighing those 'contrary proofs' and *you* are holding to 'positions that are not probable' *just the way Locke said?*"

Martin turned toward her, in his eyes a mute appeal. "Do you think I am?"

Celia said quietly, "Yes, I do."

"I'm sorry you . . ." He choked on the words and she scarcely recognized his voice. Now he said faintly, "Then . . . I give up."

Martin had broken. The quotation from Locke, his idol—turned against him by Celia—had pierced him to the heart. More than that, like a suddenly failing machine that turns inward, devouring itself, he had lost control. His face was ashen, his mouth hung open, and his jaw sagged. Disconnected words emerged. ". . . tell your people to end it . . . let them close down . . . I *do* believe, but maybe I'm not good enough, not alone . . . What we've looked for will be found . . . it will happen, must happen . . . but somewhere else . . ."

Celia was aghast. *What had she done?* She had sought to shock Martin into what she perceived as reality, but had neither intended, nor wanted, to go this far. Clearly the accumulated strain over more than two years, the lonely and awesome responsibility he had carried, had exacted its toll, which was visible now.

Again Martin's voice. ". . . tired, so tired . . ."

Hearing the defeated phrases, Celia had an overwhelming desire to take him in her arms and comfort him. Then, with the suddenness of a revelation, she knew what would happen next. "Martin," she said decisively, "let's get out of here."

A passing waitress glanced toward them curiously. Celia, standing, told her, "Put the meal on my bill. My friend isn't well."

"Certainly, Mrs. Jordan." The girl eased their table outward. "Do you need help?"

"No, thank you. I'll manage." She took Martin's arm and propelled him toward the lounge-bar outside. From there a stairway ascended to a series of guest rooms. Celia's room was near the head of the stairway. She used her key to open it. They went inside.

This portion of the building, too, had been preserved from Jacobean days. The rectangular bedroom had a low strapwork ceiling, oak-paneled walls and a fireplace framed in stone. Leaded-light windows were small, their smallness a reminder that in the seventeenth century glass was an expensive luxury.

The bed was a roomy four-poster with a canopy. During the dinner hours a maid had been here, neatly turning down the bedsheets and leaving a negligee of Celia's draped across a pillow.

Celia wondered how much history—of ancient families: their births and deaths, illnesses, loving passions, joys and sorrows, quarrels, assignations—this room had seen. Well, she thought, tonight there would be something more to add.

Martin was standing, still dazed and suffering, regarding her uncertainly. She picked up the negligee and, turning toward the bathroom, told him softly, "Get undressed. Get into bed. I'll join you."

As he continued to look at her, still unmoving, she came close and whispered, "You want this too, don't you?"

His body heaved with a groaning, gasping sigh. "Oh my God, *yes!*"

While they held each other, she comforted him as she would a child. But not for long.

She felt Martin's passion rise, and her own accompanied it. Just as Martin had wanted this moment, Celia knew that she had sought it too. In a way, it had been inevitable, ever since their first meeting at Cambridge when something far stronger than instant, mutual liking had flashed between them. From then on, Celia realized, the question had never been "if," but merely "when"?

The choice of consummation here and now had, in one sense, been accidental. It had happened because of Martin's sudden breakdown and despair, his obvious, urgent need to draw on outside strength and solace. Yet, if what was occurring now had not occurred tonight, some other time would have seen the same conclusion, with each of their meetings bringing the fateful moment closer.

As Martin kissed her ardently, and she responded, feeling his rigid masculinity against her, she knew in a crevice of her mind that sooner or later moral issues must be faced and consequences weighed. *But not now!* There was no strength left in Celia for anything but the fulfillment of desire. Her own desire, all-encompassing, burning, blissful, overwhelming, coalesced with Martin's.

Moments later they cried out to each other, lovingly, and with exquisite joy.

Afterward they slept, Martin—it seemed to Celia—deeply, and no longer troubled. In the early morning hours they awakened and, this time more tenderly but with equal pleasure, made love again.

When next Celia awoke, daylight was streaming in through the old-fashioned windows.

Martin had gone. She found the note soon after.

Dearest:

You have been, and are, an inspiration.

Early this morning while you were sleeping—oh, so beautifully!—an idea, a "perhaps" solution to our research impasse, came to me. I am going to the lab, even though I know I don't have long, to see if it has promise.

Either way I shall keep the faith, carrying on until the eviction order comes.

What happened between us will be safely secret and a lovely memory. Don't worry about anything. I know that Paradise Found only happens once.

I suggest you do not preserve this note.

Yours always,
Martin

Celia showered, ordered breakfast, and began packing for the journey home.

6

On the British Airways *Concorde*, after luncheon had been served, Celia closed her eyes and marshaled her thoughts.

Personal things first.

During the eighteen years of her marriage to Andrew, never—until last night—had she had sexual relations with another man. It was not that opportunities had not arisen; they often had. She had even been tempted occasionally to avail herself of proffered sex, but always thrust the notion away, either out of loyalty to Andrew or because, in business terms, it seemed unwise. Sometimes her reasoning was a combination of the two.

Sam Hawthorne had indicated, more than once, that he would enjoy an affair with Celia. But she had decided long ago that it would be the worst thing for them both, and discouraged Sam's rare overtures with politeness, but firmly.

Martin had been different. From the beginning, Celia admired him, and also—she now admitted to herself—had wanted him physically. Well, that wish had been fulfilled, and the result was as good as any lover could have hoped for. There could also be, Celia knew—if their circumstances were different—a good deal more between herself and Martin.

But Martin had wisely recognized that there was no future in their loving, and Celia saw that too. That is, unless she was prepared to abandon Andrew and risk estrangement with her children, which she wasn't, and never would be. Besides, she loved Andrew dearly. They had been through so much together, and Andrew had rich qualities of wisdom, tenderness and strength that no one else Celia knew—not even Martin—could ever come close to.

Therefore Martin, sounding more like a poet than a scientist, had said it all that morning. *"What happened between us will be safely secret and a lovely memory . . . I know that Paradise Found only happens once."*

She supposed there were people who would believe she ought to feel guilty about what happened last night. Well, she didn't—quite the reverse!—and that was that.

Her thoughts moved from herself to Andrew.

Had Andrew, she wondered, ever indulged in extramarital sex? Probably yes. He, too, would have had opportunities, and he was a man whom women found attractive.

Then how, Celia asked herself, did she feel about *that?*

Not happy, of course, assuming it had happened, because it was difficult, if not impossible, to be logical in such matters. On the other hand, she would never let herself become concerned over something that she didn't know about.

Celia had once heard someone say cynically at a Morristown cocktail party, "Any normal man who has been married twenty years and claims not to have had some sex on the side is either a liar or a nebbish." It wasn't true, of course. For plenty of men such opportunities never arose, while others stayed monogamous from choice.

Nonetheless, statements like the one she remembered held a core of truth. Celia knew from gossip, and sometimes public indiscretions, that there was plenty of sleeping around in the medical circles where she and Andrew moved, and in the pharmaceutical business too.

Which led to a further question: Did occasional sexual side excursions matter in a solid marriage? She didn't think so—providing they were neither intensely serious nor became lasting affairs. In fact, Celia believed, many marriages broke up needlessly because spouses were prudish or jealous, or both, about what was often no more than some harmless sexual fun.

Finally, about Andrew, she thought that whatever he had or hadn't done outside their marriage, he would always be considerate and discreet. Celia intended to be equally discreet, which was why she accepted the *fait accompli* of no more clandestine meetings between herself and Martin.

End of personal lucubration.

Now about Harlow. What, Celia asked herself, should her recommendation be, the recommendation she would make to Sam tomorrow?

Obviously there was only one line for her to take: Close the institute. Admit that opening it had been a mistake. Cut losses quickly.

239

Accept that Martin's mental aging project had been a disappointing failure.

Or *was* it the only course? Or even the best one? Even now, despite all that she had seen and heard at Harlow, Celia was unsure.

One thing in particular kept coming back to her: It was something Martin had said in his distress last night, moments before they left the Churchgate Hotel dining room. Since this morning, beginning while she was being driven by limousine to London Airport, Celia had repeatedly played Martin's words over in her mind as if they were recorded on tape. *"What we've looked for will be found . . . it will happen, must happen . . . but somewhere else."*

When the words were spoken, she had taken little heed of them. But somehow, now, their significance seemed greater. Could Martin still be right and everyone else wrong? And where was "somewhere else"? Another country? Another pharmaceutical firm? Was it possible that if Felding-Roth abandoned Martin's mental aging research, some other company—a competitor—might pick it up and see it through to a successful conclusion, "successful" implying production of an important, profitable new drug?

There was also the question of research, on the same subject, being done in other countries. Two years ago Martin had mentioned scientists working on projects in Germany, France, New Zealand. Celia knew from her inquiries that research in those other countries was continuing—though apparently with no more success than at Harlow.

But supposing, after Harlow was discontinued, one of those other scientists had a sudden breakthrough, a breathtaking discovery which *might* have happened at Harlow had they carried on. If it turned out that way, how would Felding-Roth feel? And how would Celia feel—and appear to others in the company—if she recommended closing Harlow now?

Therefore, for an array of reasons, there was a temptation for her to do nothing—"nothing," in this case, meaning: recommend carrying on at Harlow in the hope that something might develop.

Yet, Celia reasoned, didn't that kind of decision—or, rather, indecision—represent merely the *safest* way to go? Yes! It was a take-no-action-now, but wait-and-see philosophy which she had heard both Sam Hawthorne and Vincent Lord describe caustically as prevailing at FDA in Washington. All of which brought her full circle to Sam's

pre-departure instruction: *"If you need to be tough and ruthless . . .
do it!"*

Celia sighed. It was no good wishing she did not have this difficult
choice to make. The fact was, she did. Equally to the point: tough
decisions were part of top-management responsibility, which she had
once coveted, and now had.

But when the *Concorde* landed at New York, she was still not
positive about which way her advocacy should go.

As it turned out, Celia's meeting with Sam Hawthorne was delayed
by a day because of Sam's own heavy schedule of appointments. By
then, her conclusion about Harlow was strong and unequivocal.

"Well," Sam said, wasting no time with preliminaries after she was
seated facing him in the presidential office suite, "do you have a
recommendation for me?"

The direct question, and Celia's own instincts, made it clear that
Sam was in no mood for details or a background briefing.

"Yes," she said crisply. "Weighing everything, I believe it would be
a shortsighted, serious mistake to close the Harlow institute. Also, we
should carry on with Martin's mental aging research, certainly for
another year, and possibly for longer."

Sam nodded and said matter-of-factly, "All right."

The lack of any strong reaction, and an absence of questions, made
it clear that Celia's recommendation was accepted *in toto*. She also
had a feeling that Sam was relieved, as if the answer she had given
was what he had hoped for.

"I've written a report." She put a four-page memo on his desk.

Sam tossed it in a tray. "I'll read it sometime. If only to help me
handle questions from the board."

"Will the board give you a hard time?"

"Probably." Sam gave a tired half smile and Celia sensed his current strain from pressures he was working under. He added, "Don't
worry, though; I'll make it stick. Did you inform Martin we'll be
carrying on?"

She shook her head. "He thinks we're going to close."

"In that case," Sam said, "one of the pleasant things I shall do today
is write to tell him otherwise. Thanks, Celia."

His curt nod made it clear the interview was ended.

One week later a large bouquet of roses appeared in Celia's office. When she inquired about them, her secretary said, "There was no card, Mrs. Jordan, and when I asked the florists, they said all they had were telegraphed instructions to deliver the roses to you. Would you like me to try again to find out who sent them?"

"Don't bother," Celia said. "I think I know."

7

To Celia's relief, her travels diminished during the remainder of 1975. While she worked hard, it was mostly at Morristown, which meant that she could spend more time with Andrew, and also visit Lisa and Bruce at their schools.

Lisa, in her final year at Emma Willard, had been elected senior-class president and as well as maintaining a high grade average was involved in a wide range of school activities. One, of her own devising, was an intern program under which senior class members worked a half day each week in offices of the state government at Albany.

The program got started after Lisa, demonstrating a belief that if you wanted something you went to the top to ask, wrote a letter to the governor of New York. An aide showed it to the governor, who was amused and—to the surprise of everyone at the school except Lisa—answered personally and positively. When word filtered back to Andrew, he observed to Celia, "No doubt about it; that girl is your daughter."

Organization, it seemed, came to Lisa as naturally as breathing. Recently she had applied for admission to several universities, though her ambitions centered on Stanford.

Bruce, now in his sophomore year at the Hill, had become more than ever a history buff, an interest which occupied him so exclusively that sometimes he barely managed a passing grade in other subjects. As Bruce's house master explained to Celia and Andrew during one of their visits to the school, "It isn't that Bruce is a poor scholar; he could be an excellent all-around one. It's simply that sometimes we have to pry him loose from the history books and insist that he study other things. What I think you have on your hands, Dr. and Mrs. Jordan, is a future historian. I expect to see your son's name on published works before many years have passed."

While cautioning herself not to become smug, Celia reflected with relief that it was possible to be a working mother and still have successful, well-balanced children.

An important part of it, of course, was that Winnie and Hank March had run the family house, as they continued to do, with cheerful efficiency. During a celebration of Winnie's fifteenth year of employment, which coincided with her thirty-fourth birthday, it was Andrew who remembered Winnie's long-abandoned plan to move on to Australia. He remarked, "What the Aussies lost, the Jordans gained."

Only one adverse note obtruded on Winnie's sunny nature: her failure to have a child, which she dearly wanted. She confided to Celia, "Me an' 'Ank keep tryin'. Lordy, how we try!—some days I'm fair wrung out. But it don't ever click."

At Celia's urging, Andrew arranged fertility tests for Winnie and her husband. The tests proved positive in each case. "Both you and Hank are capable of having children," Andrew explained one evening while he, Winnie and Celia were together in the kitchen. "It's simply a matter of timing, in which your gynecologist will help, and also luck. You'll have to go on trying."

"We will," Winnie said, then sighed. "But I won't tell 'Ank till termorrer. I need *one* good night's sleep."

Celia did make a brief trip for the company to California in September and she was in Sacramento, by chance standing not far from President Ford, when an attempt was made on the President's life. Only the ineptitude of the woman would-be assassin, who did not understand the firearm she was using, prevented another historic tragedy. Celia was shattered by the experience, and equally horrified to learn of a second assassination attempt, in San Francisco, less than three weeks later.

243

Talking about it at home, with the family gathered for Thanksgiving, she declared, "Some days I think we've become a more violent people, not less." Then rhetorically: "Where do ideas about assassinations start?"

She had not expected an answer, but Bruce supplied one.

"Considering the business you're in, Mom, I'm surprised you don't know that historically they started with drugs, which is what the word 'assassin' means. It's from the Arabic *hashīshī*, or 'hashish-eater,' and in the eleventh to thirteenth centuries an Islamic sect, the Nizārī Ismāʿīlīs, took hashish when committing acts of religious terrorism."

Celia said irritably, "If I don't know, it's because hashish isn't a drug that's used pharmaceutically."

"It was once," Bruce answered calmly. "And not so long ago, either. Psychiatrists used it against amnesia, but it didn't work and they stopped."

"I'll be damned!" Andrew said, while Lisa regarded her brother with a mixture of amusement and awe.

The new year of '76 brought a pleasant interlude in February with the marriage of Juliet Hawthorne to Dwight Goodsmith, the young man Andrew and Celia had met and liked at the Hawthornes' dinner party a year earlier. Dwight, newly graduated from Harvard Law School, was about to begin work in New York City where he and Juliet would live.

The wedding was a large and plush affair with three hundred and fifty guests, Andrew and Celia among them. "After all," Lilian Hawthorne told Celia, "it's the only wedding at which I'll be a bride's mother—at least, I hope so."

Earlier, Lilian had confided her concern that Juliet, who was twenty, should be marrying so young and abandoning college after only two years. But on the day of the wedding Sam and Lilian seemed so radiantly happy that such thoughts had clearly been put away—with good reason, Celia thought. Watching Juliet and Dwight, an intelligent and talented, yet modest, unaffected couple, she was impressed with them and had a conviction that theirs was a marriage which would work.

In May of that year, something of special interest to Celia was the publication of *The Drugging of the Americas*.

244

It was a book which attracted wide attention and cataloged the shameful failure of American and other pharmaceutical firms doing business in Latin America to supply warnings about adverse side effects of their prescription drugs—warnings required by law in more sophisticated countries. Described and documented were the practices which Celia, during her years in international sales, had observed personally and had criticized at Felding-Roth.

What made the book different from routine, acerbic attacks on the industry was the scholarly thoroughness of its author, Dr. Milton Silverman, a pharmacologist and faculty member of the University of California at San Francisco. Dr. Silverman had also testified a short time earlier before a congressional committee which listened to him with respect. In Celia's view it was one more warning that the pharmaceutical business should accept moral obligations as well as legal ones.

She bought a half-dozen copies of the book and sent them to company executives who responded predictably. Typical was Sam Hawthorne who scribbled a memo:

> Basically I share Silverman's views and yours. However, if changes are made there will have to be all-around agreement. No one company can afford to put itself at a disadvantage to all other competitors—especially ourselves at the moment because of our delicate financial condition.

To Celia, Sam's seemed a specious argument, though she did not contest it further, knowing she would not win.

A considerable surprise was the response of Vincent Lord, who sent a friendly note.

> Thanks for the book. I agree there should be changes, but predict our masters will kick and scream against them until forced at pistol point to mend their ways. But keep trying. I'll help when I can.

Increasingly of late, the director of research seemed to have mellowed, Celia thought. She remembered sending him, thirteen years before, a copy of *The Feminine Mystique* which he returned with a curt remark about "rubbish." Or was it, she wondered, because Vince Lord had decided she was now high enough in the company to be useful to him as an ally?

During April, Lisa telephoned home to report excitedly that she

245

would be heading for California in the fall. She had been accepted at Stanford University. Then, in June, Lisa graduated from Emma Willard in a gracious outdoor ceremony which Andrew, Celia and Bruce attended. Over a family dinner in Albany that night Andrew observed, "Today's a high point, but otherwise I predict, worldwide, a dull year."

Almost at once he was proved wrong by a daring Israeli airborne commando raid on Entebbe Airport, Uganda, where more than a hundred hostages were held captive, having been seized by Arab terrorists aided by the treacherous Uganda President Idi Amin. As the free world cheered, delighted to share some upbeat, inspirational news for a change, the Israelis freed the hostages and flew them back to safety.

The dullness did return, however—as Andrew was quick to point out—when, at the Democratic national convention in New York, an obscure Georgia populist, leaning heavily on being a "born-again" Southern Baptist, secured the nomination for President.

Despite the American public's disenchantment, first with Nixon, now with Ford, it seemed unlikely the newcomer could win. In the Felding-Roth cafeteria Celia heard someone ask, "Is it conceivable that the highest office in this world could be held by someone who calls himself Jimmy?"

Yet, at the Morristown corporate headquarters there was little time for thoughts of politics. Most attention was focused on the exciting new drug soon to be released—Montayne.

It was almost two years since Celia had expressed to Sam her doubts and unease about Montayne but, at Sam's urging, had agreed to keep an open mind while studying research and testing data.

In the meantime there had been voluminous material, most of which Celia read. As she did, her conviction grew that Sam was right: pharmaceutical science had made amazing advances in fifteen years, and pregnant women should not be denied a beneficial drug simply because another drug, long ago, had proven harmful.

Equally significant: the testing of Montayne—first in France, subsequently in Denmark, Britain, Spain, Australia, and now in the United States—had clearly been as cautious and complete as human care could make it. Thus, because of authenticated results and her own

246

reading, Celia was not only convinced of the safety of Montayne, but enthusiastic about its usefulness and commercial possibilities.

At home, on several occasions, she attempted to share her knowledge with Andrew, seeking to convert him to her changed opinions. But, uncharacteristically, Andrew appeared to have a closed mind. He always managed to turn their conversation to other matters, making it clear that while wishing to avoid an argument, Montayne was a subject he preferred to hold at arm's length.

In the end Celia gave up, in Andrew's presence keeping her enthusiasm to herself. There would be, she knew, many other outlets for it once Felding-Roth's sales campaign began in earnest.

8

"The important thing all of us in sales must remember and emphasize about Montayne," Celia said into the podium microphone, "is that it is a completely safe drug for pregnant women. More than that, it is *a joyous drug!* Montayne is something which women—plagued by nausea and sickness during pregnancies—have needed, longed for, and deserved for centuries. Now, at last, we of Felding-Roth have become emancipators, freeing American women from their ancient yoke, making each day of pregnancy better, brighter, happier! The drug to *end 'morning sickness' forever* is here! *We have it!*"

There was a spirited burst of handclapping from the audience.

It was October 1976. Celia was in San Francisco at a Felding-Roth regional sales meeting, attended by the company's detail men and women, sales supervisors and regional managers from nine western states, including Alaska and Hawaii. The three-day session was at the Fairmont Hotel on Nob Hill. Celia and several other senior officers of the company were staying at the elegant Stanford Court across the street. Among them was Bill Ingram, once Celia's junior at O-T-C and now, as deputy director of pharmaceutical sales, her principal assistant.

Marketing plans for Montayne were in high gear, and Felding-Roth hoped to have the product on the market by February, now only four months away. Meanwhile it was necessary that those who would be selling Montayne know as much about the drug as possible.

Among the sales force, enthusiasm about the prospects for Montayne was running high, and someone at head office had composed a song to be sung to the tune of "America the Beautiful."

> O beautiful for carefree days,
> For dreams of motherhood,
> For now in safe and simple ways,
> All mornings can be good!
> Montayne, Montayne!
> Montayne, Montayne!
> Prescribed for pregnancy;
> Let's sell it strong, proclaim its joys,
> Its riskless potency!

The words had been sung cheerfully and loudly this morning by the assembled sales people, and would be repeated often over the next two days. Celia, personally, had reservations about the song, but others in sales had argued in its favor, so she agreed to its use, not wanting to dampen buoyant spirits.

As to United States testing programs for the drug, these had been conducted over the preceding year and a half—on animals and five hundred humans—with only the mildest and occasional side effects, none medically significant. The good results were similar to those in other countries where Montayne was already on sale, enormously popular and being praised by prescribing physicians and their women patients.

Following the United States tests, the usual voluminous new drug application had been submitted to FDA's Washington headquarters, with the hope of fast approval.

Unfortunately, that hope had proved in vain. So far, FDA permission to sell the drug as a prescription product had not been given, and this was one of two small clouds now hovering over Felding-Roth's elaborate marketing scheme.

At company headquarters, however, it was considered impossible to halt all preparations until approval was granted; otherwise six

248

months or more of selling and important revenue would be lost. So the decision was made to proceed with manufacturing, preparation of advertising, and warm-up sessions like this one, on the assumption that the FDA green light would be given before the critical deadline.

Sam Hawthorne, Vincent Lord, and others were confident the needed FDA approval would be forthcoming soon. They also noted that one factor working in Felding-Roth's favor was media publicity.

Because of the progress and popularity of Montayne overseas, questions now being asked publicly were: Why was FDA taking so long to decide? Why was American womanhood being denied this beneficial medication when other women elsewhere were using it successfully and safely? The phrase "American drug lag" was once more being bandied around critically, the blame for it directed at the FDA.

One of the pointed questioners was Senator Dennis Donahue, normally a critic of the pharmaceutical industry but now recognizing which side of an issue was the popular one. In response to a reporter's query, he described the FDA's indecision over Montayne as "clearly ridiculous in the circumstances." Donahue's comment was welcomed at Felding-Roth.

The other small cloud was created by Maud Stavely, M.D., chairperson of the New York-based consumer group, Citizens for Safer Medicine.

Dr. Stavely and her CSM were aggressively opposed to American approval of Montayne, arguing that the drug might be unsafe and should be given more prolonged testing. All who would listen were bombarded with this view, which received considerable media coverage.

The basis of the Stavely argument was a civil lawsuit which had been argued several months earlier in the courts of Australia.

A twenty-three-year-old woman living in the Australian Outback near Alice Springs had given birth to a female child. The mother, during pregnancy, had been one of the early users of Montayne. Later, tests showed the baby girl to be mentally deficient, her mind described by doctors as "a blank." Also, the child was unable to make any but the feeblest physical movements, even a year after birth. Examining physicians agreed the child would forever remain a vegetable and would never walk or sit up unaided.

A lawyer hearing of the case persuaded the mother to sue the Australian company that distributed Montayne. The suit went to court and was dismissed. That judgment was appealed to a higher court, which ruled against the plaintiff, upholding the lower-court decision.

During both legal proceedings the evidence seemed overwhelming that Montayne was not responsible for the child's condition. The mother, a person of poor reputation who admitted not knowing who the baby's father was, had been taking other drugs throughout her pregnancy—methaqualone (Quaalude), diazepam (Valium), and several others. She was also a near-alcoholic, a chain smoker and a user of marijuana. An expert medical witness at the jury trial described her body as "a horrible cauldron of antagonistic chemicals from which anything could happen." He and other medical witnesses absolved Montayne from linkage with the baby's defects.

Only an Outback "flying doctor" who had treated the woman during pregnancy and delivered the child at birth testified on the mother's behalf and blamed Montayne, which he himself had prescribed. However, under cross-examination the doctor admitted having no evidence to back his claim, only what he described as "a bloody strong hunch." In light of other, expert testimony, his views were not taken seriously.

Subsequently, an Australian government-sponsored inquiry, where medical and scientific experts again testified, reached the same conclusion as the courts, confirming Montayne to be a safe drug.

The American, Dr. Stavely, a notorious publicity seeker, had no other evidence to support her opposition to Montayne.

Thus, though the Maud Stavely-CSM campaign was regarded at Felding-Roth as a nuisance, it did not represent a major problem.

Now, at the San Francisco sales meeting, after waiting for applause to subside, Celia continued her address.

"Something you may encounter," she cautioned her listeners, "is anxiety about our new drug, Montayne, from people with memories of an older drug, Thalidomide, which had terrible effects on the fetuses of pregnant women, causing them to give birth to deformed babies. I am mentioning this now, bringing it out in the open, so it is a subject we are all prepared for."

There was silence in the hall as the men and women facing Celia listened attentively.

"The differences between Montayne and Thalidomide are many and overwhelming.

"In the first place, Thalidomide was developed some twenty years ago at a time when pharmaceutical research was not as thorough, or safety regulations as informed and rigorous as they are today. Another thing—and contrary to popular belief—Thalidomide was never intended, or used specifically, as a drug for women. It was a general sedative, a sleeping pill.

"And going back to the subject of research, Thalidomide was *not* tried experimentally on a wide range of animals before it was put to human use. *After* the banning of Thalidomide, for example, experiments with animals showed that some breeds of rabbits produced the same deformed fetuses as humans, demonstrating that if those full animal studies had been done, the human tragedies would never have happened."

Celia paused, referring to her notes which she had prepared carefully for this and later occasions.

Still with the same attention focused on her, she said, "Montayne, on the other hand, has had the fullest possible range of tests—including tests on various types of animals, as well as on human volunteers—in five countries, all of which have strict laws affecting drug control. Moreover, in most of those countries Montayne has been used by many thousands of women for well over a year. Let me give you just one example of how thoroughly this research and testing program has been carried out."

Celia described the decision of Laboratoires Gironde-Chimie, the French discoverers of Montayne, to do an additional year of medical testing over and above that required by French law, to be certain of their product's quality.

"Probably no drug ever introduced before," she added, "has been tested more thoroughly for safety."

Following Celia's speech, scientific spokesmen from the company endorsed her words and answered questions from the sales force.

"How did your sales presentation go?" Andrew asked an hour or so later in the comfortable luxury of their suite at the Stanford Court. He had taken a few days off from his practice to accompany Celia westward and, at the same time, visit Lisa, now a freshman at Stanford and living on campus.

"Well enough, I think." Celia kicked off her shoes, stretched tiredly, and put her feet up on a sofa. "In some ways, regional sales meetings are like a traveling road show, so we should get better with each performance." She regarded her husband curiously. "Do you realize that was the first time you've asked me a question about anything to do with the progress of Montayne?"

"Is it?" He tried to sound surprised.

"You know it is. I'd like to know why."

"Maybe it's because you tell me everything, so I've never needed to ask."

"That isn't true," Celia said. "The truth is, you still have reservations, haven't you?"

"Look," Andrew objected, putting aside a newspaper he had been reading when she came in, "I'm not qualified to make judgments about a drug I haven't used. You've a host of scientific people, here and abroad, who know much more than I do. They say Montayne is okay. So . . ." He shrugged.

"But would *you* prescribe it for a patient?"

"I don't have to. Fortunately I'm not an obstetrician or a gynecologist."

"Fortunately?"

"A slip of the tongue." Andrew said impatiently, "Let's talk about something else."

"No," Celia persisted; there was an edge to her voice. "I want to talk about this because it's important to both of us. You always used to say no woman should take any drug during pregnancy. Do you still believe that?"

"Since you ask—yes, I do."

"Isn't it possible," Celia said, "that while you were right once, that view could now be out of date? After all, it's a long time since you began practicing medicine—twenty years—and many things have changed." She remembered something Sam had told her. "Weren't there doctors who opposed anesthesia for pregnant women because they said . . . ?"

Andrew was becoming angry. "I told you I don't want to talk about this."

She snapped back, "But I do!"

"Dammit, Celia! I'm not involved with your Montayne and don't intend to be. I've already admitted I don't have the knowledge—"

"But at St. Bede's you have influence."

"Which I will *not* use—one way or the other—about Montayne."

252

They were glaring at each other when the telephone rang. Celia swung her legs down and reached out to answer.

A woman's voice inquired, "Mrs. Jordan?"

"Yes."

"This is Felding-Roth, Boonton. Hold, please, for Mr. Hawthorne."

Sam came on the line. "Hi, Celia. How is everything going so far?"

"Very well." The positive mood in which she had left the Fairmont session returned. "The presentations have gone smoothly. Everyone in the field is keen, and anxious to begin selling Montayne."

"Great!"

"Of course, the question we're all asking is: How soon will we get FDA approval?"

There was a silence during which Celia sensed Sam hesitating, then he said, "For the moment, this is confidential between you and me. But I can say positively we *will* get FDA permission, and *very* soon."

"May I ask why you're so sure?"

"No."

"Okay." If Sam wanted to be mysterious, Celia thought, that was his privilege, though between the two of them she could see no reason for it. She asked, "Is everything good with Juliet?"

"And with my soon-to-be grandchild?" Sam chuckled. "I'm delighted to say, yes."

Three months ago, Juliet and Dwight Goodsmith had happily announced Juliet's pregnancy. The baby was due in January.

"Give Lilian and Juliet my love," Celia said, "and tell Juliet that with her next pregnancy she'll be able to take Montayne."

"Will do. Thanks, Celia." Sam hung up.

While Celia was on the telephone, Andrew had gone into the bathroom to shower, then dress, prior to a thirty-five-mile drive to Palo Alto where they were due for dinner with Lisa and several newfound Stanford friends.

During the drive and the dinner, which was relaxed and cordial, neither Celia nor Andrew referred to their argument at the hotel. At first there was a coolness between them, but it disappeared as the evening progressed. By that time, also, Celia had decided to leave well alone and not raise the subject of Montayne with her husband again. After all, everyone in the course of a lifetime had occasional mental blind spots and—though it disappointed her—this was clearly one of Andrew's.

253

9

Sam Hawthorne, replacing the telephone after his Boonton–San Francisco conversation with Celia, found himself wishing he had not made the impulsive, positive statement he had concerning FDA approval of Montayne. It was unwise and indiscreet. Why had he done it? Probably for no other reason than the human one of seeking to impress another person—in this case Celia.

He must watch himself, he decided. Especially after his discussion an hour ago with Vincent Lord and the decision they had reached jointly. It was a decision that could have disastrous repercussions if it were found out, though it must not be—*ever*. All the more reason, then, to let the FDA's approval of Montayne, when it happened, seem natural and ordained. As it should have been, and would have been, *except for that arrogant, insufferable, criminal bureaucrat at FDA!*

It was sheer bad luck that the new drug application for Montayne had drawn Dr. Gideon Mace as the reviewer.

Sam Hawthorne had not met Mace, and didn't want to. He had heard more than enough about the man from Vince Lord and others, and about the trouble Mace caused Felding-Roth, first with the unreasonable delay two years ago over Staidpace, and now with Montayne. Why should people like Mace possess the power they had, Sam fumed, and have to be endured by honest businessmen who sought, from the Maces of this world, no more than equal honesty and fairness?

Fortunately, people like Mace were a minority—at FDA a small minority; Sam was certain of that. Just the same, Mace existed. He was currently sitting on the Montayne NDA, using regulations, procedural tactics, to delay it. Therefore a way to circumvent Gideon Mace had had to be found.

Well, they had a way. At least, Felding-Roth had, in the person of Vince Lord.

Originally, when Vince had collected—no, make that *bought*—evidence of criminality by Dr. Mace, purchased it with two thousand dollars of Felding-Roth cash, the voucher for that cash now buried deep in the travel expense account where auditors or the IRS would never find it . . . at that time Sam had been angry, critical of Vince, and shocked at the thought that the material might ever be used in the way which Vince envisaged.

But not now. The existing situation affecting Montayne was too critical, too important, for that kind of scruples anymore. And *that* was another cause for anger. Anger because criminals like Mace begat criminality in others—in this case, in Sam and Vincent Lord—who had to use those same low-grade tactics for reasonable self-defense. *Damn Mace!*

Still soliloquizing silently, in the quietness of his office, Sam told himself: A penalty you paid for appointment to the top job in any large company was having to make unpalatable decisions authorizing actions which, if they happened elsewhere or in a vacuum, you would consider unethical and disapprove of. But when you shouldered responsibilities involving so many people, all of them dependent on you—shareholders, directors, executive colleagues, employees, distributors, retailers, customers—it was necessary at times to swallow hard and do what was needed, however tough, unpleasant or repugnant it might seem.

Sam had just done that, an hour ago, in okaying a proposal by Vincent Lord to threaten Dr. Gideon Mace with exposure and therefore criminal charges if he failed to expedite the approval of Montayne.

Blackmail. No point in mincing words or hiding behind euphemisms. It would be blackmail, which was criminal too.

Vince had laid his plan bluntly in front of Sam. Equally bluntly Vince declared, "If we don't make use of what we have, putting pressure on Mace, you can forget any idea of marketing Montayne in February, and maybe for another year."

Sam had asked, "Could it really be that long—a year?"

"Easily, and more. Mace has only to ask for a repeat of—"

Lord stopped as Sam waved him to silence, canceling an unnecessary question, remembering how Mace had delayed Staidpace for longer than a year.

"There was a time," Sam reminded the research director, "when you talked of doing what you're proposing without involving me."

"I know I did," Lord said, "but then you insisted on knowing where that two thousand dollars went, and after that I changed my mind. I'll be taking a risk and I don't see why I should take it alone. I'll still handle the frontline attack, the confrontation with Mace. But I want you to know about it, and approve."

"You're not suggesting we have anything in writing?"

Lord shook his head negatively. "That's another chance I'll take. If it came to a showdown, you could deny this conversation ever happened."

It was then Sam realized that what Vince really wanted was not to be lonely, not to be the only one to know what he was going to do. Sam understood that. Loneliness was something else you experienced at the top, or near the top, and Vince was simply sharing his.

"All right," Sam said. "Much as I dislike myself for it, I approve. Go ahead. Do what we have to." He added facetiously, "I assume you're not wired for sound."

"If I were," Lord answered, "I'd incriminate myself as well as you."

When the research director was on his way out, Sam called after him. "Vince!"

Lord turned. "Yes?"

"Thanks," Sam said. "Just thanks, that's all."

So all that was necessary now, Sam reasoned, was to wait. Wait, just briefly, with confidence that FDA's approval of Montayne would come quickly, inevitably, soon.

Since their previous encounter, Vincent Lord was aware, some changes had occurred in Dr. Gideon Mace. The FDA official looked older, which he was, but also better than before, which was surprising. His face was less red, the nose veins seemed less prominent. He had shed the shabby suit and bought a new one, also new glasses, so he no longer squinted. His manner seemed easier and, while still not friendly, was certainly less brusque and not aggressive. Perhaps one reason for the changes—a reason Vincent Lord had learned about through his contacts at the agency—was that Mace had stopped drinking and joined Alcoholics Anonymous.

Apart from Mace personally, other things were the same or worse. The FDA Washington headquarters was the same impersonal, shabby beehive. In the cupboardlike office where Mace was seated at his desk there was more paper than ever; it was piled high everywhere, like a rising flood tide. Even crossing the floor one had to step around paper and files, put there for lack of any other space.

Gesturing about him, Lord asked, "Is our Montayne NDA here somewhere?"

"Parts of it," Mace said. "I haven't room for it all. Montayne is what you've come about, I suppose."

"Yes," Lord acknowledged. He was seated, facing the doctor, and even now hoping there might be no need to use the photostatic copies that were in a briefcase at his feet.

"I'm genuinely worried about that Australian case." Again in contrast to the past, Mace's tone was reasonable. "You know the one I mean?"

Lord nodded. "The woman in the Outback. Yes, the case went to court where it was thrown out, and there was also a government inquiry. Both times the accusations were checked out thoroughly, and Montayne absolved."

"I've read all that stuff," Mace said, "but I want more details. I've written to Australia for them, and when they come I may have still more questions."

Lord protested, "But that could take months!"

"Even if it does, I'll be doing what I'm here for."

Lord made one last try. "When you held up our NDA for Staidpace, I assured you it was a good drug, free from adverse side effects and so —despite the unnecessary delay—it was. Now I'm promising you, based on my reputation as a research scientist, exactly the same is true of Montayne."

Mace said stolidly, "It's your opinion, not mine, that the Staidpace delay was unnecessary. In any case, that has nothing to do with Montayne."

"In a way it has," Lord said, knowing he now had no alternative, glancing behind him to be sure the outer door was closed. "It has, because I think what you are doing to us at Felding-Roth relates not to our latest NDA, but to your own state of mind. You have a lot of personal problems which are getting the better of you, creating unfair prejudices, clouding your judgment. Some of those personal problems have come to my company's attention."

Mace bridled and his voice sharpened. "What the *hell* are you talking about?"

257

"This," Lord said. He had the briefcase open and extracted papers. "These are brokerage transaction slips, canceled checks, bank statements, and other items which show you made over sixteen thousand dollars illegal profit, utilizing confidential FDA information concerning two generic drug companies, Binvus Products and Minto Labs."

Lord added the dozen sheets or so to the paper clutter already on Mace's desk. "I think you should look these over carefully. I'm aware you've seen them all before, but it may be news to you that someone else has copies. And by the way, these are copies of copies. Keeping or destroying them will do no good."

It was obvious that Mace recognized instantly the top item—one of the brokerage transaction slips. His hands were shaking as he picked it up, then followed with the other papers, inspecting them one by one and clearly with equal recognition. As he progressed, his face went ashen and his mouth worked spasmodically. Lord wondered if Mace would have a stroke or heart attack on the spot. But instead, putting the papers down, Mace asked in a whisper, "Where did you get these?"

"That isn't important," Lord answered briskly. "What matters is: we have them and are considering making them available to the Attorney General and probably the press. In that event, of course, there will be an inquiry, and if you've been involved in more incidents of the same kind, those will come out too."

From Mace's increasingly frightened expression, Lord knew his last random shot had hit home. There *were* more incidents. Now each of them knew it.

Lord remembered something he had once said to Sam Hawthorne in foreseeing what was happening now. *"When the time comes, let me do the dirty work."* Then he had added silently, *I might even enjoy it.* Well, now that it was happening, Lord realized, he *was* enjoying it. It gave him pleasure to wield power over Mace, to behold an adversary so expert in dishing out humiliation now experiencing the same, and suffering and squirming.

"You'll go to jail, of course," Lord pointed out, "and I imagine there'll be a big fine which should clean you out financially."

Mace said desperately, "This is blackmail. You could be . . ." His voice was nervous, thin and reedy. Lord roughly cut him off.

"Forget that! There are plenty of ways of handling this so our company's involvement isn't known, and there are no witnesses here, just you and me." Lord reached over, gathered up the papers he had shown to Mace, and returned them to his briefcase. He had remembered, just in time, that his own fingerprints were on them; no sense in taking a chance on leaving evidence behind.

Mace was a broken man. Lord saw with disgust there was spittle on the other man's lips which bubbled as he asked feebly, "What do you want?"

"I think you know," Lord said. "I guess you could sum up what we would like as 'an attitude of reasonableness.'"

A despairing whisper. "You want that drug approved. Montayne."

Lord remained silent.

"Listen," Mace pleaded, half sobbing now, "I meant it when I said there *is* a problem . . . that Australian case, the doubts about Montayne . . . I truly believe there may be something there . . . you ought to . . ."

Lord said contemptuously, "We've already talked about it. Better people than you have assured us the Australian case was meaningless."

Again a silence.

"If it happens . . . the approval?"

"In certain circumstances," Lord said carefully, "the papers from which the copies I have shown you were made would not be given to the Attorney General or the press. Instead they would be handed over to you with a guarantee that, to the best of our knowledge, no other copies exist."

"How could I be sure?"

"On that, you would have to take my word."

Mace was attempting to recover; there was savage hatred in his eyes. "What's your word worth, you *bastard?*"

"Forgive my mentioning it," Vincent Lord said calmly, "but you're in no position to call anybody names."

It took two weeks. Even with Gideon Mace impelling them, the wheels of bureaucracy needed time to turn. But at the end of that time, approval of Montayne was a *fait accompli*. The drug could be prescribed and sold, with FDA approval, throughout the United States.

At Felding-Roth there was joy that the company's February marketing target would now be met.

259

Taking no chances on the mail or another messenger, Vincent Lord traveled to Washington and delivered the incriminating papers personally to Dr. Mace.

Lord had kept his word. All additional copies were destroyed.

In the privacy of Mace's office, with both men standing, a minimum of words passed between them.

"This is what was promised." Lord proffered a brown manila envelope.

Mace accepted the envelope, inspected its contents, then turned his eyes toward Lord. In a voice dripping hatred, he said, "You and your company now have an enemy at FDA. I give you my warning: someday you'll regret this."

Lord shrugged, made no reply, and left.

10

In November, on a Friday afternoon, Celia visited Dr. Maud Stavely at the New York headquarters of Citizens for Safer Medicine.

The visit was an impulse decision. Celia was in Manhattan anyway, with two hours free between appointments, when she decided to satisfy her curiosity about an adversary she had never met. She did not telephone in advance, knowing that if she did, Stavely would almost certainly refuse to see her. That kind of turndown had been experienced by others in the pharmaceutical business.

Celia remembered something which Lorne Eagledon, president of the Pharmaceutical Manufacturers Association in Washington, had told her not long before. Eagledon, genial and easygoing, had been a government lawyer before his present trade association job.

"As head of PMA, representing all the major drug companies," he said, "I like to keep contact with consumer groups. Sure, we oppose each other, but sometimes they have useful things to say, and our industry should listen. That's why I invite Ralph Nader to lunch twice a year. True, Ralph and I don't have much common ground, but we talk, and listen to each other's viewpoints, which is a civilized thing to do. But when I invited Maud Stavely to have lunch for the same reason—oh, boy!"

With prompting from Celia, the PMA chief had continued, "Well, Dr. Stavely informed me she had plenty to do in her full-time fight against a thoroughly bad, immoral industry—ours—without wasting her valuable time on a big-business lackey with unacceptable opinions—me. Furthermore, she said never mind lunch—she would choke on a chocolate bar paid for with drug firms' tainted money." Eagledon had laughed. "So we never met, which I regret."

A dreary rain was falling as Celia's taxi stopped at a dingy six-story building on Thirty-seventh Street near Seventh Avenue. The building's main floor was occupied by a plumbing supplies store whose front window had been broken, then patched with tape. From a dowdy hallway with peeling paint, a tiny, arthritic elevator grumbled its way to the top floor and CSM.

As Celia left the elevator she faced an open door and, in a small room beyond, an elderly white-haired woman seated at a battered metal desk. A card facing outward read: *Volunteer: Mrs. O. Thom.* The woman had been pecking at an Underwood typewriter circa 1950. Looking up as Celia entered, she announced, "I keep telling them I won't do any more work here unless this wretched machine is fixed. It's the capital 'I' that never works. How can you write to people without an 'I'?"

Celia said helpfully, "You could try using 'we' every time instead."

Mrs. O. Thom snapped, "What about this letter, then? It's supposed to go to Idaho. Should I rename the state Wedaho?"

"I do see your problem," Celia said. "I wish I could help. Is Dr. Stavely in?"

"Yes, she's in. Who are you?"

"Oh, just someone interested in your organization. I'd like to talk to her."

Mrs. Thom looked as if she would ask more questions, then changed her mind. Getting up, she walked through another doorway and out of sight. While she was away, Celia caught glimpses of several other people working in adjoining rooms. There was a sense of busy activity, including the sounds of another typewriter clattering and brisk phone conversations. Closer to hand, brochures and leaflets, some prepared for mailing, were piled high. A stack of incoming mail awaited opening. Judging by appearances, though, CSM was not burdened with excess cash. The office furnishings, Celia thought, were either someone else's discards or had been bought at a junk dealer's. Long ago, the floors were carpeted, but now the carpeting was worn so thin it had almost disappeared, and in places bare boards were visible through holes. As in the downstairs lobby, what was left of the paint was peeling.

Mrs. Thom returned. "All right. Go in there." She pointed to a doorway. With murmured thanks, Celia did so.

The room she entered was as shabby as the offices outside.

"Yes, what is it?" Dr. Maud Stavely, seated at another dented desk, looked up from a paper she was reading as her visitor entered.

After her impression of these surroundings, coupled with what she had heard about the person she was facing, Celia was surprised to see an attractive, auburn-haired woman, slim and well groomed, with carefully manicured hands, and probably in her early forties. The voice, though incisive and impatient, was cultured, with a slight New England accent. The clothes she had on—a maroon wool skirt and a pink tailored blouse—were inexpensive, yet worn stylishly. The eyes —Stavely's strongest single feature—were blue, direct, penetrating, and conveyed to Celia that an answer to the question was overdue.

"I'm a pharmaceutical executive," Celia said. "I apologize for barging in, but I wanted to meet you."

There was several seconds' silence. The eyes boring into her had hardened, Celia thought, and were making an appraisal.

"I suppose you're Jordan."

"Yes." Celia was surprised. "How did you know?"

"I've heard of you. There aren't many women executives in that rotten industry, and certainly no one else who has sold out decent womanhood as much as you."

Celia said mildly, "What makes you so sure I've—as you put it— sold out?"

"Because you wouldn't work in the selling end of the drug business if you hadn't."

"I worked originally as a chemist," Celia pointed out. "Then, like others, I moved up through our company."

"None of that interests me. Why have you come here?"

Celia tried countering antagonism with a smile. "I meant what I said about wanting to meet you. I had an idea we might talk, hear each other's opinions. Even if we disagree, we could both gain something."

The friendliness achieved nothing. The other woman inquired coldly, "Gain what?"

Celia shrugged. "I suppose, some understanding. But never mind. Obviously it wasn't a good idea." She turned away, prepared to go, unwilling to accept further rudeness.

"What do you wish to know?"

The words were a shade less hostile. Celia hesitated, uncertain whether to go or stay.

Stavely pointed to a chair. "You're here, so sit down. I'll give you ten minutes, then I've other things to do."

In different circumstances Celia would have expressed herself forcefully, but curiosity caused her to remain low-key. "One thing I'd like to know is why you hate the pharmaceutical industry so much."

For the first time Maud Stavely permitted herself a faint smile, though it quickly disappeared. "I said ten minutes, not ten hours."

"Why not make a start in the time we have?"

"Very well. The most immoral segment of your business is precisely the one *you* are involved in—sales. Your company and all the others oversell—grossly, cynically, wickedly. You take what are essentially reasonable drugs, though with limited medical uses, then through massive, ruthless sales campaigns have those drugs prescribed for countless people who either don't need, can't afford, or shouldn't have them—sometimes all three."

" 'Immoral' and those others are strong words," Celia said. "No one disputes there's been some overprescribing, but—"

"*Some* overprescribing! Excessive prescribing is a *norm*. But it's a norm you people work for, deliberately plan for, and most likely pray for! If you want an example, consider Valium and the others like it—probably the most overused, unnecessarily prescribed family of drugs in history. And because of overblown sales campaigns, launched because of insatiable greed by companies like yours, those drugs have left behind a trail of addicts, desperate people, suicides . . ."

"Also a good many," Celia said, "who really needed the drugs and benefited from them."

"A *minority*," the other woman insisted, "who could still have had them, but without the saturation advertising and sales promotion which brainwashed physicians into believing the Valium types were a panacea for everything. I *know*. I was one of the brainwashed doctors—until I saw how *awful* the drug scene was, and gave up private practice to start this organization."

Celia said tentatively, "I know that you're an M.D."

"Yes, and an internist. I wâs trained to keep people healthy and save lives, which I'm still doing here, though on a scale much larger than before." Stavely waved a hand to dismiss herself as subject. "Come back to Valium. It represents another way in which your business is unprincipled."

"I'm listening," Celia said. "Not agreeing, but listening."

"No one needed all the different variants of Valium which competing drug firms brought out. There is *no benefit, no possible advantage* in having five different Valiums around. Yet *after* Valium was a huge financial success, other companies devoted months, even years, of research—precious scientific time, enormous sums of money—not with the aim of discovering something new and beneficial, but simply to have a Valium of their own under a different name. So they produced other Valiums—by shifting molecules around, making their drugs just different enough so they could be patented and sold profitably—"

Celia said impatiently, "Everybody knows there are 'me-too' drugs, perhaps more than there should be. But they do sometimes lead to new discoveries; also they keep pharmaceutical companies— which society needs—solvent between other big breakthroughs."

"Oh, my God!" Dr. Stavely put a hand to her head in an incredulous gesture. "Do you really believe that sophomoric argument? When it isn't just about Valium. When every major drug that one company brings out is copied by the others. *That's* why pharmaceutical research should be directed and controlled by government, though paid for by the drug firms."

"Now *I* can't believe you're serious," Celia said. "You'd want drug research controlled by the same politicians who wrecked Social Security, fill pork barrels, can't balance a budget, and would sell their mothers for votes. Why, under that arrangement penicillin wouldn't be on the market yet! Okay, let's admit capitalist free enterprise is imperfect, but it's a country-mile better, *and* more ethical, than *that.*"

Stavely went on as if she hadn't heard. "Your precious industry had to be beaten over the head with regulations before it would publish proper warnings about the *dangers* of its drugs. Even now, it fights for *minimum* warnings and usually wins. Not only that, after a new drug goes on sale, adverse effects are hidden—conveniently, callously, buried in company files."

Celia protested, "That's nonsense! We're required by law to report adverse effects to FDA. Oh, there may have been a few instances where someone neglected . . ."

"There have been *plenty* of instances which this organization knows about, and I'll bet a lot more that we don't. Illegal withholdings of information. But is it ever possible to get a prosecution launched by the Justice Department? Not when you people have that army of paid lobbyists working on Capitol Hill . . ."

Well, Celia thought, she had come here asking for opinions and she was getting them. While she continued listening, occasionally interjecting, the promised ten minutes lengthened to an hour.

At one point Stavely mentioned a recent controversy which Celia knew about. A pharmaceutical company (not Felding-Roth) had experienced problems with one of its products, an intravenous fluid used in hospitals. Some bottles containing the supposedly sterile I.V. liquid had been found to have faulty caps, permitting the entry of bacteria which, in turn, caused septicemia—a blood disorder—now blamed for several patient deaths.

The dilemma was: the number of problem bottles was known to be small, and it was possible that all affected ones had now been found; also there would be no more, since the manufacturing problem had been discovered and corrected. Meanwhile, to place a ban on the entire supply of I.V. fluid in hospital inventories would cause acute shortages and conceivably more deaths than the original problem. The issue had been debated back and forth for several weeks between the manufacturer, FDA, and hospitals. Dr. Stavely criticized what she saw as "a disgraceful example of a drug company's dragging its feet while refusing to recall a dangerous product."

"I happen to know a little about that," Celia said, "and it's something which everyone concerned has tried to solve. Just this morning, though, I heard that FDA has decided to ban any more use of the existing I.V. fluid supplies. They're preparing notifications over the weekend, and the decision will be announced at a press conference Monday morning."

Stavely looked at her visitor sharply. "Are you certain of that?"

265

"Absolutely." The information had come from an officer of the company concerned, whom Celia knew to be reliable.

Stavely made a note on a desk pad and their exchange continued. Finally they came to Montayne.

"Even now," Stavely said, "Citizens for Safer Medicine will do everything it can to stop that inadequately tested drug going on the market."

Celia had become tired of the one-sided harangue and snapped, "To call Montayne inadequately tested is ridiculous! Besides, we already have FDA approval."

"In the public interest, that approval *must* be withdrawn."

"Why?"

"There was a case in Australia—"

Celia said wearily, "We know about the Australian case." She went on to explain how medical experts had refuted the allegations made in court and, both there and at the Australian government hearing, had given Montayne a clean bill.

"I don't agree with those experts," Stavely said. "Have you read the transcript of the trial?"

"I've read reports that have dealt with it thoroughly."

"I didn't ask that. I asked if you had read the trial transcript."

Celia admitted, "No."

"Then *read it!* And do not presume to discuss Montayne until you have."

Celia sighed. "I don't believe any more discussion will get you and me anywhere."

"If you recall, that's what I told you in the beginning." For the second time there was a thin, faint smile below the other woman's piercing eyes.

Celia nodded. "And you were right. Not about much else, but certainly about that."

Dr. Stavely had already gone back to the paper she had been reading when Celia came in. She glanced up. "Good afternoon, Jordan."

"Good afternoon," Celia said, and went out through the dismal offices to the equally dismal street outside.

Later in the afternoon, driving herself back from Manhattan to Morristown, Celia reflected on the nature of Dr. Stavely.

266

Certainly Stavely was dedicated but also, to an extent, obsessed. It was equally clear that she was lacking in a sense of humor, unable to regard herself with less than total seriousness. Celia had met such people before; it was always hard to involve them in a thoughtful, objective conversation. They were so accustomed to thinking in black-and-white, antagonistic terms that they found it impossible to switch antagonism off and think in the shades of gray where much of life was lived.

On the other hand, the CSM chairperson was clearly well informed, articulate, well organized, and had a keen, possibly brilliant mind. Her medical qualifications gave her stature and an automatic right to be heard on the subject of prescription drugs. Some of her views, too, were not all that far removed from Celia's, who remembered, fourteen years ago, describing "me-too" drugs and "molecular roulette" in much the same way as Stavely. It was Sam Hawthorne who, at that earlier time, had offered the arguments in response which Celia had used this afternoon. And despite using them, she was still not wholly convinced they were valid.

But Stavely did become unbalanced when emphasizing the pharmaceutical industry's negative aspects while ignoring the many positive, humanitarian contributions to science and health the industry provided. Celia had once heard the United States drug industry described as "a national treasure," and believed the description was, on the whole true. There was also Stavely's naïve and absurd contention that drug research should be government controlled, and her gross misinformation and prejudice about Montayne.

But all in all, Stavely and CSM were formidable opponents, neither to be ignored nor to be taken lightly.

One thing Stavely had caught her out in, Celia thought ruefully, was the fact that Celia had not read the transcript of the Australian trial involving Montayne. Next week she intended to correct that omission.

Still later that day, at dinner, Celia described her CSM experience and views to Andrew and he, as usual, had some wisdom to contribute.

"You may not find those activist people—Maud Stavely, Sidney Wolfe, Ralph Nader and the others—easy to live with, and at times you may detest them," Andrew said. "But you need them, your industry needs them, just the way General Motors and the other auto companies needed Nader before he alighted on the scene. Nader

267

helped make automobiles—for all of us—better and safer because of his needling and I, for one, am grateful. Now, Stavely and Wolfe are keeping you and your people on your toes."

"I admit it." Celia sighed. "But if only they were all more moderate and reasonable!"

Andrew shook his head. "If they were that, they wouldn't be successful activists. Another thing—when *they're* ruthless and unethical, as they can be sometimes, you should ask yourself: where did they learn to be that way? The answer is: from companies like yours, my dear, because, when no one was watching them, ruthless and unethical is the way they were."

Celia would have appreciated Andrew's last remark more if she had witnessed a scene at the Citizens for Safer Medicine offices a few minutes after she left on Friday afternoon.

Summoning an assistant, Dr. Stavely asked, "Has that woman who was with me gone?"

When the answer was yes, Stavely instructed the young man, "I want a press conference called for tomorrow morning—as early as you can arrange it. You will say that the subject is an urgent, life-and-death matter affecting hospitals and patients. Make sure you get the television networks and press wire services. There'll be a news release to be issued at the same time, which I'm going to write now. Someone will have to work tonight to . . ."

The brisk, efficient instructions continued, and at 10 A.M. next morning the press conference began.

Facing reporters, and on camera, Dr. Stavely described the I.V. fluid problem she had discussed with Celia the preceding day—the bacteria-contaminated bottles and the resultant septicemia, believed responsible for several deaths. What the CSM leader did *not* mention was either Celia or the information Celia had given her, namely that the FDA had already decided to forbid further use of all existing I.V. fluid supplies from the company concerned, and that an announcement to that effect would be made on Monday.

Instead, Stavely declared, "Citizens for Safer Medicine deplores the inaction both of the Food and Drug Administration and the manufacturer of this potentially deadly material. Further, we demand—yes, *demand!*—that all supplies of this I.V. fluid be banned from use and recalled . . ."

268

The effect was immediate. The major TV networks carried the story on their evening national news, while next day's Sunday newspapers gave it prominence, in many cases using an Associated Press photo of Stavely in action. Thus on Monday, when FDA delivered its announcement, most reporters—not bothering to check—began their stories, "Today, responding swiftly to a demand by Dr. Maud Stavely and her Citizens for Safer Medicine, the FDA announced a ban on further use by hospitals of . . ."

It was a triumphal *coup d'éclat* for CSM and, soon afterward, was used prominently in a mailed brochure appealing for donations.

Celia, who followed the sequence of events with some embarrassment, kept the knowledge of her own involvement to herself. She had learned a lesson. She had, she realized, been foolishly indiscreet, and then had been made use of by a master tactician.

11

To Celia's surprise there was not, anywhere at Felding-Roth headquarters, a trial transcript of the Australian court case which had involved Montayne. Nor could the company's legal department locate one in the United States. There were plenty of reports that quoted it, but now Celia wanted to read the proceedings in their entirety. Although, obviously, Maud Stavely had a copy, Celia felt disinclined to ask Citizens for Safer Medicine to lend it; she therefore instructed the legal department to cable a correspondent law firm in Australia and have one sent by air.

Meanwhile there were plenty of other things to do. The promotional program that would launch Montayne was now proceeding at a frantic tempo as the February deadline neared. Celia, aided by her deputy, Bill Ingram, was responsible for the several million dollars spent already; still more money was allocated for the months ahead.

Elaborate advertising—expensive four-page multicolor inserts—was appearing in a profusion of medical magazines, while an avalanche of direct mail was going out to the nation's physicians and pharmacists. Among promotional items being sent was a cassette tape—on one side, a recording of the beautiful Brahms "Wiegenlied" (Lullaby), on the other, a clinical description of Montayne. Backing up the advertising and direct mail, the company's detail men and women were delivering thousands of sample packages of Montayne to doctors, at the same time dropping on their desks golf tees and ball markers imprinted with "Montayne."

At all levels of the company, as with any new drug launching, there was a mix of excitement, circus, nervousness and hope.

Also creating hope, in an even wider dimension, was some news from the Felding-Roth Research Institute in Britain. There, it seemed, Martin Peat-Smith's scientific team had successfully broken through the technical barrier which had baffled them for so long. Complete details were lacking—Martin's report had been brief and in general terms only—but it appeared the now demolished barrier was the one of which Dr. Rao Sastri had said, when talking with Celia eighteen months earlier, "There are no techniques to take us further . . . possibly in ten years from now . . ."

Celia was delighted to learn that, in this specific at least, Sastri had been wrong and Martin right.

What *was* known, via a letter from Nigel Bentley, the Harlow administrator, was that the British technical achievement involved purification of a brain peptide mixture obtained from rats, and maze tests on rats had shown it to be effective in improving the memories of older animals. More experimental work was proceeding.

Clearly, while a medication to improve human memory was an unknown number of years away, it was much more of a possibility than at any previous time.

The news was timely in that it forestalled the latest attempt, by some members of the board, to close the Harlow institute—again because of high costs and an absence of results. Now, with some positive results, Harlow and the mental aging project appeared safe for the time being.

This, too, pleased Celia, who felt happier in having recommended against closure of Harlow a year and a half earlier.

In mid-December the Australian trial transcript for which Celia had asked arrived on her desk. It was a bulky typewritten volume, several hundred pages long. By then, however, the pressures on Celia were such that she was obliged to put it aside for later reading. The transcript still had not been read by early January, when another event occurred which was totally unexpected and seemed likely to push her reading even farther into the future.

Now that President-elect Carter had surprised the world by securing the White House tenancy for the next four years, outriders for the new administration were urgently recruiting candidates for the many government posts which Republicans would soon vacate. Among those recruited was Felding-Roth's corporate vice president for sales and merchandising, Xavier Rivkin.

Xav Rivkin, a lifelong Democrat and more recently an ardent Carter supporter, had given time and money in the election campaign; he also knew the new President, having served with him in the Navy. From all this, a reward now arrived—the offer of a post as assistant secretary in the Department of Commerce.

Within Felding-Roth, news of the offer was at first kept secret, as was the fact that Xav wanted to accept. Sam Hawthorne and a few members of the board, between whom the matter was discussed privately, believed he should. There was an awareness that it would do the company no harm to have a friend in Washington at Commerce. Quietly, a special and generous early pension arrangement was made, with Rivkin due to leave soon after the January 20 presidential inauguration.

In the second week of January, Sam sent for Celia and informed her of the Rivkin arrangements, of which she had not heard previously but which would be common knowledge in a day or two.

"Quite frankly," he said, "no one, including me, expected this to happen so soon but when Xav leaves, you'll move up to be vice president of sales and merchandising. I've had discussions with the same members of the board who approved the arrangements about Xav, and we realize this has happened at an awkward time, with Montayne about to—" Sam stopped. "Is something wrong?"

"Not really," Celia said. They had been standing, in his office, and she asked, "Do you mind if I sit down?"

"Of course. Please do." He waved her to a chair.

"And give me a minute to get my gears engaged." Her voice was

271

huskier than usual. "You may not realize it, but you did just drop a thunderbolt."

Sam looked contrite. "Oh, hell, I'm sorry! I should have made this more of an occasion. Some days I operate in such a damned hurry that—"

Celia said, "This way is fine. In fact any way is fine. You were saying about Montayne . . ."

But the words were coming from a part of herself that was detached. Her mind whirling, she was remembering an occasion seventeen years earlier when the then vice president of sales, Irv Gregson, now long departed, had ordered her angrily from the company's New York sales convention while an audience of hundreds watched . . . and Sam had saved her—from the vice president and all the others—and now it was Sam who . . . Dammit! I'm not going to cry, she told herself. But she did, a little, and looked up to see Sam holding out a handkerchief and smiling.

"You earned it, Celia," he said gently. "All on your own, every step of the way, and what I should have said sooner is—congratulations! I told Lilian at breakfast and she's as pleased as I am; she said to tell you we'll all get together soon."

"Thank you." She took the handkerchief, wiped her eyes, then said matter-of-factly, "Please thank Lilian; and I thank you too, Sam. Now about Montayne."

"Well," he explained, "because you've been so close to the plans for launching Montayne, I and those board members I spoke of would like you to see them through, even while you're taking over the bigger responsibility. It will mean a heavy load on you . . ."

Celia assured him, "That won't be a problem. And I agree about Montayne."

"At the same time," Sam pointed out, "you should think about a successor as director of pharmaceutical sales."

"Bill Ingram," Celia said without hesitation. "He's good and he's ready. He's also been working on Montayne."

The hitching-your-wagon-to-someone-else's-star principle, she thought, just as she had described it to Andrew on their honeymoon —also long ago. Celia had followed Sam upward, and how successfully her plan had worked! Now Bill had followed Celia; and who, she wondered, had already attached themselves to Bill?

With an effort—her mind for the moment split in two—she concluded her discussion with Sam.

272

That evening, when Celia told Andrew of her impending promotion, he hugged her and said, "I'm proud of you! But then I always have been."

"Most of the time," she corrected him. "There were moments when you weren't."

He grimaced. "That's all behind us." Then, with a brief, "Excuse me," he went to the kitchen, returning moments later with a bottle of Schramsberg champagne. Winnie March followed, beaming, with glasses on a tray.

Andrew announced, "Winnie and I are going to drink to you. You can join us if you like."

When the glasses were filled, Andrew raised his. "To you, my dearest love! To everything you are, have been, and will be."

"Me too, Mrs. Jordan," Winnie said. "God bless you!"

Winnie sipped her champagne, then looked at the glass and hesitated. "I'm not sure I should drink the rest of this?"

Celia asked, "Whyever not?"

"Well . . . it may not be good for the baby." With a glance at Andrew, Winnie blushed, then giggled. "I just found out I'm preggers—an' after all this time."

Celia ran to embrace her. "Winnie, that's *wonderful* news! Much more important than mine!"

"We're happy for you, Winnie," Andrew said. He took the champagne glass from her. "You're right. You should do without this stuff now. We'll open another bottle when your baby's here."

Later, when Celia and Andrew were getting ready for bed, Celia said tiredly, "It's been quite a day."

"A joyous day all around," Andrew pronounced. "I hope everything stays that way. No reason why it shouldn't."

He was wrong.

The first hint of bad news came precisely a week later.

Bill Ingram, still boyish despite the passage of years, came into Celia's office, which would soon be his. Running a hand through his red hair, unruly as ever, he said, "I thought you should see this, even though I don't believe it's important. A friend in Paris sent it."

"This" was a newspaper clipping.

273

"It's a news item from *France-Soir*," Ingram explained. "How's your French?"

"Good enough so I can understand."

As Celia took the paper and began reading, she experienced a sudden sense of chill and premonition, felt a physical shiver as if her heart had skipped a beat.

The news story was brief.

A woman in a small French town, Nouzonville, near the Belgian border, had given birth to a female child, now one year old. Doctors had recently diagnosed the baby girl as having a central nervous system disorder which permanently precluded any normal movement of the limbs; also, tests showed a lack of any brain development. No possible treatment was foreseen. The child was—in the terrible descriptive term—a vegetable. The examining doctors expected her to remain one.

During pregnancy the mother had taken Montayne. Now, she and others in her family were blaming the drug for the baby's birth defects. There was nothing in the news item to indicate whether or not this view was shared by doctors.

The *France-Soir* report concluded with a cryptic sentence: *Un autre cas en Espagne, apparemment identique, a été signalé.*

Celia stood silent, meditating, weighing the significance of what she had just read.

. . . another case, apparently identical, in Spain.

"Just as I said," Bill Ingram assured her, "I don't think there's any reason we should get concerned. After all, *France-Soir* is known for sensational reporting. It's not as if it was printed in *Le Monde.*"

Celia did not reply. *First Australia. Now France and Spain.*

All the same, common sense told her Bill was right. There *was* no reason for concern. She reminded herself of her own convictions about Montayne, the painstaking French research, the multicountry, lengthy testing, assurances sought after and obtained, Montayne's remarkable record of safety. No cause for concern, *of course.*

And yet . . .

She said decisively, "Bill, I want you to find out, as quickly as possible, everything there is to know about those two cases, then report back to me." She touched the French news clipping, then put it on her desk. "I'll keep this."

"Okay, if it's what you want." Ingram glanced at his watch. "I'll telephone Gironde-Chimie. There's still time today, and I have the name of one of their guys I've spoken to before. But I still don't think—"

"Do it," Celia said. "Do it *now!*"

Bill reported back cheerfully an hour later.

"Not to worry!" he pronounced. "I've had a long talk with my friend at Gironde-Chimie. He knew all about the two cases mentioned by *France-Soir;* he says they've been investigated thoroughly and there is no cause for alarm, or even doubts. The company sent a medical-scientific team to Nouzonville, and flew the same people to Spain to look into the incident there."

Celia asked, "Did he give you more details?"

"Yes." Bill consulted a page of notes he had been carrying. "Incidentally, both cases seem remarkably similar to that Australian one which turned out to be a phony. You remember?"

"I know about the Australian report."

"Well, both women—the mothers of the babies born with CNS disorders—were taking a hodgepodge of other drugs and large amounts of alcohol throughout their pregnancies. Also, in the case of the French birth there's a history of mongolism in the family, while in Spain the baby's father, and *his* father, are epileptics."

"But both mothers *were* taking Montayne?"

"That's true. And my French contact—his name is Jacques Saint-Jean, with a Ph.D. in chemistry—told me Gironde-Chimie was enormously concerned at first, just as you were. As he pointed out, their company has as much at stake as Felding-Roth, maybe more."

Celia said tersely, "Get on with it!"

"Well, the verdict is: Montayne had absolutely nothing to do with the birth deficiencies of either baby. The scientists and doctors, including consultants from outside the company, were unanimous about that. What they *did* find was that some of the other drugs being taken by both women are dangerous in combination and could have . . ."

"I want to read the reports," Celia said. "How soon can we get copies?"

"Both reports are here."

"Here?"

Bill nodded affirmatively. "In this building. Jacques Saint-Jean told me that Vincent Lord has them. They were sent a couple of weeks

275

ago, as part of Gironde-Chimie's policy of keeping everyone informed. Would you like me to ask Vince—"

"No," she said. "I'll get them. That's all, Bill."

"Listen." His voice was troubled. "If you don't mind my saying so, I don't think you should get too exercised about—"

She snapped, unable to control her mounting tension, "I said *that's all!*"

"Why do you want to see them?" Vincent Lord asked Celia.

She was in the research director's office where she had come to ask for the recent reports about Montayne that she and Bill Ingram had discussed.

"Because I think it's important that I read that kind of information for myself, rather than just hear about it secondhand."

"If, by 'secondhand,' you mean through me," Lord observed, "don't you think I have more qualifications to read those kind of reports, then make a judgment—as I already have?"

"What *was* your judgment?"

"That in neither incident was there any possible involvement of Montayne. All the evidence supports that, and it was evidence investigated thoroughly by qualified, competent people. My additional opinion—now shared by Gironde-Chimie, by the way—is that the families concerned were simply trying to extort money. It happens all the time."

Celia asked, "Has Sam been told about the reports—the incidents in France and Spain?"

Lord shook his head. "Not by me. I didn't consider them significant enough to bother him."

"All right," Celia said. "At this point I'm not questioning your decision. But I'd still like to read the reports myself."

Lord's increased friendliness of late had cooled noticeably during their conversation. Now he said acidly, "If you have some pretensions about possessing scientific knowledge and making judgments yourself, let me remind you that your scrubby B.S. chemistry degree is a long way behind you, and out of date."

While surprised at the research director's reluctance to let her have what she had asked for, Celia had no intention of turning this into an argument. She said quietly, "I have no pretensions, Vince. But *please!*—may I have the reports?"

What came next also surprised her. She had assumed the reports would be in a general office filing system and that Lord would send for them. Instead, with a sour expression, he used a key to open a locked drawer of his desk from which he extracted a folder. Withdrawing papers, he handed them to Celia.

"Thank you," she acknowledged. "I'll let you have these back."

That evening, though tired when she arrived home, Celia stayed up late to read the Gironde-Chimie reports and most of the trial transcript from Australia. The latter caused her most concern.

There were several significant points in the full transcript which the abridged, summarized version she had read earlier did not contain.

The woman in the Australian case had been stated—in the abridged version—to be of poor character, a heavy drug user (apart from Montayne), a near-alcoholic, and a chain smoker. All true.

But also true, and *not* appearing in the abridged report, was that despite her background the mother of the deficient child was intelligent, a fact to which several witnesses testified. Furthermore, there was no known history of mental impairment or physical deformity in the woman's family.

A second piece of information new to Celia was that the woman had had two previous pregnancies which produced normal, healthy children.

The abridged Australian report had stated that the woman did not know who was the father of her latest child.

But—the full trial transcript revealed—she *did* know that the father had to be one of four men, all of whom were questioned by an investigating doctor. In no case, among the men or their families, was any history of mental or physical problems found.

The French and Spanish reports, obtained from Vincent Lord, were much as Bill Ingram had described them earlier in the day. The detail they contained also confirmed Lord's opinion that the Gironde-Chimie investigations had been done thoroughly by competent people.

Just the same, the totality of all three documents heightened, rather than diminished, the unease in Celia's mind. For what was inescapable, despite all other considerations and opinions, was the fact that three women, in widely separated places, had produced deformed and mentally defective babies—and all, during pregnancy, had taken Montayne.

By the end of her reading she had reached a decision: Despite Vincent Lord's reluctance, Sam Hawthorne must be informed, not only of all known facts, but of Celia's personal, growing anxiety about Montayne.

12

It was late afternoon next day.

A memo, flagged "URGENT," from Celia to Sam Hawthorne had reached him by midmorning. Soon after that, Sam summoned a senior management conference for 4:30 P.M.

Now, as Celia approached the president's suite, she could hear through a doorway open to the corridor the sound of boisterous male laughter. At this moment, she thought it seemed incongruous.

As she entered the outer office, one of Sam's two secretaries looked up and smiled. "Hello, Mrs. Jordan."

"Sounds like a party, Maggie," Celia said.

"In a way, it is." The secretary smiled again and motioned to another open doorway. "Why don't you go in? There's some news I think Mr. Hawthorne would like to tell you himself."

Celia entered a room in which the air was heavy with cigar smoke. Sam was there; so were Vincent Lord, Seth Feingold, Bill Ingram, and several vice presidents, including Glen Nicholson, a company veteran who ran manufacturing, a Dr. Starbut from safety evaluation, and Julian Hammond, a youngish MBA in charge of public affairs. All were puffing at cigars, Ingram with some uncertainty; Celia had never seen him smoke before.

"Hey, here's Celia!" someone called out. "Sam, give her a cigar!"

"No, no!" Sam said. "I've something different for the ladies."

Beaming, he went around to the far side of his desk, behind which was a small pile of chocolate boxes—Turtles. He handed one to Celia.

"In honor of my grandson who"—Sam consulted his watch—"is now twenty minutes old."

For the moment, her seriousness evaporated. "Sam, that's wonderful news! Congratulations!"

"Thank you, Celia. I know it's usually fathers who do the cigar-and-chocolates routine, but I decided to begin a new tradition to include grandfathers."

"A damn good tradition!" Nicholson, the manufacturing chief, said, and Celia added, "The Turtles were thoughtful—they're my favorites." She noticed that Bill Ingram, looking slightly pale, had stopped smoking his cigar.

She asked, "Is everything okay with Juliet?"

"Absolutely," Sam said happily. "I had a call from Lilian at the hospital just a few minutes before you all came, which is how I got the good news—'mother and a seven-pound baby boy, both doing well.'"

"I'll go to see Juliet myself," Celia said. "Probably tomorrow."

"Fine! I'll tell her to expect you. I'll be leaving for the hospital myself right after this meeting." It was clear that Sam was on a euphoric high.

Dr. Starbut asked, "Why don't we postpone?"

"No," Sam said, "we may as well get this over with." Then, glancing at the others, "I assume it won't take long."

Vincent Lord said, "No reason why it should."

Celia had a sudden sinking feeling, a conviction that all of this was going wrong, that the juxtaposition of the Montayne issue and Sam's grandchild was the worst thing that could have happened at this time. Sam's happy state, which others here were sharing, would eclipse their seriousness of purpose.

Preceded by Sam, they moved to an office conference area, arranging themselves in chairs around a table. Sam was at the head. Without preliminaries, clearly wishing not to waste time, he began.

"Celia, I sent a copy of your memo, late this morning, to everyone who's here. A copy went also to Xav Rivkin, who was about to leave on a two-day trip to Washington, which he offered to postpone so he could be with us; however, I assured him that would not be necessary." Sam moved his gaze around the table. "Has everyone read what Celia wrote?"

There were affirmative nods and murmurs.

Sam acknowledged, "Good."

Celia, having drafted it carefully, was glad her memorandum had been read. In it she had referred to the Australian court proceedings concerning Montayne, setting out the facts that she had discovered during her reading of the trial transcript and that had not appeared in the summary version circulated through the company earlier. She also described the recent French and Spanish incidents which had resulted in accusations against Montayne, accusations receiving publicity in *France-Soir* and probably elsewhere. Finally, she explained the reasoning of Gironde-Chimie and the French company's conviction that all three allegations about Montayne were unjustified and need not cause alarm.

What Celia did not do in her memorandum was offer any conclusions of her own, leaving those for this meeting, after hearing what others had to say.

"Let me state right away, Celia," Sam said, "that you were absolutely correct in bringing these matters to our attention. They are important because others will hear of them and we must be ready to tell our side of the story—the true side—when Montayne goes on sale three weeks from now." He looked questioningly at Celia. "I'm sure that was your objective. Right?"

The query was unexpected and she answered awkwardly, "Well, that *is* part of it . . ."

Sam, still in a hurry, nodded and went on. "Let's clear up something else. Vince, why wasn't I told of those Gironde-Chimie reports Celia referred to?"

The research director's face muscles twitched. "Because, Sam, if I sent you every query that comes in concerning all of our products, in the first place I wouldn't be doing my job of assessing what's important scientifically and what isn't, and in the second you'd have a stack of paper on your desk so high you'd get no other work done."

The explanation appeared to satisfy Sam because he instructed, "Give us your opinion of those reports."

"They're both self-canceling," Lord declared. "They show, with a thoroughness that satisfies me entirely, that Gironde-Chimie's conclusion about the non-involvement of Montayne in either incident is correct scientifically."

"And the case in Australia? Do those extra points Celia raised have any bearing on the earlier conclusion?"

Celia thought: *We're sitting here, all of us, speaking casually of "incidents" and "cases" and "conclusions" when what it's really about—even if Montayne is not involved—is babies who'll be "vegetables" throughout their lives, unable to walk or even move their limbs or use their brains in any normal way. Are we really so indifferent, or is it fear that stops us from using the real, unpalatable words? Perhaps, too, we're relieved those babies are in distant places, and we shall never see them . . . unlike Sam's grandson, close at hand, whose birth we're celebrating with chocolates and cigars.*

Lord was answering Sam's question, his displeasure with Celia only thinly veiled. "Those 'extra points,' as you choose to dignify them, change nothing whatsoever. In fact, I fail to see the slightest reason for bringing them up."

There was an audible murmur of relief around the table.

"While we're here, though, and for the record," Lord continued, "I've prepared a commentary, from a scientific viewpoint, of the three incidents—Australian, French and Spanish." He hesitated. "I know we're in a hurry . . ."

Sam asked, "How long will it take?"

"I promise to be no more than ten minutes."

Sam glanced at his watch. "Okay, but limit it to that."

This is all wrong! Celia's mind was pleading, silently and frantically. *This entire issue is too vital, too important to be hurried in this way.* But she checked her racing thoughts, concentrating instead on Vincent Lord's words.

The research director was at once authoritative, convincing, reassuring. Examining the backgrounds of the three defective babies and their parents, one by one, he pointed out how any one of many causes may disrupt a normal pregnancy, causing damage to a fetus. In particular, "an unregulated mix of chemicals in the human body, especially drugs and alcohol together," could have disastrous effects, of which examples were tragic and frequent.

In all the cases under review, Lord argued, there were so many adverse possibilities, some of them compelling, that it became unreasonable and non-scientific to blame Montayne, especially when the worldwide record of Montayne was so immaculate and other probabilities so strong. He used the words "hysteria" and "probable fraud" in describing attempts to pin responsibility on the drug, plus the accompanying publicity.

The other men listened gravely and seemed to be impressed. *As*

281

perhaps they are right to be, Celia thought. She wished she could be as unequivocal and confident as Vince. She truly wanted to be, and recognized that Lord's qualifications to make the judgments he had were far greater than her own. Yet she, who until only yesterday had been one of Montayne's strongest supporters, simply wasn't sure.

Lord concluded eloquently. "With any new drug that is introduced, there are *always* claims that it is doing harm, that adverse side effects exist, outweighing benefits. Such claims may be responsible and based on genuine concern by qualified professionals, or they may be irresponsible, made by unqualified people, based on nothing.

"Yet each submission, both in the public interest, and to protect companies like ours which *cannot afford* to produce a dangerous drug, must be examined carefully, unemotionally, scientifically. For —make no mistake!—no complaint, no criticism concerning any pharmaceutical product can be totally ignored.

"What *must* be determined, of course, is whether an adverse reaction in someone who has taken a particular drug is from that drug or from some other source, remembering there are *many* sources where adverse happenings can originate.

"Well, I am satisfied that the most careful examinations have been done in the instances we are discussing. The charges have been examined and the bad effects described did *not,* it has been found, originate with Montayne.

"Finally, there is one more fact it is essential to remember: If a drug should be *falsely* blamed for an adverse effect it has not caused, and because of that false accusation be withheld from general use, then countless people would be deprived of its therapeutic benefits. In my opinion they should *not* be so deprived of the benefits of Montayne."

It was an impressive conclusion, as Celia admitted to herself.

Sam clearly expressed the feeling of others when he said, "Thank you, Vince. I think you've made us all feel better." He eased his chair back from the table. "I don't believe we need any formal resolution. I am satisfied that it is perfectly safe to continue full speed ahead with Montayne, and I presume everyone else agrees."

There were nods of assent from the other men.

"Well," Sam said, "I guess that's everything. Now, if you'll all excuse me . . ."

"I'm sorry," Celia said, "but I'm afraid that isn't everything."

Heads turned toward her.

Sam said impatiently, "What is it?"

"I'd like to ask Vince a question."

"Well . . . if you must."

Celia looked down at notes she had made. "Vince, you stated that Montayne was *not* the cause of the three babies in Australia, France and Spain being born as 'vegetables'—babies, we ought to remember, who cannot move their limbs and lack normally functioning brains." *If others were afraid of putting unpleasant truths into words, she decided, she would not be.*

Lord said, "I'm glad you were listening."

She ignored the unpleasant tone and asked, "Since Montayne was not the cause of those deformities, what was?"

"I thought I made clear it could be one of several, or even many, causes."

She persisted, "But which one?"

Lord said exasperatedly, "How do I know which one? It could have been a different cause in each case. All I know is, based on scientific judgment by experts on the spot, the cause was not Montayne."

"So the truth is, no one knows with certainty what did damage those fetuses and cause the deformed births."

The research director threw up his hands. "For God's sake, I've already said so! In different words, maybe, but—"

"Celia," Sam interjected, "just what are you getting at?"

"What I'm getting at," she answered, "is that despite everything Vince has said, I'm uncomfortable. No one *knows*. I'm still not satisfied. I'm having doubts."

Someone asked, "What kind of doubts?"

"About Montayne." It was Celia's turn to survey the faces around her. "I have a feeling—if you like, call it instinct—that something is wrong, something we don't yet know about. Also that there are questions to which we ought to know the answers, but we don't."

Lord sneered, "A woman's instinct, I suppose."

She snapped, "What's wrong with that?"

Sam ordered sharply, "Everybody cool it!" He told Celia, "If you have a suggestion, let's hear it."

"My suggestion," she said, "is that we should delay the launching of Montayne."

She was conscious of everyone in the room regarding her with incredulity.

Sam's lips had tightened. "Delay for how long, and precisely why?"

Celia said deliberately and carefully, "I suggest a postponement of six months. In that time there may be no more instances of defective births. Or there could be. I hope it doesn't happen, but if it does there could be information we do not have now, and which would give us, perhaps, greater confidence to proceed with Montayne."

There was a shocked silence which Sam broke. "You can't be serious."

"I am very serious." She met his eyes directly. *When she came here she had been uncertain of her own feelings. She had been uneasy— but with ambivalence. Now she was ambivalent no longer because, far from reassuring her, Vincent Lord's emphatic certainty—too much certainty!—had reinforced her doubts.*

And yes, she admitted to herself, in taking the stand she had just declared, she was relying on her instincts, and little more. But her instincts had been right before.

Celia knew there was a difficult task ahead of her to convince the others, with Sam the most important. But they *had* to be convinced. They must be persuaded that it was now in everyone's best interest to delay Montayne's American debut—in the interest of pregnant women who might take the drug and have their babies endangered; of the company, Felding-Roth; and of all of them here who were responsible for what the company did.

"Do you have *any idea,*" Sam was asking, still shocked, "what a delay in launching Montayne would involve?"

"Of course I do!" Celia let her own voice take on an edge. "Who would know better than me? Has anyone been more involved with Montayne than I have?"

"No," Sam said. "That's why what you're saying is so unbelievable."

"It's also why you can be sure I'm not making the suggestion lightly."

Sam turned toward Seth Feingold. "What do you estimate it would cost us to delay Montayne?"

The elderly comptroller looked uncomfortable. He was Celia's friend. Also he was out of his depth where scientific matters were concerned and plainly wished he were not involved. Bill Ingram, too, appeared discomfited; Celia sensed that Bill was torn by inner conflicts—loyalty to her and probably his own ideas about Montayne. Well, we all have our problems, she thought, and I, at this moment, certainly have mine.

284

One thing had been resolved, though. There was no longer any sense of haste. Clearly, Sam and others had accepted that the issue raised by Celia must be resolved, however long it took.

Feingold had his head down and was making calculations with a pencil. Looking up, he advised, "In round figures we've committed thirty-two million dollars to Montayne. Not all of it has been spent, so perhaps a quarter would be retrievable. But there are substantial general costs I've not included. As to the real cost of a delay, it's impossible to guess. It would depend on the length of delay and the eventual effect on projected sales."

"I'll tell you one effect there would be," Hammond, of public affairs, declared. "If we delay Montayne now, the press will have a field day. They'll discredit the drug and it might never recover."

Sam acknowledged, "I've thought of that too. Delay at this point would, in some ways, be as bad as canceling."

He swung back to Celia, his tone accusing. "If we did as you suggest —and for the vaguest of reasons—have you given *any* thought to the questions and angry reaction there would be from the board of directors and stockholders? And have you considered our employees who would have to be laid off, who might lose their jobs permanently?"

"Yes," she said, trying to stay calm, concealing the agony this was causing her, "I have thought of all that. I thought about it last night and through most of today."

Sam grunted skeptically, then returned to Feingold. "So one way or another we'd be taking a chance of losing twenty-eight millions, more or less, to say nothing of a much greater loss of anticipated profits."

The comptroller glanced regretfully at Celia as he answered, "That's the potential loss, it's true."

Sam said grimly, "And we can't afford it, can we?"

Feingold shook his head sadly. "No."

"However," Celia pointed out, "the loss could be greater still if we ran into trouble with Montayne."

Glen Nicholson said uneasily, "There *is* that to think about." It was the first support, even if tentative, which Celia had received and she shot the manufacturing chief a grateful glance.

Vincent Lord chimed in, "But we don't expect to have trouble. That is, unless the rest of you"—he surveyed the others—"are willing to accept the lady as our ranking scientific expert."

There was some halfhearted laughter, quickly snuffed out at an impatient gesture from Sam.

"Celia," Sam said, "please listen to me carefully." His voice was serious, but more controlled than a few moments ago, and again their eyes met directly. "I'd like you to reconsider. It could be that you've spoken hastily and made a judgment without weighing all the implications. Each of us here does similar things at times. I certainly have, and have had to swallow my pride and backtrack, admitting I've been wrong. If you were to do that now, none of us would think an iota the worse of you, and what happened here will end here. I promise that, just as I urge you to change your mind. What do you say?"

She was silent, not wanting to rush into a commitment either way without considering it first. Sam had just offered her—easily, graciously, as was his way—a dignified route out. All she had to do was utter a word, a phrase, and the impasse would be over, a crisis averted as swiftly as it came. The offer was extraordinarily tempting.

Before she could answer, Sam added, "You have a lot at stake personally."

She knew exactly what he meant. Her appointment as corporate vice president of sales and merchandising had not yet been confirmed. And if what was happening here proceeded to its logical conclusion, it might never be.

Sam was right. There *was* a lot at stake.

She took a moment more to consider, then told him quietly and decisively, "Sam, I'm sorry. I *have* weighed everything. I do know what's at stake. But I must still recommend that we delay the introduction of Montayne."

It was done. As Sam's face clouded, then suffused with anger, she knew that now there could be no turning back.

"Very well," he pronounced tautly. "At least we know where we stand." He considered, then went on, "Earlier I said there would be no formal vote here. Cancel that. I want us to go on record. Seth, please take notes."

The comptroller, his expression still sad, again produced his pencil and held it poised.

"I have already made my own position clear," Sam said. "I am, of course, in favor of continuing our introduction of Montayne, as planned. I wish to know who agrees or disagrees. Those who agree, raise their hands."

Vincent Lord's hand shot up. Those of Dr. Starbut, Hammond, and two other vice presidents followed. Nicholson, apparently overcoming his doubts, raised his hand too. Bill Ingram hesitated; he looked at Celia in mute appeal. But she turned away, refusing to help him; he must make his own decision. After a second more, Bill's hand went up.

Sam and the others were looking at Seth Feingold. The comptroller sighed, put down his pencil and waveringly raised his hand.

"That's nine to one," Sam said. "It doesn't leave any doubt that this company will continue with the launching of Montayne."

Once more there was a silence, this time awkward, as if no one knew what to do or say next. Amid it, Sam stood up.

"As you know," he said, "when all of this began, I was about to leave to see my daughter and grandson at the hospital. I'll go there now." But the earlier joy had left his voice. Sam nodded to the other men, but pointedly ignored Celia as he left.

She remained in her seat. Bill Ingram, now standing, moved toward her. "I'm sorry . . ." he began.

She waved him to silence. "It doesn't matter. I don't want to hear."

Suddenly, unexpectedly, she realized that everything she had built up for herself within the company—her position, authority, reputation, future prospects—had come tumbling down. Could she even survive here now? She wasn't sure.

Bill said, "I have to ask this. What are you going to do?" When she didn't answer, he went on. "Surely, now that you've made your protest, now that everyone knows where you stand about Montayne . . . surely you can go on directing sales?"

Celia responded dully, not wanting to make decisions now, "I don't know. I just don't know." But she did know that, at home tonight, she would have to think her position through.

Seth Feingold told her, "I hated to vote against you, Celia. But you know how it is—I don't understand anything scientific."

She glared at him. "Then why did you vote at all? You could have said that, and abstained."

He shook his head regretfully, and left.

One by one the others followed until Celia was alone.

13

"I know something is wrong," Andrew said at dinner, breaking a lengthy silence, "and my guess is, seriously wrong."

He stopped, and when Celia made no immediate reply, continued. "You've been quiet since I came in, and I know your moods pretty well, so I won't bug you. But when you want to talk, and need me . . . well, my love, I'm here."

She put down her knife and fork alongside the meal she had scarcely touched, and turned to him, her eyes brimming.

"Oh, darling! *How* I need you!"

He reached out, covering her hand with his, and said gently, "Take your time. Finish dinner first."

She told him, "I can't eat."

Soon after, in their living room and sipping a brandy which Andrew poured, Celia described the past two days' events, culminating in her failure to convince Sam and others this afternoon that the launching of Montayne should be delayed.

Andrew listened carefully, injecting an occasional question. At the end he told her, "I don't see what else you could have done."

"There *was* nothing else," Celia said. "But what I have to decide is —what do I do now?"

"Do you have to make a decision, at least right away? Why not take some time off? I could get away too, and we'll take a trip somewhere." He urged, "Away from pressures, you could think everything through, then do whatever seems right when you get back."

She smiled gratefully. "I wish it would keep that long. But it's something I can't put off."

Andrew came to Celia and kissed her, then assured her, "You know I'll help in any way I can. But remember one thing. I've always been proud of you, and I'll go on being that, whatever you decide."

Looking at her husband fondly, she thought: A lesser man would have reminded her of their argument in the hotel in San Francisco, when Andrew had refused to concede his doubts about Montayne, or the use of any drug by pregnant women. That was when Celia had suggested—maliciously, as she saw it now—that his medical reasoning might be prejudiced or outdated, maybe both.

Well, Celia was now the one who had come around to having doubts, but Andrew was too big a person ever to say, "I told you so."

If she were to apply Andrew's standards to her own present dilemma, she wondered, which way would it be decided?

She didn't even have to ask. She knew.

She remembered, too, some advice given to her years earlier.

"There is something you have: a gift, an instinct, for judging what is right . . . Use your gift, Celia . . . When you have power, be strong to do what you believe . . . Don't let lesser people dissuade you."

Emotion surged as she remembered Eli Camperdown. The long-ago president of Felding-Roth had spoken those words, near death, in his home at Mount Kemble Lake.

Andrew asked, "More brandy?"

"No, thank you."

She finished what was in her glass, met Andrew's eyes, then declared decisively, "I cannot take part in marketing Montayne. I'm going to resign."

In all of her twenty-four years at Felding-Roth, it was the most painful thing she had ever done.

Celia's letter, handwritten and addressed to Sam, was brief.

> *With the greatest personal regret I am resigning as Director of Pharmaceutical Sales and from Felding-Roth.*
>
> *This letter will terminate my connection with the company.*
>
> *You are aware of my reasons. It seems unnecessary to repeat them.*
>
> *I wish to say that my years of employment here have been pleasurable and privileged. Not least among the privileges have been your support and friendship for which I have been—and remain—most grateful.*

I am leaving without bitterness. I wish Felding-Roth Pharmaceuticals and its people success in every way.

Celia sent the letter, hand delivered, to the president's office and followed it herself a half hour later. She was shown in immediately to Sam's inner office. Behind her a door closed quietly.

Sam looked up from a paper he was reading. His features were set grimly and his voice was cold. "You asked to see me. Why?"

She responded uncertainly, "I've been with the company a long time, most of it working for you. I felt I couldn't just walk out . . ."

He cut in, with a savage anger she had never seen before, "But that's exactly what you are doing! Walking out on all of us—your friends, colleagues, others who've depended on you. Quitting disloyally at the worst possible time, an important merchandising time, when the company needs you."

She protested, "My leaving has nothing to do with loyalty or friendship."

"Obviously not!"

She had not been asked to sit down, so continued to stand.

"Sam," she pleaded, "please understand! I cannot, simply cannot, help to sell Montayne. It's become a matter of conscience."

He retorted, "You call it conscience. I could apply other names."

She asked, curiously, "Other names like what?"

"For one: feminine hysteria. For another: phony, uninformed self-righteousness. Spitefulness at not getting your own way, so you quit."

Sam glared as he went on. "Why, you're behaving no better than women who carry placards in the streets or chain themselves to fences. The truth is, you've been duped, made a sucker by that know-nothing bitch, Stavely."

He motioned to that morning's *New York Times,* which lay open on his desk, turned to a news item featuring a statement by Dr. Maud Stavely who, too, had learned of the deformed baby cases in France and Spain and was using them in her own campaign to delay Montayne. Celia had read the *Times* story earlier.

"What you just said isn't the truth," Celia insisted, "and I have not been duped." She decided to ignore the petty anti-feminist remarks.

As if he had not heard Celia's disclaimer, he sneered, "Now, I suppose you'll go to join Stavely and her gang."

"No," Celia said. "I'll be joining nothing, seeing no one, making no statement whatever about why I'm leaving." She added, in a voice she hoped was reasonable, "After all, I admitted yesterday that most of what I feel is instinct."

Never before had she seen Sam in a mood so ugly. Despite it, she decided to make a last appeal, one final try.

"I'd like to remind you," Celia said, "of something you once told me. It was when I was in London after we recruited Martin Peat-Smith."

Earlier today, thinking about this meeting, she had remembered Sam's words when she managed to lure Martin into the Felding-Roth orbit after Sam had failed. Before it happened, Sam warned her against mentioning money to Martin, but Celia ignored the warning and it was money which, in the end, had tipped the balance where Martin was concerned. On learning the news, and on the telephone from Boonton, Sam declared, "If ever, someplace down the road, you and I differ on a matter of judgment that's important, you have my permission to remind me of this incident, and that your judgment was right and mine wrong."

She reminded him now, and it was as if she had addressed an iceberg.

"Even if that's true," he snapped, "and though you say it is, I don't remember, it's merely proof your judgment has gone to pieces in the meantime."

Suddenly, great sadness and emotion seized her, so she had difficulty in speaking, but managed to say, "Goodbye, Sam."

He didn't answer.

At home, it seemed extraordinary to Celia that the act of leaving Felding-Roth had been so simple. She had merely cleared her desk of personal things, said goodbyes to her secretary and a few others in the office, some of whom had been tearful, then driven away.

In a way, she supposed, her abrupt departure had been inconsiderate, but in another it had been essential. In recent weeks almost all of Celia's work had centered on Montayne, and since it was work she could no longer do in good conscience, staying on would have achieved nothing. There was also the fact that everything in her department was in order; therefore Bill Ingram, who would have taken over anyway in a few weeks' time, could move in at once without disruption.

The thought reminded her that she would never, now, be a corporate vice president—a poignant disappointment since the cup had come so close. But, she told herself, it was a disappointment she would learn to live with.

Andrew telephoned Celia twice during the day, first at her office, then later at home. On learning that her resignation had already taken effect, he announced he would be home early, and arrived in time for afternoon tea which Celia prepared. The experience was new for her. She supposed that from now on she would be doing it more often.

They greeted each other lovingly.

Soon after, as Andrew sipped his tea, he told her gently, "You need a rest from decisions, so I've taken some for us both. One is that you and I are going to live a little."

He produced a large manila envelope. "I stopped at a travel agency on the way home, about one of my other decisions. We are going on a tour."

"To where?"

"To everywhere. A world tour."

She threw up her hands. "Oh, Andrew, you're wonderful! You're a comfort just to be with."

"Let's hope you feel that way after six months of togetherness on ships and in hotels." He began pulling brochures from the envelope. "To begin, I thought we'd fly to Europe, do some touring there— France, Spain, Italy, anywhere else that interests either one of us— then take a ship through the Mediterranean . . ."

Despite her depression from the past few days, Celia's spirits lifted. A world tour was something they had often talked about, but always vaguely, as something for the future. She thought: so why *not* now? Would there ever be a better time?

Andrew—with a small boy's enthusiasm, she observed affectionately—was already making the idea come alive. "We should go to Egypt and Israel, then stop at the United Arab Emirates . . . India, of course . . . Japan's a must, so is Singapore . . . we have to include Australia and New Zealand . . ."

She said, "It's a *magnificent* idea!"

"Something I'll have to do," Andrew explained, "is get another doctor in the practice—a *locum tenens*—to help out while I'm away. That will probably take a month to arrange, so we can get away by March." There would be no problem concerning the children, both

292

of them knew, because Lisa and Bruce had committed themselves to summer jobs away from home.

They went on talking, Celia aware that the pain of today would inevitably return, and perhaps never disappear entirely, but at the moment—with Andrew's encouragement—she succeeded in pushing it away.

Later that evening Andrew asked, "I know it's early, but have you given any thought to what you'll do now that you're through at Felding-Roth? I can't see you staying at home forever."

"No," she said, "I'm sure I won't do that. But as for anything else, I just don't know. I need time to think—which you're giving to me, darling."

That night they made love, not with grand passion but with a sweet gentleness in which Celia found peace.

During the several weeks that followed, Celia kept her word about making no public statement concerning the reason for her departure from Felding-Roth. Not surprisingly, news of her resignation filtered quickly through the industry and became known to the business press. There was a good deal of curiosity, which remained unsatisfied. *The Wall Street Journal, Business Week,* and *New York Times* all telephoned Celia, requesting interviews. She refused. She also politely turned aside questions from her own and Andrew's friends.

Only to Lisa and Bruce did Celia confide everything, and that on Andrew's urging. "You owe it to them," he told her. "The children admire you, just as I do. They're entitled to know why they can go on doing that. They should not be left wondering."

It meant special trips, to Stanford in the case of Lisa, and to Pottstown where Bruce was now in his junior year at the Hill School, and in a way the diversion was good for Celia. Her days were no longer active and filled. The adjustment to having more time on her hands than she could use did not come easily.

Lisa was sympathetic but practical. "You'll find something else to do, Mom, and whatever it is will be important. But the best thing that could happen right now is you and Daddy going on that world tour."

But it was Bruce who, with a sensitivity beyond his years, summed up the situation best. "If you're comfortable with yourself, Mom . . . if, now that time's gone by, you're sure what you did was right, that's all that matters."

After talking with both children, Celia decided that she *was* comfortable, and in that mood, in early March, flew from New York to Paris with Andrew for the beginning of their get-away-from-it-all odyssey.

14

In his house at Harlow, Martin Peat-Smith had gone to bed for the night, but couldn't sleep. It was Saturday, a few minutes short of midnight, and the culmination of an exciting, eventful week.

Deciding that sleep would come when it was ready, he lay relaxed and wakeful, letting his mind roam.

Science, he thought whimsically after a while, could be like a woman who withholds her favors from a suitor until eventually he is close to giving up, ready to abandon hope. Then, in a sudden switch of mood, without warning, the woman capitulates, opens her arms, lets her clothing fall away, revealing and offering everything.

Carrying the metaphor further, Martin mused, sometimes a whole series of orgasms followed (wasn't "rippling" the word women used?) as more and more of the hitherto unknown, and only dreamed of, continued to come clear.

Why the hell, he asked himself, *am I doing all this sexual fantasizing?*

Answering his own question: *You know damn well why! It's because of Yvonne. Every time she comes near you in the lab, your mind leaps to one thing, which might be biology but sure as hell isn't science.*

So why haven't you done something about it?

Why indeed? *Come back to that question later.*

For the moment, Martin returned to thoughts of his own scientific pursuit and the truly remarkable progress made since . . . when was it?

Well, the breathtaking, breakthrough part had begun barely a year ago.

His mind went back. To that point and beyond.

The visit to Harlow by Celia Jordan had been two years earlier, in 1975. Martin remembered showing her films of chromatograms and explaining, "Where bands appear, we have a peptide . . . you'll see two columns of dark lines . . . at least nine peptides."

But the problem—insurmountable, it seemed—was that the mixture of peptides discovered in brains of younger rats occurred in amounts too small to be purified and tested. Also, the mixture contained extraneous material, causing Rao Sastri to describe it as "nonsense" peptides.

Attempts to purify the mixture had continued, but results were desultory at best, seeming to confirm Sastri's view that the required techniques were a decade or more away.

Among other members of the Harlow scientific team, morale had declined, along with faith in Martin's basic theory.

It was then, at a time of lowest ebb, that it happened.

After working patiently, using larger quantities of brains from young rats, they achieved partial purification. Then the new, enriched mix—of fewer peptides—was injected into older rats.

Almost at once there was a startling improvement in the ability of the elderly rats to learn and to remember. Maze tests showed this clearly.

Smiling as he remembered, Martin thought of the laboratory maze.

It was a miniature of the mazes in which humans for centuries had amused themselves by entering, attempting to get out, then becoming lost or blocked by dead ends before the exit was attained. Probably the world's most famous maze, created in the seventeenth century, supposedly for Britain's King William III, was at Hampton Court Palace, west of London.

The plywood maze in the Harlow labs was a small-scale version of Hampton Court's, remarkably accurate in detail, and had been built by an institute scientist in his spare time. Unlike Hampton Court, however, it was used exclusively by rats.

The rats, one at a time, were placed in the maze entrance, prodded if necessary but otherwise left to find their own way out. At the end a reward of food awaited them, and their ability to reach the food was observed and timed.

Until the most recent series of tests, results had been predictable. Young and old rats introduced to the maze for the first time had trouble finding the exit, but eventually did. However, a second time around the young rats got out and reached the reward faster, a third time faster still, and so on.

The young rats clearly learned from each experience, remembering which turnings to take or not take.

In contrast, the old rats either failed to learn or were much slower than the younger animals.

Until the injection of the latest peptide solution.

After that, the improvement was extraordinary. When in the maze for the third or fourth time, the old rats literally raced through it, for the most part without hesitation or errors. There was now little difference in performance between the young rats and the old.

As tests continued with the same results, excitement among the watching scientists became intense. One or two, after a spectacular performance by an elderly, fat rat, shouted with joy. At one point Rao Sastri wrung Martin's hand. "My goodness! All along you were right. It entitles you to say to the rest of us, 'O ye of little faith.' "

Martin shook his head. "I was beginning to lose faith too."

"I do not believe that," Sastri said. "Like the gentleman you are, you are attempting to make your humbled colleagues feel better."

"Either way," Martin said, delighted himself, "I think we have something worth reporting to America."

This report reached Felding-Roth in New Jersey at the time when preparations for launching Montayne were in high gear, and shortly before Celia's doubts about the wisdom of proceeding with that drug.

Yet even while the report was being reviewed in New Jersey, at Harlow a new problem was having to be faced.

Despite favorable signals, the latest peptide mix presented difficulties. Like its predecessor, it was available only in limited amounts. For the work of further refining, and to identify and isolate the single, critical memory peptide, larger quantities were essential.

The route Martin chose to greater supplies was through the production of antibodies. These would bind with the desired peptide and isolate it. For that purpose rabbits would be used, since they produced antibodies in large amounts, more so than rats.

Enter Gertrude Tilwick.

The institute's supervisor of animals, a technician, was a severe, tight-lipped woman in her forties. She had been hired, fairly recently, by Nigel Bentley, and until the incident that brought them together, she and Martin had had little to do with each other directly.

At Martin's request, Miss Tilwick brought several rabbits in cages to his personal lab. He had previously explained to her that the crude peptide mixture in an oily solution—an "adjuvant"—would have to be injected into the rabbits' paws—a painful process. Therefore each animal must be held securely while it was done.

Along with the rabbits, Tilwick brought a small flat board with four straps fastened to it. Opening a cage, she seized a rabbit and placed it on the board, belly up. Then, with the creature spread-eagled, she swiftly strapped each of its legs to the board's four corners.

Throughout, her movements were rough and careless, her attitude indifferently callous. While Martin watched with horror, the terrified animal screamed—he had not realized before that a rabbit *could* scream; the sound was awful. Then there was silence and, by the time the fourth leg was secured, the animal was dead. Clearly, it had died from fright and shock.

Once again, over an animal, Martin's rare anger surfaced and he ordered Tilwick from the lab.

Exit Miss Tilwick.

Martin then sent for Nigel Bentley and informed the administrator that no one as insensitive to suffering as the animals' supervisor could continue working at the institute.

"Of course," Bentley agreed. "Tilwick must go, and I'm sorry about what happened. Her technical qualifications were good, but I didn't check her for TLC."

"Yes, tender loving care is what we need," Martin said. "Can you send me someone else?"

"I'll send Tilwick's assistant. If she's satisfactory we'll promote her."

Enter Yvonne Evans.

Yvonne was twenty-five, slightly overweight but cheerful and attractive, with long blond hair, innocent blue eyes and a milk-and-roses skin. She came from a small country town in the Black Mountains of Wales called Brecon, the locale reflected in her lilting voice. Yvonne also had stunning breasts and, quite obviously, she wore no brassiere.

Martin was fascinated by Yvonne's ample bosom from the beginning, and especially when the series of injections began.

"Give me a minute or two first," Yvonne told him. She ignored the strap board brought to the lab by Gertrude Tilwick and, while Martin waited with a hypodermic syringe ready, she lifted a rabbit gently from a cage, held it close to her face and began crooning to it, comforting it, murmuring soft words. Finally she pillowed the rabbit's head in her bosom and, holding the lower paws toward Martin, said, "Go ahead."

In a remarkably short time six rabbits had been injected with the oily solution—one injection going into each toe pad. Though distracted by the closeness of those breasts, and though at moments Martin found himself wishing his own head were there instead of a rabbit's, he worked carefully and in unison with Yvonne.

The animals were clearly soothed by her loving care, but there was some suffering, and after a while she asked, "Does it *have* to be the toe pads?"

Martin grimaced. "I don't like it either, but that's a good site for making antibodies. Though the injection's painful, and it continues to irritate, the irritation attracts antibody-producing cells."

The explanation seemed to satisfy Yvonne. When they had finished he said, "You care about animals."

She looked at him in surprise. "Of course."

"Not everyone does."

"You mean Tilly?" A frown crossed Yvonne's face. "She doesn't even like herself."

"Miss Tilwick doesn't work here anymore."

"I know. Mr. Bentley told me. He also said to tell you that my qualifications are okay, and if you like me I can do the supervisor's job."

"I like you," Martin said, then surprised himself by adding, "I like you very much."

Yvonne giggled. "Goes both ways, Doctor."

Although, after their first encounter, others took over the animal injections, Martin continued to see Yvonne around the labs. Once, with his mind more on her than on the question, he asked, "If you love animals so much, why didn't you go to veterinary college?"

She hesitated, then with unusual terseness said, "I wanted to."

"What happened?"

"I failed an exam."

"Just one?"

"Yes."

"Couldn't you take the exam again?"

"I couldn't afford the waiting time." She looked at him directly and he had no choice but to move his eyes upward, meeting hers.

Yvonne continued, "My parents didn't have money to support me and I had to start earning. So I became an animal technician—the next best thing." Then she smiled softly and he knew she was aware of where his eyes had been lingering.

That was several weeks ago, and in between, Martin had become preoccupied with other matters.

One was a computer analysis of continued tests in the rat maze; it showed that the earlier performances were no fluke and had remained consistent over intervening months. That alone was excellent news but, to top it, there had been a successful refinement of the peptide mix, eventually allowing isolation of a single active peptide. This—the much-sought-after peptide—proved to be the seventh band on the original chromatogram films and was immediately referred to as Peptide 7.

Both successes were reported by telex to New Jersey and a congratulatory message came back promptly from Sam Hawthorne. Martin wished he could have communicated also with Celia, but news of her resignation from Felding-Roth had reached him a short time earlier. Though he had no idea what prompted her departure, the fact of it saddened him. Celia had been so much a part of the research project and the Harlow institute, it seemed unfair she would not share in the fruits of what she helped to begin. He knew, too, that he had lost a friend and an ally and wondered if the two of them would ever meet again. It seemed unlikely.

Scientifically, only one factor troubled Martin as he lay in bed reviewing these events. It concerned the older rats that had been receiving regular peptide injections over several months.

While the rats' memories had improved, their general health had apparently deteriorated. The animals had lost weight noticeably, becoming lean, almost emaciated. After so much recent success, certain newer possibilities were alarming.

Could it be that Peptide 7, while beneficial to the mind, was harmful to the body? Would the peptide-treated rats continue to suffer weight loss, become enfeebled, and fade away? If so, Peptide 7 would be unusable, either by animals or humans, and all the scientific work so far—four years of it at Harlow, plus Martin's earlier labors at Cambridge—were tragically in vain.

While the specter haunted Martin, he had tried to put it from his mind, at least for a few hours over the weekend.

Now, on this Saturday night . . . *No! It had just become Sunday morning* . . . he shifted his thoughts back to Yvonne, returning to the question he had asked a short time earlier: *So why haven't you done something?*

He could telephone her, he supposed, and wished he had considered it sooner. It was too late now. Or was it? *Hell! Why not?*

To his surprise, the call was answered on the first ring.

"Hello."

"Yvonne?"

"Yes."

"This is . . ."

"I know who it is."

"Well," he said, "I was lying here, couldn't sleep, and just thought . . ."

"I couldn't sleep either."

"I wondered if we might meet tomorrow."

She pointed out, "Tomorrow's Monday."

"So it is. Then how about today?"

"All right."

"What time would be best?"

"Why not now?"

He could hardly believe his good luck as he asked, "Shall I drive over to get you?"

"I know where you live. I'll come to you."

"You're sure?"

"Of course."

He felt he had to say something else.

"Yvonne."

"Yes?"

"I'm glad you're coming."

"So am I." He heard her soft laugh. "I thought you'd never get around to asking."

300

15

In the words of a book title Martin recalled, it was a night to remember.

Yvonne's arrival was at once delightful and uncomplicated. After she and Martin kissed warmly, and she had petted the several animals surrounding them in the hallway, she asked, "Where's your bedroom?"

"I'll show you," he said, and she followed him upstairs, bringing with her a small overnight bag.

In the softly lighted bedroom, Yvonne quickly removed all her clothing, revealing her nakedness while Martin watched, his pulse racing, admiring what he saw—especially those marvelous breasts.

When she joined him in bed, they came to each other uninhibitedly, joyously, lovingly. Martin sensed within Yvonne a guileless and generous physical love, seeming to arise from some wellspring of her nature. Perhaps it was a love of life itself, and of all living creatures, but it expressed itself now in her warm tongue, which seemed everywhere, and in her soft, moving lips which ceaselessly explored him, and in pressures and rhythms of her body, prompting him to respond in kind and in ways which had been alien until this night, but were suddenly instinctive.

She murmured, "Don't hurry! Make it last."

He whispered back, "I'll try."

Despite the wish, before too long their mutual hunger swept them to a climax. Then the urgency receded, and a sense of peace and comfort came to Martin such as he had seldom known before.

Even then his questioning, scientist's mind sought causes for the exceptional serenity. Perhaps, he reasoned, what he felt was simply a relief from built-up tensions. Yet instincts which were non-scientific told him it was something more: that Yvonne was a rare woman blessed with inner peace transmittable to others . . . and with that thought, soon afterward, he fell asleep.

He slept deeply and awoke to the sight of daylight and sounds of activity from his kitchen below. Moments later Yvonne appeared, wearing a dressing gown of Martin's and carrying a tray with a teapot, cups and saucers, and toasted crumpets with honey. Surrounding her was the house collection of two dogs and three cats, who seemed to recognize a newfound friend.

Yvonne put the tray on the bed where Martin had just sat up.

Smiling, she touched the dressing gown. "I hope you don't mind."

"It looks better on you than me."

She sat on the bed and began pouring. "You like milk in your tea, but no sugar."

"Yes, but how did you—"

"I asked at the lab. In case I needed to know. By the way, your kitchen is a mess." She passed him the tea.

"Thank you. Sorry about the kitchen. It's because I live alone."

"Before I go today, I'll clean it."

The dressing gown had fallen open and Martin said, "About going. I hope you're not in any hurry."

Allowing the garment to stay the way it was, she smiled again. "Mind your fingers on the plate; it's hot."

He told her, "I'm not sure I believe all this. Breakfast in bed is a luxury I haven't had in years."

"You should have it often. You deserve it."

"But you're the guest. I should have done this for you."

She assured him, "I like it this way. More tea?"

"Maybe later." He put down his cup and reached out for her.

Yvonne shrugged off the dressing gown, let it slide to the floor, and came to him. Holding her, and this time unhurriedly, he moved his hands, exploring, over her breasts and thighs.

Kissing her, he said, "You have a beautiful body."

"Too much of it." She laughed. "I need to take off weight." Reaching downward, she pinched a thigh and held a roll of creamy flesh between her thumb and forefinger. "What I need is some of your Peptide 7. Then I could be thin, the way those rats are."

"Not necessary." Martin's face was in her hair. "I like everything you have, just the way it is."

As the minutes passed, their passion of the night before rekindled and grew. Martin was erect, Yvonne eagerly clasping him to her as he prepared to enter her.

She urged, "Go on! Do it!"

But instead he stopped abruptly, his arms loosening. Then he grasped Yvonne's shoulders and held her away.

"What did you say?"

"I said, do it!"

"No. Before that."

She pleaded, "Martin, don't torture me! I want you *now.*"

"What did you say?"

"Oh, shit!" Frustrated, the mood between them shattered, she let herself fall back. "Why did you do that?"

"I want to know what you said. About Peptide 7."

She answered petulantly, "Peptide 7? Oh, I said that if I took some, maybe I could be thin like the rats. But what . . ."

"That's what I thought." He leaped from the bed. "Hurry up! Get dressed."

"Why?"

"We're going to the lab."

She asked incredulously, *"Now?"*

Martin had thrown on a shirt and was pulling on trousers.

"Yes. Right now."

Could it be true, he asked himself. Could it *possibly* be true?

Martin stood, looking down from above, at a dozen rats that had taken turns in running through the maze. At his request, Yvonne had brought them from the animal room. They were a group which, for several months, had been injected with the partially purified peptide mix, and more recently with Peptide 7. All of the rats were thin—far thinner than when the injections had begun. Now Yvonne was returning the last rat to its cage.

It was still early Sunday morning. Apart from the two of them and a watchman they had spoken to on the way in, the institute was silent and deserted.

Like the other animals that preceded it, the twelfth rat began eating from a container in its cage.

Martin observed, "They still feed well."

"They all do," Yvonne agreed. "Now, will you tell me what this is about?"

"All right. Because the rats we gave peptides to have lost weight, got thin, and some of them are gaunt, all of us here assumed their general health is poorer." He added ruefully, "It wasn't very scientific."

"What difference does it make?"

"Possibly a lot. Supposing their health *hasn't* worsened. Suppose they're all perfectly well? Maybe more so than before. Suppose Peptide 7, as well as improving memory, caused a *healthy weight loss.*"

"You mean . . ."

"I mean," Martin said, "we may have stumbled on something for which people have been searching for centuries—a way to metabolize food in the body without producing fat and therefore weight gain."

Yvonne regarded him openmouthed. "But that could be terribly important."

"Of course—if it's true."

"But it's something you weren't looking for."

"Lots of discoveries have happened when scientists were seeking something else."

"So what do you do next?"

Martin considered. "I need advice from specialists. Tomorrow I'll arrange to get them here."

"In that case," Yvonne said hopefully, "can we go back to your house now?"

He put his arm around her. "I never heard a better idea."

"I'll send you a detailed report, of course," the visiting veterinarian informed Martin, "and it will include measurement of body fat, blood chemistry, urine and stool analyses done in my own lab. But I can tell you right now that those are some of the healthiest rats I've come across, particularly remembering their advanced age."

"Thank you, Doctor," Martin said. "It's what I'd hoped for."

Today was Tuesday and the veterinarian, Dr. Ingersoll, an elderly specialist in small mammals, had come from London on a morning train. He would return that afternoon.

Another expert, a nutritionist from Cambridge, was due at the Harlow institute two days later.

"I suppose," Dr. Ingersoll said, "you wouldn't care to tell me precisely what it is you've been injecting into those rats of yours?"

304

"If you don't mind," Martin replied, "I'd prefer not. At least not yet."

The veterinarian nodded. "I rather thought you'd say that. Well, whatever it is, my dear fellow, you are obviously onto something interesting."

Martin smiled, and left it there.

On Thursday, the nutritionist, Ian Cavaliero, provided information that was even more intriguing.

"Possibly what you have done in treating those rats," he pronounced, "is change the functioning of either their endocrine glands or their central nervous systems, or perhaps both. The result is, the calories they take in with food are converted to heat instead of fat. If not carried to extremes, there's no harm in that. Their bodies simply get rid of the excess heat through evaporation or some other means."

Dr. Cavaliero, a young scientist whom Martin had known at Cambridge, was widely regarded as a leading authority on nutrition.

"New data are emerging," he reported, "showing that different individuals—or animals—have differing efficiencies for utilizing calories. Some calories go into fat, but a lot get used for the kind of body work we never see or feel. For example, cells pumping ions, such as sodium, out of themselves and into the blood in a continuous cycling process."

The nutritionist continued, "Other calories *must* go into heat, just to maintain body temperature. It's been discovered, though, that the *proportion* going to heat, metabolic work, or fat varies widely. Therefore if you can change and control that proportion—as you appear to be doing with these animals—it represents a major advance."

A small group whom Martin had invited to join the discussion with Cavaliero listened intently. It comprised Rao Sastri, two other staff scientists, and Yvonne.

Sastri interjected, "That fat-work-heat variation is undoubtedly why some fortunate persons can eat large meals, yet never put on weight."

"Exactly." The nutritionist smiled. "We've all met, and probably envied, those kind of people. But something else may be affecting your rats also—a satiety factor."

Martin said, "Through the CNS?"

"Yes. The central nervous system is, of course, highly regulated by brain peptides. And since you inform me that the injected material affects the brain, it could be reducing brain signals of hunger . . .

305

So, one way or another, your compound plainly has a desirable anti-obesity effect."

The discussion continued and, next day, Martin used Cavaliero's words, "desirable antiobesity effect," in a confidential report sent directly to Sam Hawthorne.

"While an enhancement of memory through Peptide 7 remains our primary objective," Martin wrote, "we will experiment additionally with what, at first glimpse, appears as a positive, promising side effect which may have clinical possibilities."

While the report was restrained, excitement among Martin and his Harlow colleagues was at fever pitch.

FOUR

1977–1985

1

Majestically, and with a solid dignity no other form of transportation yet devised could match, the cargo liner SS *Santa Isabella* edged its way along Fort Armstrong Channel and into Honolulu Harbor.

Andrew and Celia were on deck, standing with other passengers, below the bridge and forward.

Andrew, with binoculars, was already scanning the dockside and port buildings coming into view. His scrutiny had a purpose.

As the Aloha Tower loomed ahead, made golden by Hawaiian sunshine from an azure sky, the ship swung smoothly to starboard, tugs fussing beside it. Ships' whistles sounded. Among the *Santa Isabella's* crew, landing preparations intensified.

Lowering the binoculars, Andrew stole a sideways glance at Celia. Like himself, she was bronzed and healthy, a consequence of almost six months of leisure, spent largely in the open air. She was relaxed too, he could see, as he thought of the accumulated tensions that had preceded their departure. No doubt about it: their tour, the comparative isolation and a total absence of pressures had been good for them both.

He raised the binoculars again.

"You seem to be looking for something," Celia said.

Without turning his head, he answered, "If I see it, I'll tell you."

"All right." She sighed. "I can hardly believe it's almost over."

And it was. Their long journey, which had taken them through fifteen countries, essentially would finish here. After a brief stopover they would fly directly home from Honolulu, ready to resume their lives amid whatever changes awaited them, though such changes would be mainly those affecting Celia.

She wondered what they might be.

Deliberately, since leaving home in early March, she had excluded thoughts of the future from her mind. Now it was mid-August and the future must be faced.

Touching Andrew's arm, she said, "For the rest of my life I'll

309

remember this time; all the places we've been, everything we've done and seen . . ."

Celia thought: There was *so much* to remember. In her mind, scenes flooded back: Yes, truly magic moonlight on the Nile, and sand and searing heat in the Valley of the Kings . . . walking the labyrinthine cobbled streets of Lisbon's Alfama, nine centuries old, and flowers everywhere . . . Jerusalem—*"The hill nearest heaven, where a man can cup his hand to the wind and hear the voice of God."* . . . Rome's paradoxical mingling of the earthy and ethereal . . . Greek islands, diamonds in the Aegean, a montage memory of dazzling light, white terraced villages, mountains, olive groves . . . Oil-rich, thriving Abu Dhabi and a happy reunion with Celia's younger sister, Janet, her husband and young family . . . India, subcontinent of savage contrasts, its pleasures weighed against appalling filth and degradation. One picture-postcard scene: Jaipur, the pink city . . . Then the Great Barrier Reef, Australian coral kingdom, a snorkeler's Fantasia . . . and near Kyoto, Japan: the fragile, dreamlike beauty of the Shugakuin Imperial Villa, an emperor's hideaway and a place of poetry, still guarded from the tourist mainstream . . . Hong Kong's frenetic pace, as if time were running out, *and so it was!* . . . In Singapore—amid enormous wealth—the humble hawker food stalls, a gourmet's paradise, with *nasi beryani* served at Glutton's Corner, aptly named . . .

In Singapore, too, Andrew and Celia had boarded the *Santa Isabella* for an unhurried journey through the South China Sea and into the Pacific, a journey which was ending in Hawaii, here and now.

There had been twenty or so other passengers aboard, most of them savoring the leisurely shipboard pace and comfortable accommodations without the hectic, organized jollity of a conventional cruise ship.

As the cargo liner continued moving slowly, Celia's musing drifted on . . .

Despite her conscious efforts at the exclusion, until now, of thoughts about the future, inevitably there had been some about the past. In recent days especially she had asked herself: was she wrong in quitting Felding-Roth so abruptly? Her resignation had been impetuous and instinctual. Had it also been unwise? Celia wasn't sure, and *that* thought made her wonder whether sometime soon she would experience regrets and anguish even greater than her present doubts.

310

Clearly her departure had not affected the company or the drug Montayne in any serious way. In February, as scheduled, Montayne was launched, apparently with great success. According to trade-press reports which Celia read before leaving with Andrew on their tour, Montayne was at once widely prescribed and popular, especially with women who continued to be employed during pregnancy and to whom relief from morning sickness was critically important. It seemed obvious that the new drug was a bonanza for Felding-Roth.

Similarly, she had learned while in France that the same was proving true for the French originators of Montayne, Laboratoires Gironde-Chimie.

The *France-Soir* news stories out of Nouzonville and Spain, it seemed, had not harmed the reputation of Montayne. Nor, in the United States, had Dr. Maud Stavely's anti-Montayne arguments been given much credence or impeded sales.

Celia's thoughts turned back to the ship, which was close to the dockside now, approaching Pier 10 where they would disembark and clear Customs.

Suddenly, beside her, Andrew exclaimed, "There!"

"There, what?"

He handed over the binoculars and pointed. "Focus on that second big window—above the dock and left of the clock tower."

Puzzled, she did as instructed. "What am I looking for?"

"You'll see."

The group around them had thinned out. In addition to Andrew and Celia, only two or three passengers remained, the rest having returned to their cabins to prepare for going ashore.

Celia adjusted the binoculars and moved them, exploring. Almost at once she cried, "I *do* see! And I don't believe it . . ."

"You can believe it," Andrew said. "They're real."

"Lisa and Bruce!" Joyously, Celia shouted her children's names. Then, holding the binoculars with one hand, she began waving frantically with the other. Andrew joined in. Behind the plate glass, in the spot where Andrew had observed them, Lisa and Bruce, laughing and excited, waved back.

Celia was incredulous. "I don't understand. We weren't expecting the children. How did they get here?"

"*I* was expecting them," Andrew told her calmly. "In fact, I arranged it. It took several phone calls from Singapore when you weren't around, but . . ."

311

Celia, still overwhelmed, seemed hardly to hear. "Of course, I'm happy to see them. But Lisa and Bruce have summer jobs. How could they get away?"

"That was easy too—when I explained why it was I wanted them here." He retrieved the binoculars and put them in a case.

"I still don't understand," Celia said. "*You* wanted the children?"

"That's right," Andrew assured her. "It was so that I could keep a promise. One made many years ago."

"A promise to whom?"

"To you."

She looked at him, perplexed.

Andrew said gently, prompting, "It was on our honeymoon. We were talking, and you told me why you'd preferred a honeymoon in the Bahamas, rather than Hawaii. You said Hawaii would have made you sad. Then you explained about your father, and his dying at Pearl Harbor, going down with the *Arizona.*"

"Wait!" Celia's voice was barely a whisper. *Yes, now she did remember . . . remembered after all these years.*

On that honeymoon day on a Bahamas beach, she had described her father to Andrew, described the little she remembered of Chief Petty Officer Willis de Grey . . . "When he was home the house was always noisy, full of fun. He was big, and with a booming voice, and he made people laugh, and loved children, and was strong . . ."

And Andrew, who had been understanding then and ever since, had asked, "Have you been to Pearl Harbor?"

She had answered, "Though I'm not sure why, I'm not ready yet. You'll think this strange, but one day I'd like to go to where my father died, though not alone. I'd like to take my children."

It was then that Andrew promised, "One day, when we have our children and they can understand, then I'll arrange it."

A promise . . . twenty years ago.

As the *Santa Isabella* eased alongside Pier 10 and mooring lines snaked out, Andrew informed Celia quietly, "We're going tomorrow; it's all arranged. Going to the *Arizona* Memorial, to your father's ship and where he died. And just as you wanted, your children will be with you."

Celia's lips trembled. Speech seemed beyond her as she reached out and grasped both Andrew's hands. Her eyes rose to his, and in

312

them was a look of adoration such as few men in their lifetimes ever see.

When she could manage it, her voice heavy with emotion, she declared, "Oh, you beautiful, *beautiful* man!"

2

At 10 A.M. a driver and a rented limousine ordered by Andrew were waiting for the family outside the Kahala Hilton Hotel. The late August day was warm, though not oppressive, with a light breeze from the south—Kona weather, Hawaiians called it. A few scattered tufts of cumulus dotted an otherwise clear sky.

Earlier, Lisa and Bruce had joined their parents for breakfast in a pleasant suite that overlooked Waialae golf course and the Pacific Ocean to the south. Today and yesterday there had been a steady, happy stream of talk as the four of them filled in, with descriptions, experiences, and animated questioning, the six-month gap during which they had been apart. Lisa had completed, with happy enthusiasm, her freshman year at Stanford. Bruce, soon to enter his final year at the Hill, had applied for entry to Williams College in Massachusetts—itself historic, in keeping with what continued to be his main academic interest.

As part of that interest, and in anticipation of today, Bruce announced he had recently completed a study of the 1941 Japanese attack on Pearl Harbor. He informed the others matter-of-factly, "If you have any questions, I think I can answer them."

"You're insufferable!" Lisa had told him. "But since your service is free, I may condescend to use it."

Celia, while managing to keep up with family banter over the breakfast table, felt within herself an unusual sense of detachment. It was a feeling difficult to define but somehow, on this day, it seemed as if a part of her past had returned—or shortly would—to join the

313

present. On waking this morning she had been conscious of a sense of occasion that had persisted, and she had dressed accordingly, carefully selecting a crisp white pleated skirt and a tailored blouse of navy blue and white. She wore white sandals and would carry a white straw handbag. The effect, which she intended, was neither casual nor unduly formal, but smart and . . . the words came to her: caring and respectful. Inspecting herself before joining the others, a thought about her father sprang to mind, a thought she tried to resist at first, then allowed to take shape: *If only he had lived to see me now —his daughter, with my family!*

As if sensing something of Celia's feelings in advance, the others had dressed less casually than usual. Lisa, who the day before had worn jeans, today had on a simple but attractive flowered voile dress; it brought out her young and glowing beauty, and for a moment Celia saw herself at Lisa's age—nineteen—twenty-seven years ago.

Andrew had chosen a lightweight suit and, for the first time in many days, was wearing a tie. Her husband, Celia thought, who would be fifty soon and whose hair was now entirely gray, looked increasingly distinguished as years went by. Bruce, still boyish though with serious ways, was handsome in a Hill School blazer with an open shirt.

As the Jordan family approached the limousine, the driver touched his uniform cap politely and held a rear door open. He addressed Andrew. "Dr. Jordan? You're going to the *Arizona,* I believe."

"That's right." Andrew consulted a paper. "But I was told to tell you not to go to the Visitor Center first, but to the private dock of CINCPACFLT."

The driver raised his eyebrows. "You must be a V.I.P."

"Not me." Andrew smiled and looked toward Celia. "My wife."

Inside the limousine, as they moved away, Lisa asked, "What's CINC—whatever you said?"

It was Bruce who answered. "Commander-in-Chief Pacific Fleet. Hey, Dad, you pulled wires!"

Celia gazed at Andrew curiously. "How did you arrange all this?"

"I used your name," he told her. "In case you don't know, my dear, it still cuts ice, and you have a lot of people who admire you."

When the others pressed him, he admitted, "If you must know, I telephoned the Felding-Roth regional manager in Hawaii."

Celia injected, "Tano Akamura?"

"That's right. And he asked me to tell you that you're greatly missed. Anyway, it happens that Akamura's wife has a sister married to an admiral. The rest was easy. So we're going to the *Arizona* in an admiral's barge."

"Dad," Bruce said, "that's great staff work!"

His father smiled. "Thank you."

"Thank *you*," Celia said. Then she asked, "When you were talking to Tano, did you by any chance ask him how things were?"

Andrew hesitated. "You mean at Felding-Roth . . . and about Montayne?"

"Yes."

He had hoped she wouldn't ask, but answered, "Apparently very well."

"That's not all you found out," Celia insisted. "Tell me the rest."

Reluctantly Andrew added, "He said Montayne is a big success and, in his words, 'selling like crazy.'"

Celia nodded. It was really no more than everyone expected, and confirmed the earlier news given out after Montayne's launching. But it did reinforce the recent question in her mind: had her resignation been hasty and foolish? Then, determinedly for today—this special day—she pushed such thoughts aside.

The limousine moved swiftly, using the Lunalilo and Moanalua freeways and passing downtown Honolulu with its modern high-rise buildings. In about twenty minutes they left the freeway near Aloha Stadium, entering, soon after, the U.S. Navy Reservation at Aiea Bay. The smallish CINCPACFLT private dock was in a pleasant land-scaped area used by military families.

A fifty-foot navy utility boat—the so-called admiral's barge—was waiting at the dock, its diesel motors running. The boat was operated by two naval ratings in dress whites. A half-dozen other passengers were already seated under a main-deck canopy.

One of the ratings, a young woman with "bowhook" duty, cast off the moorings after the Jordans were aboard. The coxswain, on a control bridge midships, eased the boat from the dock and into the busy stream of Pearl Harbor traffic.

The breeze felt earlier on land was stronger on the water, and wavelets slapped the utility boat's hull, sending occasional light spray inboard. The harbor water was a dull gray-green, with little or nothing visible beneath the surface.

The woman sailor provided a commentary as they circled Ford Island counterclockwise. Andrew, Lisa and Bruce listened attentively, but Celia, preoccupied with private memories, found her thoughts wandering and caught only snatches.

"Sunday morning, December 7, 1941 . . . Japanese dive bombers, with torpedo and fighter planes, and midget submarines, attacked without warning . . . first wave at 7:55 A.M. . . . at 8:05 explosions rocked Battleship Row . . . 8:10, *Arizona*, hit in the forward magazine, exploded and sank . . . by 8:12 *Utah* had rolled over . . . *California* and *West Virginia* settled to the bottom . . . *Oklahoma* capsized . . . casualties, 2,403 killed, 1,178 wounded . . ."

It was all so long ago, she thought—thirty-six years; better than half a lifetime. Yet never, until this moment, had it seemed so close.

The navy boat, rolling in a slight chop near the Pearl Harbor entrance channel, altered course as it rounded the southern tip of Ford Island. Suddenly, directly ahead, was the *Arizona* Memorial, white in bright sunshine.

Here is where it happened, and I have come at last. Lines from a poem sprang to Celia's mind. *"Give me my scallop-shell of quiet . . . And thus I'll take my pilgrimage."* As she looked ahead, beyond the bow of the boat, an incongruous thought intruded: *The Memorial was unlike what she had expected. Instead, it resembled a long, white railway boxcar, deflated in the middle.*

The commentary again: "The architect's words: 'The form, wherein the structure sags in the center but stands strong and vigorous at the ends, expresses initial defeat and ultimate victory' . . . *Had the architect thought of that before or after? But either way, it didn't matter. The ship was what mattered, and now its shape was becoming visible—incredibly, only a few feet below the surface of the gray-green water.*

". . . and the Memorial spans the sunken battleship."

My father's ship. His home when he was away from home, and where he died . . . when I was ten years old, five thousand miles away in Philadelphia.

Andrew reached out, took Celia's hand and held it. Neither spoke. Among all the passengers on the boat there seemed a constraint, a quietness, as if common sensibilities were shared.

The coxswain laid them neatly alongside a pontoon dock at the Memorial entrance. The woman sailor secured the moorings, and the Jordan family, along with others, disembarked. As they moved inward, there was no longer movement beneath their feet since the

Memorial rested on pilings driven into the harbor bottom. No part of it touched the ship.

Near the Memorial's center, Celia, Andrew and Lisa stood at an opening in the concrete structure gazing downward at the main deck of the *Arizona,* now clearly visible, awesome in its closeness.

Somewhere beneath us are my father's bones, or what remains of them. I wonder how he died. Was it swift and merciful, or some other, awful way? Oh, how I hope it was the first!

Bruce, who had moved away, returned to them. He said quietly, "I've found grandfather's name. I'll show you." His parents and sister followed until, standing beside many others, all subdued, they faced a marble wall, a sea of names and ranks.

In that fierce few minutes of the Japanese attack, 1,177 had died on the Arizona *alone. Later it had proved impossible to raise the ship which became—for more than a thousand of the dead—their final grave.*

An inscription read:

TO THE MEMORY OF THE GALLANT MEN
HERE ENTOMBED

Bruce pointed. "There, Mom."

W F DE GREY   CEM

They stood respectfully, each with individual thoughts; then it was Celia who led the way back to where they had been earlier, looking down on the sunken hull from which the superstructure had long since been removed. The closeness of it fascinated her. While they watched, a bubble of oil rose from somewhere far below. The oil spread itself, like a petal on the water's surface. A few minutes later, eerily, the process was repeated.

"Those oil bubbles are from what's left in fuel tanks," Bruce explained. "They've been coming up like that since the ship went down. No one knows how long the oil will last, but it could be another twenty years."

Celia reached out to touch her son.

This is my son, your grandson. He is explaining to me about your ship.

"I wish I could have known Grandfather," Lisa said.

Celia was about to speak when suddenly, without warning, her emotional defenses wavered and collapsed. It was as if Lisa's simple,

317

moving remark was the last iota added to a barely balanced scale before it tipped. Grief and sadness overwhelmed Celia—grief for the father she had known so briefly, but had loved and whose memory these poignant moments at Pearl Harbor had brought flooding back; memories of her mother who had died ten years ago this month; and, combining with those older griefs revived, Celia's nearer sorrow from her own failure, her great misjudgment as it now appeared, the recent ignominious end to her career. The last thought had, for six months or more, been resolutely thrust away. Now, like dues delayed but later to be paid, it added to the emotion and she broke. Oblivious to all else, she wept.

Seeing what was happening, Andrew moved toward her, but Lisa and Bruce were faster. Both children embraced their mother, comforting her, and unashamedly were crying too.

Andrew, gently, put his arms around them all.

The family assembled for dinner that night in the Maile Room of the Kahala Hilton. On sitting down, Celia's first words were, "Andrew dear, I would like us to have champagne."

"Of course." Beckoning a sommelier, Andrew ordered Taittinger, which he knew to be his wife's favorite, then told her, "You look radiant tonight."

"It's how I feel," she responded, beaming at them all.

Since this morning, little had been said about their excursion to Pearl Harbor. On the Memorial during the few minutes of Celia's breakdown, other people nearby had considerately looked away, and Andrew sensed that the *Arizona* setting, which evoked sad, sometimes tragic memories in so many who went there, had seen frequent and similar scenes of grief.

Through most of the afternoon Celia slept, then later had gone shopping in one of the hotel stores, buying herself a stunning red-and-white long dress, Hawaiian style. She was wearing it now.

"When you get tired of that dress, Mom," Lisa said admiringly, "I'll be glad to take it over."

At that moment the champagne arrived. When it was poured, Celia raised her glass and said, "To you all!—I love you dearly, and thank you! I want you to know that I shall never forget what happened today, and your comfort and understanding. But you should

318

also know that now I am over it. In a way, I suppose, it was a cleansing process, a—what's that word?"

"Catharsis," Bruce said. "Actually it's Greek and means purification. Aristotle used it to . . ."

"Oh, cool it!" Lisa, leaning across the table, slapped her brother's hand. "Sometimes you're *too much!*"

Andrew laughed and the others joined in, including Bruce.

"Go on, Mom," Lisa urged.

"Well," Celia said, "I've decided it's time to stop feeling sorry for myself, and to put my life back together. It's been a wonderful holiday, the finest ever, but it will be over in two more days." She regarded Andrew fondly. "I imagine you're ready to get back into practice."

He nodded. "Ready and keen."

"I can understand it," Celia said, "because I feel the same way. So I won't stay unemployed. I intend to find work."

Bruce asked, "What will you do?"

Celia sipped her champagne before answering. "I've thought a lot about it, and asked myself questions, and come up each time with the same answer: The pharmaceutical business is what I know best, so it makes sense that I should stay in it."

Andrew assured her, "Yes, it does."

"Could you go back to Felding-Roth?" It was Lisa's question.

Her mother shook her head. "I burned my bridges. I'm sure there's no way Felding-Roth would have me now, even if I wanted it. No, I'll try other companies."

"If some of them don't jump and grab you, they need their business acumen examined," Andrew said. "Have you considered which ones?"

"Yes." Celia went on thoughtfully, "There's one company, above all others, which I've admired. It's Merck. If you were to look for a 'Rolls-Royce' of the drug industry, Merck's the one. So I shall apply there first."

"And after that?"

"I like SmithKline, also Upjohn. Both are companies I'd be proud to work for. After that, if it's needed, I'll make a longer list."

"I predict you won't have to." Andrew raised his glass. "Here's to the lucky company that gets Celia Jordan!"

Later, over dinner, Bruce asked, "What do we do tomorrow?"

319

"Since it's our last full day in Hawaii," Celia suggested, "how about a lazy time on the beach?"

They agreed that a lazy day was what they wanted most.

3

In the bedroom of the Jordans' suite, a few minutes before 6 A.M., a bedside telephone rang stridently. The ringing stopped, then began again.

Celia was sleeping soundly. Beside her, Andrew, crossing the boundary from sleep to wakefulness, stirred at the phone's insistence.

The night before, on going to bed, they had left the sliding glass doors to a balcony open, admitting a soft breeze and the murmur of the sea. Now, outside in the grayness of pre-dawn, objects were becoming visible—as if a stage director were going slowly from black, lighting a new scene. In another fifteen minutes the sun would begin ascending over the horizon.

Andrew sat up, awake, the phone having penetrated his consciousness. He reached out to answer it.

Celia stirred and asked sleepily, "What's the time?"

"Too damned early!" Andrew said into the phone, "Yes—what is it?"

"I have a person-to-person call for Mrs. Celia Jordan." An operator's voice.

"Who's calling her?"

A different female voice came on the line. "Mr. Seth Feingold of Felding-Roth, New Jersey."

"Does Mr. Feingold know what time it is out here?"

"Yes, sir. He does."

Celia was sitting upright, awake now also. "Is it Seth?" When Andrew nodded, she said, "I'll take it."

He handed her the phone. After another operator exchange, Celia heard the elderly comptroller's voice. "Is that you, Celia?"

"Yes, it is."

"I've just been told we awakened you, and I apologize. But it's noon here. We simply couldn't wait any longer."

She said, puzzled, "Who is 'we'? And wait longer for what?"

"Celia, what I have to tell you is exceedingly important. Please listen carefully."

Feingold's voice sounded strained. She told him, "Go ahead."

"I'm calling you on behalf of the board of directors, and at the board's request. I am instructed, firstly, to inform you that when you resigned—for reasons which we all know—you were right, and everyone else . . ." The voice faltered, then continued, "All the rest of us were wrong."

She wondered, with bewilderment, whether she was hearing correctly, or was truly awake. "Seth, I don't understand. You can't be speaking about Montayne."

"Unfortunately, I am."

"But from what I've read and heard, Montayne is a spectacular success." She remembered the positive report, relayed only yesterday by Andrew, from Tano, the Felding-Roth Hawaii manager.

"That's what we all thought, up to just a short time ago. But everything has changed—a sudden change. And now we have a terrible situation here."

"Wait a moment, please."

Covering the phone mouthpiece, she told Andrew, "Something important has happened. I'm not sure what. But listen on the extension."

There was one in the bathroom. Celia waited while Andrew went to it, then said, "Seth, go on."

"What I just told you was the first thing, Celia. The second is this: The board wants you to come back."

Still, she could scarcely believe what she was hearing. After a pause she said, "I think you'd better start at the beginning."

"All right. I will."

She sensed Seth organizing his thoughts and, while she waited, wondered why he was calling, and not Sam Hawthorne.

"You remember the reports of damaged babies. Vegetable babies —that awful word. The reports from Australia, France and Spain?"

"Of course."

321

"There have been many more—from those countries and others. So many more, there can't be any doubt Montayne has been the cause."

"Oh, my God!" Celia's free hand went to her face. Her shocked first thought was: *Don't let it be true! This is a bad dream and isn't happening. I don't want to be proved right, not this awful way.* Then she saw Andrew through the open bathroom door, his face set grimly, and noticed the increasing light of dawn outside, and she knew that what was happening was no dream, but real.

Seth continued, reciting details. ". . . began two and a half months ago with some scattered reports . . . cases similar to those earlier ones . . . then the numbers increased . . . more recently, a flood . . . all the mothers had taken Montayne during pregnancy . . . nearly three hundred defective births worldwide, so far . . . obviously more to come, especially in the United States where Montayne has been on sale only seven months . . ."

Celia closed her eyes as the tale of horror grew. *Hundreds of babies who could have been normal, but now would never think, or walk, or sit up unaided or, through their lifetimes, behave in any normal way . . . And still more to come.*

She wanted to weep bitter tears, to cry aloud in anger and frustration. But whom to cry to? No one. And weeping and anger were useless and too late.

Could she, herself, have done more to prevent this grisly tragedy? *Yes!*

She could have raised her voice after resigning, gone public with her doubts about Montayne, instead of keeping silent. But would it have made any difference? Would people have listened? Probably not, though *someone* might have, and if *one baby* had been saved, her effort would have been worthwhile.

As if reading her mind from five thousand miles away, Seth said, "All of us here have asked ourselves questions, Celia. We've had sleepless, conscience-ridden nights, and there isn't one of us who won't carry some guilt to his grave. But your conscience can be clear. You did everything you could. It wasn't your fault your warning was ignored."

Celia thought: It would be so easy and comfortable to accept that view. But she knew that to the end of her days she would always have doubts.

Abruptly, a new and troubling thought occurred to her.

322

"Is everything you've told me, Seth, being made widely known? Is there urgent publicity going out? Have there been warnings to women that they should stop taking Montayne?"

"Well . . . not exactly in that form. There's been some scattered publicity, though—surprisingly—not much."

That would account, Celia thought, for the fact that she and Andrew had heard nothing adverse about Montayne while on their tour.

Seth went on, "Apparently no one among the news people has pieced the whole story together yet. But we're afraid it will happen soon."

"You're *afraid* . . ."

Obviously, she realized, there had been no attempt to create massive publicity, which meant that *Montayne was still being sold and used*. Again Celia remembered Andrew's report yesterday; in quoting Tano he had spoken of Montayne "selling like crazy." A shiver ran through her as she asked, "What has been done about withdrawing the drug and recalling all supplies?"

Seth said carefully, "Gironde-Chimie have told us they'll withdraw Montayne in France this week. I understand the British are preparing an announcement. And the Australian government has already stopped sales there."

Her voice rose to a shout. "I'm talking about the United States."

"I assure you, Celia, we've done everything the law requires. Every bit of information coming into Felding-Roth has been passed on promptly to the FDA in Washington. Everything. Vince Lord attended to that personally. Now, we're waiting for a decision from FDA."

"Waiting for a decision! In the name of God, why wait? What other decision *can* there be but to withdraw Montayne?"

Seth said defensively, "Our lawyers advise us strongly that at this stage it will be better to have the ruling from FDA first."

Celia was close to screaming. Holding herself in, she replied, "The FDA is *slow*. Their machinery could take weeks."

"I suppose that's possible. But the lawyers insist—if we make the withdrawal on our own, it could be an admission of error and therefore of liability. Even now, the financial consequences . . ."

"What does finance matter when pregnant women are still taking Montayne? When unborn babies . . ."

Celia stopped, realizing that argument was useless, that the con-

323

versation was going nowhere, and wondering again why she was talking with the comptroller and not Sam Hawthorne.

She said decisively, "I must speak with Sam."

"Unfortunately, that isn't possible. At least, not now." An uneasy pause. "Sam is . . . well, not himself. He has some personal problems. That's one of the reasons we want you—need you—back."

Celia snapped, "Double-talk. What does it mean?"

She heard a long, deep sigh.

"I was going to tell you this later because I know it will distress you." Seth's voice was low and sad. "You remember . . . just before you left us, Sam had a grandchild."

"Juliet's baby. Yes." Celia recalled the celebration in Sam's office in which she had shared, though she dampened it later with her doubts about Montayne.

"It seems that when Juliet was pregnant, she suffered a good deal from morning sickness. Sam gave her Montayne."

At Seth's last words, Celia went icy cold. She had a horrible foreboding of what was coming next.

"Last week the doctors established that Juliet's baby was adversely affected by the drug." Seth's voice was close to breaking. "Sam's grandson is mentally defective and has limbs that won't function—a vegetable like all the others."

Celia emitted a strangled cry of grief and anguish, then incredulity replaced it. "How could Sam have done it? At that time Montayne wasn't approved for use."

"There were physicians' samples, as you know. Sam used them, telling no one except Juliet. I suppose he had so much faith in Montayne, he assumed there was no risk. There was some personal involvement too, and maybe pride. If you remember, Sam acquired Montayne himself from Gironde-Chimie."

"Yes, I remember." Celia's thoughts were whirling—a mélange of frustration, anger, bitterness and pity. Seth interrupted them.

"I said we need you, Celia, and so we do. As you can imagine, Sam is torn with grief and guilt and, at the moment, isn't functioning. But that's only part of it. Everything here is a mess. We're like a damaged, rudderless ship, and we need you to assess the damage and take charge. For one thing, you're the only one with sufficient knowledge and experience. For another, all of us—including the board—respect your judgments, especially now. And, oh yes, you'd come back as

324

executive vice president. I won't go into the financial arrangements, but they'd be generous."

Executive vice president of Felding-Roth. Only one rung below the presidency, and higher than she would have been as vice president of sales, the promotion she had forfeited by resigning. There was a time, Celia thought, when the offer just made would have been a cause for rejoicing, a shining landmark in her life. How strange that suddenly it meant so little.

"You may have guessed," Seth said, "that some others—a few members of the board—are with me, listening to this conversation. We're waiting here, hoping your answer will be yes."

Celia became aware of Andrew signaling to her from the bathroom. For the second time since the conversation began, she said into the telephone, "Wait, please."

Andrew hung up the extension and came out. As before, with her phone mouthpiece covered, she asked him, "What do you think?"

He told her, "You'll have to make the decision. But remember this: If you go back, it won't matter that you resigned and have been away. Some of the Montayne mess and responsibility will rub off on you."

"I know." She considered. "But I was with the company a long time. They were good years, and now they need me. I'll only go back, though, if . . ."

She returned to the phone.

"Seth, I've listened carefully to what you've said. I will accept, but under one condition."

"Name it."

"Montayne must be withdrawn from sale by Felding-Roth today, and a public statement made about its dangers. Not tomorrow, not next week, and no more waiting while the FDA makes up its mind. *Today.*"

"Celia, that's impossible. I explained the warnings from our lawyers, the question of liability. We could be inviting millions of dollars' worth of lawsuits—enough to break the company."

"There'll be lawsuits anyway."

"We know that. But we don't want to make the situation worse. Withdrawal is bound to happen soon. Meanwhile, with you here we could discuss it . . ."

"I don't want it discussed. I want it done. I want it on national TV and radio today, and in every newspaper in the country within

325

twenty-four hours. I'll be watching and listening. Otherwise, no deal."

It was Seth's turn to say, "Just a moment."

Celia could hear a muted discussion at the other end. There was some obvious dissension, then she heard Seth say, "She's adamant," and a moment later, "Of course she means it. And remember, we need her more than she needs us."

The debate in New Jersey continued for a few minutes more, most of it inaudible to Celia. Finally, Seth returned to the phone.

"Celia, your terms are met. What you insist on will be done at once —within the hour. I guarantee it personally. Now . . . how soon can you be back?"

She told him, "I'll get the first flight out of here. Expect me in the office tomorrow."

4

They managed to get four coach seats on a United Airlines 747, leaving Honolulu at 4:50 P.M. The flight was a nonstop to Chicago, where they would change to another flight due in New York at 9 A.M. local time the following day. Celia intended to get what sleep she could en route, then go to Felding-Roth headquarters that same morning.

Lisa and Bruce, who had planned to spend two more days in Hawaii, made the decision to return east with their parents. As Lisa put it, "We haven't seen you for so long, we want to be with you as much as we can. Also, if I'm by myself I know I'll be sad, and probably cry, thinking about those poor deformed babies."

Over a hurried breakfast in Andrew's and Celia's suite, interrupted by several telephone calls relating to their departure, it was Andrew who had explained the tragic situation to the children.

"I *will* talk about it," Celia had said, "but if you don't mind, not any more for a while. I guess you could say I'm shell-shocked at this moment." Even now, she wondered whether she had done the right thing by agreeing to go back, then reminded herself that her insistence on having Montayne withdrawn at once would save at least some babies and mothers from their otherwise terrible fate.

That Felding-Roth's promise to Celia had been kept became evident shortly before they left the Kahala Hilton for Honolulu Airport. A radio music program was interrupted for a special news bulletin. It reported the withdrawal of Montayne from public sale because of "possible harmful effects which are being investigated," and added a warning that doctors should cease prescribing the drug and pregnant women should stop taking it.

On a regular newscast, soon after, an amplified report had Montayne's withdrawal as the top item and, at the airport, an afternoon edition of the *Honolulu Star-Bulletin* carried an Associated Press news story on the subject on its front page. It seemed clear that a barrage of publicity had begun and was likely to continue.

For the Jordan family it proved a very different day from the quiet one on a beach which they had planned the night before.

The airplane was crowded, but their four-abreast seats in the aft section at least allowed some private conversation and after a while Celia told the others, "Thank you for being patient. Now you can ask questions if you wish."

Bruce was first.

"How could something like this happen, Mom, with a drug being okayed, then having so much bad effect?"

She organized her thoughts before answering.

"What you have to remember first," Celia said, "is that a drug, *any* drug, is an alien chemical in the human body. It's put there—usually when a doctor prescribes it—with the aim of correcting something that's *wrong* in the body. But as well as doing good, it may also do harm. The harmful part is called a side effect, though there can be harmless side effects too."

Andrew added, "There's also something known as 'risk versus benefit.' A physician has to judge whether the risk of using a particular drug is worth taking in order to get results that he and the patient want. Some drugs involve more risks than others. But even with simple aspirin there's a risk—a serious one at times, because aspirin can cause internal bleeding."

"But surely," Lisa said, "drug companies test drugs before they're

327

sold, and the FDA is supposed to find out about risks—what they are and how bad."

"Yes, all of that's true," Celia acknowledged. "But what often *isn't* understood is that there are limitations with testing, even nowadays. When a new drug is tested, it's used first on animals. Then if the animal data looks okay, it's tried on human volunteers. All of that takes several years. But at the end of human trials, when everything about the drug may appear to be fine, it has still been used by only a few hundred, or perhaps a thousand people."

"And none of those people," Andrew said, "may have suffered any adverse effects—or only minor, unimportant ones."

Celia nodded agreement, then went on, "But when the drug is on the market, and being taken by tens of thousands, maybe millions, adverse reactions can show up in a *few people,* sometimes a tiny percentage of the population—reactions that *could not have been foreseen* during testing. Of course, if the percentage proves large enough and the new reactions are serious or fatal, the drug has to be withdrawn. The big point is, there's no way to be certain how safe a drug is until it has been used widely."

"Those reactions," Bruce said. "They're supposed to be reported, aren't they?"

"Yes. And if a drug company hears about any, in this country the law requires us to report them to the FDA. Usually that happens."

Lisa's forehead wrinkled. "Only 'usually'?"

Celia explained, "That's because it's difficult sometimes to decide what is a true adverse reaction to a drug, and what's caused by something else. Often it's a matter for scientific judgment, with room for genuine, honest disagreement. Something else to remember is that a hasty decision could cause the loss of a good, perhaps lifesaving medication."

"In the case of Montayne, though," Andrew reminded them, "everything went the other way." He told Lisa and Bruce, "Your mother's judgment was right about those disputed reactions, the other judgments wrong."

Celia shook her head. "Even that isn't quite true. Mine was an instinct, not a scientific judgment, an instinct which *could* have been in error."

"But it wasn't," Andrew said. "That's the important thing. More than that, you stuck with what you believed, and had the moral

courage to resign on principle, which few people ever do. And for all of that, my dear, this family is proud of you."

"I'll say it is!" Bruce echoed.

Lisa leaned over and kissed her mother. "Me too, Mom."

A meal was served. Picking at the contents of his tray without enthusiasm, Andrew observed, "The one thing you can say about airline food is that it helps to pass the time."

Soon after, they returned to what was on all their minds.

Bruce said, "Something that's hard to believe, Mom, is that newspapers and TV didn't know what's been happening about Montayne —at least not the big picture, and not until today."

It was Andrew who answered.

"It can happen, and it's happened before, almost in the same way. The other occasion was with Thalidomide, which is something I've done a lot of reading about."

For the first time in many hours, Celia smiled. "This family has two history buffs."

"In 1961 and '62," Andrew said, "the American press ignored what was already a Thalidomide disaster in Europe. Even when an American physician, Dr. Helen Taussig, testified before Congress, and showed slides of deformed babies that made congressmen shudder, not a word appeared in American newspapers."

"That's incredible," Lisa said.

Her father shrugged. "It depends on your view of the press. Some reporters are lazy. Those assigned to that hearing weren't in their seats, and afterward didn't read the transcript. But one who wasn't lazy was Morton Mintz, a *Washington Post* reporter. He put all the pieces together, then broke the Thalidomide story, beating everyone else. Of course it immediately became big news, just as Montayne is becoming now."

"I should tell you both," Celia said to the children, "that your father was opposed to Montayne all along."

Lisa asked, "Dad, was that because you thought Montayne would do the awful things it did?"

Andrew answered, "Absolutely not. It was simply because, as a doctor, I don't believe a drug should be taken for anything that is just uncomfortable or self-limiting."

"What does 'self-limiting' mean?" Lisa again.

"Sickness during pregnancy is an example. It's limited, normally, to the early months of pregnancy and before long will go away,

leaving nothing harmful behind. To take any drug at that time—unless there's some other medical emergency—is foolish and always a risk. Your mother didn't, with either of you. I made sure of that." Andrew eyed his daughter. "When your time comes, don't *you* take anything, young lady. And if you want a sound, healthy baby—no liquor, wine, or smoking either."

Lisa said, "I promise."

Listening, Celia was struck by an idea that might perhaps, in time, turn Felding-Roth's Montayne experience into something positive.

Andrew was still talking.

"We doctors are at fault in a lot of ways about drugs. For one thing, we prescribe too often—much of the time unnecessarily, and in part because it's well known among us that there are patients who feel cheated if they leave a doctor's office without a prescription. Another thing, writing a prescription is an easy way to end a patient interview, to get that patient out of the office and another one in."

"This sure is confession day," Bruce said. "What else do doctors do wrong?"

"A lot of us are not well informed about drugs—certainly not as much as we ought to be, especially about side effects or the interactions of one drug with others. Of course, it's impossible to carry all that information in your head, but doctors usually don't bother, or are too proud, to open a reference book while a patient is with them."

Celia said, "Show me a doctor who isn't afraid to look something up in the presence of a patient, and I'll show you a secure, conscientious doctor. Your father is one. I've seen him do it."

Andrew smiled. "Of course, I've had some advantages where drugs are concerned. That comes from living with your mother."

"Are there bad mistakes made by doctors with drugs?" Lisa asked.

"Plenty of times," Andrew said. "And there are other times when an alert pharmacist will save a doctor from his own mistake by querying a prescription. Generally, pharmacists know a lot more about drugs than doctors do."

Bruce asked shrewdly, "But are there many doctors who admit it?"

Andrew answered, "Unfortunately, no. As often as not, pharmacists get treated as an inferior breed, not the colleagues in medicine they really are." He smiled, then added, "Of course, pharmacists make mistakes too. And sometimes patients themselves mess up by

doubling or trebling a prescribed dose to get—as they explain later in the ambulance—a quicker effect."

"And all of that," Celia said firmly, "is more cans and more worms than this tired drug person can handle in one day. I think I'll try to sleep."

She did, and remained asleep through most of the remaining journey to Chicago.

The connecting flight to New York was uneventful—though more comfortable because the family's reservations were in first class, which had not been possible from Honolulu.

Then, to Celia's surprise, a Felding-Roth company limousine and chauffeur were waiting at Kennedy Airport to drive them to Morristown. The chauffeur, whom she knew slightly, saluted and handed her a sealed envelope which contained a letter from Seth Feingold.

Dear Celia:
Welcome home!—in every sense.

The car and chauffeur are with the compliments of the board of directors, and for your exclusive, regular use as executive vice president.

Your colleagues and subordinates—this one included— look forward to meeting you when you are rested from your journey.

Yours,
Seth

At the Jordans' Morristown house there was a joyous reunion with Winnie and Hank March—Winnie hugely extended and in her final weeks of pregnancy. As Lisa and Bruce, then Celia and Andrew, embraced her, Winnie cautioned, "Don't squeeze me too 'ard, m'loves, or little thingummy might pop out right now."

Andrew laughed. "I haven't delivered a baby since I was an intern —a long time ago—but I'm willing to try."

Hank, never talkative like his wife, beamed at them happily and busied himself unloading baggage.

It was a little later, with the trio of Winnie, Celia and Andrew exchanging news in the kitchen while other activity was going on outside, that a sudden shocking thought occurred to Celia.

331

Almost afraid to ask, she said, "Winnie, while you've been pregnant, have you been taking anything?"

"You mean for bein' sick in the mornin'?"

With growing dread, Celia answered, "Yes."

"Like that Montayne?" Winnie pointed to a copy of that morning's *Newark Star-Ledger* spread open on a countertop, a news story about Montayne prominent on the front page.

Dully, Celia nodded.

"Me doctor give me some samples an' told me to take it," Winnie said. "I would 'ave, too. I was always bein' sick in the mornin's. 'Cept . . ." She glanced at Andrew. "Is it okay to say, Dr. Jordan?"

He assured her, "Yes."

" 'Cept, before you both went away, Dr. Jordan told me—'e said it was a secret between us—if I was given any of that Montayne, not to take it, but flush it down the loo. So that's what I did."

Winnie's eyes, brimming with tears, went to the newspaper, then to Andrew. "I'd an 'ard enough time gettin' this baby. So . . . oh, God bless you, Dr. Jordan!"

Celia, relieved and grateful, took Winnie in her arms and held her.

5

Sam Hawthorne had the appearance of a walking ghost.

The sight of him, during her first day back at Felding-Roth, so shocked Celia that she found it impossible to speak. For that reason, Sam spoke first.

"Well, how does it feel to return in glory, proved right and virtuous when all the rest of us were wrong and evil? Pretty good, eh?"

The unfriendly words, in a rasping voice she scarcely recognized, added to her shock. It was seven months since Celia had seen Sam. In that time he appeared to have aged at least ten years. His face was haggard and pale, with flesh around his cheekbones hanging loose.

His eyes were dull and seemed to have receded; beneath them were dark, baggy rings. His shoulders drooped. He had lost weight dramatically so that the suit he was wearing was ill-fitting.

"No, Sam," Celia said, "I don't feel good. Only sad for all of us, and I'm desperately sorry about your grandson. As to coming back, I'm simply here to help."

"Oh, yes, I thought you'd get around to being . . ."

She interrupted. "Sam, can't we go somewhere more private?"

They had encountered each other in a corridor where others were passing as they talked. Celia had just come from a meeting with Seth Feingold and several directors.

The president's office was a short distance away. Without speaking, Sam walked toward it. Celia followed.

Inside, with the outer door closed, he swung toward her. The rough, sour voice persisted. "What I started to say was—I thought you'd get around to being sorry. That's so easy. Now, why don't you go on to say what you're really thinking?"

She said quietly, "You'd better tell me what you think I'm thinking."

"I know damn well! That I was criminally irresponsible in giving Montayne to Juliet when the drug wasn't even approved. That *I'm* the one, *I alone*, who caused Juliet's and Dwight's baby, my grandson, to be the way he is—a useless mockery of a human being, nothing but a . . ." Sam choked on the final words and turned away.

Celia stood silently, torn by sorrow and compassion, weighing what to say. Finally she spoke.

"If you want the truth, Sam—and this seems to be a moment for it —yes, I did think that. I suppose I still do."

Sam was looking at her directly, hanging on her every word, she realized, as she continued.

"But then there are other things you get around to remembering. That it's easy to have twenty-twenty hindsight. That all of us make mistakes in judgment . . ."

"*You* didn't make them. Not this one. Not a whole series of mistakes as big as mine." Still the bitterness.

"I've made others," Celia said. "Everyone with responsibility does. And it's often bad luck that makes some mistakes turn out worse than others."

"This is one of the worst." Sam moved behind his desk and

333

slumped into a chair. "And all those other babies, including the unborn ones. I'm responsible . . ."

"No," she said firmly. "That isn't true. As far as the rest, you were guided by the lead of Gironde-Chimie and by scientific advice. You weren't alone. Other responsible people felt the same way."

"Except for you. What made *you* so special that you weren't taken in?"

She reminded him, "I was, to begin."

Sam put his head in his hands. "Oh, Christ! What a mess I've made." He looked up. "Celia, I'm being unfair and rotten to you, aren't I?"

"It doesn't matter."

His voice became lower, losing its edge. "I'm sorry, and I mean that. I suppose if I tell the truth, I'm jealous of you. That, and wishing I'd listened, taken your advice." Disjointed words followed. "Haven't been sleeping. Lie awake hour after hour, thinking, remembering, feeling guilty. My son-in-law won't speak to me. My daughter doesn't want to see me. Lilian tries to help us all, but doesn't know how."

Sam stopped, hesitated, then went on, "And there's something else. Something you don't know."

"What don't I know?"

He turned his head away. "I'll never tell you."

"Sam," Celia said firmly, "you have to take hold. Nothing will be gained, for you or anyone, by torturing yourself."

As if he had not heard, he said, "I'm finished here. You know that."

"No. I don't know it at all."

"I wanted to resign. The lawyers say I mustn't, not yet. I have to stay in place." He added dourly, "The façade must be preserved. To protect the company. So as not to provide more fodder for the jackal-lawyers with their damage suits, closing in. That's why I'm still to be president for a while, sitting in this chair, for the sake of shareholders."

"I'm glad to hear it," Celia said. "You're needed to run the company."

He shook his head. "You're going to do that. Haven't you been told? The board decided."

"Seth just told me some of it. But *I* need you."

He looked at her, unspoken anguish in his eyes.

Making a sudden decision, Celia went to the outer door. It could be locked with a bolt. She turned it. There was a similar bolt on a door to the secretaries' office. Celia locked that too. Lifting up a telephone, she said, "This is Mrs. Jordan. I'm with Mr. Hawthorne. We are not to be disturbed."

Sam was still at his desk, unmoving.

She asked him, "Since this happened, have you cried?"

He seemed surprised, then shook his head. "What good would that do?"

"Sometimes it helps."

She came close, leaned down, and put her arms around him. "Sam," she whispered, "let yourself go."

For a moment he eased away, peering into her face, uncertain, wavering. Then suddenly, as if a dam had broken and like a child, he laid his head on her shoulder and wept.

Following Celia's first-day session with Sam, it quickly became evident that he was a tragically broken man, his former spirit shattered, and that he would contribute little to the top-echelon running of the company. While caring deeply, Celia was obliged to accept the situation as it was.

Sam came in each day, still driving his silver-gray Rolls-Bentley and parking it on the garage catwalk level. Occasionally he and Celia would arrive there at the same time, Celia in her chauffeured company car, for which she was grateful since it enabled her to work, reading papers, during her journeys to and from home. At such moments she and Sam would walk together to the main headquarters building, using the glassed-in ramp to reach the special elevator to the executives' eleventh floor. Between them there might be some small talk but, if so, it was Celia who started it.

Once in his office, Sam mostly stayed there. No one inquired exactly what he did, but apart from a few innocuous memos, nothing of any consequence emerged. At management conferences—though informed of them in advance—Sam was noticeably absent.

Thus, from the second day after her return, there was not the slightest doubt that Celia was in charge.

Top-level issues requiring policy decisions were referred to her. Other problems, which had been hanging in abeyance, were brought to her attention for solution. She dealt with them all, using the promptness, common sense and strong purpose that had always been her hallmark.

Conferences with lawyers occupied much of her time.

The first lawsuits were being filed as a result of publicity concerning Montayne and the drug's withdrawal. Some of the lawsuits appeared genuine. A few babies, among them premature ones, had already been born in the United States with deformities similar to those in other countries where the mothers of defective children had taken Montayne during pregnancy.

Inevitably, this list of genuine cases would increase. A confidential, in-house estimate of the total number of U.S. babies who would be born malformed because of Montayne was slightly more than four hundred. This figure had been reached using statistics coming in from France, Australia, Spain, Britain and other countries. It took into account the length of time Montayne had been on sale in those countries, the quantity of the drug sold, and comparative figures for the United States.

Of the other lawsuits, some were filed on behalf of Montayne-taking mothers who had not yet given birth; these were based on fear of what might happen and, for the most part, charged Felding-Roth with negligence. A small remainder were believed frivolous or fraudulent, though all would have to be dealt with formally—the whole involving enormous legal time and cost.

As to cost overall, Celia—who had had to learn quickly about a subject entirely new to her—discovered that Felding-Roth carried product liability insurance amounting to a hundred and thirty-five million dollars. As well, the company had an internal reserve, for the same purpose, of another twenty million dollars.

"That hundred and fifty-five million sounds a lot, and might cover all the claims we'll settle," Childers Quentin, a lawyer, told Celia. Then he added, "On the other hand, I wouldn't count on it. The likelihood is, you'll need to raise more elsewhere."

Quentin, an avuncular white-haired figure in his seventies, with courtly manners, was head of a Washington law firm specializing in pharmaceutical matters, especially defense against damage claims. The firm had been retained on the advice of Felding-Roth's regular lawyers.

Quentin, Celia learned, was known among colleagues as "Mr. O. C. Fixit," the initials denoting "out of court." This because of his negotiating skill—"he has the nerve of a high-stakes poker player," a company lawyer commented—in knowing just how far to go in getting claims resolved without court proceedings.

Celia decided early that she would trust Childers Quentin. It also helped that she liked him.

"What you and I must do, my dear," he informed her as if addressing a favorite niece, "is make swift settlements that are reasonable and generous. Those last two points are essential in containing a disaster situation such as this. About being generous, remember the worst thing that could happen is for *one* Montayne case to go into civil court and result in a multimillion-dollar jury award. It would set a precedent for other awards which could break your company."

Celia asked, "Is there really a chance of settling everything out of court?"

"A better one than you might think." He went on to explain.

"When grievous, irreversible damage is caused to a child, such as is happening with Montayne, the first reaction of parents is despair, the second, anger. In their anger the parents want to punish those who caused their grief; therefore they seek a lawyer's help. Above all, the parents want—as the cliché goes—their day in court.

"But we lawyers are pragmatic. We know that cases which go to court are sometimes lost, and not always for just reasons. We also know that pretrial proceedings, crowded courts, as well as defense-engineered delays, may cause it to be years before a case is heard. Then, even if won, appeals can drag on for years more.

"Lawyers know, too, that after that first flush of anger their clients will become weary and disillusioned. Trial preparations can dominate their lives. These are personally consuming, an ever-present reminder of their sorrow. Invariably, people wish they had settled early and resumed, as best they could, their normal living."

"Yes," Celia said, "I can understand all that."

"There's more. Personal-injury lawyers, which is the kind we'll be dealing with, look to their own interests as well as clients'. Many take a damage-claim case on a contingency fee basis, so they receive a third, sometimes more, of what is won. But the lawyers have their own bills to pay—office rent, their children's college fees, mortgage installments, last month's American Express account . . . ." Quentin shrugged. "They are as you and I. They would like their money soon, not doubtfully in the distant future, and that is a factor in achieving settlement."

"I suppose so." Celia's mind had drifted during the last exchange, and now she said, "Some days, since coming back here, I get a feeling

337

of being cold and calculating, thinking only in money terms about Montayne and all that's happened."

Quentin said, "I already know you well enough to believe that will never occur. Also, my dear, in case you think otherwise I assure you I am not indifferent, either, to this terrible tragedy. Yes, I have a job to do, and I will do it. But I am a father and a grandfather, and my heart bleeds for those destroyed children."

From this and other sessions, a target was set for a further fifty million dollars to meet possible settlements.

Also looming was an estimated cost of eight million dollars for the withdrawing, recalling and destruction of all supplies of Montayne.

When Celia relayed these totals to Seth Feingold he nodded gravely, but seemed less alarmed than she expected.

"We've had two fortuitous happenings since the beginning of the year," the comptroller explained. "One is exceptionally good results from our O-T-C products, where sales are much greater than anticipated. There also is a large, unexpected and 'once only' profit from foreign exchange. Ordinarily, of course, our shareholders would benefit. As it is, both windfalls will have to go toward that added fifty-million reserve."

"Well, let's be grateful to both sources," Celia said. She remembered that this was not the first time O-T-C products, which she once disdained, had helped keep Felding-Roth solvent in time of trouble.

"Another thing that seems to be working for us," Seth continued, "is the promising news from Britain. I assume you're aware of it."

"Yes. I've read the reports."

"If it becomes necessary, on the strength of them the banks will lend us money."

Celia had been delighted to learn of progress at the Harlow institute from where an exciting new drug, Peptide 7, seemed likely to emerge soon—"soon" in drug-development parlance meaning another two years before submission to regulatory agencies for approval.

In an attempt to reinvolve Sam in company policy, Celia had gone to him to discuss the latest U.K. news.

Because the British institute had been Sam's idea, and he had fought to keep it funded, she assumed he would be pleased to have his faith confirmed and hoped, too, it would help offset his deep depression. Neither idea worked out. Sam's response was indifference. He also rejected a suggestion that he fly to Britain to talk with

338

Martin Peat-Smith and judge the significance of what was happening.

"Thank you, no," he told Celia. "I'm sure you can find out what you need by other means."

But even Sam's attitude did not change the fact that Harlow could now loom large in Felding-Roth's future.

And something else.

Vincent Lord's long years of research into what was known chemically as "the quenching of free radicals," the elimination of dangerous side effects from otherwise good drugs, had at last shown positive results. These were so auspicious—with all the indications of a major scientific breakthrough, something Lord had always coveted—that a massive research effort in Felding-Roth's U.S. laboratories was now being directed toward final development.

While the British Peptide 7 was clearly the drug that would be ready first, Vincent Lord's creation, provisionally named Hexin W, was likely to be only a year or two behind.

The second development had another effect. It made Lord's future more secure at Felding-Roth. Celia had at first considered—in view of Lord's strong advocacy of Montayne, and for other general reasons —replacing him when an opportunity arose. Yet now he seemed too valuable to lose.

Thus, surprisingly, and despite the overhanging shadow of Montayne, the company climate suddenly looked brighter.

6

At Harlow, Yvonne Evans and Martin Peat-Smith were spending an increasing amount of time together.

Although Yvonne still kept a small apartment she had rented when beginning work at the Felding-Roth institute, she was seldom there. Every weekend and most weeknights she was at Martin's house, where she happily took over the domestic side of Martin's life as well as attending to his—and her own—sexual needs.

Yvonne had reorganized the kitchen, which was now orderly and gleaming. From it she produced appetizing meals, exercising a talent as a versatile cook which seemed to come to her naturally and which she enjoyed. Each morning before they left, separately, for work, she made the bed she and Martin shared, seeing to it that the linen was clean and changed more frequently than in the past. She left notes with instructions for the "daily," the cleaning woman, with the result that the remainder of the house took on the immaculate appearance that comes from an eye for detail, which Yvonne had, and proper supervision.

Some changes in the pet *ménage* were also made by Yvonne.

She added a Siamese cat of her own. Then, one Saturday when Martin was working but Yvonne wasn't, she brought a saw and other tools with which she constructed a hinged "cat flap" in a rear down-stairs door. It meant that the cats were free to come and go at any time, the effect being healthier for the pets and for the household.

Also, when Yvonne stayed overnight she exercised the dogs in the early morning, supplementing the regular exercise Martin gave them every evening.

Martin loved it all.

Something else he loved was Yvonne's cheerful, usually inconse-quential chatter. She talked about a multitude of subjects, few of great importance—current films, the private lives of stars, pop musi-cians and their offstage antics; which London stores were having sales, and the latest buys at Marks and Spencer; the telly; gossip of the institute—who had become engaged, was pregnant, or about to be divorced; sexual excesses of the clergy, as reported in the vigilant British press; even a political scandal or two . . . Yvonne absorbed such matters, garnered from listening and selective reading, like a sponge.

Strangely, not only did Martin not object to hearing all this, at times he found it refreshing and a change and, at other times, like background music.

The point was, he decided when he thought about it, he was sur-rounded so much of the time by intellectuals whose conversation was on a serious scientific plane, with trivia excluded, that he grew weary of it. When he listened to Yvonne he could coast contentedly, leaving his brain in neutral.

One of Yvonne's interests—a near-passion—was the Prince of Wales. His much-publicized romances fascinated, though sometimes worried her. She discussed them endlessly. A name linked with Charles's at the time was Princess Marie-Astrid of Luxembourg. Yvonne refused to take the gossip seriously. "A marriage would never work," she assured Martin. "Besides being a Catholic, Marie-Astrid isn't right."

"How do you know?" he asked.

"I just do."

Another touted candidate, Lady Amanda Knatchbull, found more favor. "She could be okay," Yvonne conceded. "But if only Charles will be patient, I'm sure someone else will come along who's more right for him, even perfect."

"He's probably worrying himself, so why not write and tell him?" Martin suggested.

As if she hadn't heard, Yvonne declared thoughtfully and with a touch of poetry, "What he needs is an English rose."

One night after Yvonne and Martin had made love, he teased her, "Were you pretending I was the Prince of Wales?"

She answered mischievously, "How did you know?"

Despite her penchant for chitchat, Yvonne was no birdbrain, Martin discovered. She showed interest in other things, including the theory behind the mental aging project, which Martin patiently explained and which she seemed to understand. She was curious about his devotion to the writings of John Locke, and several times he found her with an open copy of Locke's *Essay,* her forehead creased in concentration.

"It isn't easy to understand," Yvonne admitted.

"No, not for anyone," he said. "You have to work at it."

As to their liaison and possible gossip, Martin was sure that some was circulating—Harlow was too small a place for that not to happen. But at the research institute he and Yvonne were discreet, never communicating with each other unless their work required it. Apart from that, Martin took the view that his private life was his own affair.

He had given no thought as to how long the relationship between himself and Yvonne would continue, but from their casual remarks it was clear that neither saw it as demanding, or more than temporary.

An enthusiasm they shared was the progress of the Harlow research.

As Martin wrote in one of his rare reports to New Jersey: "The

341

structure of Peptide 7 is now known. The gene has been made, inserted into bacteria, and large amounts have been prepared." The process, he noted, was "much like the preparation of human insulin."

At the same time, tests for Peptide 7's safety and effectiveness continued via injections into animals. A vast amount of animal data was accumulating, to the point where permission for human trials would be sought within the next few months.

Perhaps inevitably, rumors about the institute's research leaked out and reached the press. Though Martin declined requests to give interviews, arguing that anything printed would be premature, reporters found other sources and newspaper accounts appeared anyway. On the whole they were accurate. Speculation about a "wonder drug to delay growing old, now being tried on animals" was given prominence, as well as "the drug's remarkable weight-reducing effect." All of this aroused Martin's anger because clearly someone on the scientific staff had been indiscreet.

On Martin's instruction, Nigel Bentley attempted to find out who had talked, but without success.

"Actually," the administrator pointed out, "the publicity hasn't done much harm, if any. The scientific world already has a good idea of what you're doing—remember those two consultants you had in. And titillating the public now could help sales of Peptide 7 later on."

Martin was unconvinced, but let the matter drop.

One unwelcome effect of the publicity was a flood of letters, pamphlets and petitions from "animal-rights" crusaders—extremists who objected to experiments of any kind on animals. Some described Martin and his Harlow staff as "sadists," "torturers," "barbarians" and "heartless criminals."

As Martin told Yvonne after reading samples of the more vituperative mail at home, "All countries have their anti-experimentation kooks, but Britain is the worst." He picked up another letter, then put it down in disgust. "These people don't just want animal suffering kept to a minimum—which I'm in favor of, and I believe in laws to enforce it. But they want our kind of science, which *has* to use animals, to come to a screeching halt."

Yvonne asked, "Do you think there'll be a time when research won't need animals at all?"

"Someday perhaps, yes. Even now, in places where we used to use animals we're using methods like tissue cultures, quantum pharmacology, and computers instead. But doing without animals entirely

. . ." Martin shook his head. "It could happen, but not for a long time."

"Well, don't let it get to you." Yvonne collected the protest letters and stuffed them back into a briefcase. "Besides, think of *our* animals. Because of Peptide 7, they're healthier and smarter."

But her words failed to change Martin's mood. The recent mail influx had depressed him.

Overall at the institute, however, the contrast to the early days of groping—when there was so little progress and only negative results —was so great that Martin confided to Rao Sastri, "I'm worried. When anything goes this well, a major setback can be just around the corner."

His words proved prophetic—and sooner than expected.

It was the following weekend—early Sunday morning, shortly after 1 A.M—when a telephone call awakened Martin. Yvonne was still asleep beside him.

When Martin answered, the caller was Nigel Bentley.

"I'm at the institute," the administrator said. "The police called me. I think you'd better come."

"What's wrong?"

"It's bad news, I'm afraid." Bentley's voice sounded grim. "But I'd rather you see for yourself. Can you get here quickly?"

"I'm on my way."

By now, Yvonne was awake. As Martin began to throw on clothes, she hurriedly dressed too.

They went together, in Martin's car. At the institute, other vehicles were outside, two of them police cars with blue lights flashing. A third flashing light was on a fire engine, just leaving. The institute's front doors were open.

Bentley met them inside. A uniformed police inspector was with him. If Bentley was surprised to see Yvonne, he effectively concealed it.

"We've been raided," he announced. "By animal lovers."

Martin's brow creased. *"Animal lovers?"*

"Actually, sir," the policeman said, "the people who did it call themselves the Animal Rescue Army. They've given us trouble before." The inspector, approaching middle age, had the resigned,

343

sardonic manner of one who had watched many human follies and expected to see more.

Martin said impatiently, "Did what? What's happened?"

"They broke in," Bentley answered. "And then they released all the animals. Some are still loose in the building, but most were taken outside, the cages opened, and of course they're gone. Then they collected all the files and records they could find, carried them outside, and poured petrol on."

"They started a fire, Doctor," the inspector said. "Someone in another building saw it and phoned in an alarm. When the fire brigade came and put it out is when we got here too. We were in time to catch two suspects, a woman and a man. The man's been in prison, he admits, for another similar offense."

"The two the police caught are being held in my office," Bentley continued. "There seems to have been a gang of six. They overpowered our watchman and locked him in a cupboard. They also knew how to deactivate the burglar alarm."

"The whole operation was carefully planned," the police inspector said. "That's one of the hallmarks of these people."

Martin scarcely heard. His eyes were on four rats which had scampered into a corner of the reception area and were huddled there. Now, frightened by voices, the rats ran through another open door. Martin followed, heading for the laboratories and animal rooms.

Mess and confusion confronted him. Animal cages had either been removed or were open and empty. Loose-leaf reference books were gone. File drawers had been pulled out, some of their contents scattered on the floor. Many files were missing. Presumably they had been burned outside.

Bentley, the inspector, and Yvonne had followed Martin.

Yvonne murmured, "Oh, my God!"

Martin, emotional, despairing, could only ask, *"Why?* Oh, why?"

The inspector suggested, "Maybe you should put that question to the pair we've arrested, Doctor."

Martin nodded without speaking, and the policeman led the way to the administrator's office. Inside, a young police constable was guarding a man and a woman.

The woman, in her mid-thirties, was tall and slim. She had aquiline, haughty features and her hair was trimmed short. A lighted cigarette drooped from her lips. She wore tight jeans, a lumberjack shirt, and plastic, thigh-length boots. As the inspector and the others came in, she regarded them disdainfully, seemingly unconcerned about her capture.

The man, of about the same age, was slight and in other circumstances could have been thought of as meek and mild. He looked like a clerk, was balding, slightly stooped, and wore steel-rimmed spectacles. He smiled thinly at the newcomers—and defiantly.

"These are the pretty pair," the inspector said. "They've been cautioned legally, but they seem to want to talk. Real proud of themselves, they are."

"And so we should be," the man said. His voice was reedy and unsteady; he coughed nervously to clear it. "We've done a noble deed."

Martin exploded, his voice close to shouting. "Do you have *any* idea what you've done? How much important work you've wrecked and wasted?"

"What we do know," the woman said, "is that we've saved some fellow creatures from the vivisectionists—tyrants like you who exploit animals for your selfish ends."

"If you think that, you're ignorant fools." Martin wanted to lash out physically at the two in front of him, but restrained himself. "All the animals you released were born in captivity. Those outside can't survive. They'll die horribly. And those inside will have to be destroyed."

"Better that," the woman said, "than suffer your inhumane cruelty."

"He isn't inhumane! He isn't cruel!" It was Yvonne, her face flushed, her voice pitched high. "Dr. Peat-Smith is one of the kindest men who ever lived. He loves animals."

The man sneered. "As pets, I suppose."

"We don't approve of animals as pets," the woman said. "That's a master-slave relationship. We believe animal rights are equal to human rights. Furthermore, animals should not be restricted, confined, or have to suffer, merely to make humans happier or healthier." Her voice, measured and assured, had the tone of one blessed with total moral certainty.

The man said, "Something else we believe is that the human species has no superiority over other species."

"In your case," the inspector said, "I'd say that's true."

Martin addressed the woman. "You and your fellow lunatics have just destroyed scientific research which will take years to repeat. And

345

for all that time you'll have deprived thousands, maybe hundreds of thousands, of decent, deserving people of a medicine to make their lives better, more bearable . . ."

"Well, good for the Animal Rescue Army!" Scornfully, the woman interrupted, spitting words at Martin. "I'm delighted to hear our effort was successful. And if what you call scientific research, and I call barbarous atrocities, is repeated, I hope you die in agony doing it."

"You maniac!" The words were a scream, spoken as Yvonne dived forward, hands extended. There was a second's stillness in which no one else realized what was happening, then Yvonne was attacking the woman fiercely, fingernails raking her face.

Martin and the inspector between them pulled Yvonne away.

Now the Animal Rescue woman screamed. "That was an assault! A criminal assault." As two long red weals, one of them bleeding, flared on her face, she demanded of the two policemen, "Arrest that bitch! She must be criminally charged."

"Arrest this lady?" The inspector seemed pained. He glanced toward Yvonne who was trembling and seemed in shock. "Arrest her for what? I didn't see any assault." He looked toward the constable. "Did you?"

The other policeman answered, "No, sir. I reckon the prisoner got those marks on her face from the animals when she was opening some of those cages."

Martin put his arm around Yvonne. "Let's get out of here. There's nothing to be gained by talking to these people."

As they left, they heard the inspector ask, "Now how about being reasonable, and giving me the names of those others with you?"

"Go screw yourself, copper," the woman said.

Bentley had followed Martin and Yvonne. He told them, "Those two will go to jail."

Yvonne said, "Oh, I hope so."

"They will," the administrator assured her. "And they'll join others from that Animal Rescue Army who are there already because of other raids like this. The whole bunch see themselves as martyrs. I've read a lot about them. Supposedly they have hundreds of followers around the country." He added, glumly, "I'm sorry. I should have foreseen this."

"None of us could have," Martin said. He sighed. "Tomorrow we'll start cleaning up and see what's left."

346

7

The dispiriting task of assessing damage at the Harlow research institute took several days. At the end, Martin estimated that the "animal-rights" raid had caused a two-year setback.

From the ashes of a burned pile of papers and other records outside the building, some assorted material was salvaged, but not much. Later, Nigel Bentley reported to Martin, "Those nut cases apparently knew what they were looking for, and where everything was. That means they had inside help which, according to the police, fits the pattern of other raids they've made. What they do, I'm told, is persuade people like cleaners and maintenance staff to become informers. I'll try to find out who were our Judases, though I haven't much hope."

Bentley was also putting into effect strong and expensive security precautions for the future. As he expressed it, "In a way, it's an exercise in stable-door shutting, but those self-righteous people don't give up easily and could be back."

Martin, in turn, reported to New Jersey by telephone the day after the raid. He talked with Celia Jordan. A few days earlier Martin had been delighted to learn of Celia's return to the company; now he expressed regret that their first conversation should involve bad news.

Celia was shocked to learn of the Harlow devastation—so much in contrast to the recent heady progress reports concerning Peptide 7. She questioned Martin sharply about his estimate of delay.

"What we'll have to do," he advised her, "is repeat all the animal experiments to recover our data, which will be needed, of course, to accompany any drug application the company eventually makes. It's a terrible time waste and cost, but there isn't any choice."

347

"Are you sure about two years?"

"That's the worst case. If we can shave a few months from that time, we will. We know a great deal more than we did two years ago, and some shortcuts may appear. We'll all do our best."

"I want you to know," Celia said, "that Peptide 7 has become tremendously important to us here. Do you remember a conversation you and I had at your home? When you said that given more time, you'd produce an important medication which could make Felding-Roth enormously rich? Those last two words were yours."

At the Harlow end of the line, Martin grimaced. "I'm afraid I do remember. I wasn't behaving like a scientist, and I hope that conversation doesn't go further than the two of us."

"It won't. But I remind you of it because the first part of your prediction came true. Now we desperately need the rest."

"Two years to get back where we were," Martin repeated. "Shortcuts or no, it won't be much less."

But the conversation spurred him to hasten reorganizing. Replacement animals were ordered promptly from supply houses, and as they arrived the institute staff commenced the tiresome rote of repeating work begun long ago. As a result, within three weeks the data recovery process was moving at full speed.

Through the entire ordeal, from the night of the raid onward, Yvonne sustained Martin in body and spirit. She took total charge of his domestic life, asking him nothing, doing everything, so that neither his attention nor energy was diverted from the institute. At other times she comforted him, seeming to know instinctively when to be silently attentive or, at other moments, to amuse him with cheerful chatter. Once, after an especially grueling day, she told him at bedtime to lie face down, and when he did, gave him a slow Swedish massage which sent him into a deep sleep that lasted until morning.

When Martin asked next day how she learned to do such things, she answered, "I once roomed with a friend who was a masseuse. She taught me."

"I've noticed something about you," he said. "You never miss a chance to learn. The same way you did by working at John Locke. Have you read any more from him lately?"

"Yes." Yvonne hesitated, then said, "I found something he wrote which kind of fits those 'animal-rights' people. About enthusiasm."

Martin said curiously, "I'm not sure I remember. Can you find the passage?"

Locke's *Essay* was across the room, but without bothering to get it, Yvonne began:

"Immediate revelation being a much easier way for men to establish their opinions and regulate their conduct than the tedious and not always successful labor of strict reasoning, it is no wonder that some have been very apt to pretend to revelation, and to persuade themselves that they are under the peculiar guidance of heaven in their actions and opinions . . ."

As she recited, obviously from memory, Martin regarded her with astonishment. Observing him, she stopped, blushed slightly, then continued.

"Their minds being thus prepared, whatever groundless opinion comes to settle itself strongly upon their fancies is an illumination from the Spirit of God and presently of divine authority; and whatsoever odd action they find in themselves a strong inclination to do, that impulse is concluded to be a call or direction from heaven . . ."

Yvonne stopped, giggled, then said with embarrassment, "That's enough."

"No, no!" Martin urged, "Go on, please! If you can."

She said doubtfully, "You're making fun of me."

"Not in any slightest way."

"All right." She recited again.

". . . enthusiasm, which, though founded neither on reason nor divine revelation, but rising from the conceits of a warmed or overweening brain . . . men being most forwardly obedient to the impulses they receive from themselves . . . For strong conceit, like a new principle, carries all easily with it, when got above common sense, and freed from all restraint of reason . . ."

Yvonne concluded the passage, then stopped, those blue, innocent-appearing eyes fixed on Martin, making clear she was still wondering about his reaction, doubtful of herself.

349

He said, his tone incredulous, "I do recall that quotation now. And I don't believe you got a single word wrong. *How did you do it?*"

"Well . . . I remember things."

"Anything? And always in such detail?"

"I suppose so."

It reminded Martin that even when reporting trivial gossip, Yvonne always seemed to have the details right—names, dates, places, sources, background facts. He had noted that subconsciously, but without significance until now.

He asked, "How many times do you have to read something until you've memorized it?"

"Once, mostly. But with Locke it was twice." Yvonne still looked uncomfortable, as if Martin had uncovered a guilty secret.

He said, "I want to try something."

Going to another room, he found a book he was sure Yvonne had not seen before. It was Locke's *The Conduct of the Understanding*. Opening it to a page he had once marked, he told her, "Read this. From here to here."

"Can I read it twice?"

"Of course."

She put her head down, her long blond hair tumbling forward while she frowned in concentration, then she lowered the book. Martin took it from her and instructed, "Now tell me what you read."

He followed the words as she repeated them.

"There are fundamental truths that lie at the bottom, the basis upon which a great many others rest, and in which they have their consistency. These are teeming truths, rich in store, with which they furnish the mind, and, like the lights of heaven, are not only beautiful and entertaining in themselves, but give light and evidence to other things, that without them could not be seen or known. Such is that admirable discovery of Mr. Newton that all bodies gravitate . . ."

She went on for several paragraphs more, Martin finding each word exactly as printed in the book he held.

At the end, Yvonne pronounced, "That piece is beautiful."

"So are you," he told her. "And so is what you have. Do you know what it is?"

Again that unease, the hesitation. "You tell me."

350

"You've a photographic memory. It's something special and unique. Surely you must have known."

"In a way. But I never wanted to be different. Not a circus freak." There was a break in Yvonne's voice. For the first time since he had known her, Martin sensed tears not far away.

"Who, in God's name, ever said you were a freak?"

"A teacher at school."

Under Martin's tender questioning the story came out.

She had written an examination and, because of that photographic memory, many of her answers were identical with material in textbooks. The woman teacher who marked the paper accused Yvonne of cheating. Later, Yvonne's denial was disbelieved. In desperation she had given an example of memorizing similar to the one Martin just witnessed.

The teacher, angry at being proved wrong, had scoffed at Yvonne's ability, describing her as a "circus freak" and her kind of learning as "worthless."

Martin interrupted. "It isn't worthless if you understand what you've learned."

"Oh, I *did* understand."

"I believe that," he assured her. "You've a good brain. I've seen it function."

But after her clash with the teacher, Yvonne not only concealed her gift, she attempted to discard it. When studying, she consciously tried not to memorize sentences and phrases and, in part, succeeded. But doing so also lessened her understanding of what she was required to learn, with the result that she did poorly in examinations and failed the one that might have got her into veterinary college.

"Teachers can do a lot that's good," Martin said. "But stupid ones can do great harm."

Yvonne, looking sad as she remembered, said nothing, and a silence followed during which Martin concentrated, thinking.

At length he said, "You've done so much for me. Maybe, for a change, I can do something for you. Would you still like to be a vet?"

The question took her by surprise. "Is it possible?"

"Many things are possible. The point is: do you *want* it?"

"Of course. It's what I've always wanted."

"Then let me make some inquiries," Martin said. "Let's see what I find out."

351

It did not take long.

Two days later, after dinner at home which Yvonne prepared, Martin said, "Let's sit and talk. I have things to tell you."

In the small living room, he relaxed in his leather armchair while Yvonne curled up on the rug in front. Despite her good intentions, she still had not shed her surplus weight, though Martin made clear it didn't bother him; he liked the fullness of Yvonne's body and its curves, which he regarded fondly at this moment.

He told her, "You *can* apply to veterinary college, and the chances are good that you'll get in. Also, some financial aid, which you'll need to live reasonably, is possible, even probable, with help from the institute. But if you don't get helped financially, I'm sure I could work something out."

She said, "But I'd have to do other work first and pass exams."

"Yes, and I've found out what you need. You'll have to pass three 'A' levels—one in chemistry, another in physics, a third in zoology, biology or botany. With your experience, zoology makes most sense."

"Yes, it does." A note of doubt crept in. "Would it mean giving up my job?"

"Not necessarily, while you're preparing for the 'A' levels. You can study during evenings and weekends. I'll help you. We'll work together."

Yvonne said breathlessly, "I can hardly believe it."

"You'll believe it when you find out how much there is to do."

"Oh, I'll work hard. I promise. I really will."

Martin smiled. "I know. And with that memorizing mind of yours, you'll sail through it all, and you'll pass the exams without trouble." He paused, considering. "One thing you'll have to learn is to change the textbook language so it isn't identical when you sit the exams. No sense in making examiners suspicious the way your teacher was. But you can practice that beforehand. And there are techniques to passing exams. I can show you those too."

Yvonne jumped up and threw her arms around him, "Oh, my love, you're wonderful, and the idea is so exciting. This has to be the best thing that ever happened to me."

"Well," he said, "since you mention it, I've been feeling the same way about you."

8

At Felding-Roth, New Jersey, the mood of mild euphoria which developed soon after Celia's rejoining the company did not last long.

The animal-raid news from Britain, reported by Martin Peat-Smith, first shattered it. Then, closer to home, a sudden, dramatic tragedy cast an overhanging pall of gloom.

It was an accident—at least, "accident" was how the Boonton police eventually classified it—and it happened on a workday, three weeks exactly after Celia's return.

A few minutes before 9 A.M., Celia's chauffeured company car brought her to the catwalk level of the Felding-Roth parking garage, near the entrance to the glassed-in ramp that led to the main office building. Celia's driver had pulled in close to the ramp, on the left, because—as he told it later—he had observed in his rearview mirror, while at street level, Mr. Hawthorne's Rolls-Bentley a short distance behind. Knowing that the company president would be driving to his normal parking slot, which was against an outer wall and to the right of where Celia's car had stopped, the driver left access to it clear.

Celia did not see Sam's car until she got out of her own, with the chauffeur holding the door open. At that time she saw first the distinctive hood cresting the top of the ramp from the parking floor below, then the rest of the car as it reached the catwalk level.

Expecting to walk with Sam across to the executive elevator, as on other days, Celia paused while the handsome automobile—for many years Sam's pride and joy—moved forward at a safe, slow speed.

Then it happened.

With a sudden roar from the powerful Rolls-Royce engine, accompanied by a screech of tires, the heavy car shot forward, attaining high speed instantly as no lesser vehicle ever could. It passed Celia and her driver in a blur of silver-gray, went through the parking slot

353

assigned to Sam, and without stopping smashed into the wall directly ahead. The shoulder-high wall, open at the top, was the only separation between the parking floor and the outside air, with the ground some fifty feet below.

With a reverberating crash, the wall crumbled and the car went through it, disappearing.

Immediately after, and for what seemed to Celia the longest time, there was a silence. Then from below, and out of sight, came a heavy thud, and a tortured rending of metal and a shattering of glass.

The chauffeur raced to the ragged opening in the wall, and Celia's first impulse was to follow him. She curbed it. Instead, thinking quickly, she got back inside her car, which had a mobile telephone, and used it to call police emergency. She gave the address and asked for police officers, a fire truck, and an ambulance to be sent to the scene urgently. Then, making a second call to Felding-Roth's switchboard, she instructed that any medical doctors available—the company employed several—were to hurry to the west side ground level of the parking garage. Only after that did Celia go to the gaping hole through which Sam's car had crashed, and look downward.

What she saw horrified her.

The once-handsome automobile was upside down and totally wrecked. Clearly, it had fallen first on its front end which, from the force of impact after the fifty-foot fall, had been thrust back into the main body of the car. The concertinaed whole had then rolled over onto the roof, which collapsed too. Smoke was rising from the wreckage, though it had not caught fire. A twisted wheel was spinning crazily.

Fortunately, where the car had fallen was part of a vacant lot. No one had been below. There was nothing to damage but some shrubs and grass.

Several people were now running toward the demolished vehicle, and Celia could hear approaching sirens. It seemed impossible, however, that anyone inside what was left of the Rolls-Bentley could have survived.

And that was how it was.

It took more than an hour to pry Sam's body loose, a grisly task over which the fire department rescue squad did not hurry since a doctor, reaching inside, had confirmed the obvious—Sam was dead.

Celia, taking charge, had telephoned Lilian, breaking the news as gently as she could, though urging Lilian not to go to the scene.

"If you like," Celia volunteered, "I'll come over now."

There was a silence, then Lilian said, "No. Let me stay here for a while. I need to be alone." Her voice sounded remote and disembodied, as if coming from another planet. She had suffered already and now would suffer more. *What women have to bear,* Celia thought.

Lilian said, "After a while I'll go to Sam. You'll let me know where he's been taken, Celia?"

"Yes. And I'll either come to get you or meet you there."

"Thank you."

Celia attempted to phone Juliet, then Juliet's husband, Dwight, but could not reach either.

Next she summoned Julian Hammond, the public affairs vice president, to her office and instructed, "Issue a press statement immediately about Sam's death. Describe it as a tragic accident. I want the word 'accident' stressed, to head off other speculation. You might say something about the probability that his accelerator jammed, causing the car to go out of control."

Hammond protested, "No one will believe that."

Wanting to weep, controlling her emotions by a thread, Celia snapped, "Don't argue! Do it the way I say. And *now.*"

The last service she would do for Sam, she thought as Hammond left, was—if she could—to save him the indignity of being labeled a suicide.

But to those closest to him, suicide it plainly was.

What seemed most likely was that Sam, finally overwhelmed by his burden of despair and guilt about Montayne, had seen the parking garage wall ahead, thought suddenly of a way to end his life, and floored the accelerator pedal, steering for the relatively fragile wall. It would be typical of Sam, his friends said privately, to have remembered the vacant lot below and therefore the absence of danger to anyone else.

Celia had some questions and guilt feelings of her own. Had Sam, she wondered, contemplated on previous occasions doing what he did, but allowed sanity to prevail? Then, seeing Celia that day as his car topped the ramp—Celia confident and in control, wielding authority which would have remained his had circumstances not reversed their roles so drastically—had Sam then . . . ? She could not bring herself to complete the question, the answer to which she would never know.

355

One other thought kept coming back to her: The occasion in Sam's office, the first day of Celia's return, when he had said, ". . . *there's something else. Something you don't know."* And a moment later, *"I'll never tell you."*

What *was* Sam's other secret? Celia tried to guess, but failed. Whatever it was must have died with him.

At the family's request, Sam's funeral was private. Celia was the only company representative. Andrew accompanied her.

Seated on an uncomfortable folding chair in an undertaker's chapel, while an unctuous clergyman who had not known Sam intoned religious platitudes, Celia tried to blot out the present and recall the richer past.

Twenty-two years ago—Sam hiring her as a detail woman . . . Sam at her wedding . . . Her selection of him as the one to follow on the company ladder . . . At the New York sales meeting, risking his job in her defense: "I'm standing up here to be counted. If we let Mrs. Jordan leave this way, we're all shortsighted fools" . . . *Sam, overcoming opposition, placing her on the fast track . . . promoting her to O-T-C, later to Latin-American Director:* "International is where the future is." . . . *Sam, on his own promotion and his two secretaries:* "I think they dictate letters to each other." . . . *Sam the Anglophile, who was farseeing about a British research institute:* "Celia, I want you as my right hand." . . . *Sam, who had paid for a judgmental error with his reputation, and now his life.*

She felt Andrew move beside her. He passed a folded handkerchief. Only then did Celia realize that tears were streaming down her face.

Again at their request, only Lilian and Juliet accompanied the coffin to the graveside. Celia spoke to both briefly before leaving. Lilian was pale; there seemed little life left in her. Juliet's face and eyes were hard; she appeared not to have cried during the service. Dwight was conspicuously absent.

In the days that followed, Celia persisted in her effort to have Sam's death officially declared an accident. She succeeded, mainly because —as she explained to Andrew—"No one seemed to have the heart to argue otherwise. Sam didn't carry life insurance, so financially it didn't matter."

After a decent interval of two weeks, the Felding-Roth board of directors met to elect a new president. Within the company it was assumed this was a formality only, and that Celia would be appointed.

Seth Feingold came to her office a few minutes after the directors' meeting ended. His expression was grim.

"I've been deputed to tell you this," he said, "and I hate doing it. But you aren't going to be president."

When Celia failed to react, he went on, "You may not believe this and, by God, it isn't fair, but there are still some men on the board who don't like the idea of a woman heading the company."

"I believe it," Celia said. "Some women have spent their lives discovering it."

"There was a long argument, heated at times," Seth said. "The board was split, and there were several who spoke out strongly in your favor. But the objectors wouldn't budge. In the end, we had to compromise."

A president *pro tempore* had been appointed, Seth revealed. He was Preston O'Halloran, a retired bank president who for many years had been a member of the Felding-Roth board. He was seventy-eight and nowadays walked with the aid of a cane. While respected and a financial expert, the new president's knowledge of the pharmaceutical business was limited and largely confined to what he learned at board meetings.

Celia had met O'Halloran several times, though without knowing him well.

She asked, "What's with the *pro tem?*"

"O'Halloran has agreed to serve for six months at the most. Sometime between then and now the board will make a permanent appointment." Seth grimaced. "I may as well tell you there's talk of looking for someone outside the company."

"I see."

"I suppose I shouldn't say this. But frankly, Celia, if I were in your position I'd say, 'To hell with 'em all!' Then I'd walk out of here— right now."

She shook her head negatively. "If I did, someone else would say, '*How like a woman!*' Besides, I agreed to come back to do a cleanup job, and so I will. When it's finished, though . . . well, let's wait until then."

The conversation reminded her of one she had had years before with Sam, when Celia had been made assistant director of Sales Training instead of director, because—as Sam expressed it at the time —"There are some in the company who can't swallow quite that much. Not yet."

Plus ça change, plus c'est la même chose, she quoted silently to herself. The more things change, the more they remain the same.

"Do you feel terribly hurt?" Andrew asked at dinner.

Celia thought before answering. "Yes, I suppose so. The injustice gets to me. Yet in another way, strangely, I find I don't care as much as I would have a few years ago."

"That's what I thought. Would you like me to tell you why?"

She laughed. "Please do, Doctor."

"It's because you're a fulfilled woman, my love. Fulfilled in every way. You're the best wife any man could have, and a superb mother, and you're smart, responsible and competent at work, and can run rings around most men. You've proved a thousand times how good you are. So you don't, anymore, need the trappings and the titles because everybody who knows you knows your worth—including those chauvinist boobs on the Felding-Roth board, not one of whom is worth your little finger. That's why what happened today shouldn't cause you a second's anguish, because those who made the decision are the losers, and sooner or later they'll find out."

Andrew stopped. "Sorry. I didn't mean to make a speech. I just wanted to state some truths and maybe cheer you up."

Celia got up from her chair and threw her arms around him. As she kissed him she said, "As, indeed, you have."

Winnie's baby—a healthy son—was born the following day. The event delighted not only Winnie and Hank, but the entire Jordan family, Lisa phoning Winnie enthusiastically from California, Bruce from Pennsylvania.

Winnie, as usual, took everything in stride. "Looks like I 'it the jackpot," she contended happily from her hospital bed. "Now p'raps 'Ank an' me should try fer twins."

9

Vincent Lord was a changed man. He radiated energy and happiness.

After almost twenty years of scientific dedication to a single idea, of pursuing a dream which few other than himself believed in—designing that drug to quench free radicals—the dream had at last come true. The decades of dedication were about to be rewarded.

What was now feasible, needing only the completion of trials on animals and humans to satisfy the law's requirements, was a drug which would make other drugs, hitherto dangerous, beneficial and safe.

Hexin W—Lord's provisional name for his creation had, so far, persisted—was being discussed avidly within the industry, although full details remained a Felding-Roth secret. Other pharmaceutical firms, which kept surveillance on patent filings and understood the implications of this one, were already letting their interest be known.

As the head of a major competitive company expressed it in a telephone call to Celia, "Naturally we wish our own researchers had discovered what Dr. Lord appears to have done, but since they didn't, we want to be first in line when you people are ready to talk deals."

Of equal interest was that the new drug would be usable in either of two ways. It could be included as an active ingredient when other drugs were formulated—that is, mixed in during manufacturing. Or it could be made up as a separate tablet, to be taken with other medication.

Thus, Hexin W would be an "across-the-board" drug. Expressed another way, it was a drug-scientist's drug, to be used by developers of other pharmaceutical products, and marketed, not by one company, but by many. The other companies would operate under license, with royalties—presumably enormous—being paid to Felding-Roth.

Among principal beneficiaries from Hexin W would be arthritis and cancer patients. Many strong potions for those conditions already existed, but were prescribed sparingly, or not at all, because of dangerous side effects. With Hexin W, those effects and dangers would be removed or markedly reduced.

Vince Lord explained to Celia and several others during a sales planning session what would happen with arthritis. He used non-scientific language.

"Sufferers get inflammation in the joints which causes immobility and pain. It occurs when the disease condition generates free radicals which, in turn, attract leukocytes—white blood cells. The leukocytes pile up, creating and worsening the inflammation.

"But Hexin W," Lord continued, "stops free-radical production, so leukocytes are not attracted. Result—there is no inflammation, and pain disappears."

The effect of Lord's statement was such that several of his listeners clapped their hands. He flushed with pleasure.

Lesser ailments, he added, would also have new choices of treatment, because of Hexin W.

The big breakthrough with his research had come to Vince Lord some three months earlier. It marked a gloriously satisfying victory in a laborious, wearying process of trial and error—a process frequently heartbreaking and strewn with repeated failures.

The process itself was another measure of Lord's achievement because nowadays, by some, it was regarded as outdated.

Expressed simply: the system developed new drugs from old drugs, making use of organic chemistry. Beginning with an existing active compound, the drug's chemistry was modified, then modified again . . . and again, and again, and again . . . if necessary to infinity. Always, the search was for a new effective drug, derived from the old, and with no, or low, toxicity. Looking back, Lord remembered how, two years ago, after trying nearly a thousand different compounds—all unsuccessful—he vowed he would never give up.

A differing, newer approach—employed by Sir James Black, the distinguished developer of SmithKline's Tagamet—was to decide which biological disorder might be corrected pharmaceutically, then create a totally new drug. Martin Peat-Smith, at Harlow, was using genetic methods which were newer still. However, even the last two involved years of experimentation and could end in failure, though when they succeeded, revolutionary new drugs resulted.

But Lord had decided the older method was more suited to his purpose and temperament and, by God!, he reminded himself, he had been right.

What caused his more immediate happiness was the small army of specialists—chemists, biologists, physicians, clinical pharmacologists, physiologists, toxicologists, veterinarians, pathologists, and statisticians—who, at Felding-Roth, were working together, exercising their talents to bring Hexin W to its final form.

Even so, because of a complex testing program in animals and humans, it would be another two years before an application for general use of Hexin W could be made to FDA.

While not saying so aloud, Lord had been pleased to hear of the setback to Peat-Smith's Peptide 7 program. This, because a two-year delay at Harlow meant Hexin W might now be on the market first.

Lord's upbeat mood had even caused him to take an initiative in making peace with Celia. Soon after her return to the company, he went to her office. Offering congratulations on her new appointment, he told her, "I'm glad to see you back."

"For that matter," Celia said, "congratulations to you. I've just read the report on Hexin W."

"I expect it to be recognized as one of the major discoveries of the century," Lord acknowledged matter-of-factly. Even a certain mellowing with the passage of years had not dimmed his appreciation of his own worth.

In his conversation with Celia, Lord did not choose to admit she had been right about Montayne, and himself wrong. His reasoning was that she had merely made a lucky, unscientific guess; therefore she deserved no more intellectual credit than did the holder of a winning lottery ticket.

Despite the tentative rapport with Celia, he was relieved when, after Sam Hawthorne's death, she did not become president. That would have been too much to live with. For once, he thought, the board of directors had shown some sense.

As the world entered the new year of 1978, Hexin W continued to be a strong center of hope at Felding-Roth.

361

The appointment of Preston O'Halloran as Felding-Roth president *pro tem* made little difference, if any, to Celia's responsibilities and day-by-day routine. The day after the special board meeting, O'Halloran had been open and frank with her.

They met—just the two of them—in the president's office suite. The sight of a new tenant in quarters which until so recently had been occupied by Sam was a poignant reminder to Celia of her grief at Sam's death, which she still had difficulty accepting.

Speaking carefully with his well-bred New England accent, the elderly O'Halloran said, "I would like you to know, Mrs. Jordan, that I was not one of those adamantly opposed to your becoming president. I'll be equally honest in admitting I did not support your candidacy, but would have gone along with a majority in your favor, had that been possible. I even went so far as to inform the other board members of that."

"I'm interested to know you regard that as 'going far,' " Celia acknowledged, with a touch of acidity she could not resist.

"Touché!" The old man smiled and she thought: at least he has a sense of humor.

"All right, Mr. O'Halloran," she continued briskly, "so both of us know where we stand, and I appreciate that. What I need from you, in addition, are instructions on how you wish me to operate, and our division of duties."

"My close friends call me Snow." Again a wry smile. "The name originates from a misspent youth when I did a great deal of skiing. I'd be glad to have you use it, and perhaps I may call you Celia."

"Okay—you Snow, me Celia," Celia said. "Now let's lay out how we work." She knew she was being bitchy, but didn't care.

"That's easy. I would like you to carry on exactly as you have until now—and I am aware that is with great competence and resourcefulness."

"And you, Snow? What will you be doing while I'm being competent and resourceful?"

He chided her gently, "The president does not have to account to the executive vice president, Celia. It is the other way around. However, so there is no misunderstanding between us, let me concede that my knowledge of the pharmaceutical business is in no way comparable with yours, in fact far less. What I do know a great deal

362

about—almost certainly more than you—is company finance. It is an area needing special attention at this time. Therefore reviewing money matters is how I shall spend most of the six months, or less, I will be occupying this chair."

Celia admitted to herself that she had been dealt with courteously and with patience. She said, more pleasantly than earlier, "Thank you, Snow, I'll do my best to keep up my end of that arrangement."

"I'm sure you will."

The new president did not come into the office every day, but when he did he developed a financial master plan for Felding-Roth, covering the next five years, which Seth Feingold described to Celia as "a gem, a real contribution."

The comptroller added, "The old codger may need a cane to walk, but not for his mind, which is still sharp as a razor blade."

At the same time, Celia came to appreciate O'Halloran herself—his support of everything she did, and his unfailing courtesy. He was truly, in an outmoded description she remembered, "a gentleman of the old school."

Consequently she was sorry, in the last week of January, 1978, to learn of his confinement to bed with influenza, and genuinely sad a week later when Snow O'Halloran died of a massive coronary occlusion.

This time there was no two-week delay in appointing a successor. The matter was settled the day after O'Halloran's funeral.

No viable outside candidate had appeared, even though the president *pro tempore* had served more than four of his agreed six months.

There was only one possible choice and the board of directors made it, taking less than fifteen minutes to decide what should have been decided the previous September: Celia Jordan would become president and chief executive officer of Felding-Roth.

10

The raw idea had come to her on the flight back from Hawaii last August. A remark of Andrew's had triggered it.

He had said to Celia, Lisa and Bruce: *"I don't believe a drug should be taken for anything that is just uncomfortable or self-limiting."* The subject was pregnancy. The Montayne disaster, fresh in all their minds, had prompted the remark.

Andrew had added, advising his own daughter, *"When your time comes, don't you take anything . . . And if you want a sound, healthy baby—no liquor, wine, or smoking either."*

Those words were the foundation of what Celia was now ready to propose as a fixed company policy. She had a name for what she planned: the Felding-Roth Doctrine.

She had considered bringing the idea forward sooner, during her time as executive vice president, but decided against it for fear of being overruled.

Even after her appointment as president she waited, biding her time, knowing that what she intended would require approval of the board of directors.

Now, seven months later, in September, she was prepared to move.

Bill Ingram, recently promoted to vice president of sales and marketing, had helped with the wording of the Felding-Roth Doctrine, of which the draft introduction read:

FELDING-ROTH PHARMACEUTICALS INCORPORATED
solemnly pledges:

Article 1: This company will never research, manufacture, distribute, or market directly or indirectly, any pharmaceutical product intended for use by women during

364

pregnancy and aimed at treating any natural, self-limiting condition, such as nausea and sickness, relating to a normal pregnancy.

Article 2: Felding-Roth will actively advocate, in all ways open to it, that no pregnant woman shall have prescribed for her, or shall obtain and use directly, during a normal pregnancy, any such product as described in Article 1 and originating elsewhere.

Article 3: Felding-Roth will advise pregnant women to avoid the use of all prescription and non-prescription drugs—its own and those of other companies—throughout their pregnancies, except those drugs prescribed by a physician for exceptional medical needs.

Article 4: Felding-Roth will further actively advocate that pregnant women abstain, throughout their pregnancies, from the use of alcoholic beverages, including wine, and from cigarette and other smoking, including the inhalation of smoke from other persons . . .

There was more. Another reference to physicians was included— in part to uphold the advisory-trust relationship between doctor and patient; also as a sop to doctors who, as prescribers, were Felding-Roth's best customers. There were references to special conditions, such as medical emergencies, where the use of drugs might be essential or overriding.

As Bill Ingram put it, "The whole thing makes more sense, Celia, than anything I've read in a long time. Someone in this business should have done it years ago."

Ingram, who had voted against Celia and for Montayne at the critical meeting prior to her resignation, had been penitent and uneasy at the time of her return to Felding-Roth. Several weeks later he had admitted, "I've been wondering if, after all that happened, you want me working here at all."

"The answer is yes," Celia told him. "I know how you work, also that I can trust and rely on you. As to what's past, you made a mistake in judgment, which all of us do at times. It was bad luck that it turned out to be a mistake with awful consequences, but you weren't alone, and I imagine you've learned from the experience."

"Oh, have I learned! And suffered, too, wishing I'd had the intelligence and guts to stick with you."

"Don't necessarily stick with me," she advised. "Not even now. There'll be times when I'll be wrong, and if you think I am, I want to hear about it."

After Celia's elevation to the presidency, there was a restructuring of duties, along with several promotions. Bill Ingram's was among them. He was already doing well in his new senior post.

Celia, now a full-fledged member of the board of directors, prepared carefully for the meeting which would consider her proposed Felding-Roth Doctrine.

Bearing in mind what Sam once told her about his problems with the board, and remembering the resistance there had been, years before, to Sam's controversial plan for a British research institute, Celia expected opposition.

To her surprise, there was little, almost none.

One member of the board—Adrian Caston, who was chairman of a financial trust group and a cautious thinker—did ask, "Is it wise or necessary to block ourselves off permanently from a field of medicine which, at some future time, might see new and safer developments of a highly profitable nature?"

They were meeting in the boardroom at company headquarters, and Celia answered, looking down the long walnut table, "Mr. Caston, I believe that is *exactly* what we should do. We should do it because we will also be blocking ourselves, and others who succeed us here, from the temptation, the chance, and the risk of involving this company with another Montayne."

There was an attentive silence as she continued. "Memories fade quickly. Many young women now at the age of motherhood do not remember Thalidomide, indeed have never heard of it. In a few more years, that will be equally true of Montayne, at which point pregnant women will again take *anything their doctors prescribe*. But if it happens, let *us* have no part of it, remembering that the entire history of influencing, by drugs, the normal course of pregnancy has been burdened with disaster.

"Time and experience have demonstrated pregnancy as *the single health condition* which is best left to nature alone. At Felding-Roth we are living with a pregnancy-drug disaster, paying dearly for it

366

now. For the future we will do better—morally and financially—to seek our profits elsewhere and urge others to do likewise."

Clinton Etheridge, a veteran director and lawyer, from whom Celia had expected antagonism, then spoke in her support.

"Speaking of profits, I like Mrs. Jordan's idea of turning our Montayne debacle into a commercial advantage. In case the rest of you haven't noticed, this so-called doctrine"—the director held it up —"is damned clever. It's a smart piece of merchandising promotion for the other drugs we sell. It will have a strong dollar value, as I think we'll find in time."

Inwardly Celia winced, then reminded herself that support was worth having, even if for wrong reasons. She also wondered about Etheridge, whom she knew to be a friend and ally of Vincent Lord's, and who sometimes brought the research director's viewpoints to board meetings, as Sam had discovered long ago. Lord knew about the Felding-Roth Doctrine, was aware it would be considered today, and he and Etheridge would almost certainly have discussed it. So . . . was the support she was now receiving a remote way of Lord's acknowledging to Celia his regrets about Montayne? She supposed she would never know.

There was more discussion by the board members, mostly questions about how the doctrine would be put into effect. But it was the TV-radio network czar Owen Norton who had the final word.

Looking at Celia from the opposite end of the boardroom table, Norton, who a few days earlier had celebrated his eighty-second birthday, observed dryly, "You may have noticed, Mrs. Jordan, that we are finally getting around to respecting your womanly judgment. I can only say, for myself and others like me, I am sorry we took so long."

"Sir," Celia said, and meant it, "you have just made my day."

The vote that followed, establishing the doctrine as official company policy, was unanimous.

The impact of the Felding-Roth Doctrine was substantial, though, with the general public, not as great as Celia had hoped.

Doctors, with a few exceptions, liked it. One obstetrician wrote:

> Kindly send me some extra copies, one of which I shall
> have framed to hang on my office wall. I intend to point to it

when pregnant patients suggest I am serving them less than adequately if I decline to write a prescription for some palliative which, in my opinion, they would be better off without.

You have, by your highly ethical stand, strengthened the hands of some of us who do *not* believe there is a drug for every occasion. More power to you!

The extra copies were sent—to that doctor and many others who requested them.

Physicians who objected did so on the grounds that they, and not a pharmaceutical company, should advise patients about which drugs to take, or not, and when. But judging by the volume of mail, they were a small minority.

The Felding-Roth Doctrine was featured widely in the company's advertising, though this was confined to medical and scientific magazines. Celia at first favored advertising in newspapers and general publications, but was persuaded this would create antagonism from organized medicine which, along with FDA, frowned on direct approaches to consumers about prescription drugs.

Perhaps because of this absence, newspapers gave only minor attention to the Felding-Roth Doctrine. The *New York Times* ran a short two-paragraph story amid its financial news, the *Washington Post* buried a similar report in a rear section of the paper. Elsewhere, in other newspapers, brief items appeared if there happened to be room. Television, despite public relations attempts to persuade producers otherwise, paid no attention at all.

"If we market a drug that turns out to have harmful side effects we didn't expect," Bill Ingram complained to Celia, "those TV news types take our skins off. But when we do something positive like this, all we get is yawns."

"That's because TV journalism is simplistic," she responded. "Its people are trained to look for strong, quick impact, so they avoid the thoughtful, the cerebral, which take too much air time. Don't worry, though. At times that policy can help us."

Ingram said doubtfully, "Be sure to tell me when it does."

Reaction to the Felding-Roth Doctrine from other drug firms was mixed.

Those who marketed products for use by women during pregnancy were openly hostile. "A cheap shot, shoddy publicity, nothing

368

more," was how a spokesman for one such company described the doctrine publicly.

From others came suggestions that Felding-Roth had attempted to be "holier than thou," and might have harmed the industry, though in what way was not made clear. However, one or two competitors were openly admiring. "Frankly," Celia was told by a respected industry leader, "I wish we'd thought of it first."

"None of which proves anything," she confided to Andrew, "except you can't please everyone."

"Be patient," he urged. "You've done something good, and you've started ripples which are spreading. In time, you'll be surprised how far they go."

Other rings of ripples were resulting from Montayne. One had its origin on Washington's Capitol Hill.

Aides to a congressional veteran, Senator Dennis Donahue, had spent a year, on and off, reviewing the Montayne matter and now declared it an ideal subject for their leader to focus on at a Senate investigative hearing. "Ideal," in this case, meant with wide public interest, generous exposure and, almost certainly, television coverage. As the senator was apt to remind those closest to him politically, "Let's never forget TV is where the masses and the votes are."

Accordingly, it was announced that the Senate Subcommittee on Ethical Merchandising, of which Donahue was chairman, would begin hearings in Washington, D.C., early in December. Witnesses, the senator stated during an October news conference, were already being subpoenaed. Others with firsthand knowledge of the subject were invited to communicate with the committee's staff.

When Celia heard the initial report, she telephoned Childers Quentin, the Washington lawyer.

"That really is bad news," he affirmed. "I'm afraid that your company, and probably you as its chief spokesman, Mrs. Jordan, are in for a rough time. If you'll consider some advice, I urge you to begin preparing for the hearings now, with help from legal counsel. I know how these things work, and I assure you the senator's staff will dig up and place on view every unsavory fact and rumor they can find."

11

If the word demagogue, or *dēmagōgos,* had not been coined by the Ancient Greeks around the time of Cleon, it would have been invented, out of necessity, to define United States Senator Dennis Donahue. No more striking example of the breed existed.

He was born to wealth and privilege but posed, and regularly described himself, as "a son of the common people, truly one of them, and 'of the earth, earthy.'" No description could have been more inaccurate but, like anything repeated often enough, it became accepted and believed by many.

Another way the senator liked to be portrayed was as "a spokesman for the poor and suffering; a foe of their oppressors." Whether, inside his soul, he really cared about the poor and suffering, only Donahue himself knew. Either way, he made good use of them.

Anywhere in the nation, where there happened to be a newsworthy David vs. Goliath struggle, Donahue hastened to the scene, stridently siding with the Davids, even on occasions when—to thoughtful people—Goliath was clearly in the right. "There are always more Davids, and they're useful at election time," an aide once explained in a moment of unguarded frankness.

Perhaps for the same reason, in any labor dispute Donahue unfailingly supported organized labor, never favoring business even if labor excesses were involved.

The labor and unemployment scenes were fertile fields for an ambitious politician, he had discovered early. Which was why, at times of higher than normal unemployment, the senator sometimes joined lines of job-seekers outside employment offices, talking with them. Ostensibly this was to "see for himself, and find out how the unemployed felt"—an admirable aim to which no reasonable person could object. Interestingly, though, the media always learned of the

370

senator's intentions, so that TV crews and press photographers awaited him. Thus his familiar face, wearing its most soulful expression as he discoursed with the unemployed, was on network news that night and in next day's newspapers.

As to other "common man" matters, the senator had discovered a recent, fruitful one in his objections to first-class, tax-deductible air travel by businessmen. If people wanted that kind of special privilege, he argued, they should pay for it themselves, and not be subsidized by other taxpayers. He introduced a Senate bill to make first-class air travel non-deductible for tax purposes, though knowing full well the bill would die somewhere in the legislative process.

Meanwhile, the amount of news coverage was remarkable. Keeping the idea afloat, Senator Donahue made a point of traveling tourist class himself, by air, informing the press before each journey. However, no first-class passenger ever had as much attention lavished on him as Donahue, back in his tourist seat. One thing he failed to mention publicly was that the bulk of his air travel was in the luxury of private aircraft—either chartered through a family trust fund or made available by friends.

In appearance, Donahue was stocky, and had a cherubic face which made him look younger than the forty-nine he was. He was overweight without being fat, and referred to himself as "comfortably upholstered." Most of the time, especially when on public view, he exuded friendliness, expressed through an easy grin. His dress and hairstyle had a studied untidiness, conforming with the "common man" image.

While objective observers saw Donahue for the opportunist he was, he was genuinely liked by many people, not only members of his own party, but political opponents. One reason was that he had a sense of humor and could take a joke at his own expense. Another was that he was good company, always interesting to be with.

The last made him attractive to some women, a situation Donahue had a reputation for taking advantage of, even though he had a secure marriage and was seen frequently in the company of his wife and teenage children.

This was the Senator Donahue who, shortly after 10 A.M. on the first Tuesday of December, gaveled to order the Senate Subcommittee on Ethical Merchandising, and announced that proceedings would begin with a short statement of his own.

The committee was meeting in Room SR-253 of the Old Senate

Office Building, an impressive setting. The chairman and fellow senators sat behind an elevated U-shaped desk, facing witnesses and the public. Three large windows overlooked the Senate park and fountain. There was a marble fireplace. Beige curtains had printed on them the Great Seal of the United States.

"All of us here," Dennis Donahue began, reading from a prepared paper, "are aware of the ghastly, worldwide tragedy involving children whose brainpower and other normal functions have allegedly been destroyed by a drug which, until recently, was prescribed and sold in this country. The name of that drug is Montayne."

The senator was a strong, commanding speaker, and the hundred or so people in the room were attentively silent. TV cameras were focused on him. Besides Donahue, eight other senators were present —five from Donahue's own majority party, and three from the minority. To the chairman's left was Stanley Urbach, the committee's chief counsel, a former district attorney from Boston. Behind the senators were fifteen members of the committee staff, some seated, others standing.

"What these hearings will investigate," Donahue continued, "is the responsibility for this series of events, and whether . . ."

Celia, who was scheduled to be the first witness, listened as the opening statement continued along predictable lines. She was seated at a green-baize-covered table and beside her was her counsel, Childers Quentin. She had persuaded the courtly Quentin to accept this extra responsibility because, as she told him, "There's no other lawyer who knows more than you do, now, about Montayne, and I have confidence in your advice."

That advice, relating to today, had been specific and forthright. "Describe the full facts as honestly, clearly and briefly as possible," Quentin insisted, "and do not attempt to be smart, or to score off Dennis Donahue."

The last admonition had been in response to Celia's wish to bring out in evidence the fact that, more than two years earlier when Montayne's U.S. introduction was being delayed at FDA—some thought unreasonably—Donahue had been among those protesting the delay, describing it then as "clearly ridiculous in the circumstances."

"Absolutely not!" Quentin had ruled. "For one thing, Donahue will have remembered that remark; if not, his staff will remind him, so he'll be ready to deal with it. He'd probably say he was one more victim of drug company propaganda, or something of the kind. And, for another, you'd arouse his antagonism, which is extremely unwise."

The lawyer then outlined for Celia some Washington facts of life.

"A United States senator has enormous power and influence, in some ways even more than a President because the exercise of power is less visible. There isn't a government department a senator can't reach into and have something done, providing it isn't outrageous or illegal. Important people inside and outside government will fall over themselves to do a senator a favor, even if that favor is harmful to someone else. It's a system of trades and, within that system, a senator's power—which can be used benevolently or to destroy—is the biggest trading chip of all. Which is why it's a foolish person indeed who chooses to make an enemy of a U.S. senator."

Celia had taken the advice to heart and cautioned herself to remember it in any exchange with Dennis Donahue, whom she already detested.

Also accompanying Celia was Vincent Lord, now seated on the other side of Quentin. While Celia would make a statement on behalf of Felding-Roth and then be cross-examined, the research director's role was solely to answer questions if required.

Senator Donahue concluded his remarks, paused briefly, then announced, "Our first witness is Mrs. Celia Jordan, president of Felding-Roth Pharmaceuticals of New Jersey. Mrs. Jordan, do you wish to introduce your associates?"

"Yes, Senator." In a few words, Celia introduced Quentin and Lord.

Donahue nodded. "Mr. Quentin we know well. Dr. Lord, we are glad to have you with us. Mrs. Jordan, you have a statement, I believe. Please proceed."

Celia remained seated at the witness table as she began, speaking into a microphone in front of her.

"Mr. Chairman and members of the subcommittee: First and foremost my company wishes to express its great sorrow and sympathy for those families which have been part of what Senator Donahue, a few moments ago, described correctly as a worldwide tragedy. While the full scientific evidence is not yet in, and may take years to assemble, it now appears certain that the drug Montayne was responsible for damage to fetuses in wombs of pregnant women—in a very small section of the total population, and in circumstances impossible to

373

foresee during the extensive testing of that drug, originally in France, later in other countries, and before its official approval by FDA for use in the United States."

Celia's voice was clear, but low-keyed and deliberately not forceful. Her statement had been carefully drafted and worked on by several people, though principally by herself and Childers Quentin. She stayed with the text as she read, merely adding an occasional phrase where appropriate.

"Something else my company wishes to point out is that it has, in all matters concerning Montayne—at every stage of testing, distribution, and reporting—complied with the law. Indeed, when serious doubts were raised about the drug, my company went beyond requirements of the law, and withdrew Montayne voluntarily, without waiting for a decision by the FDA."

Celia continued, "I now wish to go back and review the origins of Montayne in France, where it was developed by Laboratoires Gironde-Chimie, a company of excellent reputation and with a long history of successful . . ."

As well as being precise, the report being delivered was impersonal. That, too, had been decided after discussions at Felding-Roth headquarters and at Childers Quentin's offices in Washington.

Quentin had asked Celia, "How do you wish to handle the matter of your resignation over Montayne?"

"Not at all," she had replied. "My resignation was personal, a matter of instinct and conscience. Now that I'm back, I'm representing the company, reporting what the company did."

"And where is your conscience in all that?"

"Still intact, still in place," she responded sharply. "If I'm asked about my resignation I'll answer honestly. It's simply that I don't propose to bring it up, simply to make myself look good."

Celia had reminded Quentin, too, of the lack of any scientific grounds for her resignation—a weakness she had been aware of at the time, and her reason for not going public.

She now informed the Senate subcommittee, "No doubts whatever about the safety of Montayne arose until a report from Australia in June 1976. Even then, there seemed no reason for concern because an Australian government investigation . . ."

Step by step she traced the Montayne story. The recital took forty minutes, at which point Celia concluded, "My company has complied with committee subpoenas by supplying documents confirm-

374

ing all that I have said. We remain ready to cooperate in any other way, and to respond to questions."

The questions began at once, the first from the committee counsel, Stanley Urbach, long-faced and thin-lipped, who gave the impression of smiling only on rare occasions.

"Mrs. Jordan, you referred to the first Australian report that raised possible doubts about Montayne. That would be seven to eight months before your company placed the drug on sale in the United States. Is that correct?"

She calculated mentally. "Yes."

"Mentioned in your statement were two other adverse reports, one from France, another from Spain, both also occurring before your company's U.S. marketing of Montayne. Again correct?"

"Not entirely, Mr. Urbach. You called them adverse reports. What they were—at that point—were allegations which had been investigated by Laboratoires Gironde-Chimie and declared unsubstantiated."

The lawyer made an impatient gesture. "If we are quibbling about words, let me ask you this: Were the reports *favorable?*"

"No, and perhaps I can save us time. In the pharmaceutical business 'adverse reports' has a specific meaning. In that sense, those from France and Spain were not."

Urbach sighed. "Would the witness settle for 'critical reports?'"

"I suppose so." Celia already sensed this was going to be difficult, and that she was in for a hard time.

Senator Donahue cut in. "The point counsel is making is perfectly clear. Were you people—your company—aware of those three reports prior to Montayne's being placed on sale here?"

"Yes, we were."

"Yet you still went ahead and marketed the drug?"

"Senator, with any new drug there are *always* negative opinions. All of them must be examined carefully and assessed . . ."

"*Please*, Mrs. Jordan. I am not asking for a lecture on the practices of the pharmaceutical industry. My question requires a simple 'yes' or 'no.' I repeat: Knowing about those reports, did your company go ahead and sell that drug to pregnant American women?"

Celia hesitated.

"We are waiting, Mrs. Jordan."

"Yes, Senator, but . . ."

"The answer 'yes' will be sufficient." Donahue nodded to Urbach. "Carry on."

"Would it not have been better and more prudent," the subcommittee counsel asked, "for Felding-Roth to have done more investigating of those reports and delayed the launching of Montayne?"

Celia thought wryly: that had been her argument which, later, caused her to resign. Remembering her role here, she answered, "With hindsight, yes. Of course. But at the time, the company was proceeding on scientific advice."

"Whose advice?"

She considered before answering. It had, of course, been Lord's advice, but she wanted to be fair. "Our director of research, Dr. Lord, but he was acting on what seemed authentic data from Gironde-Chimie."

"We will ask Dr. Lord about that later. Meanwhile . . ." Urbach consulted notes. "Did the decision to go ahead, and not to delay Montayne despite those adverse . . . excuse me, critical reports have any relation to anticipated profits?"

"Well, profits are always a factor . . ."

"Mrs. Jordan! Yes or no?"

Inwardly, Celia sighed. *What was the good?* Every question was a trap, a contrived progression toward a preconceived conclusion.

She conceded, "Yes."

"Were those profits critical to your company?"

"It was believed so, yes."

"What were those profits expected to be?"

The remorseless, loaded questions continued. Yet, she found time to ask in a corner of her mind: Were they so unfairly loaded when touching so very close to truth? Wasn't there a time, not long ago, when she would have asked those same questions herself? And wasn't it ironic that she was appearing here in place of Sam Hawthorne who ought to have had these questions put to him, but was dead? For the first time since Hawaii, she was reminded of Andrew's cautioning words: "*If you go back . . . the Montayne mess and responsibility will rub off on you.*" As happened so often, Andrew had been right.

Her ordeal was interrupted by a lunch recess, Senator Donahue informing her, "Mrs. Jordan, you may stand down, but please be available for more questions later." The senator then announced, "The next witness after lunch will be Dr. Vincent Lord."

376

12

Quentin and Celia ate a sandwich lunch and drank coffee from a thermos in the rear of a limousine which had been waiting for them outside the Old Senate Office Building. "It's faster and more private than we'd get elsewhere," Quentin had said when announcing the arrangement. Now they were parked on Jefferson Drive, not far from the Smithsonian, with the uniformed chauffeur pacing to and fro outside.

Vincent Lord had been invited for the limousine lunch, but declined, having made other arrangements.

"You're being made to look bad, and I mean bad personally," Quentin said, after a while. "How do you feel about that?"

Celia grimaced. "How would anyone feel? I don't like it."

"What's happening is a tactic." The lawyer sipped his steaming coffee. "Any investigation of this type, which is a political exercise, requires a showcase villain. Representing your company, you happen to be the one available. But I could do something to change that."

"Do what?"

"Let me explain some background first. Donahue and his staff know about your stand within the company against Montayne, and your resignation because of it. There's no way they wouldn't know; they're thorough people. They probably know, too, the terms you insisted on when coming back, and they're certainly aware of the Felding-Roth Doctrine, and that you were its author."

"Then why . . ."

"Hear me out. Also, try to look at it their way." Quentin nodded to a group of passing tourists who had peered into the limousine, then he turned his attention back to Celia. "Why should Donahue's people concern themselves with bolstering your image? And if they did, who else could they focus on critically? Certainly not a dead man; he's beyond their reach."

"I suppose I understand all that, and I know you said this is a political exercise," Celia admitted. "Just the same, isn't the truth important at all?"

"If I were a lawyer on the other side," Quentin said, "I'd answer your question this way: Yes, truth is always important. But concerning Montayne, the truth lies in what the company—Felding-Roth—did, because it marketed Montayne and is responsible. As to you individually—yes, you did resign. But you also came back and, in doing so, accepted your share of responsibility for Montayne, even after the fact." Quentin smiled grimly. "Of course, I could argue the whole thing the other way and be equally convincing."

"Lawyers!" Celia's laugh was hollow. "Do they ever believe in anything?"

"One tries to. Though perpetual ambivalence is a hazard of the profession."

"You said there was something you could do. Just what?"

"On the subcommittee," Quentin pointed out, "are several minority members friendly to your industry. There's also a minority counsel. None of them have spoken up yet, and probably won't, because doing so might suggest they were in favor of Montayne—an impossible position. But what one of them will do, if I request it as a favor, is have questions asked to bring out your personal record and make you look good instead of awful."

"If that happened, would it help Felding-Roth?"

"No. Probably the reverse."

Celia said resignedly, "In that case, let's leave it alone."

"If you insist," the lawyer said sadly. "It's your head, and your blood on it."

Vincent Lord took over the microphone reserved for witnesses when the afternoon session began.

Once more, Urbach led off the questioning, having Lord first describe his scientific background. The subcommittee counsel then proceeded through the early stages of Montayne, Lord responding to all questions in a confident, relaxed manner.

After about fifteen minutes, Urbach asked, "When Montayne was close to being marketed in the United States, and those reports from

378

Australia, France and Spain were known within your company, did you recommend a delay?"

"No, I did not."

"Why was that?"

"A delay at that point would have been a management decision. As director of research, my involvement was solely scientific."

"Please explain that."

"Certainly. My responsibility was to provide a scientific evaluation of the information then available, and supplied by Laboratoires Gironde-Chimie. On that basis I had no reason to recommend delay."

Urbach persisted. "You used the phrase 'scientific evaluation.' Apart from science, did you have any feeling, any instinct, about those three reports?"

For the first time Lord hesitated before answering. "I might have had."

"You might have had, or *did* have?"

"Well, I was uneasy. But, again, there wasn't anything scientific."

Celia, who had been relaxed while listening, suddenly paid closer attention.

Urbach was continuing. "If I understand you correctly, Dr. Lord, you were in something of a dilemma?"

"Well, yes."

"A dilemma between science on the one hand and, on the other, your 'unease'—I am using your word—as a human being? Is that correct."

"I guess you could say that."

"It is not a matter of guessing, Dr. Lord, nor what I would say. It is what *you* would say."

"Well . . . all right, I would say it."

"Thank you." The subcommittee counsel glanced down at his notes. "And for the record, Doctor, after your reading of those reports we spoke of, did you *advocate* the marketing of Montayne?"

"No, I did not."

The series of replies jolted Celia. *Lord was lying.* Not only had he supported going ahead with Montayne, he had voted for it at the meeting held by Sam, sneering at Celia's doubts and her plea for a postponement.

Senator Donahue leaned in toward a microphone. "I'd like to ask the witness this question: If your responsibility had been a management one, Dr. Lord, and not just science, would you have recommended a delay?"

Again Lord hesitated. Then he answered firmly, "Yes, Senator, I would."

The bastard! Celia began scribbling a note to Quentin: *That isn't true* . . . Then she stopped. What difference did it make? Supposing she questioned Lord's honesty and a debate ensued, with accusations and denials flying—what would it change? At this hearing—nothing. Disgusted, she crumpled the paper on which she had begun to write.

After a few more questions, Lord was thanked for his evidence and excused. He left the hearing room at once, without speaking with Celia or looking in her direction.

Dr. Maud Stavely was called as the next witness.

The chairperson of Citizens for Safer Medicine strode confidently forward from the rear of the room and went to a microphone at the witness table, some distance from Celia and Quentin. She did not glance their way.

Senator Donahue welcomed the witness cordially, after which Dr. Stavely read a prepared statement. It described her medical qualifications, the structure of the New York-based organization, CSM's negative views about drug firms, and the group's early opposition to Montayne.

While Celia disliked the statement's emphasis and some allusions, she conceded mentally that Stavely sounded professional and impressive. As when the two of them had met two years earlier, the CSM leader was attractive and well groomed, and today was stylishly though simply dressed in a maroon tailored suit.

About Montayne, Stavely declared, "Unfortunately our protests were handicapped by a lack of funds. CSM does not have the enormous resources—multimillions of dollars—which companies like Felding-Roth can pour into sales propaganda, deluding doctors and the public into believing that drugs such as Montayne are safe, yet knowing—as they did with Montayne—that indications argue otherwise."

As Stavely paused, Dennis Donahue interjected, "I imagine, Doctor, that since your opinions about Montayne have been proved correct, contributions to your organization have increased."

"Indeed they have, Senator. And we hope, after these hearings which we welcome, they will become greater still."

Donahue smiled without replying, and Stavely continued.

To Celia's distress, her own visit to CSM headquarters was referred to. It introduced a complication she had hoped would be avoided.

The matter came up again during Stanley Urbach's cross-examination of Dr. Stavely.

The subcommittee counsel asked, "What was the date of Mrs. Jordan's visit to Citizens for Safer Medicine?"

Stavely consulted notes. "November twelfth, 1978."

"Did Mrs. Jordan state her purpose in coming to see you at that time?"

"She said she wanted to talk. One of the things we talked about was Montayne."

"At that point, I believe, while Montayne had been approved by FDA, it had not yet gone on sale. Is that correct?"

"Yes, it is."

"Is it also correct that, at that time, Citizens for Safer Medicine was actively seeking to have the FDA approval canceled?"

"Yes. We were strong about that, working hard at it."

"Did that strength, those efforts you were making to stop Montayne, appear to worry Mrs. Jordan?"

"Well, she certainly wasn't pleased. She argued *for* Montayne, saying it was safe. Of course, I disagreed."

"Did she say *why* she believed the drug was safe?"

"I remember very clearly—she did not. Of course she has no medical qualifications to make that kind of judgment—not that that stops sales-happy people like Jordan making them." Stavely's voice conveyed disdain, then she added, "Just the same, I was shocked at how little she did know."

"Can you be specific as to why you were shocked?"

"Yes. You remember, at the time, the Australian case against Montayne had already received wide attention?"

Urbach smiled politely. *"I'm* supposed to be asking the questions, Doctor."

Stavely smiled back. "Excuse me. The point I'm making is that Jordan had not even read the Australian trial transcript. She admitted it. I urged her to go away and do so."

"Thank you, Doctor. Now, during your conversation, did you get

381

the impression that Mrs. Jordan had come representing her company, Felding-Roth?"

"Very definitely, yes."

"And again referring to the effort by Citizens for Safer Medicine to have the FDA approval of Montayne withdrawn, did you also form an impression that Felding-Roth had become anxious about that, and therefore sent Mrs. Jordan to you with a plea to ease up?"

"Well, it did occur to me, though I can't prove it. However, if that *was* the woman's purpose, she must have seen immediately that there was not the slightest chance of its happening."

Listening and watching, Celia thought: Unlike Vince Lord, Stavely had not lied. But what a difference the selection of items, a tone of voice, and emphasis seasoned with opinion could make to a subsequent report of *any* conversation!

Senator Donahue, holding a paper, spoke into his microphone. "Dr. Stavely, I have in my hand a document described as 'The Felding-Roth Doctrine.' If you have not seen it, I will have this copy handed to you."

"I have seen it, Senator, and once is enough."

Donahue smiled. "I take it you have an opinion. We would like to hear it."

"I believe the so-called doctrine is a nauseating, shameless piece of sales promotion which capitalizes on a ghastly tragedy and is an insult to the children and families who have been victims of Montayne."

Celia, hot with anger and ready to leap to her feet, felt Quentin's hand on her arm, restraining her. With an effort she stayed seated, her face flushed, seething.

A minority member of the subcommittee, Senator Jaffee, observed mildly, "But surely, Dr. Stavely, if a company, in effect, admits an error and promises for the future . . ."

Stavely snapped, "I was asked my opinion and gave it. If a piece of hocus-pocus like that deceives you, sir, it doesn't me."

Senator Donahue, with a half smile, put his paper down.

After a few more questions, Dr. Stavely was thanked and excused.

The first witness on the following day, it was announced, would be Dr. Gideon Mace from FDA.

That evening, in her suite at the Madison Hotel, Celia received a telephone call. The caller was Juliet Goodsmith who announced she

382

was downstairs in the lobby. Celia invited her to come up, and when Juliet arrived embraced her affectionately.

Sam's and Lilian's daughter looked older than her twenty-three years, Celia thought, though that was not surprising. She also appeared to have lost weight—too much of it, prompting Celia to suggest they have dinner together, but the offer was declined.

"I only came," Juliet said, "because I'm in Washington, staying with a friend, and I read about those hearings. They're not being fair to you. You're the only one in the company who showed any decency about that filthy drug. All the others were greedy and rotten, and now *you're* being punished."

They were seated facing each other, and Celia said gently, "It wasn't, and isn't, quite like that."

She explained that as the company's senior representative, she was the immediate target for Senator Donahue and his aides; also that her personal actions had had no effect on the marketing of Montayne.

"The point is," Celia said, "Donahue is trying to make Felding-Roth look like a public enemy."

"Then maybe he's right," Juliet said, "and the company *is* a public enemy."

"No, I won't have that!" Celia said emphatically, "The company made a bad mistake over Montayne, but has done enormous good in the past and will do the same again." Even now she was thinking, with excited optimism, about Peptide 7 and Hexin W.

"Also," Celia went on, "whatever mistake your father made— which he paid for dearly—he wasn't either of those things you said: 'rotten' or 'greedy.' He was a good man who did what he saw as right at the time."

"How can I believe that?" Juliet retorted. "He gave me those pills without telling me they weren't approved."

"Try to forgive your father," she urged. "If you don't, now that he's dead, you'll achieve nothing and it will be harder on you." As Juliet shook her head, Celia added, "I hope you will, in time."

She knew better than to inquire about Juliet's son, now almost two years old and in an institution for the helpless and incurable, where he would spend the remainder of his life. Instead, she asked, "How is Dwight?"

"We're getting a divorce."

"Oh, no!" The shock and concern were genuine. Celia remem-

383

bered her conviction, at Juliet's and Dwight's wedding, that theirs would be a strong marriage which would last.

"Everything was great until our baby was a few months old." Juliet's voice held the flatness of defeat. "Then, when we found out how he was, and why, nothing seemed to work anymore. Dwight was bitter at my father, even more than me. He wanted to sue Felding-Roth and Daddy personally, savaging them in court, handling the case himself. I could never have agreed to that."

"No," Celia said. "It would have torn everyone apart."

"After that we tried to put things together for a while." Juliet said sadly, "It didn't work. We weren't the same two people anymore. That's when we decided on divorce."

There seemed little to say, but Celia thought, How much sadness and tragedy, beyond the obvious, Montayne had wrought!

13

Of all the witnesses to appear before the Senate Subcommittee on Ethical Merchandising during its investigation of Montayne, Dr. Gideon Mace suffered the hardest time.

At one dramatic point during the cross-examination of Mace, Senator Donahue pointed an accusing finger and thundered in a voice matching Jehovah's, "*You* were the one who, representing government and all the safeguards government has set, unleashed this scourge upon American womanhood and helpless unborn children. Therefore do not expect to leave this place unscathed, uncensured, or unburdened of a guilty conscience which should stay with you through all your days."

What Mace had done a few minutes earlier, astounding all who heard, was admit that prior to recommending FDA approval of Montayne, he had had serious doubts about the drug, based on the earliest Australian report—doubts which never left him.

Urbach, conducting the cross-examination, had almost shouted, "Then *why* did you approve it?"

To which Mace answered, emotionally but lamely, "I . . . I just don't know."

The answer—the worst he could have given—produced from spectators in the hearing room an audible shock wave of disbelief and horror, and Donahue's tirade a moment later.

Until that point, Mace had appeared—while plainly nervous—to be in control and able to account for his actions as the FDA reviewer who had overseen the Montayne new drug application. He had begun with a short statement of his own, describing the enormous amount of data submitted—125,000 pages in 307 volumes—followed by details of his various queries of that data, which resulted in delay. These queries, he stated, were eventually resolved to his satisfaction. He did not refer to the report from Australia; that only came out later, in response to questions.

It was during questioning, when the Australian matter was reached, that Mace became emotionally disturbed, then seemed suddenly to go to pieces. The awful admission—*"I just don't know"*—had followed.

Despite an awareness of Mace's weak position, Celia felt some sympathy for him, believing the load of blame on Mace was disproportionate. Later she spoke of it to Childers Quentin.

"It's at times like this," the lawyer commented, "that the British system of drug approvals is shown as clearly superior to ours."

When Celia asked why, Quentin explained.

"In Britain a Committee on the Safety of Medicines advises the Minister of Health, and it's the minister who grants a new drug license. Civil servants are among those counseling the minister, of course, but the minister has responsibility, so if anything goes wrong he, and he alone, must face Parliament and take the blame.

"A minister in the British government would not do anything as cowardly as we let happen here—allow a civil servant like Mace to carry the can and go to Capitol Hill, accepting blame. If we had the same strong moral system, the Secretary of Health, Education, and Welfare would be up there, facing Donahue. But where is the Secretary now? Probably skulking in his office or conveniently out of town."

There was another weakness in the United States system, Quentin believed.

"One effect of what you see happening is that FDA's people become ultracautious, not wanting to be dragged before a congressional committee and maybe crucified. So instead of approving drugs which ought to be available, they sit on them and wait, sometimes far too long. Obviously some caution—a lot of caution—about new drugs is needed, but too much can be bad, delaying progress in medicine, depriving doctors, hospitals and patients of cures and other aid they ought to have."

When Mace's ordeal was finally over and a recess ordered, Celia was relieved. At the same time, because of her earlier sympathy, she got up and walked across to him.

"Dr. Mace, I'm Celia Jordan of Felding-Roth. I just wanted to say . . ."

She stopped, confounded and dismayed. At the mention of Felding-Roth, Mace's features contorted into a look of blazing, savage hatred such as she had never seen before. Now, eyes glaring, teeth clenched, he hissed, "Stay away from me! Do you hear! Don't ever, *ever*, come near me again!"

Before Celia could collect her thoughts and answer, Mace turned his back and walked away.

Quentin, close behind, asked curiously, "What was all that about?"

Shaken, she answered, "I don't know. It happened when I used the company name. He seemed to go berserk."

"So?" The lawyer shrugged. "Dr. Mace doesn't like the manufacturer of Montayne. It's understandable."

"No. It's something more than that. I'm sure."

"I wouldn't worry about it."

Yet that expression of hatred stayed with Celia, troubling and puzzling her, for the remainder of the day.

Vincent Lord had stayed on in Washington for an extra day and Celia had a showdown with him about his testimony the previous afternoon. It took place in her hotel suite where she accused him bluntly of lying, and asked, "Why?"

To her surprise, the research director did not dispute the accusation and said contritely, "Yes, you're right. I'm sorry. I was nervous."

"You didn't appear to be nervous."

"It doesn't have to show. All those questions were getting to me. I wondered what that guy, Urbach, knew."

"What could he know?"

Lord hesitated, groping for an answer. "Nothing more than we all do, I guess. Anyway, I figured that how I answered was the quickest way to end the questions and get out."

Celia was unconvinced. "Why should you, more than anyone else, have to get out quickly? Okay, what's happening is unpleasant for everyone, including me, and we all have consciences to answer. But nothing illegal was ever done about Montayne." She stopped, a sudden thought striking her. "Or was it?"

"No! Of course not." But the response was a second late and a shade too strong.

Some words of Sam's, as they had once before, came back to Celia: *"There's . . . something you don't know."*

She regarded Lord quizzically. "Vince, is there anything, anything at all, about Montayne and Felding-Roth that I've not been told?"

"I swear to you—nothing. What could there be?"

He was lying again. She knew it. She also knew that Sam's secret, whatever it might be, had not died with him—that Lord had shared it.

But at the moment, she could go no further.

The subcommittee hearings lasted four days. There were other witnesses, among them two doctors—neurologists who had examined babies damaged by Montayne. One of the doctors had been to Europe to study cases there and showed slides of children he had seen.

Outwardly, there was nothing to suggest that the photographed children were other than normal. But most were lying down and, as the specialist explained, "Any but the smallest movement will always have to be made for them. Additionally, all these infants suffered serious brain damage during their embryonic stage."

Some of the children's faces were beautiful. One—older than the others—was a two-year-old boy. Supported by an unseen hand behind him, he was looking into the camera with what seemed soulful eyes. His expression was blank.

"This child," the neurologist informed his silent audience, "will never think like you or me, and almost certainly will have no awareness of what is going on around him."

The young face reminded Celia sharply of Bruce at the same age,

387

sixteen years ago. Bruce, who had written only a few days before from Williams College, which he was now attending.

> Dear Mom and Dad:
> College is great! I love it here. What I like most is, they want you to *think, think, think* . . .

Celia was glad the lights had been lowered for the slides, then realized she was not alone in using a handkerchief to wipe her eyes.

Senator Donahue, when the doctor had finished, seemed to be having trouble with his voice. Yes, Celia thought, despite all his grandstanding and politics, he cares too.

Whatever softness there had been in Donahue had clearly vanished when, on the afternoon of the hearing's fourth and final day, Celia was recalled as a witness. Even in exchanges with his own staff, the senator seemed impatient and irritable. Before Celia was called, Quentin whispered to her, "Be careful. The great man sounds as if he ate something during lunch which disagreed with him."

Celia was questioned by subcommittee counsel Urbach concerning other testimony as it related to her own, earlier.

When queried about Vincent Lord's assertion that he would have delayed Montayne had the responsibility been his, she replied, "We have since discussed that. My own recollection differs from Dr. Lord's, but I see no point in disputing his statement, so let it stand."

As to her visit to the headquarters of Citizens for Safer Medicine, Celia said, "There are differences in interpretation. I went to see Dr. Stavely on impulse and with friendly intentions, thinking we might learn something from each other. It did not turn out that way."

Urbach asked, "Did you go there intending to talk about Montayne?"

"Not specifically."

"But you did discuss Montayne?"

"Yes."

"Did you hope to persuade Dr. Stavely and Citizens for Safer Medicine to cease, or moderate, their campaign to have the FDA's approval of Montayne withdrawn?"

"I did not. The thought never occurred to me."

"Was your visit an official one, on behalf of your company?"

388

"No. In fact, no one else at Felding-Roth knew of my intention to call on Dr. Stavely."

In his seat beside Urbach, Donahue seemed displeased. He asked, "Are all those truthful answers, Mrs. Jordan?"

"All my answers have been truthful." Anger seized her as she added, "Would you like me to take a polygraph test?"

Donahue scowled. "You are not on trial here."

"Excuse me, Senator. I hadn't noticed."

Glowering, Donahue motioned for Urbach to continue.

The questioning moved on to the Felding-Roth Doctrine.

"You have heard Dr. Stavely describe the document as a 'shameless piece of sales promotion,' " Urbach said. "Do you agree with that assessment?"

"Of course not. The doctrine has no objective other than the declared, straightforward one of charting future company policy."

"Oh, really. Are you convinced, then, it will have no sales promotion value at all?"

Celia sensed a trap being sprung. She decided to be wary.

"I didn't say that. But if—as an honest declaration—it eventually has that kind of value, it was not the original intention."

Donahue was fidgeting. Urbach turned to him inquiringly. "Senator?"

The chairman seemed uncertain whether to intervene or not. Then he said dourly, "It all comes down to interpretation, doesn't it? Whether we should believe a selfless, dedicated person like Dr. Stavely, or a spokeswoman for an industry which is so obsessed with profit that it regularly kills people or mutilates them, using drugs it knows in advance to be unsafe?"

There were gasps from spectators. Even Donahue's aides looked uneasy, sensing he had gone too far.

Ignoring all else, Celia asked acidly, "Is that a question directed at me, Senator? Or is it what it appears to be: a totally biased, unsupported statement, revealing this hearing as a charade which reached its verdict before any of us arrived?"

Donahue pointed to Celia, as he had to Mace. "Let me warn the witness: there is an offense in this place called contempt of Congress."

Not caring anymore, she shot back, "Don't tempt me!"

The senator thundered, "I order you to explain that remark!"

Celia had progressed beyond all caution. Scarcely hearing a whispered plea from Quentin, and shaking off his hand, she leaped to her feet.

"I explain it by pointing out that you, who sit here in judgment of Montayne and Felding-Roth and FDA, are the same person who, two years ago, complained about a delay in approving Montayne, and described it as ridiculous."

"That is a lie! Now you *are* in contempt, madam. I made no such statement."

Celia felt a wondrous glow of satisfaction. *Donahue had forgotten.* It was hardly surprising—he made so many statements on so many subjects. And his aides, if they knew of what was said earlier, had failed to brief him. On both counts, Quentin had been wrong.

There was a folder in front of her which she had not opened until now. She had brought it, just in case. From it Celia produced a batch of press clippings stapled together. She chose the one on top.

"This is from the *Washington Post* of September 17, 1976." She was still standing as she read:

> "Referring to the drug Montayne, now under review at FDA and intended for women during pregnancy, Senator Dennis Donahue today described the FDA's lack of a decision as 'clearly ridiculous in the circumstances.'"

She added, "The same report was in other newspapers."

Celia stopped. "And there is something else, Senator." She selected another paper from her folder.

Donahue, who had flushed a deep brick red, reached for his gavel. As he did, Senator Jaffee on the minority side called out, "No, no! Let the lady finish. I want to hear."

"You accused our industry of killing people," Celia said, addressing Donahue. "I have here your voting record on tobacco subsidies ever since you entered Congress eighteen years ago. Every one of those years you voted 'yes' for subsidies. And with those votes, Senator, you have helped kill more people from lung cancer than the pharmaceutical industry has killed in most of its history."

The last few words were lost in a tumult of confused shouting, some of it Donahue's as he banged his gavel, declaring, "This hearing is adjourned."

390

14

What started, for Celia, as a dismal experience ended—or so it seemed—as a personal triumph.

The same evening as her explosive clash with Senator Donahue, the television networks—ABC, CBS and NBC—carried almost the entire dramatic scene on their evening newscasts. As a critic subsequently wrote, "It was great theater, and TV at its immediate best."

Newspapers, next day, accorded the story similar prominence. The *New York Times* headed its report:

A Spunky Lady Bests a Senator

The *Chicago Tribune* had it:

Sen. Donahue Crosses Jordan
Afterward Wishes He Hadn't

There was other emphasis.

In this instance, it emerged, reporters—both for television and the press—had done their homework and some digging. As one explained it to Julian Hammond, who passed the information on to Celia, "Most of us found out about Mrs. Jordan's resignation over Montayne, also her insistence when she came back that the drug be withdrawn without waiting for the FDA. What no one seemed sure of was how to use that bit of background, so we saved it. As it turned out, holding it proved more effective in the end."

Thus, most reports after the showdown had Celia standing tall in two ways. First, both her departure from Felding-Roth and her return—now recorded publicly—revealed her as a person of strong moral principle. Second, her refusal to make herself look good at the Senate hearings at the expense of her employer demonstrated a noteworthy loyalty.

391

The Wall Street Journal began an editorial:

> There is usually more honor in business than business receives credit for. How pleasant it is, then, to have some honor not only plainly shown but widely acknowledged.

A few days after her return from Washington, Celia and Julian Hammond were together in her office. The public affairs vice president had brought in, happily, a newly received batch of press clippings which he spread over Celia's desk. Moments later, the arrival of Childers Quentin was announced.

Celia had not seen the Washington lawyer since their final day on Capitol Hill. His visit now was to review, with her, some more proposed settlements of Montayne lawsuits.

She told her secretary to send him in.

He looked tired and sounded moody, she thought as they greeted each other and she asked him to be seated.

Hammond said, "I was just leaving, Mr. Quentin." He pointed to the news clippings. "We were savoring the spoils of victory."

Quentin appeared unimpressed. "Is that what you call them?"

"Certainly." The public affairs chief seemed surprised. "Wouldn't you?"

The answer came grouchily. "If you think that, then you're both shortsighted."

There was a silence, after which Celia said, "All right, counselor. You've something on your mind. Tell us."

"All of that," Quentin motioned to the clippings, "as well as the TV coverage you've had, is heady stuff. But in a few weeks, most will be forgotten. The publicity will count for nothing."

It was Hammond who asked, "What *will* count?"

"What will count is that this company—and you personally, Celia —have acquired a formidable enemy. I know Donahue. You made him look a fool. Worse, you did it on his own home ground, the Senate, and—as it turned out—with millions watching. He'll never forgive that. Never. If, any time in the future, he can do harm to Felding-Roth or to you, Celia, he'll do it and enjoy it. He may even look for ways, and a United States senator—as I told you once—has levers of power he can pull."

It was, Celia thought, as if she had suddenly taken an icy shower. And she knew that Quentin was right.

She asked, "So what do you suggest?"

The lawyer shrugged. "For the moment, nothing. For the future, as best you can, be cautious. Don't put yourself—or Felding-Roth—in any situation where Senator Donahue can do you harm."

15

"What's Mrs. Jordan like?" Yvonne asked Martin.

He thought before answering. "Attractive. Strong. Intelligent. Extremely good at her job. Direct and honest, so that when you deal with her, you always know where you stand."

"I'm already nervous about our meeting."

He laughed. "No need to be. I predict you'll like each other."

It was a Friday evening in July and the two of them were in Martin's house at Harlow, into which Yvonne had moved completely almost a year before. She abandoned her small apartment because it seemed a needless expense.

In the living room at this moment, books and papers were spread around—a clutter from Yvonne's studies for "A" level exams, now six months away. A year and a half had passed since, at Martin's urging, she had taken on the heavy work load which eventually, they hoped, would launch her into veterinary medicine.

The studying had gone well. Yvonne, loving what she was doing, had never been happier. Her joy pervaded the household and was shared by Martin. As well as continuing to work at the Felding-Roth Research Institute by day, she was having outside tutoring during some evenings and weekends. Martin—as he had promised—helped Yvonne, supplementing her learning with his practical experience.

Another reason for pleasure was progress at the institute. Since the devastating "animal-rights" raid, the reassembly of data had gone far faster than expected. Now, not only was all of it recovered, but development of Peptide 7 had advanced to the point of being ready for a management product review.

Celia, along with several others from New Jersey, would arrive at Harlow for that purpose on Wednesday of the next week.

At this moment, however, thoughts of Celia were a digression. Martin continued to frown, as he had for several minutes, over a textbook—Murray's *Principles of Organic Chemistry*.

"They've rewritten this since I studied it for my degree. Some of the new stuff is unrealistic. You'll learn it, then ignore it afterward."

Yvonne asked, "You're talking about those systematic chemical names?"

"Of course."

The Geneva system for chemicals had been devised by the International Union of Pure and Applied Chemistry, abbreviated to IUPAC and pronounced "U-pak." The idea was that the name of any chemical compound should also indicate its structure. Thus, *iso*-octane became 2,2,4-trimethylpentane, acetic acid—common vinegar —was ethanoic acid, and ordinary glycerin, propane-1,2,3-triol. Unfortunately, chemists who were supposed to use the IUPAC names seldom did, though examiners required them. Thus Yvonne was learning the new names for the exams, the old for future lab work.

She asked, "Don't you use IUPAC names in the lab?"

"Not often. Most of us can't remember them; also they're unwieldy. Anyway, let me test you on both."

"Go ahead."

Successively, Martin called off twenty chemicals, sometimes using the old name, with others the newer code. Each time, without hesitating, Yvonne recited the alternate.

Martin closed the book, shaking his head. "That memory of yours still amazes me. I wish I had one like it."

"Is my memory why you won't let me take Peptide 7?"

"That's part of it. Mostly, though, I don't want you running any risks."

A month ago, Martin had posted a notice at the institute. It was headed: *Volunteers Wanted*.

The notice requested that any staffers who were willing to have Peptide 7 injected into them, for the first series of tests on healthy humans, should sign their names below. The objectives and potential risk were carefully spelled out. Before posting the notice, Martin signed himself.

Rao Sastri signed immediately after. Within a few days there were fourteen more signatures, including Yvonne's.

From the final list, Martin chose a total of ten volunteers. Yvonne was not among them. When she inquired about her omission, he put her off with, "Perhaps later. Not yet."

The purpose of the early human testing was not to study positive results from Peptide 7, but to look for any harmful side effects. As Martin explained to Celia by telephone at the time, "We're allowed to do this kind of testing in Britain on our own, though in America you'd need approval from the FDA."

So far, after twenty days' monitoring of the volunteers, who continued to receive daily doses of Peptide 7, there had been no visible side effects whatever. Martin was delighted, though knowing that much more human testing needed to be done.

Yvonne sighed, "I'd like to have some Peptide 7 soon. It's probably the only way I'll ever take my extra weight off. By the way, I bought us kippers for tomorrow."

Martin beamed and told her, "You're an angel." Kippers were his favorite breakfast on weekends, when he could take time to enjoy them.

His voice became more serious. "I'm going to see my mother tomorrow. I talked to my father today and he told me the doctors say she hasn't long."

While the deterioration of Martin's mother had been slow, the progression of her Alzheimer's disease had been relentless. A few months earlier, Martin had had her moved into a Cambridge nursing home where she now floated dimly on the outer edge of life. Martin's father continued to live in a small but pleasant flat that Martin had rented for his parents soon after joining Felding-Roth.

"I'm sorry." Yvonne reached out, touching his hand in sympathy. "Yes, I'll come. If you don't mind my studying in the car."

They arranged to leave immediately after breakfast. Martin wanted to stop at his office, briefly, on the way.

Next morning at the institute, while Martin glanced through mail and read a computer printout from the day before, Yvonne wandered into the animal room. He found her there later.

She had paused in front of a cage containing several rats and Martin heard her exclaim, "You horny old devil!"

He asked, amused, "Who is?"

Yvonne turned, then pointed to the cage. "This bunch are some of the horniest little beasts I've ever seen. Just lately, they can't seem to get enough of each other. They'd sooner have sex than eat."

While Martin watched, the rat over whom Yvonne had exclaimed continued copulating with a submissive female, while another pair in an adjoining cage amused themselves likewise.

He glanced at typed descriptions on both cages. All the rats, he noted, were receiving the most recent, refined batch of Peptide 7.

"You said they were horny 'just lately.' What does that mean?"

Yvonne hesitated, then looked sharply at Martin. "I suppose . . . since they've been getting their injections."

"And they're not young rats?"

"If they were human, they'd draw old-age pensions."

He laughed and said, "It's probably coincidence." Then he wondered, *was it?*

As if reading his mind, Yvonne asked, "What will you do?"

"On Monday, I'd like you to check the breeding rate of rats which have had Peptide 7. Let me know if it's average, or above."

"I don't have to wait until Monday. I can tell you now, it's way above normal. Up to this moment, though, I didn't connect—"

Martin said sharply, "Don't connect! Assumptions can lead down false alleys. Just send me what figures you have."

She said submissively, "All right."

"After that, set up two new groups of male and female older rats. Keep the groups separate, but let each group cohabit. One group will receive Peptide 7, the other won't. I want a computerized study of the mating habits of both."

Yvonne giggled. "A computer won't tell you how many times . . ."

"I suppose not. But it will keep track of litters. We'll settle for that."

She nodded, and Martin sensed that her mind was on something else. He asked, "What is it?"

"I was thinking about a funny thing that happened yesterday. While I was buying those kippers. Mickey Yates is one of your volunteers, isn't he?"

"Yes." Yates, a lab technician, was the oldest of the Peptide 7 volunteers. He had gone out of his way to be helpful to Martin ever since the incident, several years earlier, involving Celia and the guillotined rat. Being in the testing program was Yates's latest contribution.

"Well, I saw his wife in the market and she said how good it was that Mickey's work was making him feel young again."

396

"Meaning what?"

"I asked her. So she went red and said nowadays Mickey was feeling so 'bouncy and energetic'—those were her words—he was keeping her busy in bed."

"Did she mean just recently?"

"I'm sure of it."

"And he hadn't before?"

"According to her, hardly ever."

"I'm amazed she'd talk about it."

Yvonne smiled. "You don't know women very well."

Martin was thoughtful, then he said, "Let's get in the car. We'll talk on the way to Cambridge."

At first, while driving, they listened to the news on the radio, which was mostly of politics. It was an exciting, optimistic time in Britain. Two months earlier, a general election had brought to power the first woman prime minister in British history. Now, Margaret Thatcher and her government were injecting new enterprise into a nation which had suffered from too little of it since World War II.

At the end of the news, Martin switched off the radio and returned to closer concerns.

"I'm worried," he said, "and I don't want any general talk about what we've discussed this morning. You're to keep to yourself what you told me about those rats breeding. Also, don't tell anyone else about the new study. We have to do it, even though I don't like the idea, but keep the results locked up until you give them to me. And no more stories about Mickey Yates and his wife."

"I'll do all of that," Yvonne said. "But I don't understand why you're worried."

"Then I'll tell you. It's because we've produced a drug which I hope will be significant, be taken seriously, and become an important disease fighter. But if word gets around that it's some kind of aphrodisiac—as *well* as inducing weight loss, which may or may not be good after all—it could be the worst thing to happen. It would throw everything we've done into disrepute, could make us look as if we reinvented snake oil."

"I think I understand," Yvonne said. "And now you've explained it, I won't talk. But it'll be hard to stop others."

Martin said grimly, "That's what I'm afraid of."

397

It was midmorning when they reached Cambridge. Martin drove directly to the nursing home where his mother was being cared for. She was in bed, which was where she spent most of her time, having to be lifted out when necessary. She remembered nothing, not even the simplest things, and—as had been the case for many years—gave no flicker of recognition when Martin came close.

His mother, Martin thought as he stood with Yvonne beside him, seemed visibly to be wasting away day by day. Her body was emaciated, cheeks gaunt, hair thinning. Even in the earlier declining years —around the time when Celia had visited the old house in the Kite— some vestige of a younger beauty still remained. But now that, too, was gone.

It was as if the Alzheimer's, which had eaten away his mother's brain, was devouring her body too.

"It's been my dream," Martin said softly to Yvonne, "to help find something to prevent most, or some, of this. It will be years, of course, before we know if we've succeeded. But it's because our research into aging has been so important that I don't want anything to cheapen what we've found."

Yvonne said, "I do understand. Especially now."

On previous occasions when Martin had brought Yvonne to see his mother, Yvonne had taken the older woman's hands and sat holding them, saying nothing. Though no one could be sure, Martin had had an impression it gave his mother comfort. Today Yvonne did the same thing, but even that thin communication seemed no longer there.

From the nursing home, they drove to see Martin's father. The flat rented by Martin was northwest of the city, not far from Girton College, and they found Peat-Smith, Senior, in a tiny work area behind the building. The tools of his old trade were spread around, and he was chipping experimentally at a small piece of marble, using a chisel and a mallet.

"I think you know," Martin said to Yvonne, "that my father used to be a stonemason."

"Yes. But I didn't know you were still working at it, Mr. Peat-Smith."

"Ain't," the old man said. "Fingers get too damn stiff. Thought, though, I'd make an 'eadstone for your ma's grave, son. About the only thing left to do for 'er." He looked at Martin inquiringly. "Is that all right, seein' she ain't dead yet?"

Martin put his arm around his father's shoulders. "Yes, it is, Dad. Is there anything you need?"

"I need an 'unk of marble. Costs a bit, though."

"Don't worry about that. Just order what you want, and get them to send the bill to me."

When Martin looked at Yvonne, he saw that she was crying.

16

"I agree with you totally about the sex stimulant effect," Celia told Martin. "If Peptide 7 became thought of as some kind of aphrodisiac, it would fall into disrepute as a serious product."

"I think the chances are fair that we can keep it to ourselves," Martin said.

"I'm less sure," Celia acknowledged, "though I hope you're right."

It was the second day of her visit to the Harlow institute, and she was having a private meeting with Martin in his office. Earlier, he had advised her formally, "I can report that we have what appears to be a beneficial medication to retard mental aging and aid acuity, the two things going together. All signs look good."

It seemed, Celia thought, a long way from the time when, on Sam's instructions, she had visited Harlow to consider closing the institute, and even longer—it was seven years—since the memorable first meeting at Cambridge between Sam, herself and Martin.

She said, "There doesn't seem much doubt that you've achieved something great."

They were relaxed and comfortable with each other. If either, from time to time, remembered the intimacies of their night as lovers, it was never mentioned. Clearly that was a moment, an interlude, belonging solely to the past.

While Celia was having her talk with Martin, a half-dozen other executives who had accompanied her from Felding-Roth headquarters were having separate, specialized discussions about the future of Peptide 7. These covered a range of subjects—manufacturing, quality control, materials and sources, costs, packaging, product management—all facets of what would become a master plan determining how the drug would be introduced and marketed worldwide. Rao Sastri, Nigel Bentley, and other Harlow staff were responding to questions from the U.S. team.

Although more than a year of clinical trials still lay ahead and, after that, approval for Peptide 7's use had to be obtained from governments, many decisions about the future had to be made now. A major one was the extent of Felding-Roth's investment in a new manufacturing plant, which would be either a costly, unprofitable gamble or a shrewd, successful act of faith.

The way in which the drug would be ingested by those who used it was also important.

Martin told Celia, "We've researched this exhaustively, and recommend delivery by nasal spray. This is the modern, coming system. There'll be more and more medicines taken that way in future."

"Yes, I know. It's being talked about for insulin. Anyway, I'm thankful you've not produced an injectable."

As both knew, it was a pharmaceutical fact of life that any drug delivered by injection never sold as well as one which could be taken easily by patients at home.

"To be used as a nasal spray," Martin explained, "Peptide 7 will be in an inert saline solution mixed with a detergent. The detergent assures the best absorption rate."

Several detergents had been experimented with, he disclosed. The best nontoxic one, creating no irritation of nasal membranes, had been found to be a new Felding-Roth product recently available in the United States.

Celia was delighted. "You mean we can keep it all in-house?"

"Exactly." Martin smiled. "I thought you'd be pleased."

A normal dosage, he continued, would be twice daily. Two medical doctors, recently added to the Harlow staff, would coordinate clinical trials in Britain, beginning at once. "We shall concentrate on the age ranges of forty to sixty, though in special circumstances that can be

400

varied either way. We'll also try the drug on patients in the early stages of Alzheimer's. It will not reverse the disease—there's no hope of doing that—but may retard it."

Celia, in turn, reported plans for North American testing. "We want to begin as soon as possible. Because of preliminaries and the need for FDA permission, we'll be a little behind you. But not much."

They continued with their hopeful, exciting plans.

Out of the Harlow talks came a conclusion that a small plastic bottle with a push top would be the best container for Peptide 7. A suitable dose could result from the throw of a finger pump.

Such a container system opened up possibilities for attractive, interesting packaging.

It seemed likely that Felding-Roth would not manufacture the containers, but would contract them out to a specialist supplier. A decision, though, would be made in New Jersey.

While Celia was at Harlow, Martin arranged dinner for her with himself and Yvonne. Showing his sensitivity, Celia thought, he did not take them to the Churchgate, but to the dining room of a newer hotel, the Saxon Inn.

At first the two women inspected each other curiously, but after a short while, and despite the difference in ages—Celia was forty-eight, Yvonne twenty-seven—they seemed to slip into an easy friendship, perhaps because of their affinity with Martin.

Celia was admiring of Yvonne's decision to apply to veterinary college. When Yvonne pointed out that if accepted, she would be older than most students, Celia advised, "You'll do better because of that." And she told Martin, "We've a fund at Felding-Roth, set up to help employees who want to improve their education. I think we can bend the rules sufficiently to give Yvonne some financial aid."

Martin raised his eyebrows. "Yvonne, it looks as if your cost of living just got paid."

When she expressed gratitude, Celia waved it away and said, smiling, "From what I've been told, you contributed a lot to getting Peptide 7 where it is."

Later, when Yvonne had left the table briefly, Celia said, "She's

401

special and delightful. It's none of my business, Martin, and you can tell me so if you like—but are you going to marry her?"

The question startled him. "That's highly unlikely. In fact, I'm sure neither of us has thought about it."

"Yvonne has."

He disagreed. "Why should she? She has a whole career ahead of her—a good one. It will take her to different places where she'll meet other men, closer to her own age. I'm twelve years older."

"Twelve years means nothing."

Martin said obstinately, "Nowadays it does. It's a whole generation gap. Besides, Yvonne needs to be free, and so do I. At the moment we've an arrangement which suits us, but that can change."

"Men!" Celia said. "Some of you certainly get the best of your 'arrangements.' But you can be blind too."

The discussion was ended by Yvonne's return. It was not resumed before Celia and her group went back to New Jersey a few days later.

On the day that Celia left, Martin's mother died. She slipped away from life quietly, without warning or fuss. As a doctor at the nursing home expressed it to Martin later, "She went like a small boat that drifts off into the night on a calm sea."

The calmness, Martin thought, with feelings of mixed sadness and relief, had been present for his mother far too long. It was mental turbulence, not calm seas, that gave life its zest. Alzheimer's had deprived his mother of that zest, and the thought revived, once more, his hopes for the future of Peptide 7.

Only Martin, his father and Yvonne attended the simple funeral, and afterward Peat-Smith, Senior, went back to chipping at the block of marble he had ordered and which had been delivered several days before. Martin and Yvonne drove back to Harlow in companionable silence.

In the several months that followed, important decisions were taken at Felding-Roth, New Jersey, punctuated by many transatlantic journeys by headquarters staff.

The active ingredient of Peptide 7, which would appear as a white crystalline powder, was to be manufactured in the Republic of Ireland at a new plant for which a site had been chosen and architects' plans were being rushed to completion. The plant would be the first of Felding-Roth's to specialize in molecular biology. Space would be allowed on the site for later manufacturing of the chemical base for Hexin W.

Final production of Peptide 7, in its liquid form and ready for insertion in containers, would be in an existing plant in Puerto Rico. The containers, manufactured as expected by another company, would be shipped there. The overseas arrangements had substantial tax advantages compared with manufacturing in the United States.

The overall plan involved an enormous investment which, after doubts and discussions, was approved by the board of directors. At dinner one night Celia explained the doubts to Andrew. "It's money we don't have. Everything's going to be borrowed, and if it goes down the drain, so does Felding-Roth. But we've agreed we have to do it. We've bet the company, and we're in a now-or-never mood."

There were other decisions, of smaller dimension but important. One concerned a product name for Peptide 7.

Felding-Roth's advertising agency—still Quadrille-Brown of New York—began a costly, exhaustive study during which existing brand names were examined and new, suggested ones brooded over, with many being rejected. Finally, after several months of work, a top-level review session took place at Felding-Roth headquarters. On the company side it was attended by Celia, Bill Ingram and a half-dozen others.

A small agency contingent was headed by Howard Bladen, now president of Quadrille-Brown, who attended, as he expressed it, "a lot for old time's sake." Before the proceedings, Celia, Ingram and Bladen reminisced about the session sixteen years before, when they had all met, and which resulted in the "happy-momma plan" for New Healthotherm, still a steady O-T-C seller and revenue producer.

Storyboards and easels were set up in the boardroom to display eight suggested names, each presented in succession, in several type styles.

"Among possibilities we've narrowed down," an agency account executive announced, "are names which relate to the brain or human understanding." These followed and were: Appercep, Compre, Percip, and Braino. The first three, it was pointed out were derived from "apperception," "comprehension," and "percipience."

The fourth name was speedily withdrawn when Bill Ingram commented on its similarity to a household product—Drano.

"I'm embarrassed," Bladen said, "and how we all missed that, I'll never know. But no excuses. I apologize."

Then there were names which, the account exec said, "suggest something bright—shining with high intelligence." Those were: Argent and Nitid.

Two others were: Genus and Compen. The second, it was said, implied that the drug would "compensate" for what might otherwise be missing.

An hour's discussion ensued. Bill Ingram liked Appercep, disliked Nitid, was lukewarm about the others. Three people on the company side favored Argent. Bladen expressed himself a supporter of Compen. Celia held back, listening to the others, letting the arguments flow, reflecting at one point on the thousands of dollars all this was costing.

It was Bladen who eventually asked, "What's your opinion, Mrs. Jordan? You're one who's had some splendid ideas in the past."

"Well," Celia said, "I've been wondering why we don't call our new drug Peptide 7."

Only Ingram had the seniority, and knew Celia well enough, to laugh aloud.

Bladen hesitated, then a slow grin crossed his face. "Mrs. Jordan, I think what you've suggested is nothing short of brilliant."

Celia said tartly, "Just because I'm the client doesn't make it brilliant. It's simply sensible."

After the briefest further discussion, it was agreed that the product name of Peptide 7 would be Peptide 7.

A year flew by.

Clinical trials of Peptide 7, moving much faster than anyone expected, had proved outstandingly successful in Britain and the United States. Older patients responded positively to the drug. No adverse side effects appeared. Now, all accumulated data had been sent to the Committee on the Safety of Medicines in London, and to the FDA in Washington.

After careful discussions both at Harlow and in Boonton, involving Martin Peat-Smith, Vincent Lord, Celia and others, it was decided not to seek an official "indication" of the antiobesity effect of Peptide

404

7. This meant that while the known weight-reducing effect of the drug would be disclosed in information given to physicians, Peptide 7 would not be *recommended* for that use.

Some doctors, it was realized, might prescribe it for that purpose. However, if they did it would be the doctors' own responsibility, not Felding-Roth's.

As to a sexual stimulant effect, while repeated tests on animals showed that such an effect existed, it had not been sought during human testing, and was listed as inconspicuously as possible in all submitted data.

In both cases the thinking continued to be: Peptide 7 was a serious drug, intended to retard mental aging. Any "frivolous" uses would detract from this important role and diminish the drug's reputation.

In view of the flawless results from clinical testing, and the fact that extra indications were not sought, it appeared unlikely that official approval of Peptide 7 would be long delayed.

Meanwhile, work on the Irish plant and changes at Puerto Rico were near completion.

At Harlow, Martin, while keenly interested in the outcome of clinical trials, had left the details to the medical staff. He was working on modifying Peptide 7, exploring the possibilities of making other brain peptides, a spectrum which the earlier success had opened.

Martin and Yvonne were still living together. In January 1980, Yvonne had taken her A level examinations and, to her own and Martin's great joy, passed with A's in all subjects. She had also taken, and passed, the Cambridge Colleges' Examination, this because she had applied to Lucy Cavendish College in that university, and been accepted, subject to exam results. The admissions prospectus had pleased Yvonne with its reference to a "society for women, with a particular concern for those whose studies have been postponed or interrupted."

In September, having resigned from Felding-Roth, she began attending Lucy Cavendish where she would read Veterinary Medicine.

It was now October and she had become accustomed to driving daily to and from her Cambridge classes, an hour's journey.

Apart from her studies, a source of pleasure to Yvonne was the blossoming royal romance between the Prince of Wales and "Lady Di," as all of Britain now called her. Yvonne tirelessly discussed the subject with Martin. "I said all along that if he waited, he'd find an English rose," she declared. "And so he has."

Martin continued to listen to Yvonne's gossipy news, which now included the Cambridge University scene, with affectionate amusement.

During January of the following year, as President Reagan was inaugurated four thousand miles away, a license to market Peptide 7 in Britain was granted by the Minister of Health. Two months later, approval for United States use of the drug was announced by FDA. Canada, as it often did, followed the FDA lead.

In Britain, the drug was scheduled to go on sale in April, in the United States and Canada in June.

But in March—before its marketing anywhere—an event occurred that confirmed earlier fears and placed in jeopardy, it seemed, the entire future of Peptide 7.

It began with a telephone call to Felding-Roth's Harlow institute from a London newspaper, the *Daily Mail*. A reporter making the call sought to speak with Dr. Peat-Smith or Dr. Sastri. When informed that neither was available that morning, he left a message which a secretary typed out and placed on Martin's desk. It read:

> The *Mail* has learned you are about to unveil a miracle drug which will rejuvenate people sexually, cause them to lose weight, and make the middle-aged and old feel young again. We will have a story in tomorrow's paper and would like a statement from your company as soon as possible today.

When Martin read the message it was a half hour before noon, and he reacted with shock and fear. Was *some damn newspaper, concerned only with printing a sensational one-day story*, about to lay in ruins all his work and dreams?

His immediate impulse was to telephone Celia, and he did—at home. In Morristown it was 6:30 A.M., and she was in the shower. Martin waited impatiently while she dried and put on a robe.

At the sound of Celia's voice, he relayed what had happened and read out the reporter's message. His tone conveyed his anguish. Celia was concerned and sympathetic, but also practical.

"So the Peptide 7 sex thing is out in the open. I always thought it would happen."

"Can we do anything to stop it?"

406

"Obviously not. The report has a basis of truth, so we can't deny it totally. Besides, no newspaper will give up that kind of story, once they have it."

Martin, sounding unusually helpless, asked, "So what shall I do here?"

She told him, "Call the reporter back and answer questions honestly, though be as brief as possible. Be sure to emphasize that the sexual results have been observed in animals only, which is a reason we are not recommending the drug for sexual use by humans. The same applies to use for weight loss." Celia added, "Maybe, that way, they'll run a short item which won't get much notice anywhere else."

Martin said gloomily, "I doubt it."

"So do I. But try."

Three days after Martin's call, Julian Hammond reported to Celia with a summary of media attention to Peptide 7. The public affairs vice president began, "It's as if that first British news story opened a floodgate."

The *Daily Mail* had headed its report:

SCIENTIFIC BREAKTHROUGH
Soon!—A New Miracle Medicine
To Make You Sexy, Younger and Slim

What followed played up the acknowledged sexual effect of Peptide 7, but glossed over the fact that, so far, it had been officially recorded in animals only. The word "aphrodisiac," which Martin and others at Felding-Roth had dreaded, was used several times. Even worse, from the company's point of view, the newspaper had somehow learned about Mickey Yates and interviewed him. A photograph headed, "Thank you, Peptide 7!" showed the elderly Yates beaming after boasting of his revived sexual powers. Beside him, his wife, smiling demurely, had confirmed her husband's claim.

Something else in the news report, not known previously by Felding-Roth officials, was that several others among the Harlow Peptide 7 volunteers had experienced unusual sexual stimulus. They, too, were named and quoted.

Celia's dim hope that the story might be confined to one newspaper proved merely a hope, and nothing more. Not only was the *Mail*'s story picked up by the remainder of the British press and

407

television, all wire news services flashed it overseas. In the United States, instant interest was aroused, with Peptide 7's sexual and anti-obesity effects being mentioned in most newspapers and discussed on TV.

From the moment the story broke in the United States, Felding-Roth's switchboard was swamped with calls from press, radio and TV seeking details about Peptide 7's release. Though reluctant to respond to what was felt to be a wave of harmful sensationalism, the information was given. There was no alternative.

Few callers inquired about the true, anti-mental-aging purpose of the drug.

Following the tide of media calls came a second one: questions from the public. Most concerned only the drug's sexual or weight-loss properties, and callers were read a short statement to the effect that Peptide 7 was not recommended for such uses. Phone operators reported that the answer did not appear to satisfy.

Some calls were obviously from cranks. Other callers were sexually explicit or obscene. As Bill Ingram commented, "Suddenly, everything we so carefully planned has been turned into a sideshow."

It was this circus effect that most worried Celia. Would doctors, she wondered, not wanting to be associated with something which already appeared disreputable, decide not to prescribe Peptide 7 at all?

She consulted Andrew, who confirmed her fears. "I'm sorry to have to say this, but quite a few physicians will feel that way. Unfortunately, all the publicity suggests that Peptide 7 is in the same league with laetrile, ouzo and Spanish fly."

Celia said unhappily, "You make me wish I hadn't asked."

Thus, less than a month before what had been foreseen as a strong but dignified introduction of Peptide 7, Celia was weary, dismayed and apprehensive.

In Britain, Martin was in deep despair.

408

17

"As it turned out," Celia was apt to reminisce much later, "we really did have problems—extremely serious ones—during the early months after Peptide 7's introduction. Among all of us in charge at Felding-Roth there were plenty of tense, anxious hours, biting of fingernails, and sleepless nights. Yet the strange thing was, the problems that happened were not the ones we expected." Then she would laugh and add, "What it all showed is that you can never be certain how people will react to *anything.*"

The problems Celia referred to concerned supply.

From the moment Peptide 7 was available—obtainable, with a doctor's prescription, from druggists—for months there was never enough to meet the amazing, unprecedented demand. Long lines formed in front of pharmacy counters, and when customers were turned away because supplies ran out, they would go to other drugstores and stand in lines there.

A reason that was revealed later—this time quoting Bill Ingram—was that "the damn doctors and druggists were using the stuff themselves and cornering some of the rest for friends."

The shortage, which for a while was desperate, occurred in Britain as well as the United States. Long-timers in the company had never known anything like it. It resulted in frantic phone calls between New Jersey, Ireland, Harlow, Puerto Rico, Chicago and Manchester —the last two where plastic containers were being made and finger pumps assembled. Puerto Rico in particular, said a Felding-Roth purchasing agent, was "always screaming for containers, which they filled and shipped as fast as they came in."

Both the Irish and Puerto Rican plants were working around the clock, with extra shifts. At the same time, chartered jet aircraft flew on several occasions from Ireland to Puerto Rico, carrying the precious active Peptide 7 ingredient.

It was Ingram who bore the brunt of that difficult time, overseeing all arrangements while, in his words, "We lived from hand to mouth, juggling what supplies we had, trying to keep the multitudes who demanded Peptide 7 as happy as we could."

Then, looking back on those frantic days, he too would laugh, the anxiety long behind him, and say, "Bless everybody, though! All of our people pitched in, doing everything they could. Even those doctors and druggists, playing favorites, helped Peptide 7 become the golden success it is."

The word golden was appropriate. As *Fortune* magazine headlined a feature article a year after the new drug swept, like a tornado, upon the pharmaceutical scene:

**FELDING-ROTH
FINDS RICH
IS BETTER**

Fortune estimated that the first year of Peptide 7 sales would bring in revenues of six hundred million dollars. That and earlier estimates caused Felding-Roth shares, traded on the New York Stock Exchange, to go, in one broker's words, "through the roof into the stratosphere." Immediately after the drug's introduction the share price tripled in a month, doubled again within a year, and redoubled during the eight months following. After that, directors voted for a five-to-one split to keep the share price within a reasonable trading range.

Even so, when accountants finished their arithmetic, the *Fortune* estimate proved low by a hundred million dollars.

Something else *Fortune* said was, "Not since SmithKline's remarkable ulcer drug, Tagamet, was introduced in 1976 has there been any industrial product comparable with the phenomenon of Peptide 7."

The success was not confined to money.

Thousands upon thousands of middle-aged and elderly men and women were taking the drug, spraying it into nasal passages twice daily and proclaiming that they felt better, their memories were sharper, their general vigor enhanced. When asked if "vigor" included sexual energy, some replied frankly, yes, while others smiled, declaring that to be a private matter.

The enhanced memory factor was regarded by medical experts as the most important. People taking Peptide 7 who once suffered from forgetfulness now remembered things. Many who previously had difficulty in recalling other people's names found that problem disappearing. Telephone numbers were recollected without effort. Husbands who formerly forgot them began remembering their wives' birthdays and wedding anniversaries. One elderly gentleman claimed to have memorized, without even trying, an entire local bus schedule. When put to the test by friends, he proved it true. Psychologists who devised "before and after" memory checks confirmed to their satisfaction that Peptide 7 worked.

Though considered secondary to memory, the drug's antiobesity effect quickly became indisputable and advantageous. Fat people, including those in lower age groups, lost unwanted weight and gained in general health. The effect was soon so widely accepted medically that Felding-Roth applied, in the United States, Britain and Canada, for an official weight-loss "indication" to be added to Peptide 7's authorized use. There seemed little doubt the applications would be approved.

Throughout the world, other countries were rushing to approve Peptide 7 and obtain supplies.

It was too early yet to know whether the drug would reduce the incidence of Alzheimer's disease. Such knowledge was several years away, but many lived in hope.

One critical question was being asked. Was Peptide 7 being overprescribed, as had happened with other medications in the past? The answer: almost certainly, yes. Yet what made Peptide 7 different from those others was that even when not needed, it did no harm. It was not addicting. Incredibly, adverse reports about its effects were almost nil.

One woman wrote from Texas, complaining that each time she took a dose, and afterward had sexual intercourse, she ended with a headache. The report was passed routinely by Felding-Roth to the FDA, and also investigated. The matter was dropped when it was discovered the woman's age was eighty-two.

A California man went to Small Claims Court, demanding that Felding-Roth be made to pay for a new wardrobe since his previous clothes were no longer usable after Peptide 7 caused him to lose thirty pounds of weight. The claim was contested and dismissed.

Nothing more serious was reported.

As for doctors, their enthusiasm seemed to have no limits. They

411

recommended Peptide 7 to patients as being beneficial, safe, and one of history's great medical advances. Hospitals were using it. Doctors who enjoyed active social lives rarely went out to dinner or to a cocktail party without a prescription pad in pocket, knowing they would be asked for Peptide 7, and that obliging a host or hostess, or their friends, could lead to other invitations.

On the subject of doctors, Celia said to Andrew, "For once you were wrong. Doctors weren't put off by all that publicity. In fact, it seems to have helped."

"Yes, I was wrong," her husband admitted, "and you'll probably remind me of it for the rest of my life. But I'm happy to be wrong, and happiest of all for you, my love. You—and Martin, of course—deserve everything that's come about."

The publicity seemed to continue unabated, perhaps, Celia thought, because Peptide 7 was causing so much renewal of human happiness. In newspapers there were frequent references to the drug's effects, and on television it was talked about often.

Bill Ingram reminded Celia, "You once told me the nature of TV would help us one day. It certainly has."

Ingram, who had been promoted a year earlier to executive vice president, was carrying much of the load that Celia formerly had. Celia's main preoccupation nowadays was what to do with the money that was pouring in and, presumably, would continue to accumulate for years to come.

Seth Feingold, now retired, had been retained as a consultant and appeared occasionally. During one meeting with Celia, a year and a half after Peptide 7's U.S. introduction, Seth cautioned, "You have to speed up decisions about how to spend some of that cash. If you don't, too much will be swallowed by taxes."

One way of using cash was to acquire other companies. On Celia's urging, the board approved purchasing the Chicago firm which was making Peptide 7's containers. That was followed by acquisition of an Arizona concern specializing in new drug delivery systems. Negotiations to buy an optical company were under way. Many more millions would be spent on a new genetic engineering research center. There would be expansions overseas.

A new company headquarters was planned, since the existing Boonton building had run out of space and some departments were housed in distant, rented quarters. The new structure would be in Morristown, with a hotel as part of a Felding-Roth high-rise complex.

One purchase was a jet airplane—a Gulfstream III. Celia and Ingram used it on their North American journeyings, more frequent now because of the company's widening activities.

During Celia's meeting with Seth, he also said quietly, "One thing that's good about all this money coming in is that some of it can be used to settle claims about those poor Montayne-deformed children."

"I'm glad of that too," Celia said. She had been aware for some time that the existing reserve fund being used by Childers Quentin for Montayne settlements was almost exhausted.

Seth said sadly, "I'll never feel free from my guilt about Montayne. Never."

Sharing the sober, reflective moment, Celia thought: Amid an enormous therapeutic and financial success, it was necessary and chastening to be reminded that grim failures were also part of pharmaceutical history.

Through all of Peptide 7's bountiful triumph, Martin Peat-Smith was, as the cliché went, in seventh heaven. Not even in the most optimistic moments had he ever imagined so much would be accomplished by his research into aging. Martin's name was now widely known, his person admired, respected and in demand. Praise and accolades poured in. He had been elected a member of the Royal Society, Britain's oldest scientific body. Other learned societies sought him as a speaker. There was talk of a future Nobel. A knighthood was rumored.

Amid the attention, Martin managed to retain some privacy. His home telephone number was changed and unlisted. At the institute, Nigel Bentley arranged for Martin to be shielded from all but the most important calls and visitors. Even so, it was clear that Martin's earlier, inconspicuous life would never be the same again.

Something else changed too. Yvonne decided to cease living with Martin, and to move into a flat in Cambridge.

There was no quarrel or difficulty between them. It was simply that she resolved, quietly and calmly, to go her separate way. Recently Martin had been away from Harlow a good deal, leaving her alone, and at such times it seemed pointless to make the daily two-way Harlow-Cambridge journey. When Yvonne explained her reasoning, Martin accepted it uncritically, with understanding. She had expected him to put up at least a token argument, but when he failed to do so, she did not show her disappointment. They agreed they would see each other occasionally and remain good friends.

Only Yvonne, when the moment came to leave, knew how sad, how torn she was inside. She reminded herself how happy she was with her veterinary studies; her third year had just begun.

Immediately following the separation, Martin was away for a week. When he returned, it was to a darkened, empty house. It was more than five years since it had been that way, and he didn't like it. He liked it even less as another week passed. He found that he was lonely and missed the sight and cheerful chatter of Yvonne. It was, he thought on going to bed one night, as if a light in his life had abruptly gone out.

Next day, Celia telephoned from New Jersey on a business matter and, near the end of their conversation, observed, "Martin, you sound depressed. Is anything wrong?" It was then, in a burst of confidence, that he told her about missing Yvonne.

"I don't understand this," Celia said. "Why did you let her go?"

"It wasn't a question of letting her. She's free, and she decided."

"Did you try to talk her out of it?"

"No."

"Why not?"

"It didn't seem fair," Martin said. "She has her own life to live."

Celia agreed, "Yes, she does. And she undoubtedly wants more out of it than you were giving her. Did you consider offering her something more—like asking her to marry you?"

"As a matter of fact, I did consider it. The day Yvonne left. But I didn't, because it seemed . . . ."

"Oh, God help us!" Celia's voice rose. "Martin Peat-Smith, if I were over there I'd *shake you*. How can anyone bright enough to find Peptide 7 be so dumb? You fool! She loves you."

Martin said doubtfully, "How do you know?"

"Because I'm a woman. Because I hadn't been five minutes in her company before it was as plain to me as it's plain now that you are being obtuse."

There was a silence, then Celia asked, "What are you going to do?"

"If it isn't too late . . . I *will* ask her to marry me."

"How will you do it?"

He hesitated. "Well, I suppose I could phone."

"Martin," Celia said, "I am your superior officer in this company, and I am *ordering* you to leave that office you are in, right now, and get in your car, and drive to find Yvonne wherever she is. What you do after that is your affair, but I'd advise you to get down on your knees, if necessary, and tell her you love her. The reason I'm telling you this is that I doubt whether, in all your future life, you'll find anyone who's better for you, or who'll love you more. And, oh yes, you might consider stopping on the way to buy some flowers. At least you know about flowers; I remember you sent some once to me."

Moments later, several employees in the Harlow institute were startled to see the director, Dr. Peat-Smith, running full tilt down a corridor, racing through the outer lobby, then jumping in his car and speeding away.

The wedding present from Celia and Andrew to Martin and Yvonne was an engraved silver tray on which Celia had included lines from *To a Bride* by the Essex-born seventeenth-century poet Francis Quarles:

> *Let all thy joys be as the month of May,*
> *And all thy days be as a marriage day:*
> *Let sorrow, sickness, and a troubled mind*
> *Be stranger to thee.*

And then there was Hexin W.
It was due to appear on the market in a year.

18

The clinical trials of Hexin W produced a few side effects in patients who had taken the drug in conjunction with other chosen drugs—such combinations being the route to effective medication via the quenching of free radicals. There were scattered reports of nausea and vomiting, and separate occurrences of diarrhea, dizziness or elevated blood pressure. None of this was unusual or a cause for alarm. The incidents were not severe, nor did they appear in more than a tiny percentage of patients. It was rare for any drug to be free from occasional side effects. Peptide 7 had been a notable exception.

The Hexin W trials, which occupied two and a half years, were overseen personally by Dr. Vincent Lord. In doing so he handed over other responsibilities to subordinates, leaving himself free for what had become a task of total dedication. At this vital, near-final stage he wanted nothing to go wrong with the launching of his brainchild. Nothing which, through someone else's neglect or inefficiency, might diminish his scientific glory.

Lord had watched with mixed feelings the enormous, continuing success of Peptide 7. On the one hand he experienced some jealousy of Martin Peat-Smith. But on the other, Felding-Roth was now a stronger company because of Peptide 7, and thus better equipped to handle another product that looked as if it could be equally, or even more, successful.

Results from the Hexin W trials had delighted Lord. No major adverse side effect appeared. Those minor ones which did were either controllable, or unimportant in relation to the drug's positive, excellent uses.

In what was known as Phase III testing, where the medication was given to patients who were ill, under conditions similar to those foreseen for later use, the outcome had been uniformly good. The drug had been taken, over substantial periods of time, by more than six thousand persons, many in hospitals under controlled conditions —an ideal setup for test purposes.

Six thousand was a larger number than in most Phase III's, but was decided on because of the need to study Hexin W's effects when taken with various other drugs, hitherto unsafe.

Arthritis patients, as had been hoped, responded particularly well. They were able to take Hexin W not only alone, but with other strong anti-inflammatory drugs that formerly had been denied them.

Coordinating the testing, in several widely separated locations, had been a mammoth task for which extra help had been recruited, both inside the company and out. But now it was done. Enormous amounts of data were assembled at Felding-Roth headquarters and, before submitting it to the FDA in the form of a new drug application, Lord was reviewing as much of the material as he could.

Because of his personal interest, he found the process mostly a pleasure. Yet, suddenly, it ceased to be when he encountered one set of case reports.

What Vince Lord read, then reread more carefully, at first caused him concern, after that perplexity, and eventually blazing anger.

The reports in question were from a Dr. Yaminer who practiced medicine in Phoenix, Arizona. Lord did not know Yaminer personally, though he was familiar with the name and knew a little about the doctor's background.

Yaminer was an internist. He had a substantial private practice and held staff appointments at two hospitals. Like many other doctors involved in the Hexin W testing program, he had been employed by Felding-Roth to study the effect of the drug on a group of patients— in his case one hundred. Before such studies began, the patients' permission had to be obtained, but this was seldom difficult.

The arrangement was a normal one, used routinely by pharmaceutical companies wishing to field-test new drugs. Yaminer had done work for Felding-Roth before, and for other drug firms too.

Doctors who contracted to do such work liked the arrangement for one of two reasons, sometimes both. Some were genuinely interested in research. All enjoyed the substantial money it brought in.

For a little extra labor, spread over several months, a doctor would receive between five hundred and a thousand dollars per patient, the amount varying with the drug company involved and the importance of the medication. For his Hexin W case studies, Yaminer had received eighty-five thousand dollars. A doctor's own costs for such work were small, therefore most of the money was profit.

But the system had a weakness.

Because the work was so lucrative, a few doctors were tempted to take on more of it than they could properly handle. This led to corner cutting and—with surprising frequency—falsification of data.

In a word: fraud.

Dr. Yaminer, Lord was certain, had perpetrated fraud in sending in reports about the effects of Hexin W.

There were two possibilities as to what had happened. Either Yaminer had failed to do the studies he was supposed to on the patients he had named, or some, perhaps most, of the hundred listed patients did not exist, except in the doctor's imagination. He had made them up, invented them, as well as their test "results."

Making a guess based on experience, Lord believed the second to be true.

Either way, how did he know?

One reason—Yaminer had done his fake reporting in a hurry and been careless. What had caught Lord's eye to begin was a close similarity between the handwriting on patient report forms on different dates. Usually such entries varied, and not only the handwriting, but the writing instrument. Even if a doctor used the same ball-point pen every day, it seldom performed with exact consistency.

That in itself was not conclusive. Yaminer *could* have made earlier notes, then transformed them patiently into neater, finished reports. But for a busy doctor it was unlikely. Which prompted Lord to look for more.

He found it.

Among tests performed on patients receiving experimental drugs was one to measure urine pH—acidity or alkalinity. For an average person the result would be expressed in the range 5 to 8. But each measurement, on separate days, was an "independent event" and usually varied, meaning that a reading of 4 on Tuesday did not make likely another 4 in the same person on Wednesday. Expressed a different way: over five successive days, the likelihood of pH measurements being identical was only one in four. Long odds.

Yet, repeatedly, Dr. Yaminer's reports on patients showed identical pH readings day after day. Highly unlikely, even with one individual. *Impossible* in the case of fifteen patients—the number reviewed by Lord from the Yaminer study.

418

To be absolutely sure, Lord selected fifteen other patient names and made a similar review of blood studies. Again identical figures repeated with unnatural frequency.

There was no need to go further. Any medical investigator would accept the pattern already uncovered as evidence of falsification—in this instance, criminal fraud.

With silent, seething anger, Lord cursed Dr. Yaminer.

The overall report presented by Yaminer made Hexin W look extremely good. *But it was unnecessary.* The drug would have looked good anyway, as was demonstrated by every other report which Lord had read.

Lord knew what he ought to do.

He should immediately inform the FDA, laying everything before them. After which Dr. Yaminer would be officially investigated and almost certainly prosecuted. It had happened to other doctors before, and some had gone to prison. If Yaminer was found guilty he could go there too and also, perhaps, lose his license to practice medicine.

But there was something else which Lord knew.

If the FDA became involved, with Yaminer's work thrown out, *all* of it would have to be done again. And allowing for new arrangements that would have to be made, it would take a year and would delay Hexin W's introduction by the same amount of time.

Again Lord cursed Yaminer for his stupidity and the dilemma now created.

What to do?

If it had happened in connection with a drug about which there were doubts, Lord told himself, he wouldn't have hesitated. He would have thrown Yaminer to the FDA wolves and offered to give evidence at Yaminer's trial.

But there *wasn't* any doubt about Hexin W. With or without the false report, it was going to be a beneficial, successful medication.

So why not let the fake study go in with the other genuine ones? It was a safe bet that no one at FDA would notice; the sheer volume of an NDA made that unlikely. And if Yaminer's papers were looked over by an FDA examiner, there was no reason to suppose the deception would be seen. Not everyone was as quick to notice things as Vincent Lord.

Lord would have preferred to omit the study altogether, but knew

419

he couldn't. Yaminer's name was listed in other material already sent to FDA.

He also hated the idea of letting Yaminer get away with what he had done, but there seemed no other way.

So . . . all right. *Let it go.* Lord initialed the Yaminer study and placed it on a pile of others previously reviewed.

He would make sure though, Lord vowed, that the bastard never worked for Felding-Roth again. There was a departmental file for Yaminer. Lord found it and stuffed his own rough work sheets in, the pages he had used to figure out the fakery. If he ever needed them, he would know exactly where they were.

Lord's assessment of the situation proved to be correct.

The NDA was submitted and, in a satisfyingly short time, approved.

Only one thing briefly troubled Vincent Lord, making him nervous. In FDA's National Center for Drugs and Biologics at Washington, D.C.—formerly the Bureau of Drugs—Dr. Gideon Mace was now a deputy director. Compared with earlier days, Mace was a changed and better person, a strict teetotaler, at last with a good marriage, and respected at his work. His bad experience at the Senate hearing appeared to have done him no harm. In fact, soon afterward he had been promoted.

Word reached Lord that Mace, while not directly involved with the Hexin W application, had taken an interest in it, as apparently he did with anything coming into the agency from Felding-Roth. Almost certainly, Mace still bore the company a grudge and hoped one day to get even.

But nothing happened as a result of Mace's interest, and when FDA approval to market Hexin W was given, Lord's nervousness evaporated.

As with Peptide 7, it was decided that the developmental name of Hexin W would be its product name also.

"It comes easily off the tongue and will look good on packaging," Celia declared when it was time for the matter to be decided.

Bill Ingram agreed, adding, "Let's hope it brings us the same kind of luck we had before."

Whether luck helped or not, Hexin W was an immediate success. Physicians, including some in prestigious teaching hospitals, hailed it as an important medical advance which opened up new therapies for treating seriously ill patients. Medical journals praised both the drug and Vincent Lord.

Many doctors in private practice began prescribing Hexin W, including Andrew, who reported to Celia, "It looks as if you have a live one there. It's as much a breakthrough, I think, as Lotromycin in its time."

As more and more doctors discussed the drug with each other, and patients expressed gratitude for the relief it brought them, Hexin W's use expanded and sales zoomed.

Other pharmaceutical companies, some of which had been wary at first, began using Hexin W under license, incorporating it in their own products to improve their safety. A few drugs that had been developed years before but were never marketed because of high toxicity were brought down from the shelf and subjected to experiments with Hexin W added.

One such was an anti-arthritic drug named Arthrigo. The patent owner was Exeter & Stowe Laboratories of Cleveland, whose president, Alexander W. Stowe, was well known to Celia. A former research chemist, Stowe and a partner had formed their company a decade earlier. Since then, while the firm remained small, it had achieved a merited reputation for high-quality prescription products.

After a licensing deal was negotiated, Stowe came personally to Felding-Roth headquarters. In his fifties, he was a genial figure who wore rumpled suits, had shaggy hair, and looked absentminded, which he wasn't. During a meeting with Celia and Vincent Lord he told them, "Our company has FDA permission to use a combination of Arthrigo and Hexin W experimentally. Since both drugs have anti-arthritic properties, we've high hopes for the outcome. Of course, we'll keep you informed as results come in."

That was six months after Hexin W's introduction.

A few weeks later, Celia and Andrew gave a Saturday evening party at their Morristown house in honor of Vincent Lord. Lisa and Bruce came home for the occasion.

It was high time, Celia reasoned, that she did something personal for Lord, if only to make clear her recognition of his outstanding contribution to the company and to signal that any antagonism between them was now over, or should be.

The party was a success, Lord more relaxed and happy than Celia had ever seen him. His thin, scholarly face became flushed with pleasure as compliments were heaped upon him. He smiled continuously and mingled easily with the guests who included Felding-Roth executives, prominent citizens of Morristown, others who had come specially from New York, and Martin Peat-Smith whom Celia had asked to fly from Britain for the occasion.

The last gesture especially pleased Lord, as did Martin's toast, proposed at Celia's request.

"The life of a research scientist," Martin declared while the other guests fell silent, "offers challenges and excitement. But also there are wearying years of failure, long hours of despair, and often loneliness. Only someone who has known those black occasions can understand what Vincent endured during his quest for Hexin W. Yet, his genius and dedication rose above them, leading to this celebration in which I humbly join, saluting—with you—a major scientific achievement of our time."

"Very gracious," Lisa commented later, when guests had gone and the Jordan family was alone. "And if all tonight's company success talk gets out, it should send Felding-Roth stock up another point or two."

Lisa, nearing her twenty-sixth birthday and four years out of Stanford, was a financial analyst, working for a Wall Street investment banking firm. In the fall, though, she would leave the money milieu to enter Wharton School of Business and study for an M.B.A. degree.

"What you should do," Bruce advised his sister, "is on Monday suggest your clients buy Felding-Roth, then on Tuesday leak to the wire services that Dr. Peat-Smith, inventor of Peptide 7, is bullish on Hexin W."

She retorted, "It would be unethical. Or don't publishers worry about such things?"

Bruce, for the past two years since graduation from Williams, had been working for a New York textbook publisher where he was an editor in the history department. He, too, had plans for the future, which involved a move to Paris and studies at the Sorbonne.

"We're concerned with ethics all the time," he said. "Which is why publishers make less money than investment bankers."

"It's nice to have you both home," Celia said, "and to know that nothing's changed."

Being president of a highly successful, wealthy company, Celia found, did not eliminate top management problems. Compared with when the company had been poor, there were just as many, sometimes more. However, their nature differed. Also, nowadays there was an exhilaration, a heady excitement lacking in the older times, on which Celia thrived.

Immediately following the social tribute to Vincent Lord, she was exceptionally busy with financial and organizational matters, all requiring travel. Consequently, nearly three months went by before she spoke to Lord again concerning the Hexin W licensing contract with Exeter & Stowe. He had come to her office about something else and she inquired, "What word is there from Alex Stowe on their Arthrigo and Hexin W?"

He answered, "Their clinical trials seem to be working well. Everything looks positive."

"How about adverse reports on Hexin W generally? I haven't seen any cross my desk."

"I haven't sent you any," Lord said, "because there's been nothing of importance. Nothing, that is, that concerns Hexin W directly."

Celia's mind, so accustomed nowadays to a diet of good news, had already moved on quickly to something else; therefore the wriggling proviso in Lord's last remark escaped her. Later, she would remember it with regret, and blame herself for missing it.

For Lord, as had been his way for many years, going back to a time long before Celia had known him, had not delivered all the truth.

19

The news, when it broke, came quietly. Deceptively casual, even then it did not reveal itself entirely, and afterward it seemed to Celia as if fate had tiptoed in, at first unheeded and wearing a prosaic scabbard from which, later, emerged a fiery sword.

It began with a telephone call when Celia was away from her office. When she returned, a message—one of several—informed her that Mr. Alexander Stowe, of Exeter & Stowe Laboratories, had phoned and would like her to call him. There was nothing to indicate the request was urgent, and she dealt with several other matters first.

An hour or so later, Celia asked for a call to be placed to Stowe, and soon after was informed by a secretary that he was on the line.

She pressed a button and said into a speakerphone, "Hello, Alex. I was thinking about you this morning, wondering how your Arthrigo-Hexin W program is going."

There was a moment's silence, then a surprised voice, "We canceled our contract with you four days ago, Celia. Didn't you know?"

Now the surprise was hers. "No, I didn't. If you told someone at your place to cancel, are you sure they followed through?"

"I handled it myself," Stowe said, obviously still puzzled. "I talked directly with Vince Lord. Then today, realizing I hadn't spoken with you, thought I should, as a courtesy. It's why I called."

Annoyed at being told something she should have known sooner, Celia answered, "I'll have something to say to Vince." She stopped. "What was your reason for canceling?"

"Well . . . frankly, we're worried about those deaths from infections. We've had two ourselves in patients we were monitoring, and while it doesn't look as if either drug—Arthrigo or Hexin W—was directly responsible, there are still unanswered questions. We're uneasy about them, so we decided not to go on, particularly in view of those other deaths elsewhere."

Celia was startled. For the first time since the conversation began, a shiver of chill ran through her. She had a sudden premonition there was more to come and she would not like hearing it.

"What other deaths?"

This time the silence was longer. "You mean you don't know about those either?"

She said impatiently, "If I did, Alex, I wouldn't be asking."

"There are four we actually know about here, though without details, except that all the deceased were taking Hexin W and died from differing types of infection." Stowe stopped, and when he resumed his voice was measured and serious. "Celia, I'm going to make a suggestion, and please don't think this presumptuous since it concerns your own company. But I think you need to have a talk with Dr. Lord."

"Yes," Celia agreed. "So do I."

"Vince knows about the deaths—the other ones and ours—because we discussed them. Also, he'll have had details, so as to inform the FDA." Another hesitation. "I truly hope, for everyone's sake in your shop, that FDA *has* been informed."

"Alex," Celia said, "there appear to be some gaps in my knowledge and I intend to fill them right away. I'm obliged to you for what you've told me. Meanwhile, there doesn't seem much point in our continuing this conversation."

"I agree with you," Stowe said. "But do please call me if there's any other information you need, or any way I can be of service. Oh, and the real purpose of my calling was to say I'm genuinely sorry we had to cancel. I hope, some other time, we can work together."

Celia answered automatically, her mind already on what must be done next. "Thank you, Alex. I hope so too."

She terminated the call by touching a button. She was about to press another which would have connected her with Vincent Lord, then changed her mind. She would go to see him personally. Now.

The first report of death where a patient had been taking Hexin W arrived at Felding-Roth headquarters two months after the drug's introduction. It had come, as was usual, to Dr. Lord. Moments after reading it, he dismissed it entirely.

The report was from a physician in Tampa, Florida. It revealed that while the deceased had been taking Hexin W in conjunction with another drug, the cause of death was a fever and infection. Lord reasoned that the death could have had no relation to Hexin W, therefore he tossed the report aside. However, later that day, instead of sending it for routine filing, he placed the report in a folder in a locked drawer of his desk.

The second report came two weeks later. It was from a Felding-Roth detail man and was mailed after a conversation with a doctor in Southfield, Michigan. The salesman had been conscientious in recording all the information he could find.

Reports about side effects of drugs, including adverse effects, came to pharmaceutical companies from several sources. Sometimes physicians wrote directly. At other times, hospitals did so as routine procedure. Responsible pharmacists passed on what they learned. Occasionally, word came from patients themselves. As well, the companies' detail men and women had instructions to report anything they were told about a product's effect, no matter how trivial it seemed.

Within any pharmaceutical company, reports of side effects of drugs were accumulated and, in quarterly reports, passed to the FDA. That was required by law.

Also required by law was that any serious reaction, particularly with a new drug, must be passed to FDA, and flagged as "urgent," within fifteen days of the company's learning of it. The rule applied whether the company believed its drug to be responsible or not.

The detail man's report from Southfield, again read by Lord, revealed that the patient, while taking Hexin W and another anti-arthritic drug, died from a massive liver infection. This was confirmed at autopsy.

Again, Lord decided that Hexin W could not possibly have been the cause of death. He put the report in the folder with the first.

A month went by, then two reports came in, separately but at the same time. They recorded deaths of a man and a woman. In both cases they had been taking Hexin W with another drug. The woman, elderly, developed a serious bacterial infection of a foot after it was cut in a home accident. As an emergency measure the foot was amputated, but the infection spread quickly, causing death. The man, who had been in poor health, died from an overwhelming infection of the brain.

Lord's reaction was one of annoyance with the two dead people. *Why* had their *damned diseases,* from which they would have expired anyway, had to involve Hexin W, even though the drug was clearly not responsible in either case? Just the same, the accumulating reports were becoming an embarrassment. Also a worry.

By this time Lord was aware of his failure to comply with federal law by not reporting the earlier incidents immediately to FDA. Now, he was in an impossible position.

If he sent the latest reports to FDA, he could not omit the earlier ones. Yet those were long overdue under the fifteen-day reporting rule, and if he sent them, both Felding-Roth and he personally would be shown as guilty of a law violation. Anything could happen. He was uncomfortably conscious of Dr. Gideon Mace probably waiting at FDA to pounce on such an opportunity.

Lord put the two latest reports in his folder with the others. After all, he reminded himself, he was the only one with knowledge of the total number. Each had arrived separately. None of the individuals making a report was aware of the others.

By the time Alexander Stowe telephoned, canceling Exeter & Stowe's contract for the use of Hexin W, Lord had accumulated twelve reports and was living in fear. He also learned—increasing his anxiety—that Stowe had somehow heard about four of those Hexin-W-related deaths. Lord did not tell Stowe that the actual number was twelve, *plus* the two Stowe knew about directly, which Lord learned of for the first time.

Since, legally, Lord could not ignore what Stowe had told him, the total of known deaths was now fourteen.

A fifteenth report came in on the day that Stowe telephoned Celia. By then, reluctantly but unable to avoid the scientific truth, Lord had gained an idea of what was causing the deaths—most of them, if not all.

Several months earlier in Celia's office, during that sales planning meeting where afterward his words had been applauded, he had described the effect of Hexin W. " . . . *stops free-radical production, so that leukocytes—white blood cells—are not attracted to a disease site . . . Result—no inflammation . . . pain disappears.*"

All of that was true.

What was also becoming clear, by deduction and some hasty new experiments, was that banishment of leukocytes opened up a weakness, a vulnerability. In the ordinary way, leukocytes at a disease site

427

killed off foreign material—bacteria. Thus leukocytes, though causing pain, were also a protection. But in their absence—an absence caused by the quenching of free radicals—bacteria and other organisms flourished, creating massive infections in various body locales.

And death.

Though it had yet to be proved, Vincent Lord was sure that Hexin W was, after all, the cause of at least a dozen deaths, perhaps more.

He also realized, too late to be of use, that there had been a weakness in the Hexin W clinical testing program. Most of the patients observed had been in hospitals under controlled conditions where infections were less apt to flourish. All of the deaths recorded in his folder had occurred *away from hospitals*, in homes or other noncontrolled environments where bacteria could live and breed . . .

Lord reached the conclusion—acknowledging his failure, shattering his dreams, reinforcing his present, desperate fears—only a few minutes before Celia arrived.

He knew now that Hexin W would have to be withdrawn. He knew, with despair, that he was guilty of concealment—a concealment causing deaths that could have been prevented. As a result he faced disgrace, prosecution, and perhaps imprisonment.

Strangely, his mind went back to twenty-seven years before . . . Champaign-Urbana, the University of Illinois, and the day in the dean's office when he had asked for accelerated promotion, which had been refused.

He had sensed then that the dean believed he, Vincent Lord, was flawed by some defect of character. Now, for the first time, peeling the layers from his soul, Lord asked himself: Had the dean been right?

Walking unannounced into Lord's office, closing the door behind her, Celia wasted no time.

"Why was I not told that Exeter & Stowe canceled their contract four days ago?"

Lord, startled by the sudden entry, said awkwardly, "I was going to tell you. I hadn't got around to it."

"How long would you have taken if I hadn't asked?" Then, without waiting for an answer, "I had to learn from outside that there have been adverse reports about Hexin W. Why haven't I heard of those either?"

Lord said lamely, "I've been studying . . . collating them."

She ordered, "Let me see them. Every one. Now."

Knowing that, at this point, nothing could be held back, Lord produced keys and opened a locked drawer of his desk.

Watching him, Celia remembered the occasion seven years ago when she had come here, wanting to see those early, dubious reports about Montayne. At that time, Lord had been reluctant to show them, but when she insisted, he had gone through the same procedure with the same locked drawer. She had been surprised even then to discover that the reports were not in the general office filing system where they would have been accessible to others.

The same process of concealment.

Celia thought bitterly, the earlier experience should have taught her something. Because it hadn't, an organizational weakness had persisted in the company, a weakness for which, as president, she was responsible.

Doubly responsible—because she had known of Vincent Lord's penchant for hiding bad news, concealing what he didn't like, and she had done nothing to guard against it.

Lord handed her a bulging folder. Celia's first impression was shock at how much it contained. Her second, as she turned pages and read while Lord watched silently, was horror. She counted groups of pages. *Fifteen deaths.* And all those who died had been taking Hexin W.

At the end, she asked the inevitable question, though knowing the answer in advance.

"Have we informed the FDA of any or all of these reports?"

Lord's face muscles twitched as he answered, "No."

"You're aware, of course, of the law and the fifteen-day rule?"

Lord nodded slowly, without speaking.

"I asked you some time ago," Celia said, "if there had been adverse reports on Hexin W. You told me there were none."

Desperately trying to salvage something, Lord replied, "I didn't say there were none. What I said was—there was nothing that concerned Hexin W directly."

Startled, Celia remembered. That was *exactly* what he had said. It had been a weasely answer, typical of Lord, whose ways she had known for twenty-seven years.

Armed with that knowledge, she should have recognized the answer for what it was—evasive—and persisted in her questioning. If she had, the adverse reports would have been out in the open months ago. And there would have been fewer of them than now—fewer deaths—because the FDA would have taken action, warnings would have issued . . .

But no! Instead, she had been caught up in euphoria, enamored of a second huge success . . . Peptide 7, then Hexin W . . . She had thought that nothing could go wrong. But it had, and now, while Vincent Lord's world was crashing down about him, so was hers.

Not expecting any reasonable reply, she asked, "Why did you do it?"

Lord began, "I believed in Hexin W . . ."

She waved away the answer. "Never mind."

Returning the papers to the folder, Celia said, "I'm taking these. Copies will be sent to Washington—the FDA—today, marked urgent, and by special messenger. I intend to telephone the commissioner to ensure they have proper attention."

She added grimly, mostly to herself, "I imagine we'll hear something back quite soon."

20

The FDA reacted quickly, almost certainly because of Celia's decision to involve the commissioner directly. An order for temporary withdrawal of Hexin W was issued, the "temporary" leaving open a possibility that the drug might be reintroduced later with more restrictive labeling. But even if that happened, it was clear: The high-flying days of Hexin W were over.

"Which is a damn shame," Alex Stowe said in a conversation with Celia soon afterward. "It's still a fine drug, and a scientific achievement quite apart from the way Vince messed up personally." He

430

added dourly, "The trouble in our society is that everyone wants drugs that are free from risk and, as you and I both know, they don't exist and never will."

Since their recent joint experience Celia had fallen into a habit of talking regularly with Stowe, who was proving a wise friend and confidante.

"You *will* see Hexin W back," he insisted, "maybe with greater safeguards, or after more development. There's a need for the quenching of free radicals, even at some risk, and it's a technique that's spreading medically. In the next few years we'll be reading more and more about it. When that happens, Celia, you can take heart that Felding-Roth was in there, pioneering."

"Thank you, Alex," she said. "Around here, right now, any cheerful thought is welcome."

Despite the melancholy surrounding Hexin W's withdrawal, the process itself went smoothly. Celia, anticipating it, had ordered preparations made in advance of the FDA order. Thus, when it came, a "Dear Doctor" letter immediately went out to all physicians advising them that the drug should no longer be prescribed. Within two weeks following that, the product was off drugstore shelves. Celia had attempted to have the Hexin W removal listed as voluntary, but the FDA demurred, choosing to exercise its authority. Because of the overhanging problem of the late reporting, Celia was advised by lawyers not to argue.

As to that problem, nothing was heard immediately, but a few weeks later the "Pink Sheet"—a weekly review of pharmaceutical affairs, published in Washington—stated:

> In the matter of Felding-Roth and Hexin W, the FDA has referred its investigation of alleged adverse report violations to the Justice Department, though it is understood no recommendation has been made as to whether a grand jury should be empaneled.

"The way I hear it, confidentially," Childers Quentin told Celia during a telephone conference call which included Bill Ingram and an in-house company lawyer, "is that you're between two factions pulling different ways inside the FDA."

At Celia's request, Quentin, through his many contacts in the capital, had put out feelers to discover what was happening. Periodically

431

the Washington lawyer relayed what he learned, and the Pink Sheet's comment had prompted his latest call.

Quentin continued, "One faction includes the commissioner and some others who are inclined to go slow, knowing that grand juries and indictments are tricky and can bounce back on the FDA's own people if their involvement was neglectful too. Another thing—the commissioner was impressed, Celia, when you were honest with him about those delayed reports." Quentin paused. "However, there's a second FDA contingent led by an associate commissioner; he has power, is a permanent bureaucrat, and will be around long after the commissioner has gone. The associate commissioner is in the corner of an FDA doctor named Gideon Mace, and it's Mace who's screaming for strong action. You may remember him. We were all on Capitol Hill together."

"I do remember," Celia said. "Dr. Mace seems to hold a grudge against Felding-Roth, though I've no idea why."

Bill Ingram asked, "Is there anything we can do about what's happening, or might happen, over at Justice?"

"Yes," Quentin said. "Just sit, wait, and hope. There are things you can meddle with in Washington and sometimes get away with doing it, but a grand jury proceeding—if it comes to that—isn't one of them."

So that was how they left it, and the waiting was unnerving.

Even more unnerving was the appearance of federal marshals at Felding-Roth headquarters with a search warrant. The warrant had been issued by the U.S. Federal Court at Newark, the nearest federal court to Boonton.

Hexin W had been withdrawn during early October. In mid-November, the U.S. Attorney for the District of New Jersey, acting on instructions from the Justice Department, sought permission before a federal magistrate to "search for and seize all memoranda, correspondence and other documents relating to the pharmaceutical product known as Hexin W."

It was an *ex parte* proceeding of which Felding-Roth had no advance knowledge; therefore the company was unrepresented when the search warrant was applied for and issued.

The search-and-seizure move was a shock to Celia and others, as was the presence of the marshals who remained for several days, finally taking away a dozen cartons of papers in a truck. Among them

432

were contents of filing cabinets in the research department, including one in Vincent Lord's office.

Lord tried to protest the intrusion into his office, but was shown the search warrant and ordered to stand aside.

Since the day when, in Lord's office, Celia had discovered the illegally withheld adverse reports, the research director had avoided, as much as possible, contact with other senior people in the company, especially Celia. It was clear to all concerned that Lord's days at Felding-Roth were numbered. Equally clear was that until the Hexin W adverse reports matter was resolved, the company, which included Lord, had no choice but to present a united front. The seizure of papers made this even clearer, therefore an uneasy truce prevailed.

While Lord was keeping his distance, Celia was formulating a plan to restructure the research organization, with a divisional president in overall charge and, reporting to him, vice presidents who would head specialist sections, including the new genetic engineering facility. She had some ideas about who the head of genetics might be.

After the mid-November activity, nothing more was heard on that subject through the remainder of the year. Shortly before Christmas, Childers Quentin reported, "Officially there's still an investigation in progress, but they've a lot of other things going on at Justice, and Hexin W isn't on their front burner."

Bill Ingram, who again listened to the report with Celia, said, "I suppose the longer that action is delayed, the less chance there is of anything serious happening."

"It's been known to work out that way," Quentin said. "Just the same, don't count on it."

The first day of the new year brought an item of happy news. The rumored knighthood for Martin Peat-Smith became reality with the appearance of Martin's name on the Queen's Honors List. The *Times* of London reported that the award was for "outstanding service to humanity and science."

The official investiture of Sir Martin Peat-Smith by Her Majesty would be at Buckingham Palace in the first week of February. Celia, learning of this during a congratulatory telephone call to Martin, said, "Andrew and I will come over the week before, and after you've been to the Palace we'll have a party for you and Yvonne."

433

Thus, near the end of January, Celia and Andrew were in London, accompanied by Lilian Hawthorne whom Celia had persuaded to join them. In the seven and a half years since Sam's death, Lilian had grown accustomed to living alone and seldom traveled. But Celia pointed out that the occasion was, in a way, a memorial to Sam since the Harlow institute had been his idea, and Martin, Sam's choice to head it.

Celia, Andrew and Lilian were staying at the latest "in" place for affluent travelers—Fortyseven Park Street in Mayfair, where hotel convenience was combined with private luxury apartments.

Lilian, who would be sixty at her next birthday, was still a strikingly handsome woman, and during a visit by the trio to the Harlow institute Rao Sastri was obviously attracted to her, despite the twenty-year difference in their ages. Sastri conducted a special tour of the labs for Lilian and afterward the two of them took off for lunch. Celia was amused to learn that they had arranged an evening in London—dinner and a theater—for the following week.

On Monday, two days before the investiture, Celia received a transatlantic call from Bill Ingram. "I'm sorry to burden you with bad news," the executive vice president began, "but Childers Quentin just called. It seems that in Washington all hell just broke loose."

The news, he explained, concerned the FDA, Dr. Gideon Mace, the Department of Justice, Senator Dennis Donahue and Hexin W.

"The way Quentin tells it," Ingram said, "is that Mace got tired of what he saw as inaction at the Justice Department. So on his own, unofficially, he took all the Hexin W papers over to Capitol Hill to one of Donahue's aides. The aide showed them to Donahue, who grabbed the whole schmear as if it were a Christmas present. According to Quentin's informant, the senator's words were, 'I've been waiting for something like this.' "

"Yes," Celia said, "I can imagine."

"The next thing," Ingram continued, "is that Donahue called the Attorney General and demanded action. Since then—again as Quentin tells it—Donahue's been calling the A.G. every hour on the hour."

Celia sighed. "That's a lot of bad news at once. Is there anything else?"

"Unfortunately, quite a bit more. First, it's now definite that a grand jury will be empaneled to look into the Hexin W delayed reports, plus something else that's come out. And the Attorney Gen-

434

eral, who's taking a personal interest because of Donahue, is sure he can get indictments."

"Against whom?"

"Vince Lord, of course. But also, I'm sorry to tell you, Celia, against you. They're going to argue that you were responsible—and that's on Donahue's urging. According to Quentin, Donahue wants your scalp."

Celia knew why. She remembered the Washington lawyer's warning after the Senate hearings. *"You made him look a fool . . . If, any time in the future, he can do harm to Felding-Roth or to you . . . he'll do it and enjoy it."*

Then she recalled some words of Ingram's spoken moments earlier and asked, "Bill, you said there was 'something else that's come out.' What?"

This time Ingram sighed. Then he said, "This gets complicated, though I'll try to put it simply.

"When the clinical testing data on Hexin W was submitted to Washington with our NDA, it contained the usual gamut of medical studies, including one by a Dr. Yaminer of Phoenix. It now turns out that Yaminer's study was a fake. He listed patients he didn't have. Much of his data was fraudulent."

"I'm sorry to hear that," Celia said, "though it happens occasionally. Other companies have had the same problem. But when you find out about the faking—*if* you do—you tell the FDA and they go after the doctor."

"Right," Ingram agreed. "What you're not supposed to do, though, is include the data in an NDA *after* discovering it to be false."

"Of course not."

"Vince did. He initialed Yaminer's report and let it go."

Celia asked, "But how does anyone know that Vince was aware—"

"I'm coming to that."

She said wearily, "Go on."

"When those federal marshals were with us, doing their search and seizure, they took away files from Vince's department. Among them was one for Dr. Yaminer. In that file were some rough notes in Vince's handwriting, showing he'd discovered Yaminer's report to be false *before he let it go to FDA*. The Justice Department now has the original report and Vince's notes."

Celia was silent. What was there to say? She wondered: was there any end to infamy?

435

"And I guess that's all," Ingram said. "Except . . ."

"Except what?"

"Well . . . it's about Dr. Mace, and the way he seems antagonistic to us. I remember you saying once that you had no idea why."

"I still haven't."

"I think Vince knows why," Ingram said. "I have an instinct. I've watched Vince too. He seems scared stiff any time Mace's name comes up."

Celia weighed what she had just heard. Then suddenly, in her mind, Ingram's words linked up with a conversation she had had with Lord at the time of the Senate hearings. She had accused him then of lying on the witness stand and . . .

Making a fast decision, she said, "I want to see him. Over here."

"Vince?"

"Yes. Tell him it's an order. He's to get on the first available plane and report to me as soon as he arrives."

Now they faced each other. Celia and Vincent Lord.

They were in the living room of the Jordans' Mayfair apartment.

Lord looked tired, older than his sixty-one years, and under strain. He had lost weight so that his face was even thinner than before. His face muscles, which earlier had twitched occasionally, were doing it more often.

Celia remembered an incident from her early days as assistant director of sales training, when she had often gone to Lord for technical advice. In attempting to be friendly she had suggested that they use first names, and Lord had replied unpleasantly, *"It would be better for both of us, Mrs. Jordan, to remember at all times the difference in our status."*

Well, Celia thought, for this occasion she would take his advice.

She said coldly, "I will not discuss the disgraceful Yaminer affair, Dr. Lord, except to say that it gives the company an opportunity to dissociate itself from you, and leave you to defend yourself about everything—at your own expense."

With a glint of triumph in his eyes, Lord said, "You can't do that because you're going to be indicted too."

"If I choose to do it, I can. And any defense arrangements I make for myself are my concern, not yours."

"If you *choose* . . ?" He seemed puzzled.

436

"I will not make any commitment. Understand that. But if the company *is* to help with your defense, I insist on knowing everything."

"Everything?"

"There's something in the past," Celia said. "Something that you know and I don't. I believe it has to do with Dr. Mace."

They had been standing. Lord motioned to a chair. "May I?"

"Yes." Celia sat down too.

"All right," Lord said, "there is something. But you won't like hearing it. And after you know, you'll be sorry that you do."

"I'm waiting. Get on with it."

He told her.

Told everything, going back to the first problems with Gideon Mace at the FDA, Mace's pettiness, the insults, the long, unreasonable delays in approving Staidpace—in the end, a good, lifesaving drug . . . Later the attempt to discover something harmful about Mace, resulting in Lord's Georgetown meeting in a homosexual bar with Tony Redmond, an FDA technician . . . Lord's purchase from Redmond of documents incriminating Mace. The cost: two thousand dollars—*an expenditure approved by Sam,* who later agreed not to disclose the information to a law enforcement agency but to hold the papers secretly, thus making Sam and Lord accessories to a crime . . . Two years later, when Mace was delaying FDA approval of Montayne, the decision, *shared by Sam,* to blackmail Mace . . . The blackmail succeeding, despite Dr. Mace's unease about the Australian report on Montayne and his honest doubts about the drug . . .

Then it was done. Now Celia knew it all and, as Lord had predicted, wished that she did not. Yet she had had to know because it affected future judgments she would make as president of Felding-Roth.

At the same time so much became clearer: Sam's despair and guilt, the real and deeper reason for his suicide . . . Dr. Mace's breakdown at the Senate hearings and, when asked why he had approved Montayne, his pathetic answer, *"I just don't know."* . . . Mace's anger at Felding-Roth and all its works.

Celia thought: If I were Mace I would hate us too.

And now that Celia knew the sorry, dismal story, what came next? Her conscience told her there was only one thing she ought to do. Inform the authorities. Go public. Tell the truth. Let all concerned take their chances—Vincent Lord, Gideon Mace, Felding-Roth, herself.

But what if she did? Where would it leave everybody? Lord and Mace would be destroyed of course—a thought which left her unconcerned. What did concern her was the realization that the company would be disgraced and dragged down too, and not just the company as a paper entity, but its people: employees, executives, stockholders, the other scientists apart from Vincent Lord. Only she herself might look good, but that was least important.

Equally to the point was the question: If she went public what would be achieved? The answer: After this length of time—nothing.

So she would not do the "conscience thing." She would not go public. She knew, without having to think about it any more, that she too would remain silent, would *join the others in corruption*. She had no choice.

Lord knew it also. Around his thin lips there was the ghost of a smile.

She despised him. Hated him more than anyone else in all her life.

He had corrupted himself, corrupted Mace, corrupted Sam. Now he had corrupted Celia.

She stood up. Emotionally, almost incoherently, she shouted, "Get out of my sight! *Go!*"

He went.

Andrew, who had been visiting a London hospital, returned an hour later.

She told him, "Something's happened. I'll have to go back right after Martin and Yvonne's party. That means a flight the day after tomorrow. If you want to stay a few days more—"

"We'll go together," Andrew said. He added quietly, "Let me handle the arrangements. I can tell you've a lot on your mind."

Soon afterward, he reported back. Thursday's *Concorde* to New York was fully booked. He had secured two first-class seats on a British Airways 747. They would be in New York, then Morristown, on Thursday afternoon.

438

21

Yvonne could scarcely believe it. Was she really inside Buckingham Palace? Was it truly herself in the State Ballroom, seated with others whose spouses or parents were about to receive honors, all of them waiting with varying degrees of excitement or expectancy for the Queen's arrival? Or was it all a dream?

If a dream, it was delightful. And set to music by the regimental band of the Coldstream Guards in the minstrels' gallery above. They were playing *Early One Morning,* that happy, jouncy tune.

But no, it was no dream. Because she had come here to the Palace with her own dear Martin, who was now waiting in an anteroom, ready to be escorted in when the ceremony began. Already Martin had gone through a brief rehearsal, guided by the Comptroller of the Household, a colonel in dress uniform.

Suddenly a pause, a stir. The band stopped, its music ceasing in midflow. All other activity halted. In the gallery, the bandmaster, his baton poised, stood waiting for a signal. It came. As liveried footmen swung double doors open, the Queen appeared.

The uniformed were at attention. All guests had stood. The baton swooped. The national anthem, sweet yet strong, swelled out.

The Queen, in a turquoise silk dress, was smiling. She moved to the center of the ballroom. Dutifully following were the Lord Chamberlain and the Home Secretary, each in morning dress. The presentation of honors began. The band played a Strauss waltz softly. All was dignified, fast-moving and efficient. No wasted time, but not an occasion that those involved were likely to forget.

Yvonne was storing every detail in her memory.

Martin's turn came soon, immediately following a Knight Commander of St. Michael and St. George who took precedence in rank. Following instructions, Martin entered, advanced three paces,

439

bowed . . . forward to a kneeling box . . . right knee on the box, left foot to the floor . . . As Martin knelt, the Queen accepted a sword from an equerry and with it touched Martin lightly on both shoulders. He rose . . . a half pace to the right, one pace forward . . . With Martin standing, his head bowed slightly, the Queen placed around his neck a gold medallion on a red-and-gold ribbon.

The Queen had spoken briefly with each person being honored. With Martin, Yvonne thought, more time was spent. Then, with three backward paces and a bow, Martin was gone.

He joined Yvonne quietly a few minutes later, slipping into a seat beside her. She whispered, "What did the Queen say?"

Smiling, he whispered back, "The Queen is a well-informed lady."

Yvonne knew that later she would find out *exactly* what the Queen had said.

Yvonne's only disappointment was that she hadn't seen or met the Prince and Princess of Wales. She had been told in advance that it wasn't likely they would even be in the palace, but had hoped. One day, though, it might happen. Now that she was married to Martin, anything could happen.

The only thing she was having trouble getting used to since the announcement of Martin's knighthood was being addressed as "my lady" by Harlow and Cambridge people, including the head porter at Lucy Cavendish. She'd asked him not to, but he insisted. Well, in time she supposed she'd adjust to that and other things. After all, Yvonne thought whimsically, quite soon there would be farmers calling for Lady Peat-Smith, veterinary surgeon, to take care of their pigs and cows.

Celia and Andrew's reception and party at the Dorchester Hotel in honor of Sir Martin and Lady Peat-Smith was a great success. It began at teatime, went on until early evening, and during that time nearly a hundred people came, including most of the Harlow institute's senior staff. Rao Sastri was there; he was escorting Lilian, and they seemed to be having fun. Twice, however, Celia saw them with their heads together, apparently engaged in serious talk. Rao, Celia knew, was unattached; according to Martin, he had never married.

Yvonne was looking lovely and radiant. She had lost weight and confided to Celia that Martin had at last allowed her to take Peptide 7. For Yvonne, as for others, the drug's antiobesity factor worked.

During the party Celia told Martin quietly, "Andrew and I are leaving tomorrow, early. When this is over, I'd like the four of us to have a few minutes by ourselves."

At last the celebration ended. With happy leave-takings, the guests dispersed.

It was already dark when Celia, Andrew, Martin and Yvonne walked the short distance from the Dorchester to Fortyseven Park. The February day had been cold, but clear and invigorating. The clearness was persisting into night.

Now they were relaxed in the pleasant living room of the Jordans' apartment.

"Martin," Celia said, "I'll come to the point because it's been a full day and I think we're all a little tired. As you know, Felding-Roth is building a genetic engineering facility. It will be in New Jersey, not far from what will be our new Morristown headquarters, and we're taking care that the labs will have everything in them to gladden a genetic scientist's heart."

"I'd heard some of that," Martin said. "The quality of what you're doing is already being talked about."

"What I'm leading up to," Celia continued, "is a question. Will you and Yvonne come to live in the United States, and will you head our genetic research as vice president and director of the new labs? I'd promise you a free hand to follow whatever scientific direction you believe we should."

There was a silence. Then Martin said, "It's a fine offer, Celia, and I'm truly grateful. But the answer is no."

She urged, "You don't have to give an answer now. Why not take time to think about it, and talk it over with Yvonne?"

"I'm afraid the answer's definite," Martin said. "It has to be because I need to tell you something else. I wish I could have picked another time, but here it is. I'm resigning from Felding-Roth."

The news shocked Celia. "Oh, no! That can't be true." Then she looked at him sharply. "Are you going to another pharmaceutical company? Has someone made a better offer? Because, if so—"

He shook his head. "I wouldn't do that to you. At least, not without discussing it first. What I'm doing is returning to an old love."

"He means Cambridge, not another woman," Yvonne said. "We're going to live there. The university is where his heart is."

441

And where I plucked him from before you knew him, Celia thought.

She had been unprepared for the news, but instinct told her there would be no dissuading Martin, so she wouldn't try. Cambridge had called; he had responded like a homing pigeon. Well, on a sunlit Sunday thirteen years earlier, she had won a victory against the university. It had proved a worthwhile victory all around. But time's wheel had spun; now it was Cambridge's turn, and Celia and Felding-Roth had lost.

Andrew spoke, addressing Martin. "I always thought that academia might call you back one day. Will you be master of a college? I read somewhere that there are vacancies."

"There are," Martin answered, "but not for me. At forty-six I'm still young for a mastership. Maybe when I'm older, grayer, more illustrious . . ."

"Goodness!" Celia exclaimed. "How illustrious do you have to be? You've had a major scientific breakthrough, accolades worldwide, a knighthood."

Martin smiled. "Cambridge has seen all those things many times. The university is not easily impressed. No, I'm going in under something called the 'New Blood Scheme.' "

It was a government-sponsored program, he explained, through which he would become an assistant director of research in one of several new, frontier areas of science. The salary in the new post, as was so often the case in academia, would not be large—to begin, less than ten thousand pounds a year. However, the Peat-Smiths would be comfortable because of Martin's substantial Peptide 7 income, and he would undoubtedly use some of it, he said, to supplement his department's research funds.

Several months earlier a settlement for Martin had been worked out by Felding-Roth's financial officers and lawyers in New Jersey. The arrangement had received Celia's approval and, later, the board's.

Under British law—the Patents Act of 1977—Martin could have applied for a court award of compensation for his Peptide 7 discovery. But he hadn't wanted to go to court, even amicably, nor had Felding-Roth. Therefore, by agreement, an offshore trust fund of two million pounds had been set up in the Bahamas from where money would flow to Martin regularly. The fund was hedged around with legal moats and barriers so that Britain's confiscatory taxation system would not, as Celia expressed it, "rob Martin of his just reward."

That just reward, she now thought ruefully, had helped open the way back to Cambridge. She suspected, though, that Martin would have made the same decision whether the Peptide 7 money were available or not.

Before Martin and Yvonne left to drive home, Celia said, "Felding-Roth will miss you both, but I hope the four of us will always stay close friends."

They agreed they would.

Prior to Celia and Andrew's departure from Britain, one final matter was arranged.

Several hours after Martin and Yvonne had gone, and close to the Jordans' bedtime, there was a knock at the apartment door. It was Lilian Hawthorne. Sensing that Lilian wanted to be alone with Celia, Andrew discreetly disappeared.

"I'm glad you talked me into coming to England," Lilian said. "You may have noticed that I've had a good time."

"Yes, I have," Celia said. She smiled. "I was pleased to see Rao enjoy himself too."

"Rao and I have discovered that we like each other—and it may be even more than that." The older woman hesitated. "I suppose you'll think, because all of it has happened so quickly, and at my age, I'm being foolish . . ."

"I think nothing of the sort. What I do think is that it's time you had fun again, Lilian, that you should enjoy life any way you want, and if that includes Rao Sastri—fine!"

"I'm pleased you feel that way because it's about that I came to see you. I want to ask a favor."

"If I can do it," Celia said, "I will."

"Well, Rao would like to come to America. He says he's wanted to for a long time. I'd like it too, and if it were possible for him to work at Felding-Roth . . ."

The sentence was left unfinished. Celia completed it. "It would be convenient for you both."

Lilian smiled. "Something like that."

"I'm certain," Celia said, "that a place can be found in the new genetic labs. In fact you can tell Rao I guarantee it."

Lilian's face lit up. "Thank you, Celia. He'll be delighted. He was hoping for that. He knows he doesn't have the leadership qualities of someone like Martin; he told me so. But he's a good support scientist—"

"I'm aware of that, which makes it easier," Celia said. "But even if he'd been less than he is, I'd still have done it. You did me a big favor many years ago, Lilian, my dear. This is a small one in return."

The older woman laughed. "You're talking about that first morning we met? When you came to the house—so young, so brash—hoping I'd help you become a detail woman, by influencing Sam?"

Then she stopped, a catch in her voice as, for both of them, so many memories flooded back.

Early the following morning a chauffeured limousine conveyed Andrew and Celia to Heathrow airport.

444

EPILOGUE

In the 747's first-class section the trappings of luncheon had been cleared away. Andrew, after leaving his seat briefly, returned.

He told Celia, "I was thinking in there"—he waved a hand in the direction of the airplane's toilets—"how we take so many things for granted. When Lindbergh made the first successful transatlantic flight, which isn't all that long ago, he had to stay in his seat and urinate into a flask."

Celia laughed. "I'm glad *that* much has changed." She regarded her husband quizzically. "Is that all? I sense some philosophy aborning."

"You're right. I've been thinking about your business—pharmaceuticals. I had a thought or two you might find cheering."

"I could use a little of that."

"People like you, hemmed in by pressures," Andrew said, "get so

445

close to what you're doing that there are times—and I think this is one—when you're apt to see the storm clouds only, and forget the rainbows."

"Remind me of some rainbows."

"That's easy. You brought one to me when our life together started. Lotromycin. It's still in place, as good a drug as when you let me be the first to use it—effective, lifesaving, needed in a doctor's toolbox. Of course, no one talks about Lotromycin anymore—it isn't news; it's been around too long. But add it to others from then onward and you have a cornucopia of drugs, so many of them since the 1950s that medicine's undergone a revolution. I've lived through it, seen it happen."

Andrew considered, then went on, "When I graduated in medicine seven years after World War II, most of the time when we had sick patients all you could do was provide support, then stand aside and hope. There were so many diseases which doctors had no weapons to fight, it used to be frustrating. Now that isn't true. There's a whole arsenal of drugs to fight with and to cure. Your industry provided them."

"I'm hearing music," Celia said. "Play more."

"Okay, take hypertension. Twenty years ago there were a few, limited ways to treat it. Often they didn't work. Lots of times hypertension was a killer. Now, treatment through drugs is unlimited and sure. The incidence of stroke, which hypertension caused, is down by half, and dropping. Drugs are preventing heart attacks. They've stopped tuberculosis and ulcers, improved the diabetic patient's life. In every other field of medicine the same is true. So many good drugs. I prescribe them every day."

"Name some."

He rattled them off. "Corgard, Procardia, Indocin, Orinase, Thorazine, Tagamet, Lasix, Tofranil, Apresoline, Staidpace, Mandol, Prednisone, Levodopa, Cytoxan, Isoniazid, Peptide 7." Andrew stopped. "You want more?"

"That should hold us," Celia said. "And the point you're making?"

"The point is that the successful, useful drugs outnumber losers. For every loser—Thalidomide, Selacryn, Montayne, Oraflex, Bendectin; those and the other few failures you hear about on TV news and '60 Minutes'—there have been a hundred winners. And it isn't just the pharmaceutical companies who are gainers. The big

446

winners are *people*—those who have health instead of sickness, those who live instead of die."

Andrew mused, then added, "If I were making a speech, which I suppose I am to an audience of one, I'd say that what your industry has done, my love—with all its faults, despite its critics—is provide a benefaction for mankind."

"Stop there!" Celia said. "That was so beautiful, so right, anything more might spoil it. You *have* cheered me." She smiled. "Now I'm going to close my eyes and think."

She did.

Ten minutes later, opening her eyes, Celia said, "Andrew dear, there are things I want to say." She paused. "You've been many things to me; now you're my confessor. First, I *am* responsible for those bad events with Hexin W. In my mind there isn't any doubt. If I'd acted sooner some deaths might not have happened. I didn't ask tough questions when I ought. I took for granted what my own experience should have warned me not to. I became heady, a little drunk with power and success—so buoyed by Peptide 7, then Hexin W, that I overlooked the obvious. In a way, it was part of what happened with Sam about Montayne. I understand that better now."

He said, "I hope you don't intend to say all that in court."

Celia shook her head. "I'd be foolish if I did. I've already said that if I'm indicted, brought to court, I'll fight. But I needed to admit my guilt to someone, which is why I'm telling you."

"And Vince Lord—if he's indicted too?"

"We'll give him legal help. I've decided that. But otherwise he'll take his chances."

Andrew said gently, "Despite everything you've told me—and I agree that most is true—don't be too hard on yourself. You're human like the rest of us. No one has a perfect record. Yours is better than most."

"Not good enough, though. But I know I can do better, and an experience like this one helps." Celia's voice had regained her old, crisp matter-of-factness. "Those are reasons I want to go on, and why I intend to. I'm only fifty-three. There's a lot more I can do at Felding-Roth."

"And you will," he said. "The way you always have."

447

There was a silence. Then after a while, when he looked sideways, he saw that Celia had closed her eyes once more and was asleep.

She slept until the flight was losing altitude for landing. Awakening, she touched Andrew's arm. He turned to face her.

"Thank you, my dearest," Celia said. "Thank you for everything." She smiled. "I've thought some more, and I've made up my mind. Whatever happens, I'm coming through. I'm going to win."

Andrew said nothing—just took her hand. He was still holding it when they landed at New York.